PERFECTION IS
EVERYTHING.

Catalyst

THE DECEPTION GAME, BOOK ONE

KRISTIN SMITH

PRAISE FOR CATALYST

"This book has everything I love in a young adult book: a strong, Harley-riding, brilliant female character, a captivating plot set in a vividly imagined futuristic city that I know and love (Las Vegas), and a scintillating romance that leaves me wanting more. It's a good thing that more has been promised in this series!"

~JESSIE HUMPHRIES, BEST-SELLING AUTHOR OF THE RUBY ROSE SERIES

"A gripping thriller with a tough, but vulnerable heroine who must fight against a corrupt underworld. High stakes and non-stop action paired with terrific writing will have you turning the pages late into the night."

~KIMBERLEY GRIFFITHS LITTLE, AWARD-WINNING AUTHOR OF THE FORBIDDEN TRILOGY (HARPERCOLLINS)

"An action-packed sci-fi thriller filled with romance, danger, and twists you won't see coming, CATALYST provides a glimpse into an eery future depicting what can go wrong when those in power attempt to make things right."

~ILIMA TODD, AUTHOR OF REMAKE

"Compelling. Intriguing. Fantastic! Catalyst gives us a view into a different world, but with relatable characters that everyone can understand. The novel's exhilarating pace only gets better as the story reaches its heart-pounding climax. A YA read reminiscent of the best that the genre has to offer. Hunger Games and Divergent, eat your heart out."

~MARK NOCE, AUTHOR OF BETWEEN TWO FIRES

"Catalyst is a stunning and unique addition to the dystopian genre. Fans of The Maze Runner and Divergent series will devour this series opener."

~SHERRY D. FICKLIN, BEST-SELLING AUTHOR OF QUEEN OF SOMEDAY

"It takes a lot to literally make my jaw drop open but Catalyst did it! Packed with adventure and emotion, this book will have you turning the pages at a frantic pace. A brilliant start to a new series."

~NERD GIRL REVIEWS

Smith, Kristin, 1980–
Catalyst : the
deception game, book one
[2016]
33305236883165
sa   02/21/17

Catalyst

BY: KRISTIN SMITH

THIS book is a work of fiction. Names, characters, places and incidents are the product of the author's imagination or are used factiously. Any resemblance to actual persons, living or dead, business establishments, events or locales is entirely coincidental.
NO part of this book may be reproduced, scanned, or distributed in any printed or electronic form without permission. Please do not participate in or encourage piracy of copyrighted materials in violation of the author's rights. Purchase only authorized editions.

Catalyst

Copyright ©2016 Kristin Smith
All rights reserved.

ISBN 978-1-63422-998-2
Cover Design by: Marya Heiman
Typography by: Courtney Knight
Editing by: Cynthia Shepp

For more information about our content disclosure,
please utilize the QR code above with your smart phone
or visit us at www.CleanTeenPublishing.com

FOR MY BOYS
YOU ARE MY HEART AND MY INSPIRATION. YOU
ARE MY LIFE.

"There are no limits, only possibilities."

-Harlow Ryder

Creator of Match 360 and Chromo 120

Chapter One

School is only good for two things—grades and social life. Considering I'm not exactly excelling in either of those areas, I'm not sure why I'm here.

Professor Armstrong walks down the aisle, his comscreen in hand. "All right, class, your test scores have been uploaded." He stops beside my desk, the smell of his cheap cologne overpowering, and stares down at me through his rimless glasses. "If you have any questions, please see me after class."

I avoid his gaze and focus on my desk-screen, dreading my latest calculus test score. The screen lights up, a digital device that displays my name, the date, and my test grade.

C minus.

Again.

Professor Armstrong continues down the aisle, and I groan inwardly, swiping the screen off.

Is it too much to ask for one good test grade?

When the bell rings, I escape into the hall. Chaz is already waiting for me.

"Hey, Sienna, you coming over to my house tonight?" He smiles, his dark round face giving way to a row of white teeth. "We still need to watch the final season of *Return to Space.*"

A group of girls glides onto the Stairway to Heaven—as they call it. I like to call them the Stairs from Hell. I avoid the see-through moving contraption of death and take the normal stairs instead. Mainly because that thing scares me, but partly because I know I'd collapse by the time I made it to the top. I watch as the girls' long legs work their way up the moving stairs—kind of like a mini-workout just getting around school. "Haven't we already watched all the episodes, like, three times?"

Chaz shrugs. "I dunno. Who's counting?"

Once we make it to the top, I stop and face him. "I am. And once was enough for me." I shift my backpack on my shoulder. "Besides, I have a ton of homework to do. I think the professors forget that not *all* of us are blessed with enhanced genetics."

Chaz snorts. "Oh, you mean the two of us who aren't?"

Chaz and I are the only ones at the Genetically and Intellectually Gifted Academy—GIGA for short—who aren't genetically gifted. Which is probably the reason we bonded in the first place. At least Chaz has the intellectually gifted thing going for him. Me? Not so much.

I guess you could say we're lucky—or cursed, depending on how you look at it—to have fathers who are professors at the school. It affords us free tuition and automatic acceptance. But for Chaz, the only boy in a sea of perfect GM girls—thanks to our segregated schools policy—life is good. Unfortunately, just because we go to this school, it doesn't mean we belong.

Case in point: Rayne Williams and her entourage of perfect human specimens. I watch as they stride past, their legs long and endless, their hair perfect, their teeth straight, and their clothes tight and curving in all the right places. These are girls who never smell and probably never even sweat, whereas I'm like an overworked sweat gland factory. How can I ever compete with that perfection? I can't. Therefore, I don't try to.

Sighing, I turn back to Chaz, whose eyes have also followed Rayne and her friends down the hall. "Dang," he says. "That sight never gets old."

I slug him in the shoulder and take off down the hall in the opposite direction of Rayne & Crew. Chaz hurries to catch up.

"I'll make you a deal," he says. "Come over after school. I'll help you with your homework, and then we can watch *Return to Space*. It's a win-win."

How can I possibly argue with that kind of logic? Especially when it comes from my best and only friend? "Let me run by my dad's room and tell him I'm riding home with you."

"Meet me at my car?" When I nod, he adds, "Don't take long, okay? You know how Destiny doesn't like to hang around school any longer than she has to."

I bite my lip to hide my smile. Destiny is Chaz's beat-up old cruiser. "I'll be so fast you won't even realize you're waiting for me." I pick up the pace and turn down another hall as Chaz keeps going straight, headed for the parking lot.

When I reach my father's classroom, my eyes flit to the nameplate on the wall outside his door. Without thinking, I place my hand on it, tracing the engraved grooves. *Ben Preston*. The name is solid, sturdy, just like my father.

I find my dad inside, hunched over his desk-screen, doing grades. His tie is loose around his neck, and the beginnings of a five o'clock shadow are already evident. He looks up and smiles when he sees me. "Hi, sweetie. You headed home?"

Tapping my finger on his screen, I eye the grades, even though I probably shouldn't. I don't really understand the purpose of giving grades when they're all nearly the same—95 or 100. That's what happens when you have a school full of genetically modified kids whose parents picked their characteristics like ordering off a drive-thru menu.

"I'm going to Chaz's house. He offered to help me with some of my homework."

Dad gives me a sympathetic smile. "Is calculus still giving you trouble?"

"It's all giving me trouble," I say, my tone wry.

"Well, hey, you know how much I love math. If you still don't understand after your study session with Chaz, maybe I could sit down with you tonight. Go over some math problems?" He winks at me, his brown eyes crinkling at the corners. "You have to give your old man a chance to prove he still knows a few things."

I laugh. "Trust me, Dad. I don't think I'm in danger of forgetting that." Leaning over, I wrap my arms around his neck. Like always, he smells of a combination of cedar and leather. He reminds me of a classroom, but he also reminds me of home. "See you tonight."

As I'm headed out the door, he calls to me. "Sienna?"

I stop and turn, one hand resting on the wooden doorframe.

My dad smiles, his hair tinged with gray, his hands lightly clasped on his desk. "I'm so proud of you. I know it's not easy…" He gestures around the room. "Being here, I mean. But I'm proud of you for sticking it out."

I smile back at him. "Thanks, Dad."

That's what I love about my dad. He always knows what to say and when I need to hear it.

When I arrive home later that evening, all the lights are on inside the house. Mom and Emily aren't here because it's Thursday night, which means Emily has dance class.

I don't know why my mom insists on taking my four-year-old sister to dance. It's mostly just a class where she learns to spin around and touch her toes. I could teach her that at home for free.

"Dad?" I call out, entering the foyer. "You home?"

I'm greeted with silence.

I walk through the living room to get to the kitchen. A comscreen broadcasts a local news channel. As I enter the kitchen, I see him. Sprawled out on his back on the kitchen floor, eyes wide open, mouth slightly parted.

My heart drops, and I fall to my knees beside my father, my fingers searching for a pulse. I cringe when I touch his skin—so cold, so very cold.

"No," I whisper, tears stinging my eyes. "No, no, no, no."

I pull my Lynk from my pocket and call rescue services. With sobs shaking my body and my words coming out in gasps, I'm not sure if they understand what I'm trying to say, but they promise to send help.

The next few minutes are a blur. I hold his hand because I don't know what else to do, but my tears stain his dress shirt and silk tie—his work clothes. *He never even had a chance to change when he got home.*

Rescue services burst through the door and begin working on him, but I can see it in their eyes. It's in the way they move, the way they whisper to one another. It's too late. But no one wants to tell me.

And then, finally, they do.

Later that night, after we've dragged ourselves home from the hospital, without Dad, because Dad will never step through that door again, I sit in a kitchen chair and stare at the spot where I found him. Mom and Emily are already in bed, but my mother's sobs trail down the hallway.

How can I ever go to sleep again? After finding my father like that, how can I ever close my eyes and dream?

Tears fill my eyes as I stare at that corner of the room. The exact spot where only this morning, my father stood, making chocolate oatmeal for my sister and me. I can practically hear his off-key humming and smell the aroma of cocoa and peanut butter. I miss it already. I miss the life I'll never have with him. I miss the years that have been stolen from us. And what about Emily? My heart breaks for her. She's too young to understand, and I think that's the saddest part of all. She doesn't even know what she's missing.

Salty tears run down my cheeks and into my mouth, but I don't bother to wipe them away. Despite the blurriness, something catches my eye, so I stumble out of the chair to get a better look. A black leather briefcase rests against the kitchen cabinet. Dad's briefcase.

I rake a palm across my face and reach for the bag, clutching it to my chest. When I breathe in, the distinct smell of leather fills my nostrils and gives way to a thousand memories. This is the smell of my father. The smell of old books, classrooms, and shoe polish. And this is all I have left of him.

Before I can stop myself, I unzip the compartments of his briefcase, searching for something, anything, I can hold. Anything to remind me of him.

In a small inner pocket, I find something. A photo. But as I stare at it, I realize it's not at all what I was hoping to find. It's odd. There are two people in the photograph—a man and a woman, both smiling, the man's arms wrapped around the woman's shoulders. This man is a much younger version of my dad, but the woman, with her long, dark hair and beautiful smile, is not someone I recognize. Strangely enough, the handwriting on the back of the picture says Mitch and Penelope.

Who are Mitch and Penelope?

Every nerve in my body tingles from exhaustion, and my head pounds from crying so much. Too drained to contemplate it further, I slip the photo in my pocket and tiptoe down the hall to Mom's room. Her lamp is on, as if she doesn't plan to go to sleep. It casts a glow over her hair, which is red like mine, untamed and uncontrollable. I quietly slip into the bed next to her, as I did so many times before when I was a small child, seeking comfort. Back then, cocooned against her bosom, every fear, every doubt, would melt away.

But now, I wrap my arms around her, trying to provide some comfort. The warmth of her body radiates through her thin nightgown, and I inhale the scent of lavender. A scent that takes me back to memories of Mom, Dad, Emily, and me, of us together as a family—summer picnics, family dinners, and nights spent stargazing.

I never knew how good I had it. How could I know I wouldn't have more days, months, or years of that life? I never dreamed things would change so drastically.

If I had known... If I had only known.

I might have been prepared.

Chapter Two

I sold my soul only weeks after my father's death. It's fitting that one year later, I would be in an underground pool hall, requesting a meeting with the Devil.

The air is thick with cigarette smoke and the pungent smell of men's cologne. I'm clearly the minority with my fiery hair and fair skin—not to mention my boobs.

Wearing the shortest, tightest skirt I own, I weave past tables full of men with lingering eyes until I reach Victor, where he stands at the back of the pool hall. With his arms crossed over his chest and his hair slicked back with grease, he looks like the average criminal. Once again, I wonder how I got mixed up with his kind.

"Good job last night," Victor says, smirking.

My eyes narrow. "If you thought you could do better, you should have done it yourself."

"A crowbar and twine? Really?" He leans close. "Next time you break in somewhere, don't be so careless and leave evidence for the Enforcers to find."

A muscle in my jaw twitches. Apparently, he saw the news this morning, just like I did.

"I did what you asked. I stole the file and got it loaded to Video Share. Now you owe me a meeting with the Devil, just as you promised."

Victor sneers, the bling in his mouth on full display. I've

never understood the desire to have gold and diamonds in your mouth, but whatever.

"How 'bout a game of pool? You win, and I'll get you that meeting."

My response is to grab the nearest cue stick and chalk the tip.

When I break the balls and two solids glide smoothly into the corner pockets, Victor nods his approval. When the next shot lands two more solids in the pockets—one in the far corner and one in the side—his jaw tightens. Victor doesn't know it, but my father taught me to play pool before I barely had the strength to break the balls.

Throughout the game, I keep an eye out for the Devil—the biggest crime lord on the Lower East Side of the city. I've often heard he owns this place, but he rarely makes an appearance. As a powerful man who has access to all kinds of information, he knows how to keep people loyal, using any means necessary. The two missing fingers on Victor's right hand are proof of that. Victor works for him and I work for Victor, so I guess that technically makes me an employee of the Devil. Even though I've never met him.

"So tell me, Sienna. Why do you keep hounding me about meeting the Devil?" Victor flashes me a gold-toothed smile as he leans over the pool table to take his turn. "Am I not good enough for you?" The cue ball shoots across the table, narrowly missing one of his stripes.

Slipping my hand in the pocket of my mini-skirt, I graze the glossy surface of the photo I've been carrying around with me for months. "I have my reasons," I say.

When it's my turn again, I lean over the pool table and eye the setup, confident I can hit the cue ball low enough to put a backspin on it and keep it from going into the pocket with the eight ball. Exhaling slowly, I relax my stiff fingers before I give a nudge with the cue stick. I sink the shot. When I turn, I confront the glaring dark eyes of Victor.

"Looks like I won." I smirk. "Now you give me the

meeting you promised."

"How 'bout another game?"

"A deal's a deal." When Victor just stands there looking at me, I add, "Should I record the results on the house ledger?" I figure he probably doesn't want people to know he was beaten by a girl.

Victor's eyes narrow. "The Devil doesn't entertain uninvited guests. You should know that, Sienna." As he leans close, his foul breath rakes over my face. "Didn't your dad strike a deal with the Devil?"

After my father died of a massive heart attack, Mom and I heard rumors that he was part of an underground gambling ring while he was alive. That he had "struck a deal with the Devil"—so to speak.

My hands tighten around the cue, my fingernails digging into my palms. "That's none of your business." Through clenched teeth, I hiss. "You promised me a meeting with the Devil."

He smiles. "What will you give me? A kiss?"

That does it. Bile rises in the back of my throat, and anger, like a hot poker, swells inside of my chest. Before I have time to react, a deep voice booms from behind Victor.

"The Devil will see you now."

A dark-skinned man the size and stature of a small bus stands a few feet behind Victor, blocking the doorway to the back room of the pool hall. Smoothing my blouse, I lift my shoulders and toss my hair. I give a stunned Victor a smug smile. He didn't think I'd gain access to the Devil, and I just proved him wrong.

Heart pounding, I follow the oversized man through the velvet-draped doorway and up a flight of metal stairs. When we confront a thick wooden door, the man raps softly, a series of knocks broken up by pauses, clearly meant as a code for the person inside.

The heavy door swings open. A man sits behind an ornate desk, his legs propped up on the reddish wood and a cigar hanging loosely from his mouth. He is older than I expected, with a bald head that reflects the light from his desk lamp and a dark goatee tinged with gray. When he speaks, I'm reminded of sandpaper, rough and grainy.

"Miss Preston, what can I do for you?" He motions a glittering hand topped with gold and diamond rings to the upholstered chair across from his desk.

I sink into the chair and inhale slowly to calm my racing heart. Now that I'm here, I'm at a loss for words. I guess because this "assignment" is personal. Like everything else, the things closest to our heart are always infinitely harder to do.

Clearing my throat and hoping my voice sounds more confident than I feel, I slide a worn photo across the smooth wood of the desk. The Devil glances at it briefly from his laid-back position, but he doesn't move to take it in his hand.

"What's this?" he asks with a raised eyebrow.

"I found this photo in my father's briefcase the day he died. I want to know who these people are." I pause. "I was hoping you could help me."

The Devil's mouth turns up into a cruel sneer. "And why would I do that?"

"Because you know everything. Everyone." I square my shoulders, trying to make myself appear larger and more formidable than my five-foot-two frame really is. "And because you knew my father. Ben Preston." Swallowing hard, I plow forward, "You struck a deal with him, and now my mother, sister, and I are suffering because of it—"

He holds up a hand to stop me. "Miss Preston, your father and I had a business arrangement years ago. Way before your time and before he even knew your mother."

"But what about the gambling ring?"

His eyes narrow. "Your father was never part of any gambling ring." He pauses, making me think I'll have to beg for more information. "I can tell you this—Harlow Ryder might be the one to answer some of your questions."

Harlow Ryder? The creator of Match 360 and Chromo 120—the genetic matchmaking and modification companies? Why would he know anything about this picture or my father?

At my confused expression, the Devil clarifies. "Your father worked for Mr. Ryder years ago."

"As a professor?"

He snickers in reply. "No, he was Mr. Ryder's lead geneticist."

My mind spins. What is he talking about? My father was no more a scientist than I am a genetically modified supermodel. "That's impossible."

The Devil gives me a wicked grin as he leans forward, his hands clasped on the desk. "How much do you really know about your father, Miss Preston?" When I don't answer, he continues. "Years ago, when things went south with his job at the Match 360 headquarters in Rubex, he came to me for help. And I helped him find a better venue."

"I don't understand—"

"You're not supposed to." He nods at his guard, who is standing in front of the door with his arms crossed over his thick chest. "Now, if you'll excuse me…"

In one swift movement, the dark-skinned guard crosses the room and grabs my elbow, applying enough pressure to convince me not to struggle. He guides me out of the chair and toward a back door hidden in the shadows.

"The Devil would appreciate it if, in the future, you left him out of your search-and-discovery sessions," he grunts.

The demon shoves me out into the night, but right before he closes the door, the Devil casually offers one last bit of information. "Oh, and Miss Preston, although I would advise against repeating it, your father's name was Mitch Hoover."

The guard slams the door, and the sound of metal against metal reverberates through the night.

Mitch Hoover.

For a moment, I stand there frozen, staring down a cliché

dark and deserted street. I just had a face-to-face meeting with one of the most dangerous and elusive men in the city. And somehow, he knows more about my father than my mother and I ever did.

Chapter Three

My bike sits several streets over from Shooters. I'm relieved to find it in the same place, resting against an abandoned casino, this one a little less recognizable than others.

Once a glittering metropolis of casinos, nightlife, and flashing lights, Legas now looks like nothing more than a pit. Gone are the glitz, glamour, and material wealth of the Casino Age. Gone are the colors of the rainbow blazing across neon signs and white lighted billboards decorating the town. Instead, many of the buildings sit vacant, a perfect place for squatters at night and vagrants during the day. Now, this is a tarnished, a broken, and a defiled city.

Obviously, I never saw this place at the height of its wealth and prosperity, but I've been told it was an unbelievable sight. But that was before. Before Pacifica's government got a "moral compass" and made gambling illegal, forcing the shutdown of all casinos. But it's funny how crime increases when things become illegal. Kind of like Prohibition all over again.

I throw my leg over my Harley and hike my miniskirt up a little further, my bare thighs pale in the moonlight. The engine roars, and I take off in the direction of the abandoned Megasphere. It was once a thrill-seeking ride, taking its victims far above the city. Now it sits, dark and desolate, lurking like a sentinel at the edge of the Gateway.

I skid to a stop in front of the Megasphere, the heat from the exhaust pipe licking at my bare legs. This is the place I like to come. To think. To get away.

The door to the empty building creaks when I open it. At night, everything looks eerie in the darkness. As I switch on my pocket light, the room in front of me glows a sickly yellow. I know this place well and could easily find my way in the dark, but I choose not to. Too many low-hanging beams and rusty pipes make it dangerous and stupid to traipse through at night.

It takes several minutes to climb to the top by way of the emergency staircase, but when I reach the roof and step outside, the breeze lifts my hair and passes over my bare arms and legs, reminding me it's worth it. I move toward my favorite spot and settle into one of the abandoned ride chairs. My legs dangle over the city. From here, I can see it all. The vastness beyond. The tiny pockets of light.

It is only here, at the top of the Megasphere, that I'm able to find peace. The peace that was ripped from me the night my father passed away—the night my world turned upside down. Even though GIGA was willing to let me stay on as a student after my father's death, I couldn't go back. I never belonged there anyway.

I stare at one light pocket in particular. The suburbs where we lived before my father died. Before we couldn't pay the mortgage and had to move to a double-wide on the outskirts of town.

When my father died and I found the photo in his briefcase, I became curious. After we found out about his supposed involvement with the Devil, I was angry. How could my father keep something like that from us?

Anger and curiosity is not a good combination.

And after months of wanting to meet with the Devil, I now know something about my father I never would have imagined.

The smell of burning wood fills the air around me, and I

squint at the valley below, trying to locate the source. Smoke rises from a burning building on the edge of the Hollow, the area where most of the government buildings outside Rubex, Pacifica's capital, are located. I'd bet anything it's the handiwork of the Fringe, an extremist group.

I suck in a breath and tilt my head back, resting it against the seat. The wind roars at this height. It drags through my hair and prickles against my skin.

I don't really like the person I've become in the last year, but circumstances necessitate this lifestyle. As a seventeen-year-old dropout, there aren't many options afforded me. Except one—the art of lying and stealing. The truth is, thugs don't really care how old you are, as long as you're willing to do the work.

A light in the distance draws my curiosity. To get a better look, I slip from the seat and ease to the edge, leaning over slightly. It's past the city, deep in the desert at the base of the mountains. I wasn't aware anyone lived all the way out there.

The sound of shoes scraping against concrete startles me, and I turn quickly, surprised to see a boy close to my age. I use the term *boy* loosely as he is built more like a man. With broad shoulders and a solid build, he looks to be about twenty.

He moves toward me, his hands out like he's trying to calm a raging sea.

"Let's not do anything hasty, okay?" His voice is smooth and deep, almost melodious.

My eyes narrow as I cross my arms over my chest. "What the hell are you talking about?"

He inches closer. "Trust me; you don't want to do this."

My heart pounds. I take a step away from him, wondering if he's mentally sound.

He continues. "Nothing can be that bad for you to want to end your life—"

End my life?

Anger flares up, hot and heavy. What is he doing here?

This is my place. My *space*.

My eyes flash, and when I don't respond, he looks doubtful.

"You *are* a jumper, right?" His eyes crinkle in concern.

"No," I practically spit out. "I'm not a jumper. And even if I was, it would be none of your concern."

His facial muscles relax in response, and his mouth turns up into a grin. I want to punch the smile off his face. Who does he think he is? I certainly don't need him to rescue *me*. I don't need anyone to rescue me.

He tilts his head and stares at me with a bemused expression. "If you're not a jumper, then why are you up here? Do you have a death wish?"

"Do you?" I retort.

The irony of the situation hits him, and he bursts into laughter. Refusing to stand there and be laughed at, I turn on my heel and stride to the stairs.

His laughter subsides, and I hear him call after me. "Wait! I'm sorry."

I pick up the pace and hurry down the stairs. He's directly behind me, which causes my heart rate to speed up. I don't think he's chasing me, but the presence of him makes me leery. I'd *really* rather not shove the heel of my hand into his nose, but I will if he tries to touch me.

My breathing comes in ragged gasps by the time I push through the exit, but the boy sounds as if he's only walked a few feet. His breathing is smooth and slow, an indication that he's most likely genetically modified—a GM.

"Listen, I wasn't trying to offend you," he persists.

I continue to ignore him as I move toward my bike across the street. His hand latches on my arm. Instinctively, I turn, prepared to deliver a forceful blow to his face. But right before my palm connects with his nose, he grabs my wrist, stopping the impact. Of course, he's quick.

I wrench my wrist free and glare at him. "What do you want?"

His mouth turns down in a frown. In the glow of the streetlights, his hair is the color of fresh wheat and his eyes are a warm chocolate brown.

"To apologize. I'm sorry I assumed you were a jumper."

I cross my arms over my chest in the most defiant stance I can muster. "Feel better now?"

"Yes. I mean, no—"

I swing my leg over my bike, suddenly self-conscious when his eyes shift to my pale bare legs. Groaning inwardly, I rev the engine.

"Look, just forget about it," I call out to him before the bike moves down the dimly lit street. Only as I turn the corner do I venture a glance in his direction. I see him re-enter the Megasphere, and it is then, as I speed away, that I wonder what he is doing there.

Chapter Four

The bio fridge hums with its latest addition—a package of dehydrated bologna.

"The shelf life for product Meat Delite expires in one month and two days," the automated voice chimes in.

I sigh in disgust. If I have to eat one more package of that crap, I'll vomit in my mouth. Seriously.

I eye the sparse contents inside the gelled portion of the fridge. The tube of yogurt looks decidedly better than the bottled pickles. And definitely better than Meat Crap Delite. I grab the purple yogurt tube, tear into it, and head back to my room.

The cold blast from the Quik Air unit stings my face as I kneel directly in front of it and suck down the creamy pomegranate-blueberry goodness. Beads of sweat run down my back as I lift my arms to allow the frigid air to flow over me. In the desert, the June heat is horrendous, making me lethargic. But with no impending assignments from Victor, and an overwhelming desire to stay indoors, it's given me plenty of time to think about my father and his connection to Harlow Ryder.

Problem is, I still don't have any answers.

Finished with the yogurt, I gather my long hair into a tangled bun on top of my head and turn, letting the icy air cool my moist neck. It's days like this that make me want to shave my thick hair down to a nub.

There was a time when summer heat meant lazy Sunday afternoons spent swimming in our pool or entertaining family friends. My dad would barbecue and my mom would flit about making sure everyone had enough lemonade to drink or snacks to eat. But now, sitting in this humming silence, with nothing keeping me cool but the air unit in front of me, that life seems light-years away.

Emily bursts into the room, her five-year-old face glowing with excitement, and a brown package resting in her hands. "Si-Si, a package came! I found it outside." When my sister was two, she couldn't say my name, so she resorted to calling me Si-Si. I love how she says it, more like see-see than sissy.

Dropping my hair, I let it fall down my back in a tangled mess and reach for the square-shaped package in her hands. I turn the box over, studying it. There's no name, no return address—nothing.

I hop up from the floor and sink onto my bed. Emily settles next to me. "What's in the box, Si-Si?"

"I'm not sure. Should we check it out?"

When I lift the wrapping on both sides, the thick brown paper falls away, revealing a silver, hexagon-shaped box beneath. It is small enough to fit in my palm, and it's weightless. Yet, when I clink my fingernail against the top, it gives off a distinct metallic sound. I think this package was left for me, but I don't understand. I always receive my assignments via secret location and from Victor. But I have a feeling this didn't come from Victor.

Taking a deep breath, I undo the magnetic latch on top and lift the lid. A holographic image bounces up and shivers in place before it's replaced by the next image, then the next. An oversized building. A keyless back entry. A glass office. A small, black box.

The words follow the images. *Secure the black box. Located in the Match 360 Legas facility. The director's office. Meet with box in hand at ten hundred hours Thursday night. Back alley of*

Wedgewood Row. You will be heavily compensated.

"What is that, Si-Si?" Emily asks. I hush her and pull her closer.

The image shrinks and dies, as if sucked back into an invisible vortex. Replacing the lid, I exhale slowly.

Thursday night? Three nights from now? That doesn't give me much time. And then it hits me—Harlow Ryder is the owner and director of all the Match 360s. I've been hired to break into his office and steal something important. A grin spreads across my face as I think of the implications—I might be able to find out information about my father while I'm there.

"Wow, that was cool," Emily whispers, her blue eyes wide with awe.

I place the metallic hexagon on my scuffed-up dresser. I'm not the least bit surprised when it bursts into flames, but Emily screams and buries her face in my pillow. I wonder if her screams will wake our mother.

"It's okay, Em," I say, wrapping my arms around her.

The metal disintegrates and turns into a fine, silver powder. It lays there in a small pile of ash on my white dresser. Emily wiggles free and moves across the room to touch it.

"No, Em," I say in a stern voice. She melts back against the bed and watches as I sweep the powder into the trash. Bored, she runs out of the room, her pink Princess Power shoes pounding down the hall.

Rubbing my fingers over the small burn mark, I wonder why this black box is important. As with each "thief-for-hire" assignment, I'm not given details, only specific instructions from Victor of what I need to do. Afterward, the payment for my services automatically appears in my bank account. I never know who hires me because Victor handles all of that. Truthfully, I prefer to keep it that way.

If the assignment didn't come from Victor, then who?

But does it matter? Because the truth is, I don't really care who hires me or where the money comes from, as long as it comes. The thought of eating Meat Crap Delite, a step above dog food, for the next month is more than enough incentive.

Biting my lip, I contemplate the task before me.

This one sounds complicated. Breaking into a secure facility is not easy. There are sure to be the three G's: guards, gates, and my least favorite—guns. Not to mention locked doors and secure access areas. I'm going to need a wingman.

I pull up Chaz on the Lynk communicator, and his face pops up on the tiny, handheld screen. Even without a genetically altered body, Chaz is a genius with computers and easily as smart as most GMs, which makes him my number one go-to guy.

Chaz breaks into a smile when he sees me. "Sienna! Girl, it's been a long time. How are you?"

I smile. It's good to see him again. "Chaz, I need a favor."

Chaz raises his eyebrows. "So this is a business call only, huh? Well, now I feel cheap."

A laugh escapes from the back of my throat. "Do you still remember how to bypass codes to get into highly secure locations?"

"Yes. Why? Are you planning to break into a secure location?" He grins like he's being funny.

I shrug. "Are you busy Wednesday night?"

"As long as this doesn't come back to me—"

"It won't. I promise."

Chaz grins and leans toward the Lynk, his round face taking up the entire screen. "Looks like you got yourself a date."

For the next two days, I don't have time to think about my father, his past, or why he changed his name. Instead, I research points of entry and the layout of the Match 360 building. Thankfully, the city planner made it easy to access architectural copies of the building's structure.

As I practice different lock-picking techniques, I ponder where the black box might be hidden in Mr. Ryder's office. I even take a few minutes to contemplate where I might find information about my father. Creating my own laser obstacle course—minus the real lasers, of course—I try to assimilate what I might face once inside the building. After a few calisthenics and stretches, I think I'm ready.

Donning my black shadow outfit, I tie my hair up into a ponytail and pull on a dark ball cap. I'm grateful the sun has long since gone down. As hot as it's been, I can't imagine wearing this outfit under its blistering glare. Not even the air coolers inside the fabric of my clothes can help on a hot day like this.

Before I leave, I check on Emily. She's asleep, the lamp with the pink shade casting a yellow glow about the room. I'm about to turn it off, but then I think better of it. If she wakes while I'm gone, the lamplight will provide her comfort until she's able to fall back to sleep.

I check on Mom next. Earlier today, she had a systemic lupus flare-up, which usually lands her in bed for a couple of days. Sure enough, she's already asleep, her worn brown quilt pulled up to her chin, despite the heat. Diagnosed a couple of months after Dad died, my mom hasn't had it easy, which is why I don't want her to have to worry about anything. And why I do whatever I can to earn a little cash.

Once outside, I grip the handlebars of my Harley and walk it down the gravel driveway until I reach the road. Now that I'm a safe distance from the house, I climb on and start the engine. Most girls my age would be content with a little Hydra, but not me. That small car seems stifling—claustrophobic, even. I prefer the open air of this antique motorcycle I found and restored after my dad died. Turns out, I may not be an academic queen, but I'm fairly good with my hands.

The wind seeps its way into my shirt, like fingers

searching for a warmer spot. Soft tendrils of hair escape from my ponytail and caress my face. I try not to think about what I'm planning to do or the consequences for getting caught.

We need this money.

Chapter five

The Match 360 facility, the Legas division, is a large, fifty-acre complex located on the outskirts of the city. Made almost completely of glass, it's one of the pockets of light viewed from the Megasphere. Barbed wire and electric fences run the length of the property, but for safety reasons, they were unable to fence a small portion of the back of the property, in case emergency vehicles need to enter the premises. A big thank you to the city planner for highlighting that detail in his survey plans.

Once I've made it past the gun-toting guard in the courtyard—with the aid of a few well-thrown, barrel-rattling rocks—I sprint soundlessly until I reach the keyless entry, the exact door I saw in the hologram. As I dial Chaz, I insert a tiny earbud into my right ear and wait until his face pops up on the screen.

"I'm here," I say, trying to catch my breath. "What do you have for me?"

The *clack, clack, clack* of his fingers rapidly typing on the keyboard is his only response. I glance around.

What if there's another guard I'm not aware of?

"Got it," he declares in triumph.

A lock clicks, and the door falls open. A good thing considering there isn't a handle on this side.

"Thanks, Chaz. You're the best."

I ease through and leave a small card in the doorjamb to keep it from completely closing. Before I take a step, I eye my surroundings.

"Do you see any lasers?" Chaz asks.

"Shh. I need to concentrate."

I don't see any lasers, but that's what makes them so dangerous. You *don't* see them. Not until it's too late.

I pull a container of baby powder from my backpack and dump some into my hand. When I fling it out onto the floor in front of me, I see them then.

Intersecting lines of lasers positioned every foot or so.

I exhale in a slow rush. *I can do this. I can beat this.*

And as long as I don't think about what these lasers can do to my skin—to my body—I can make it past.

I tighten the straps of my backpack as I ease up on my toes, flexing my calf muscles. With careful precision, I step over the first wire. I barely have enough space to stand in between the first and second, but I catch my balance and conquer the next. The ones after that are trickier because they crisscross at waist level. Using my flexibility, I limbo my way under the next two, the lasers so close to my chest, I can feel the heat through my shirt.

By the time I get to the last one, I'm a little cocky and impatient. I've wasted valuable time trying to get past this obstacle. As I hurry over the last laser, I hear the sizzle of the heat slicing through my dangling shoestring. I gape in horror at the leftover piece of shoelace on the floor, its burnt end curling up. Shuddering, I push through to the stairwell.

According to the survey plans, the director's office is located on the sixth floor. I climb the emergency stairs two at a time until I reach it. Once I've pushed through the heavy metal door, I tiptoe down the hallway of glass until I see a door with the name *Harlow Ryder* etched onto the smooth surface. But when I try the knob, my heart sinks.

Of course, it's locked.

A small, gel-like keypad sits above the doorknob. I pull

Chaz from my pocket and show him the door. "We're screwed. It's a fingerprint-activated lock."

"I think I can bypass the system," he says. "What floor are you on?"

"Six."

The clink of the keyboard becomes background noise on Chaz's side of the phone. I glance down the hall as a nervous bead of sweat dribbles between my shoulder blades. Not even the air coolers in my shirt can help right now.

"How much longer?" I hiss when the silence in the hall becomes deafening and the only sound is the swift beating of my heart.

Another pause, and then a triumphant voice announces, "You're in."

At the same time, I hear the lock click.

Relief floods me as I slide into the dark room. With my pocket light, I do a quick sweep of Harlow Ryder's office. A sleek black desk rests in the center of the room with a silver pendant light hanging above it. Two black-and-silver striped chairs sit opposite the desk, and a white couch covered with black throw pillows lounges in the corner.

I hurry to the desk and jerk each drawer open, rifling through papers as my heart pounds against my lungs. What if I can't find this box? What if it's not here? I try not to think such thoughts as I search under the desk for a trigger or key or something to indicate there's a hidden safe in the room.

The metal cabinet in the corner of the room looks like a great place to stash a small box. I pull open drawer after drawer, but all I find are data chips in their protective sleeves neatly filed in rows. My eyes skim over the names on the sleeves, searching for my father's former name—according to the Devil—but my shoulders slump when I reach the last alphabetized chip. No Mitch Hoover. And no black box.

Of course, it won't be in plain sight. Not something as important as this small box that must contain secrets. *Think, Sienna, think.*

Catalyst

I scan my light around the dark room until it rests on an elaborate oil painting of a Trojan horse.

Bingo.

I stride over to the picture frame and try to lift it off the wall, but it won't budge, almost as if held to that spot by some invisible force. With my latex-covered hands, I feel around the picture, searching for a hidden button. There's an indentation in the backside of the picture frame, and my heart thuds with excitement as I lightly press the small button. The sound of the click brings a smile to my face, and the heavy frame swings open to reveal a small safe.

I eye it. Clearly, this is an antique rotary combination lock, and they don't make them like this anymore. When I spin the dial, I hear the click of the four live locking bolts.

Shouldn't they have something more sophisticated for such an important facility? Not that I'm complaining. They just made my job a whole lot easier.

I press my ear to the safe at the exact moment that there's a noise outside. Standing slowly, I peek out the window. Three sleek vehicles pull up, their roof lights barely glowing. Enforcers step out of their vehicles, making their way to the building with their laser guns drawn. *Damn.* I must have triggered a silent alarm.

"Looks like we have company, Chaz," I mutter. I don't know if he can hear me, but I don't take the time to find out. As I rush back to the safe, I know I can't leave until I get what I came for. I probably have three minutes tops until the Enforcers reach my level of the building.

Taking a deep breath, I bend down until my ear is next to the dial. My fingers grasp onto the cool metal, and I slowly turn it. I'm greeted with silence. Swallowing hard, I try again. This time, I hear it, the faint click of the lock. The dial moves easily in the opposite direction, and again, I hear the slight clink of the discs catching.

The Enforcers will be on my level at any moment. My hands shake, and beads of sweat dot my forehead.

Stay calm, Sienna. Just stay calm.

Cursing my heart for its loud, erratic throbbing, I turn the dial again, carefully listening. After what seems like an eternity, I feel the click, like a small pulse under my fingertips. With a slight tug, I open the safe and see it.

The black box.

The engraved symbol on top of the smooth lid is one I've seen before. Similar to an infinity sign, two triangles face each other, forming a mirror image—the Match 360 symbol.

Lights bounce on the other side of the glass wall, throwing my pulse in overdrive. The Enforcers are nearing Mr. Ryder's office.

I grab the box, wrap it in the red bandana, and place it in the pack slung over my shoulder. Clearly, I can't leave the way I came. After closing the safe and the picture frame, I scan the room for an escape, spotting the windows on the far wall.

I try the first one, but it won't budge.

My chest constricts with fear as my hands move to the next one. Thankfully, it slides open easily enough. Crawling out, I inhale sharply as my eyes adjust to the darkness. The fire escape is strategically placed under the next set of windows. And there's no way I can reach it from here.

Plastering myself against the wall, I slide along the eight-inch ledge to the next window and try not to think about what will inevitably happen if I slip six stories above the ground. Each step puts me closer to my escape, but further from the safety of the window I crawled out of.

Once I reach the adjacent window, I drop five feet onto the metal fire escape below. A groan escapes as my knees take the full impact of my weight. I stumble forward, grasping for the railing. But I can't stop yet, not until I put more distance between the Enforcers and myself. Ignoring the pain, I leap down the stairs while voices shout above me.

"She's getting away! Enforcers! Stop!"

A laser bullet whizzes past my head and hits the railing, burning a quarter-sized hole in the metal. I keep moving.

Catalyst

When I reach the end of the fire escape, I plow forward, throwing myself over the seven-foot drop. Pain shoots up my arm and tiny rocks stab my skin as my body slams against the pavement. Blood trickles down my elbow, and I lay on the ground for a moment, struggling to catch my breath as another bullet whizzes past. It lands on the ground next to me and leaves a burnt hole in the pavement. The next one is so close that it singes my pant leg and grazes the skin underneath. I scream as a lightning bolt of pain sears my leg and the smell of burnt flesh and fabric assaults my nose.

Staggering to my feet, I take off running—well, hobbling mostly—as I escape into the darkness, the black box wrapped protectively in my backpack.

Chapter Six

Sitting on my bed, I lather burn cream on my leg. Thankfully, the laser burn wasn't as bad as I initially pictured, only the size of a dime. But by the time I got home last night and dialed Chaz to let him know I was okay, it had already blistered and was oozing a bile-colored liquid. Not one of my best nights, that's for sure.

A knock on my bedroom door is followed by Mom peeking into the room. She's dressed in the usual—tan sweatpants and gray T-shirt. Her bright red hair is pulled back in a high ponytail.

I quickly pull my pant leg down, but I'm too late.

"What happened, sweetie?" Crossing the room in two strides, she plops down on the bed next to me. She tries to reach for my leg, but I gently push her hands away.

"I'm fine, Mom. Just a little burn from the exhaust pipe."

She frowns and fiddles with the silver charm bracelet on her wrist, one Dad gave her a few months before he died. "You need to be more careful, honey. That thing is so dangerous."

"I will, Mom. I promise." I study her face. She looks better today than she did yesterday. "How are you feeling?"

She gives me a small smile. "Much better, thankfully." She fingers a piece of my hair that came out of my ponytail. "Just look at you. You've grown into such a mature young woman."

Biting my lip, I tuck the strand of hair back into place. "Mom, can I ask you something?"

"Sure, honey."

"Why didn't you and Dad choose to have me genetically engineered?"

Mom's eyes widen as if she wasn't quite expecting that question. "Well, your father was opposed to it. Wanted you to be free of the pressures of society, or something. I can't remember how he put it." She smiles. "But it doesn't matter, does it? Because you're perfect to me."

My chest squeezes at her words. I wrap my arms around her and hold tight. As strong as I try to be, I still need my mother's love. I want to ask her about my father's identity change, but I don't want to upset her. She's so fragile nowadays.

Mom's arms enfold me. When she pulls away, her eyes are moist.

"What are your plans for today?" she asks. "Are you still working at that doctor's office?"

No, that was like two jobs ago, but I don't expect her to keep track, especially when I never tell her the truth about my jobs. "That was only a temporary position. I'm between jobs right now. But don't worry; I should be getting another paycheck soon." I hate lying to her, I really do. But if she knew the truth, it would tear her apart.

She nods, her eyes filling with tears. "Sienna," she whispers. "Do you know how proud I am of you?"

"Mom—"

"No, listen." She takes a deep breath. "I feel awful that you dropped out of school to help provide for the family. I know I haven't been a good mother, not since your father—" She pauses, blinking rapidly. "But I want to be better. I do. It's not fair to you or your sister—"

"Mom, please."

She straightens her shoulders. "Starting tomorrow, there will be some changes around here. Maybe I can get a job again—"

"I don't think that's a good idea," I say, thinking of the numerous jobs she's had and lost since my father's death. Grabbing my mother's cold hands and squeezing them between my own, I say, "It's okay, Mom. I have it covered. You just focus on getting well."

Her smile is sad as she brushes a lock of hair from my eyes. "You are so beautiful. If only your father could see you now. He would be so proud."

Guilt fills me, and my eyes shift away from hers.

If she only knew…

On my Harley, I weave through City Square, the area of town where the wealthy live. The twinkling lights from the street lamps illuminate clean streets and rows of restaurants. Such a contrast to the far side of Legas with its broken-down buildings and darkened streets. The Gateway was once a prominent business strip, a moneymaker for Legas, but now it's merely a cesspool for drug lords, criminals, and underground gambling. I don't know why the Enforcers haven't tried harder to put a stop to it.

Up on Hampstead Hill, I spot one of the mansions that overlook the city. The home of Match 360's director, Harlow Ryder. It stands like a beacon, embodying the dream of every person.

That one man can change our future.

I snort, struggling to hold back the laughter that bubbles up. Change the future? More like ruin the future. If it weren't for Harlow Ryder, genetically modified boys and girls wouldn't be quarantined from one another like hormonal dogs in heat. If it weren't for Harlow Ryder, people would still believe in love, romance, and desire. If it weren't for Harlow Ryder, wealthy parents wouldn't be making matches for their children while they are still infants.

When Mr. Ryder first began Match 360, his genetic

matchmaking company, I'm sure he didn't anticipate the impact his genetic discovery would have on the future of mankind. Perhaps he was trying to eradicate divorce. He may even have had good intentions to reduce the number of out-of-wedlock births and fatherless families. But his invention is changing society. Where lovers once courted, kissed, and fell in love, now, strangers are analyzed, their DNA coded, and their personalities and genetic makeup matched to create the perfect compatibility.

As if matchmaking wasn't enough, twenty-one years ago, Harlow expanded his company to include genetic modification. He created the first generation of genetically modified individuals, his youngest son being the very first. Now, genetic modification is a choice the affluent make for their children, for their society of Citizens.

When wealthy parents are ready to conceive, they fill out a form at a Chromo 120 facility and the doctor handpicks those qualities from the DNA of the mother and father. Rarely do you find "surprise" pregnancies among Citizens. That simply would not be acceptable.

I park my bike against the curb and walk the few blocks to Wedgewood Row, a group of connected buildings that house a barbershop, a couple of upscale boutiques, and an electronics repair shop. This part of the Row is pitch dark and completely deserted.

The alley behind the buildings isn't much better. The large dumpsters create lurking shadows on the brick walls. My heart pounds, both from uncertainty and excitement as I glance up and down the alley. With heightened senses, my eyes slowly adjust to the shadows and my ears perk at each rustle in the breeze. I glance at my watch. It's exactly ten.

A figure emerges from the shadows. He's been there the whole time.

Watching. Waiting.

A shiver of fear shoots up my spine.

The large man with oversized shoulders and a thick,

bulging neck approaches, but he keeps to the shadows. The moonlight carves a path of light, allowing me to see his piercing, beady eyes as he opens his mouth to speak.

"Preston?"

My blood runs cold at the sound of his voice. Low and menacing.

"Yes, I'm Sienna Preston," I say, tilting my chin higher.

The man pauses. "Do you have the box?"

I nod.

"Good." He motions with his hands. Two men step from the shadows, one burly, and the other wiry.

My heart stops. Three against one. Is this a joke?

The men grab my arms, pinning them to my sides.

"Hey! What are you—" I struggle against them, but they are too large, too strong. I open my mouth to scream, but something damp covers my mouth. The smell of castor oil mixed with chloroform fills my nostrils. Gagging, I swing my leg back to kick him in the groin.

Everything goes dark.

The rickety wooden chair creaks as I shift my weight and struggle to open heavy eyelids. Dim light filters in through the slits, and then I remember—the man with the thick neck and his two goons who grabbed me.

Rough cording binds my hands behind my back and rubs against my tender wrists. I try to shrug off the fear that tightens my shoulders as my eyes scan the room where I'm held captive. Puddles of water pool on the concrete floor and a single dangling bulb illuminates the dank, musty space. I must be in a basement of some sort, but where?

The door opens, and the thick-necked man with the beady eyes enters the room. After taking a seat in the chair across from me, he holds out a water bottle.

I glare in response. "Is this really necessary?" I ask,

indicating the bindings around my wrists.

He shrugs. "Doesn't have to be." Moving behind me, he unties the rope.

Relieved to be free of that awkward position, I rub my wrists, soothing the raw marks left from the cords.

Thick Neck offers me the water bottle again. This time, I gladly take it. My throat feels like a slightly wetter version of sandpaper, and my mouth tastes like someone poured vinegar in it. But before I chug the water, I pause to sniff. Smells like nothing—a good sign for water.

Thick Neck chuckles and settles back into his seat. "We appreciate you bringing the box to us—"

My hands move instinctively to my chest where I'd hidden the box that wasn't much larger than a matchbook. There's nothing there.

"We already got it."

A deep flush spreads across my cheeks. They invaded me. They had no right to take the box without my permission. And I don't even want to think about where they had to place their hands in order to retrieve it.

"I can see that bothers you. Rest assured—we were very professional about it." He smirks.

I bite my lip to keep from saying something I'll regret. The sooner he lets me leave, the better. "So if you have the box, why am I still here? Why all this drama?"

"Because what you did was illegal and I want to know who hired you." His eyes turn cold as he crosses one leg over the other and rests his clasped hands over his knees.

My eyes narrow. "I thought *you* hired me—"

He shakes his head and laughs, a cruel sound that chills me to the bone. "No. I just intercepted the exchange."

"Who are you?"

"Can't answer that, but what I can tell you is that you've been a very naughty girl." He leans in, closing the distance between us. "Do you know what happens to naughty girls?"

My breath catches, and I try to swallow the lump that

rises in my throat. "What do you want from me?"

He leans back and resumes a relaxed position. "I want to know who hired you, nothing more, nothing less."

"Sorry, can't help you there. I have no idea."

He glances at a mirror across the room and snaps his fingers. It is then that I realize this is nothing more than an interrogation room. My pulse quickens when his two goons enter the room and move toward my chair.

"Perhaps my boys can help jog your memory."

I stifle a moan as the goons shove me out of the chair. Gripping my arms, they lead me down a dank hall to an adjacent room that has a wooden chair and a galvanized tub filled with water. Fear courses through me as they set me down on the chair and tie my hands behind my back. I study their faces as they move around me—the hanging jowls of one, the lazy eyes of the second. As I plead with my own eyes for them to have mercy on me, they barely even glance in my direction. Tears threaten, but I blink them back before they can fall. I refuse to cry in front of these monsters.

The voice of the thick-necked man comes through a speaker overhead. "I'll ask you one more time. Who hired you to steal the computer chip from Harlow Ryder's office?"

"I already told you, I *don't know!*"

He makes a *tsking* sound. "Sorry, but that's the wrong answer."

Hands on the back of my head force my face forward until it's submerged in the tub. The cold water seeps into my eyes, nose, and ears as I struggle against their hands. But they are too strong. I stop fighting and concentrate on holding my breath. They are only trying to scare me, and I can't let them.

My lungs scream. Just when I think I can't hold my breath a second longer, they yank me up by my hair. My head throbs as I gasp for breath.

"Well, Miss Preston, let's try that again. Who hired you to steal the computer chip?"

I remain silent as the water drips down my face and onto

my black pants.

"Boys, you know what to do," Thick Neck's voice instructs.

I suck in a deep breath before my head is forced under again. Even though my throat is raw and my lungs ache, I remove myself. In my mind, I am lying in a meadow surrounded by beautiful butterflies. The sunlight falls on my face, and the breeze cools my warming body—

My head jerks up with a whoosh. Blackness dots the edges of my vision as I gulp air.

"Has your memory returned, Miss Preston?" his voice challenges.

When I don't answer, staring straight ahead at the cracked plaster on the walls instead, he continues, "Perhaps Miss Preston needs some time to think about it. Why don't we give her a few minutes?" The two goons leave the room. My head flops forward, my heart thudding its own sense of relief. I breathe deeply, grateful for a few moments of uninterrupted air.

I don't know how to make this ruthless man understand that I know nothing about my clients except they are the source of my paycheck.

What can I do to convince him?

My heart sinks when I hear a noise at the door. They've returned, and I'm no closer to knowing how to stop them than I was a few minutes ago. Maybe they will tire of this game and kill me quickly. I'd almost welcome a sure, fast death as opposed to this torture.

The door pushes open. A dark-haired guy not much older than I am pops his head in and glances around. When he spots me, he slides inside and hurries over. My eyes widen in fear—this must be the man who doesn't mess around. Maybe they *have* tired of playing games and decided to kill me. I close my eyes, not wanting to see the gun or knife he will surely pull from the back of his pants.

"Hey," he says, his voice soft.

My eyes pop open. This guy can't be an assassin, not with

that smooth, deep voice that would put most baritones to shame.

"I'm here to help you," he says, his blue eyes warm and kind.

My eyes narrow. "Who are you?"

He glances behind him. "I'll explain all that later."

Removing a knife from his pants—didn't I say he would have one?—he moves behind me to cut the cord from my wrists. Once my arms are free, I push my wet hair out of my eyes.

"You know how to get out of here?" I ask.

He nods, pocketing the knife. "Follow me and try to stay close." That's when I notice the heat he's packing in the back of his pants. I was right on both accounts. A knife and a gun. Thankfully, it looks as though neither of them will be used on me.

Removing the gun, he holds it steady before opening the door and peering down the hall. He motions, and we creep down the dark corridor, our feet silent on the block tile floor. I follow him to an empty stairwell, expecting to be ambushed by the thick-necked man and his men at any moment.

It isn't until we push through a metal door and are greeted by the night air that I feel a sense of relief. But we aren't safe yet. The guy breaks into a slow jog, crossing the damp grass, and I struggle to keep up, my head still fuzzy from lack of oxygen. We jog down a deserted road, the night sky so brilliant above us that the stars feel as if they are only an arm's reach away. A black truck is parked on the side of the road a half-mile from the facility where I was held hostage. I hang back as we near the vehicle.

I'm grateful for his help, but I know nothing about him, and that dark truck parked on the side of the road looks as inviting as being water tortured by those lunatics. Not to mention the fact he has a gun… and I don't.

"You okay?" he asks, eyeing me.

I shake my head. "I'm sorry. I appreciate you busting me

out of there, but I don't know you."

He grins, flashing a pair of dimples, and then holds out his hand. "Trey Winchester."

I hesitate a moment before sliding mine in his, the rough calluses on his palms scraping against my fingers. "Sienna Preston." It is then that I notice his arm. It's a tattoo, and yet, it's not. Interweaving, knotted ropes form what looks to be a tree that snakes down his arm. But it doesn't sit on top of his skin like a normal tattoo. Instead, it seems to glow from *beneath* his skin, especially in the dark. I've never seen anything like it.

"I know," he says.

"How do you know who I am?"

Trey shifts his weight and looks down at the ground before glancing up, his eyes connecting with mine.

"Because I'm the one who hired you to steal the computer chip."

Chapter Seven

My mouth drops open. "So, it's *your* fault I was kidnapped and practically drowned by some lunatic?"

Trey nods, his eyes pained. "I'm sorry. I got to the Row in time to see those men carrying your body to their car."

"You followed them?"

"Yeah."

"What took you so long? To get me out of there, I mean? Were you waiting for them to drown me before you came and collected my body?"

"It's... complicated. I had to find a way in. I couldn't exactly walk through the front door of a government facility."

"Government facility?"

Trey glances down the dark road as his face hardens. "Yeah. Those were government bastards."

I was thinking Mr. Ryder's men had come after me, but apparently not.

Cocking my head, I study the well-built guy in front of me, trying to decide if I should trust him. His kind eyes and dimpled smile make him appear believable, but the sheer fact that he's the reason I was kidnapped in the first place makes me want to smack him.

"I don't understand how our meeting was compromised," I accuse.

"Neither do I. And I'm sorry for the trouble this has caused you."

"They took the box with the chip."

Trey sighs. "Figures. Those government officials have wanted to get their hands on that for ages, and I practically handed it over to them."

I shouldn't want to know, with the client anonymity and all, but I'm curious. "Why did you want that computer chip?"

He shakes his head, his smile wry. "I'd like to tell you, but I can't."

Pursing my lips together, I place my hands on my hips. "Considering what you made me go through, I think I deserve to know."

He exhales deeply and contemplates my request. Just when I think he'll refuse, he nods. "You're right. I guess I owe you at least that much." He runs a hand through his dark hair before he continues. "That computer chip houses all the codes used for genetic matchmaking as well as the DNA database for genetic sequencing. If it gets into the wrong hands... let's just say I was trying to make sure it never does." He gives a harsh laugh. "Looks like I failed."

"Yeah, pretty much," I say, my tone flat.

The sound of a car speeding down the dark road catches my attention. "It's them," I choke out. Tiny headlights, like pinpricks in the night, move toward us.

"I can't outrun them in my truck. We need to hide." Trey grabs my arm. "Quick. Climb underneath."

I stare at him. "Of the truck? Are you crazy? Don't you think an abandoned truck is the first place they'll check?"

"That's what I'm banking on. They'll look in here," Trey pats his truck, "but they won't think to look underneath." His mouth turns up into a crooked grin. "I know we just met, but we're about to get real cozy."

My breath catches. "I think I'd rather make a run for it," I say. As I move away from the vehicle, Trey's hand latches on my arm, pulling me back.

"You don't have time," he hisses.

I glance down the road at the approaching headlights. He's right. "If you try anything," I threaten.

"I won't. Trust me."

Hesitantly, I lie facedown on the ground, rocks embedding themselves in my palms, and work my way under the truck. Little blades of grass poke through the gravelly shoulder, tickling my chin. There are distinct smells of dirt and gasoline under here, and I picture things dripping and oozing onto my back. Making a face, I close my eyes and scoot further beneath the belly of the truck. I feel Trey slide in next to me, his shoulder and hip pressed against mine.

The sound of the car draws closer, and Trey curses under his breath. He rolls over on his side and pulls me to him, trying to minimize the shape of our bodies beneath the truck. My fists clench, but I turn and face him, my head resting under his chin and my arms crushed against his chest. Squeezing my eyes shut, I hold my breath until I can't anymore. When I finally do inhale, I breathe in the smell of his skin. Sweat and soap—a very manly smell.

The car slows as it nears Trey's truck, its headlights illuminating the pavement all around us, but my heart rate picks up speed. "Be still and don't make a sound," Trey warns as the vehicle pulls to a stop beside the truck. A couple of car doors slam and heavy footsteps cross the pavement.

"Looks like an abandoned truck," one of the goons says.

Opening my eyes, I crane my neck. Trey gives me a warning look. I watch as a pair of black boots walk around the truck and then stop, directly at my eye level.

"Scan for fingerprints, and let's see if we can pull a connection to Miss Preston." Definitely Thick Neck's voice. A slight whirring sound follows his words as the fingerprint detector is activated.

Trey curses under his breath again, but so soft I barely hear it. The footsteps move to the back of the truck, stopping at the bed. The tailgate creaks open, and the whole truck shakes as someone climbs into the back. I hear the sound of something scraping, and then stuff being thrown around. My body tenses, and Trey's hands grip me tighter. I'm praying they don't look under here next.

"Clear," someone says. The truck shakes a little more as the person jumps out, his feet thumping against the pavement.

"Check the inside," Thick Neck commands.

More doors open and there's the muffled sounds of rifling around. "There's no one here, Colonel."

"Let's go," Thick Neck says. The footsteps move away, and the whirring noise stops.

We wait until the car leaves and is only a sound in the distance before Trey loosens his hold and wriggles out from under the truck. I follow him. But when I try to stand, my legs tremble so much that I stumble forward. Too much excitement for one night.

"You okay?" Trey asks.

I nod, but even as I do, pain shoots behind my eyes. "I think the night is finally catching up to me." Trey's hands try to offer support, but I push them away. "I'm fine."

Frowning, he moves to the driver's side of his truck. "Let's get you home."

As he drives, I rest my head against the leather headrest and recite my address so he can find it on his data map.

"I know where you live, remember? The package that showed up on your doorstep?"

Ahh, right. The package that started this whole mess. How could I forget?

"And how did you get my address?"

Trey glances at me, a grin spreading across his face. "Let's just say we have a mutual friend."

Mutual friend? I only have one friend, which narrows the possibilities considerably. "Chaz? You know Chaz?" When Trey nods, I ask, "How?"

"He works for me."

I'm about to ask him what Chaz does for him when I

remember. My bike.

"I need you to take me back to the Row," I say. "My bike is parked there."

"Are you sure? What if the government bloodhounds are still looking for you?"

I chew on my lower lip as I think about my options. This Thick Neck guy doesn't seem like one to give up easily, and if he knows who I am, he can easily find out where I live. But I have to protect Mom and Emily. They need me.

"Maybe you should go into hiding," he suggests before I can say anything.

Hiding? That's not even an idea I can contemplate. Who would take care of Mom and Emily?

"I actually know of a place—" he begins.

"I can't."

Trey glances in my direction, but it's too dark to see his expression. "If they find you—"

"That's a chance I'll have to take." I fold my arms over my chest. "Besides, it's not really your concern, is it?"

"Actually," he argues, "it is. I'm the one who hired you. Therefore, I put you in danger."

"And I'm the one who accepted the assignment. I knew the dangers involved."

He heaves a deep sigh, but he doesn't say anything else.

A few minutes later, I spot my bike still parked in front of the restaurant that closed hours ago. "Right over there."

Trey pulls into a parking space beside it, idling the engine. "You sure you'll be okay to ride home?" he asks.

"I'll be fine." I climb out of the truck and sidle over to the driver's side, leaning into his rolled-down window. "Now, as far as payment goes…"

Trey shakes his head with a rueful smile. "The deal was for you to bring me the chip. Without the chip, I can't make a payment."

Clenching my fists, I curse under my breath.

"What?" Trey says.

"Looks like I'll be sneaking back into that government facility."

"You wouldn't." He stares at me, his expression serious.

I shrug. "I need the money." I won't beg. I refuse to beg. But the idea of eating Meat Delite for the next few months makes my stomach churn.

He rests his head against the seat before replying, "Maybe we can work something out."

"Like?"

He leans forward. "Let me see your Lynk."

Confused, I pull my communicator from my pocket and hand it to him. He presses our screens together and holds down the button on the side. "Now, I have your information and you have mine. I'll be in touch." Handing the device back to me, he smiles. "Send me a message if you need anything."

Pocketing my Lynk, I turn and stride to my bike. I feel Trey's eyes on me as I straddle my Harley and rev the engine. I'm sure he's admiring her chrome handlebars and sleek frame as much as all the other men who've ever seen her.

On the drive home, my mind wanders to Trey and how he knows Chaz. I never did get an answer to that question. Who is this Trey guy and why does he care so much about that computer chip?

I tighten my fingers around the handlebars, enjoying the roar of the engine on the open road. The wind cools my skin and dries my hair into a frizzy mess, but I welcome my freedom. For the moment. The sun peeks over the horizon as I approach the turn-off to my home.

I was gone all night.

As I near our double-wide trailer, exhaustion sets in. All I can think about is climbing into my twin bed with the ruffled comforter. I just want to sleep. Forever.

Reality replaces my desire for sleep when I see a vehicle parked on the road in front of our trailer. A dark SUV with tinted windows. The owner leans against the back of it, his arms crossed over his chest. My heart stops when I get a good look at the man waiting for me.

Thick Neck.

"Well, Miss Preston, you weren't too hard to find," Thick Neck calls out as he strides down the gravel road toward me.

My mind races. *Should I turn my bike around and try to outrun him?* My eyes flicker to the trailer where my mother and sister sleep. No, I can't leave them here. Not with this crazy man right outside their door.

Taking a deep breath, I cut the engine and slide off my bike. As I walk toward him, I half-expect his goons to appear at any moment and force me into that black beast of a car, but the doors remain closed. I'm not sure what game Thick Neck is playing, but I decide to play along.

I hold out my arms, expecting him to bind them, but he only chuckles. "I'm not here to take you in, Miss Preston. I have a bigger fish to fry."

My arms drop to my sides. "What do you want?"

"I have a proposition for you. A business arrangement, if you will."

Cocking my head, I cross my arms. "I'm listening."

"I can choose to ignore the illegal act you performed if you would be willing to help me with something." He pauses. "A special assignment."

"What is it?"

He holds up a hand. "Before I tell you, I feel it's my duty to enlighten you concerning something you should have learned long ago." He pauses. "Your father once worked for Harlow Ryder. In the Capital."

I stare at him, surprised he knows anything about my father or his former life.

"I know," I say.

"Do you know why he left the Match 360 headquarters twenty-one years ago?"

I shake my head.

"Because of Harlow Ryder. Your father found out something—something he didn't want to be a part of. He wanted to leave, but Harlow threatened that if he ever told anyone what he'd discovered, he would kill him."

"What did my dad discover?"

Thick Neck shrugs. "Don't know, exactly. But what I do know is that Harlow made good on his promise a year ago."

"That's not possible. My father died of a heart attack—"

"A drug-induced heart attack," he clarifies.

The world spins. I close my eyes and take a deep breath, trying to sort through my thoughts, my feelings. How do you mentally swallow that kind of information?

My father was murdered. Harlow Ryder is the one responsible.

The sure foundation I've been resting on is crumbling beneath me, and I have no way to stop it. All this time, I believed my father died of natural causes. With this new knowledge, a fire burns deep inside. It's because of Harlow Ryder, that genetic-coding swine, that I've spent the past year selling my soul. I inhale slowly and exhale even slower.

I open my eyes and glare at Thick Neck.

"Why are you telling me this?"

The man grins and leans forward, pushing up onto the balls of his feet.

"Because, Miss Preston, I want you to put an end to Harlow Ryder."

Chapter Eight

Time stands still for a moment. Like one of those out-of-body experiences where everything slows down, and I'm able to see it from different vantage points. Except this is real life. And I've just been hit with a blow beyond imagination.

Kill someone. Harlow Ryder.

"Why do you want Harlow Ryder dead? What's in it for you?"

"That's classified," he says.

Exhaling slowly, I try to ease my racing heart. I don't know who he thinks I am, but I'm certainly not a murderer. I can barely kill the scorpions that find their way into our trailer. I can't kill a man.

"No," I say, shaking my head. "I could never."

Thick Neck's face twists into a sneer. Before I have time to react, he grabs my arm hard and drags me toward his SUV. I try to dig in my heels, but he's too strong.

"Let me see if I can convince you." The door lifts open with a hiss, and I gasp. There, seated in the back, is my mother. Her eyes are wide, her mouth gagged, and her hands bound.

"Leave her out of this," I warn, yanking my arm from his grasp. I start toward her, but Thick Neck's claw-like fingers dig into my shoulder, pulling me back. He grins. "I figure your mother can serve as insurance.

A cold sweat breaks out on the back of my neck despite the heat from the rising sun. "She needs her medicine," I say through clenched teeth.

"You deliver Harlow Ryder to me, dead, and you can have your mother back. Until then, I'm sure we have anything she needs," he finishes.

"You want me to kill Harlow Ryder in exchange for my mother's freedom?"

"That's correct. And don't even think about trying to go to the Enforcers. First, they'd never believe *you*—a girl from the trailer park. And second—" He leans toward me, his lips curling into a sneer. "You have no idea who you're dealing with."

Threats and blackmail. Pure and simple.

"And neither do you," I hiss.

The man laughs, his Adam's apple bobbing up and down in his thick neck. "Name's Radcliffe. I'm a colonel in the military and head of the AIG branch of government. I have connections you can't even dream about. I practically own this city."

"So, basically, that makes you a tyrant. Not surprised."

Radcliffe's eyes narrow, and he moves abruptly to my side. Before I have a chance to defend myself, he grabs my hair, jerking my head back. I hear my mom whimper as she watches us. Pain radiates through my neck, but I refuse to give him the satisfaction of knowing he hurt me.

"Wouldn't it be awful if something happened to your dear mother and sister?" he says, his voice low, his breath reeking of garlic or onions, not sure which. My throat constricts.

Radcliffe shoves my head to the side. A dull ache spreads at the base of my neck and works its way to my brain. I suddenly wish I *had* let Trey bring me home. At least Trey has a gun.

I glance over at my mother, who is still bound and gagged in the backseat. In her eyes, I see all the confusion, sadness, and fear that I feel but can't show. I have to stay strong—for her and Emily. And now my mother will have to watch me do a deal with the *real* devil.

I clear my throat and clasp my hands together. "How would I do it?"

Radcliffe gives me a sick smile. "I figure it's only fitting for Harlow Ryder to experience the same death as your father."

"A heart attack?"

"Poison. It stops the heart almost immediately and simulates a heart attack."

An image floods my mind. My father dead on our kitchen floor, his skin cold, his eyes blank. Murdered.

How can I even entertain the idea of killing a man? Even though Harlow has my father's blood on his hands, I don't want to be his judge and jury. I don't want to be the one to snuff out his life.

"It doesn't seem like it would be a very hard decision, Miss Preston. Especially if you want your mother home safe and sound with you and your sister. I don't understand why you wouldn't want Harlow dead anyway, considering what he did to your father."

I am not a murderer. *I'm not.* But I have to protect my family.

Then again, why me? Why not someone with experience? Military training perhaps?

But I know the answer without even thinking too hard. They need a scapegoat. An *untraceable* scapegoat. If things go awry, they need someone to take the fall. Someone who will never be linked to them.

But, I'm not a murderer.

Then what are you? A thief? A liar? Does that make you any better?

It's just one man. One man who's causing a division among the people. One man who took away everything I've ever known and loved. One man who deserves to die.

Radcliffe crosses his arms over his wide chest. "Well, Miss Preston?"

Catalyst

I lick my lips and struggle to swallow the lump in my throat.

"I'll do it."

Chapter Nine

Inside the house, I find Emily still curled in her bed with no idea that her mother was taken while she was sleeping. I don't know how Radcliffe got in and out without making any noise, but there's no sign of a struggle.

I pace the tiny kitchen, chewing my lower lip and trying to come up with a plan. When Emily stumbles into the kitchen a little while later, the sun is barely peeking through the flimsy curtains nailed over the window. She yawns and rubs her eyes.

I immediately pull her into my arms and breathe in the scent of her Smashin' Strawberry shampoo. She is so small, so fragile, that she fits perfectly in my arms, her bones poking through her thin cotton nightgown.

I cling to her because she's all I have left. If anything happens to her…

"I'm hungry, Si-Si. Will you make me breakfast?"

I pull back to look at her and smooth the hair away from her face. "What would you like?"

"Can I have chocolate oatmeal?" Chocolate oatmeal was my dad's signature breakfast item. Of course, Emily doesn't remember that, only that she likes it. She doesn't remember much about the man who once rocked her to sleep and sang off-tune lullabies in her ear.

"I'm sorry, sweetie. We don't have any oatmeal, but we do

have some lovely dehydrated bologna."

Emily makes a face as I open the fridge.

"The shelf life for product Meat Delite expires in—"

"Yeah, yeah, yeah, I know," I mutter, grabbing one of the packages. It only takes a few minutes to rehydrate the meat. After placing it in a bowl in front of Emily, I take a seat next to her at the counter. I watch her take the first bite, grimacing as she swallows, her blue eyes wide awake despite the early hour.

"Is Mommy still sleeping?" she asks, peering at me.

Shaking my head, I search for the right words. I don't want to scare her, but I don't want to lie to her either. "Mommy went away for a few days."

"For work?" For a five-year-old, she sure is perceptive.

"No, sweetie. But I'm sure she'll be home before you know it."

Emily scrunches her little nose, looking like a cute bunny. "Is she okay?"

"Of course."

Cocking her head to the side, she thinks for a moment. "When Mommy comes home, will she not be so tired?"

I glance down at my hands, searching for the right words. She doesn't understand. How do I explain to my sister that her mom is physically sick, unable to care for herself and others?

I run my fingers through her curls, and she swats my hand away. "Right after Daddy died, Mommy worked so hard that she wore herself out. Now her body is trying to get better."

"When will she be better?"

I pull her close and kiss the top of her head, thinking how right now, our mother's sickness is the least of our worries. "I don't know, sweetie. I just don't know."

Taking Emily's hand in mine, we traipse across our yard together. With more sand and rocks than grass and plants, it's a typical desert landscape.

Mrs. Locke, our only neighbor, is outside watering the plants on her porch. She's a kind, elderly woman who lost her husband several years ago. She's also Emily's babysitter when the need arises.

"Hi, Mrs. Locke," I say, greeting her with a smile.

She straightens up, watering can in hand and housedress hanging around her knees. "Hello, Sienna. How are you, dear?" Her smile lights up her wrinkled face. With one weathered hand, she smooths the gray hairs back into her bun.

"You are very ambitious, Mrs. Locke, to grow flowers in this heat."

She laughs and raises a hand to shield her eyes from the blinding sun. "It's a hobby of mine. Gives me something to do."

I glance down at Emily, who clutches her favorite doll and a backpack filled with snacks. "Would you mind watching Emily for me? I have to go to work, and my mother... is out of town for a few days."

"I'd love to," she says, smiling. Like a mother hen, she ushers Emily into her trailer, the screen door creaking closed behind them.

I peek my head in and call out "Thank you," but Mrs. Locke is busy showing Emily her newest coloring screen.

As I ride my motorcycle to town, I try not to picture this man I've never met dead on the floor. I force images of his family's tears from my mind. I can't think of him as anything other than a murderer and a genetic-coding tyrant in order for me to go through with this. The thought of my father dead on *our* kitchen floor helps to fuel my cause.

I arrive at City Square only minutes before the Match 360 Extravaganza is scheduled to start. Today, Harlow Ryder will announce the betrothal of his youngest son, Zane, the first genetically modified human and Harlow's greatest accomplishment. Since birth, Zane has been matched to the "perfect" girl for him. This match has been kept secret for years, but today, all of Pacifica will tune in to the announcement of the decade. Akin to our own type of royalty, Zane and his fiancée will have a hard time avoiding the spotlight once their betrothal is announced.

Today is also an opportunity for Harlow to introduce his son to the world and show him off as the poster child he is. Whereas much of Harlow's life has been spent under the scrutiny of society, Zane has lived a more sheltered life. Very few digital images of him exist, and Harlow has always said it was to protect his son.

I'm here purely for research purposes. Before I go storming into Mr. Ryder's home to pour poison into his Scotch, I need to analyze the situation.

The benefit of being small comes into play as I weave in between the crowds of protestors who line the Square and the wealthy Citizens who adorn themselves in the latest fashion, expensive jewelry, and trendy shoes. I see more holographic jackets, vinyl, transparent skirts, metallic corsets, and five-inch heels than I care to ever see again.

My eyes rest on a girl about my age with sun-kissed hair, tan skin, and a skin-tight outfit with puffy shoulders that makes her look like a butterfly. She smiles and waves to someone she knows in the crowd, showing off a perfect set of pearly whites. I know her. The beautiful, perfect, always alluring Rayne Williams.

I used to compare myself to her and all those other girls at GIGA. I would come home after school and cry to my mother. It wasn't fair that they were smart, pretty, talented, and athletic. And I wasn't.

My mother would wipe the tears away and say, "It doesn't matter what *they* are. It only matters what *you* are. You are smart, beautiful, and courageous, and I didn't need a test tube to give me the best daughter in the world."

Her words gave me the confidence I needed to face one more day. And then another. Until eventually, I didn't have to anymore. The truth is, as much as I hated going to that school, I'd take that life—the one with my father alive, my mother home safe, my life secure, intact—over this one, any day.

Ducking through the tiny pockets the curious onlookers leave, I make my way to the roped-off area in front. A grand stage has been set up in the middle of the Square. It's adorned with extensive lighting, cameras, and a massive screen. I don't know why Harlow Ryder decided to have the Extravaganza here instead of in the Capital. Maybe because this is where Zane grew up?

I spot the triangle symbol that was etched on the black box I stole. Here, the symbol is everywhere—stamped onto the glass podium, on large, unfurled banners creating a backdrop for the outdoor stage, and flashing across the giant screen.

Two elongated Ms—one right side up and the other upside down—separate, and then move back into position, fitting together perfectly to form the symbol.

Now, the symbol makes sense. The Match 360 symbol forms a perfect match just as the company does. I groan in response to my discovery. It's fitting, but kind of cheesy in my opinion.

Shielding my eyes from the glaring sun, I glance around the Square and spot two security guards on each side of the stage. Studying the roofline behind me, I notice two more perched on the roofs of adjacent buildings. The amount of security isn't surprising. With the growing agitation of the Fringe—a terrorist group that actively takes a stand against genetic matchmaking and modification—and the many death threats Harlow Ryder has received over the years, he is a wanted man. I can attest to that.

A hush falls over the crowd as three well-dressed men in custom-tailored suits and expensive dress shoes walk onto the stage, escorted by a man in a navy suit with a wire running behind his ear and down his neck. The security guard stands a few feet away as the three Ryder men position themselves in front of a glass podium in the center of the stage. Harlow Ryder, the older gentleman with graying hair and deep-set eyes, steps up to the podium. His two sons stand to the left of him.

That is the man I'm here to analyze. The man I'm supposed to kill. And the man who ended my father's life well before his time. Anger wells up inside as I think of my sister who will never know her father and the man responsible only twenty feet from me.

Breathing deeply, I turn my attention to the other two men on stage. The older son is Steele Ryder, the one who runs the Match 360 headquarters in Rubex, and the one who *was* in line to inherit the company after his father dies. That's what everyone believed until *Reader's Daily* exposed the sordid details of his removal from power. Apparently, after Zane was born—twenty years his junior—Steele's position of authority was displaced to his younger, genetically modified brother. And even though society has heard about Steele throughout the years, his younger brother, Zane, remains a mystery.

I study Zane as Harlow Ryder begins to speak. He's a beautiful man, with wavy blond hair, a powerful frame, and a warm smile. Oddly, there's something very familiar about him.

As his father speaks, Zane's eyes sweep the crowd, locking with mine for an instant. It's then that I remember him— the boy from the Megasphere. The one who thought I was a jumper.

My cheeks flush and my eyes shift downward. I hope he doesn't recognize me.

When I think it's safe, I dare another glance in his direction. He still stares at me, his head tilted, his eyebrows raised, and the beginnings of a smile tweaking the corner of his mouth. My heart speeds up like a freight train barreling through a tunnel.

When he realizes his father is talking about him, he straightens up and takes on an air of formality.

"And now, I'd like to introduce you to my son, Zane Ryder," Harlow says, motioning with his arms.

Zane steps forward and waves in greeting amidst the cheers and catcalls. Many are from adoring girls, but from the back of the crowd, I hear the murmurs and unease of the protestors, followed by several chants of, "No more match! No more match!"

When Zane speaks from the podium, his deep voice with the melodious lilt resonates through the microphone. For a brief moment, I picture him walking toward me, hands outstretched, trying to convince me not to jump. The screen behind him lights up with a bigger-than-life image for those in the back of the crowd to see.

"Greetings, friends! Thank you for coming out today. I appreciate your support. It's not every day you meet your fiancée for the first time." The audience chuckles. "You know, I realized today that my father is a genius. A true genius. There are many out there who believe he lacks a heart, or who wonder how he can live with himself for taking away the choice of who to marry and the mystery of birth, but I believe he is the smartest man I've ever known. He saw a discrepancy in the way marriage worked. Saw a need for a change and therefore created a scientific formula to make a marriage successful. He created the ideal marriage by producing a matchmaking system unparalleled to anything ever seen before or since." Zane pauses and lifts his hand in his father's direction. "My father had a vision for our future, one of individuals who are no longer bound by disease and imperfections. So he designed a genetic codex to create perfect members of society. He is changing our future for the better. He is the matchmaker. He is the modifier. And a fine one he is."

After a few moments, Zane finishes speaking and Steele

takes the podium, flashing a wide smile at the crowd. I tune him out as he speaks. He comes across as slightly arrogant, and I'm not really interested in anything he has to say. It's amazing how two brothers can look so completely different. While Zane is blond, tan, and muscled, Steele is brown-haired, fair, and slightly overweight.

I perk up when they introduce Zane's fiancée, a young woman by the name of Arian Stratford. Arian and her parents step onto the stage and stand next to Zane. Curious, I scrutinize the young woman. She is tall and beautiful, her long, dark hair cascading down her back, her slender legs endless in her black sequined pencil skirt and six-inch heels. She looks tailor-made, almost as if she just stepped off the pages of a fashion magazine. I feel a twinge of jealousy as I admire the glamorous girl. I know I'll never look like that, no matter how hard I try.

Zane curiously eyes his new fiancée, as if seeing her for the first time. It's odd they've never met, which is what I gather from the furtive looks and lack of affection. Isn't it only natural for an engaged couple to hold hands or stand closer together? In truth, they look more like perfect strangers than a perfectly matched and engaged couple. *True compliments of the matchmaking system.*

I turn my attention to the target, Harlow, who gazes around the crowd of people with a satisfied smile on his face. When he walks to the podium to speak again, he clears his throat and proclaims he has an important announcement to make.

"Ladies and gentlemen, as you know, Zane is a miracle, not because he's handsome and smart, but because he is the first genetically modified human Chromo 120 has produced." He motions for Zane to join him next to the podium, and Zane walks forward with a confident smile.

Harlow continues, "And Arian—come on up here, dear." He waits for Arian to join him and Zane. "Arian is our first genetically modified female. She was created specifically to be a perfect match for my son, Zane. In the next few years, you will see the first generation of genetically modified individuals marrying their matches and expanding this society we live in. A society where there are no limits, only possibilities."

A commotion from behind propels me to turn and scan the crowd. A few people in the back hold signs and shout with angry force. I tune in to what they are saying as a murmur spreads through the crowd around me.

Abomination.

They shout the word over and over again in one voice, united in their hatred. Something catches the corner of my eye, and I look in time to see a small army of Enforcers making their way toward the shouting people.

Zane moves to the podium in shock, and his eyes lock with mine as he struggles for the right words to calm everyone down. His gaze is completely unnerving. I glance down at my hands, but my head snaps up when his voice comes clear and strong through the microphone.

"The purpose of our company is to better society—"

A gunshot rings out.

I gasp in horror as a bullet whizzes past Zane's head and through the screen behind him, leaving a quarter-sized bullet hole in its wake. Everything happens in slow motion. The security guard in the navy suit rushes forward, knocking Zane to the ground and shielding him with his own body. The crowd screams and pushes each other, struggling to get away from the stage. Harlow, Steele, Arian, and Mr. and Mrs. Stratford throw themselves to the ground while several plainclothes guards hurl onto the stage. A hovercraft appears from out of nowhere and lands next to the stage. The guards help the Ryders and Stratfords to their feet and usher them to the waiting craft.

I scan the crowd, looking for the source of the shot. Another shot fires, this one from the rooftop.

The mob of people run, almost knocking me to the ground. I struggle to regain my footing and push past everyone. A woman screams to my left, an ear-piercing scream that makes my blood run cold. I duck through the moving bodies until I reach the center of the Square. Blood pools around the lifeless body of a man. The lifeless body holding a gun.

I struggle to breath as a wave of nausea passes over me. His expressionless face, his unseeing eyes. It all takes me back to another time and another place.

I don't know how long my father lay on our kitchen floor, but when I found him, his body was as cold as the tile beneath him. His eyes were haunting. Unflinching. Unfeeling. Just like the ones of the man before me.

Bodies press against me, trying to get a glimpse of the dead man lying in the street. I push through the crowd of people, wanting to put distance between the man responsible for the attempted murder of Zane Ryder and myself.

And yet, here I am, about to commit the most heinous act of all. I'm about to become no better than the man lying in the Square.

Will that be my end also?

Chapter Ten

The wind that whips my face as I tear away from the city is a welcome change from the hot, stagnant air of the Square. My bike knows the way, even before I decide where I'm going.

The road leading to the dam is winding, perfect for a motorcycle. I wonder, as I have before, why more people don't restore these old relics. There is nothing like the feel of power between your thighs and searing heat only inches from your legs. Nowadays, if you want a fast ride, your only option is a jet bike. Although it is similar to a motorcycle, it lacks the few crucial components that make me feel as if I'm challenging death every time I ride—small wheels, open-air design, and a burning hot exhaust pipe.

I park in my favorite spot on the lake side of the dam. The reservoir created by the dam is the perfect place to swim— and it would be, if it were legal. Since the lake is our primary source of water, it is now a protected resource. Once a place filled with boats, jet skis, and water boarders, the lake now sits unused and unspoiled.

I slip out of my black pants and gray shirt, placing them in a pile on a nearby rock. The sun beats down on my bare skin, but I'm not worried about being seen. No one dares come to this part of the lake.

Climbing the highest rock I can find, I adjust the straps

of my pink bra. I eye the surroundings. The turquoise lake stretches for miles to my right, and the large concrete dam is in the distance to my left. I glance below me. The distinct orange line against the rocks shows the water level is lower than it has been in quite some time. The lack of rain in the coming summer months will only decrease the level.

I know this is stupid—jumping off the cliff. There could be hidden rocks submerged under the water. And the sheer fact that the water level is lower than normal does cause my heart rate to quicken.

But I love the way I feel when I cliff jump. I've jumped off these rocks a hundred times before. And I need something to remove the dead man's blank stare, the knowledge that Harlow killed my father, and the image of my mom bound and gagged from my mind.

I take a deep breath before hurling myself over the rock. The cool water stings when it hits my skin. Instead of kicking to the surface, I allow my body to sink downward, toward the bottom of the lake. My hair floats around me like red seaweed, and I stay at the bottom for who knows how long, holding my breath. It would be so easy to stay here. To forget about Harlow Ryder. To escape Radcliffe. To pretend my mother is home safe. To leave my sister—

A sob chokes the back of my throat, but I still don't kick upward. I'm not trying to kill myself. I know that. Suicide is never an honorable escape. But perhaps I'm trying to find that place, the one that exists on the cusp of death where life makes more sense. Where things seem clearer.

Before I can contemplate this, strong arms wrap around my waist and lift me upward, propelling me toward the surface.

I come up sputtering, coughing, and gasping for air. Someone is behind me, dragging me toward the rocks. When I wrench myself free and turn to confront my attacker, I come face to face with Zane Ryder.

"What the—" The absurdity of the situation hits me, and

a laugh of hysteria bubbles out. Zane Ryder, the man who was just shot at, is here at the dam, dragging me from the water.

I rub my eyes to make sure I'm not seeing things. Sure enough, Zane is treading water three feet from me.

"That's the second time I've had to save you," Zane says with a grin.

Heat rises to my cheeks despite the cool water. "I didn't need you to *save* me," I snap.

Zane cocks his head to the side and studies me. "You must be a thrill seeker. One of those people who do crazy things for a high."

Ignoring his comment, I swim past him to the rocks. I climb out, keenly aware of his eyes on my body. Turning to confront him, I raise my eyebrow. "Do you mind?" I ask as I place my hands on my hips.

He averts his eyes and mutters an apology, but not before I catch him gazing at my chest. *Boys.*

I grab my clothes and struggle back into them. It's a lot harder to dress with wet skin. Thankfully, Zane stares at something on the other side of the lake, giving me the privacy I need.

When I'm dressed, I stride to my bike. His sleek silver Mercedes Benz Aria is parked crookedly on the gravel, as if he were in a hurry to get here.

"Wait," he calls out.

Turning slowly, I watch as he swims to the side and climbs out, his boxer shorts clinging to him. I avert my eyes in embarrassment. I'm trying not to notice the dip where his shoulders and bicep connect. I don't want to admire the broadness of his shoulders or the water that glistens over his smooth skin.

He hurries into his clothes while I wait.

When he strides over to me, he's dressed in the same attire from the Extravaganza, minus the suit coat.

"What are you doing here?" I demand. He almost got

shot for crying out loud. Shouldn't he be with his fiancée or something?

"I'm here for the same reason you are. To escape." His smile adds mirth to his words, but his dark eyes remain serious.

I don't want to ask. I shouldn't care to know. But I do. "From what?"

He ignores the question. "You were at the Extravaganza?" It sounds more like a statement than a question.

I nod.

"I know. I saw you."

"So?" Defensiveness prickles through me.

"So you know what happened." He runs his fingers through his wet hair. "Kind of a wake-up call, you know?"

Again, I wonder—*Where is Arian?*

My mouth finds a way to give a voice to my thoughts.

He shrugs in response. "After I made sure everyone was okay, I left."

"You didn't get on the hovercraft?"

He shakes his head. "I had to get away. I needed time… to think."

My mouth drops open a little. "They let you leave? By yourself?" Doesn't he realize his father isn't the only one with a target on his back?

His smile shows a row of perfect white teeth. Then again, I don't know why I expect any less. He is, after all, a super human. A perfect specimen.

But I don't see anything perfect about him. His nose is too straight. His smile too white. His shoulders too broad. His waist too trim. Nope. Nothing perfect about him at all.

I shake my head in disgust. Why is he still here talking to me?

I turn to leave, calling over my shoulder, "Good luck staying alive."

"Wait. I didn't get your name." He follows me to my bike.

"That's because I didn't give it," I retort.

He grins. "I think I deserve to at least know your name, considering I've saved you twice now."

"I already told you—"

He laughs, a deep sound that bounces off the rocks around us. "I know. You didn't need saving. But that's not how it looked to me. When I see a girl jump off a cliff and not surface, what am I supposed to think?"

He has a point. But I won't admit it to *him*.

Climbing on my bike, I rev the engine. I think I see a flash of disappointment in his eyes.

As I pull away from the lake, I call over my shoulder.

"It's Sienna."

Chapter Eleven

tupid. Stupid. Stupid.

S I didn't even think about the complication Zane causes. Tonight, I'm supposed to sneak into the celebratory ball at Zane's house and poison his father. Now that Zane "knows" me, things have become infinitely harder.

When I open the package left on our doorstep, I find a black cocktail dress inside. I swallow my disgust. Can't have the poor girl looking like trailer-park trash in a multimillion-dollar mansion.

When I try on the dress, it only reaches mid-thigh. I want to curse the thick-necked man. Is this his idea of a joke?

I park several blocks from the palatial home. I figure it's best if I don't pull up to the house in my mother's beat-up Asher, its fender-wing dangling precariously by a few strips of metal. Everyone else uses the valet that waits in front of the fifteen-thousand square foot home.

I tug the dress further over my rear and try not to gape as I walk up the driveway toward the white chateau-style home. Large, arched windows and a grand balcony on the second story decorate the front. An oversized stone courtyard shows off an exquisite fountain I could practically swim in, and pencil-like spruce trees outline the property. I've never seen a house so imposing, and the very thought of going inside sends a buzz of nervous energy shooting through me.

The mahogany door swings open before I even have a chance to knock. My heart pounds, and I try to swallow the fear in my throat. I flash my fake invitation at the man I assume must be the Ryder's butler, and he offers me a warm smile and invites me in.

My gaze moves around the foyer. If entering the Ryder's home was under different circumstances, I might enjoy seeing the inside of such a beautiful estate. The curved double staircases, giant crystal chandeliers, and overflowing vases of fresh bouquets make me realize how far out of my league I am. Never in my life have I been around so many nice things or so many people with money.

Focus, Sienna. You have a job to do.

I follow several other people as they enter what must be the grand ballroom. Hundreds of wealthy Citizens mingle, eating hors d'oeuvres and socializing. Diamond-studded hands wave to friends, while the jewelry embellishing the arms, necks, and ears of the young GM women makes the room sparkle.

Taking a deep breath, I try to calm my swiftly beating heart. I don't belong here, and I know it. It's only a matter of time before they know it, too.

My eyes scan the room. I'm hoping I can avoid Zane. Tonight will be tricky enough without his questioning brown eyes. And the last thing I need is for him to ruin my only chance of getting close to Harlow Ryder.

I try not to think about what I'm going to do. It's just an assignment. A horrible, atrocious, unforgivable one, but it is still just an assignment. And it's one that will deliver swift justice and reunite me with my mother.

A tray filled with glasses of champagne moves past, and I grab one, hoping the alcohol will calm my nerves. After chugging the golden liquid, I shake my head to clear my thoughts. I search the crowd, trying to locate Mr. Ryder, but as I turn, I spot Zane instead. From across the room, he stares at me with the same amused expression I saw earlier today.

Biting my lip in frustration, I duck into a crowd of people, trying to hide from his gaze. I still don't see Mr. Ryder. He's probably in a room smoking cigars with a bunch of wealthy, old men.

I scoot to the wall and watch the GM girls in their fancy apparel—gaudy blue sequins, diamond-studded bodices, and red taffeta skirts. They talk in groups, sway to the music, and chat with their handsome GM matches, while their parents monitor their interactions from across the room. From what I understand about GMs, the amount of time they spend with their future match is minimal. Seems as if Zane and Arian are the exception; I don't think they'd ever even met until today.

A cascade of illustrious, golden hair mocks me from across the room. Rayne turns around, smiling wide, her gown barely covering all of her important parts. I try not to gape at her exposed belly and the slit in her dress. It comes up so high it shows off the entire length of one long, perfectly sculpted leg. I only hope she's wearing panties underneath.

This is a different lifestyle. A completely different way of thinking. These people have had things handed to them on a silver platter, while my family lives day to day. If I don't work, we don't eat. If I don't bring home money, we have no place to live. And if I don't kill Harlow, I'll never see my mother again.

Hot tears sting the back of my eyes when I think of my mom lying on a hard, cold surface somewhere, alone and scared. This is my fault. This is all my fault. If I had never taken the assignment to steal the computer chip, none of this would have happened. Because of my stupidity, I've placed all that I have left in this world in danger. And I don't know how to make it right other than by killing Harlow Ryder.

I hurry over to the veranda and step outside. Thankfully, it's empty except for some large potted plants and a few wrought-iron tables.

The tears I'm holding in fall on the white balustrade as

my mind churns with unanswered questions. How did I get mixed up in all of this? What did my father know that made him a threat to Harlow Ryder? How could he leave us in such a position?

The door opens behind me, and I quickly wipe the tears away.

A melodic voice speaks. "Sienna? Are you okay?"

I regret telling him my name. Why did I use my real name?

Be charming, Sienna. That's how women at these parties act. Charming.

I turn slowly and find Zane staring at me. He looks every bit the part of the Chromo 120 poster child in his expensive black tuxedo.

"I'm fine," I say, but my voice comes out tighter than I would have liked.

He eyes me as if trying to determine the truth. "You sure? Is there something I can do?"

Sure—kill your father for me?

I force a smile. "I'm fine, really. I've just had a lot on my mind lately."

Zane's smile is rueful. "I know the feeling." He stares at me, his gaze bringing heat to my cheeks. He finally speaks again. "I didn't expect to see you here tonight."

"I… I'm a freelance reporter," I say, using my preconceived cover. "And this is the biggest celebration Pacifica has seen in quite some time. Naturally, this is the place to be."

His brows lower. "You're a reporter?"

My heart pounds. He's suspicious. *Please don't let him call my bluff.*

"That's right."

"Were you on assignment at the Extravaganza today?"

I nod slowly. "Yes, I was."

Zane grimaces. "I bet you got a good story."

"Sadly, yes. People will always tune into three things: murder, political conspiracy, or betrayal." I shrug. "It's the nature of the beast. But I was hoping you might have time to chat tonight? Maybe answer a few questions?"

"Of course, I'd be happy to." He motions to a small bistro table with two metal chairs. "Shall we?"

A breeze blows across the veranda, carrying with it the scent of jasmine. The moon hangs low in the night sky as if it's trying to listen in on our conversation. I take the offered seat and pull out a transcriber from my purse, relieved I thought to put it in there earlier. Gliding my finger over the record/transcribe button, I look up at Zane. "Ready?"

"Will you take it easy on me?" He grins.

I want to roll my eyes, but instead, I force a chuckle. "I can't make any promises."

He winks at me, and I want to curse my heart when it starts to beat erratically.

"Well, then, fire away."

"What happened at the Extravaganza today?"

Zane shrugs. "Some crazy Fringe member tried to kill me. End of story."

"Do you have any idea why someone would want you dead?" *Or your father?* I hold my breath and wait for his answer.

Irritation flashes across his face. "You heard them. I'm an abomination. Abominations need to be destroyed."

"Have the Fringe always been violent toward your family and your company?"

"No, not until recently. There's growing agitation about Chromo 120 and government interference."

"Government interference?"

Zane glances at the transcriber before speaking. "Can we take this off the record?"

I switch the transcriber off and lean forward. When he speaks, Zane sounds tired and looks much older than his twenty-something years.

"A division of the government called AIG—Agency for Intelligence & Genetics—is very interested in our company.

They've been approaching my father for years, wanting to buy the company from him, but just recently—" He pauses and glances behind him. Leaning in, he speaks softer. "Recently, someone broke into our Legas facility and stole an important computer chip. This chip houses all the codes, all the information we use to run the company. With the wrong person in possession of it, I'd hate to see what would happen."

My heart skips a beat and breathing becomes a chore. Radcliffe's words fill my brain: *I'm a colonel in the military and head of the AIG branch of government.*

"What do you think might happen?" I whisper.

"Any number of things. Someone else could develop a prototype similar to ours."

"Why would this AIG be interested in it?"

"Why else? To create a perfect race. A master race. One more advanced than any other. Whereas my father is interested in eliminating diseases and bettering marriages, I think the AIG's motivation for this perfect race would be very different."

"How do you know all this?"

"Like I said before, they've been approaching my father for years. And I've done a little of my own digging."

My mind whirs. A perfect race? A race of genetically modified people? And what happens to those who aren't perfect? Are we shunned? Eliminated? Did I just make this more possible by stealing the chip?

Zane places a hand on the table and leans in. "Don't you find it odd that we keep running into each other? First the Megasphere, then the dam, now here—"

"Coincidences," I say quickly, and then force a smile to soften my harshness.

He stares at me, his eyes roving over my face until I grow uncomfortable. When he speaks, his voice is low. "I've thought about you a lot since that night." He says it casually, but his words hit me hard.

Why is he telling me this?

I pretend that I don't understand the meaning behind his words. "Off the record, why were you on top of the Megasphere? I thought I was the only one crazy enough to go up there."

His playful grin fades. "My brother and I don't always agree on how the company should be run."

"Steele?"

His jaw clenches. "Yeah. Steele. If it were up to him, we would have sold our prototype to the government ages ago. It's a good thing he spends most of his time at the Match 360 headquarters in Rubex." He shakes his head. "I like to go to the Megasphere to think. I seem to find clarity when I can look out over the whole valley." He laughs, but it's not convincing. "Seems childish, huh?"

"Not at all. Same reason for me. To think. Figure things out."

Zane's warm brown eyes widen in surprise, and then he grins. "I knew there was a reason I liked you."

Heat rises to my cheeks, and I bite down on my lip.

Before I have a chance to respond, the door leading to the veranda swings open. His brother stands in the doorway, taking up most of it. A large man, Steele looks about as cuddly as a prickly pear. His mouth is set in a hard line, and his eyes rake over Zane, announcing his disapproval.

"Zane, a word, please." Steele strides to the far corner of the veranda and waits for Zane to join him.

Zane rolls his eyes and mutters, "See what I mean?" before sauntering over to his brother.

Steele makes me wary. I don't like how he keeps glancing in my direction or the stone-cold look in his eyes. He seems like a ruthless man. One I'd rather not be involved with.

Since Zane is engrossed in a conversation with his brother, I hurry across the veranda and slip inside the ballroom. I immediately spot Mr. Ryder across the room conversing with two gentlemen in tuxedos. My heart leaps to my throat. This is it. It's time.

I picture the unfeeling glassy eyes of the dead man in the Square. Then my mind replaces the image with that of Harlow Ryder lying on the cold, marble floor. His eyes open, glassy, unmoving, and unfeeling.

I fight back a wave of nausea. I can't do it. I'm not a murderer.

How did I ever think I could go through with this?

I hurry toward a hallway on my left and push open a door, relieved to find an empty bathroom. After locking the door behind me, I lean against the bathroom counter and stare at my reflection in the mirror. A pale, almost ghost-like, red-haired girl stares back.

I splash cold water on my face and pinch my cheeks until the color returns. As much as I don't want to poison Harlow Ryder, I have to. He killed my father. This is revenge. Justice. This is what he deserves. And it's the only way to get my mom back.

I bang my fist against the counter until my hand aches. Taking a step back, I breathe deeply. *In. Out. In. Out.*

I stare once again at my reflection. My mouth is set in a firm line. My eyes are cold, unfeeling like the man in the Square.

I can do this. I have to.

Slipping the vial from my beaded purse, I fling open the bathroom door before I lose my nerve.

I repeat the following phrase in my mind: *I am hard. I am cold. I am a murderer.*

Chapter Twelve

The kitchen is bustling. Women in cocktail dresses similar to my own grab trays of hors d'oeuvres and drinks and carry them out through a second swinging door. A white server apron hangs on the wall. I quickly don it, put my purse in the pocket, and grab a tray of champagne. Another girl with short, blond tresses is restocking her own tray with beverages. She flashes me a friendly smile before exiting the kitchen.

My heart pulses frantically as I glide to the swinging door. Deep breaths. *What am I doing? What the hell am I doing?*

Before I push open the door, I pretend to adjust my apron. The cap to the vial comes off easily, and I pour the clear liquid into the closest glass.

Balancing the tray, I make my way to the ballroom. Mr. Ryder is still talking with the same group of men. I start toward him.

Twenty feet.

Ten feet.

Five feet.

My fingers slide around the glass, and I'm about to hand it to Mr. Ryder when a man in a black business suit strides over to his side. My feet stop moving when he leans down to whisper something in Harlow's ear. I take a few steps back when a confused look passes over the company owner's face.

The man takes Harlow by the arm and steers him out of the room while the guard in the navy suit from the Extravaganza stands on top of a chair to make an announcement.

"Ladies and gentleman, we hate to cut the party short, but Mr. Ryder is unable to entertain guests for the remainder of the evening. We thank you all for coming and wish you a safe trip home."

A murmur ripples through the crowd. First, the attempted murder of his son. And now this.

Swallowing hard, I shrink back against the wall. They've discovered me. They must know someone is here to kill him. Did Radcliffe rat me out? Is this all some sort of sick game? One where I end up in Confinement for the rest of my pathetic life?

I hurry to the kitchen where I dump the glasses of champagne down the sink.

"Hey! What are you doing? We could drink that," a voice exclaims behind me.

Trust me—you don't want to drink this. I turn to confront the accusing eyes of a short, pudgy woman.

"Sorry," I respond flippantly, trying to sound like a ditzy teenage girl. If only I had some gum to smack in between my teeth. "I didn't know. My bad."

Her eyes narrow. "Who are you? I don't remember you being part of my catering crew."

I shrug off the apron and hang it on the knob. "I'm not. I'm just a fill-in for tonight." Leaving the kitchen, I call over my shoulder, "Sorry about the champagne."

As I slip out the front door with the other guests, my ears perk at snatches of conversation from the brightly painted women.

"Poor man. First his wife. Now his son. It's a wonder he was able to celebrate at all tonight after what happened today in the Square."

"Such a shame. He receives death threats all the time. I bet it was another one. Or maybe a bomb threat."

And my favorite one.

"Did you get a look at that Zane Ryder? He is delicious. I'd love to take a bite out of him. Too bad he's marrying that robot."

I struggle to suppress a smile. For some odd reason, it gives me great pleasure to hear Arian referred to as a robot.

I hear the car before I see it. A black Land Rover with dark tinted windows.

The door opens, and strong arms grab me from behind and pull me in the back. I don't have time to scream. I barely have time to breathe.

My heart pounds loudly in my ears when Radcliffe gives me a wicked grin.

"Well, Miss Preston, seems like we had a minor mishap tonight."

"I don't suppose you know anything about that," I accuse.

He smirks. "What are you implying, Miss Preston?"

I glare at him. For a moment, I wish I were taller, bigger, and stronger so I could wipe the smirk off his face. "Look, I did what you asked me to do. I snuck into the party—"

"But you did not deliver. Harlow Ryder is still alive. Am I correct?"

"Yes, but—"

"Then it appears your job isn't finished. Not yet." His beady eyes bore into mine as if he is the vulture and I am the prey. The two goons from the other day twist their heads from the front seat and sneer.

He clicks on a comscreen. "And to prove it to you..."

An image of my sister, asleep in her bed, her honey-colored hair fanning around her head like angel wings, comes on the screen.

My teeth grind against each other as I glare at Radcliffe. "If you hurt her, I swear—"

"Now, now, Miss Preston. Your sister is safe. For now. And as long as you do what you're supposed to, she and your mother will remain unharmed." He leans toward me, his lips curling into a sneer. "However, if you don't complete your assignment… Well, I can't make any promises about their safety."

"My mother is sick," I choke out. "She needs to be cared for. Please, just let her go and I'll do anything."

"Sure. I'll let your mother go when Harlow Ryder is dead. End of discussion." He stares at me, challenging me to refute him.

"Since you failed," he continues, "we'll have to try a different tactic."

I hate the way he says *we*, implying we are working together for a common cause. And I don't like the look he's giving me. Like I'm disposable. A liability. *Once this is over, they have no reason to keep me around. To keep my mom or me alive.*

From a compartment, Radcliffe pulls out a needle the size of a horse tranquilizer.

Fear surges through me, turning my insides to ice. I try to swallow, but there isn't enough spit in my mouth to wet anything, like I've swallowed a handful of cotton balls. I eye the door handle, wondering if I can escape.

"This tracker will keep a tab on your whereabouts." Radcliffe grabs my arm. Even though I want to fight him, I don't. He has my mother so he will always have the upper hand. I am merely his puppet. "Try not to scream, okay?" He flashes me a twisted smile.

The inside of my forearm is exposed. I turn away so I can't see it, but I feel the cool tip of the needle press against my skin. Pressure builds at that spot until it breaks through, and pain shoots up my arm. I bite my tongue to keep from crying out and suck down the irony taste of blood. Something hard and cold slides into place under my skin before the needle is removed. The pressure is gone, but the discomfort remains.

Catalyst

"Now, I'll have eyes on you always," Radcliffe says.

The very thought creeps me out.

Radcliffe pulls another vial of poison from his pocket and hands it to me before reaching over and pushing the door open. I hurl myself out before he can change his mind, and then sprint down the street to where my mother's car sits. I want to scream. I want to hit something. I want to run forever.

Chapter Thirteen

eart thrumming against my ribs, I bang open the door to my trailer.

"Is Emily okay?" I burst out.

"She's fine. Just fine." Mrs. Locke smiles from her perch on a kitchen chair and shuffles to her feet. Emily is sitting at the table eating crackers. I choke back a sob and gather her in my arms, breathing in the scent of her. She smells sweet like strawberries, and her blonde curls tickle my nose.

"Oh, thank God," I murmur into her ringlets.

"She woke up just a few minutes ago. Had a bad dream or something. I thought the crackers would calm her."

"I can't thank you enough, Mrs. Locke."

The old woman smiles. "Anytime, dear. Anytime."

I help Mrs. Locke out the door and watch as she walks across the yard to her own trailer. When I'm certain she's made it inside and locked the door, I turn back to Emily.

"Time for bed, Em."

Once Emily is back in bed and her pink comforter is tucked under her chin, I sink onto the couch in the living room. I finger the spot where Radcliffe inserted the tracker in my arm. It's still a little sore.

Scanning the inside of our trailer, I weigh my options. I didn't deliver Harlow Ryder as a dead man, and now, it's only a matter of time before Radcliffe makes good on his promise. Emily's safe for now, but for how long? One thing is certain—I can't just sit around and wait for Radcliffe to cart her away too. Hell no. If he wants to fight, I'll bring the ring to him.

The next morning, the sun is barely high in the sky before I drop Emily off at Mrs. Locke's trailer. Straddling my bike, I dial Chaz's number, hardly daring to breathe until he answers.

"Sienna—"

I cut him off. "Chaz. A military colonel kidnapped my mother. I need to know where he might be holding her. Can you help me?"

Chaz's eyes widen, and his face moves up and down as he makes his way to a computer. "That might be difficult, Sienna. Their site is extremely secure, and I don't think they—"

"Just try. Please. His name is Radcliffe. George Radcliffe."

Chaz is quiet for a few minutes. Concentration lines his face as his fingers rapidly click the keyboard keys. "I think I have something." He glances at me. "I infiltrated the government site, and it looks like Radcliffe and his men are holed up in an underground bunker."

"Do you know where it is?"

Chaz frowns, and I hear his fingers flying over the keys again. "This infrared satellite image shows this as the only bunker in the area, so it has to be the one."

"Send it to me."

Chaz hesitates. "You're not gonna do anything stupid, are you?"

"Like what?"

"Like get yourself killed?"

"I'll try not to. Now, please, send me those coordinates."

The moment my Lynk buzzes, I thank Chaz, pocket the device, and rev the engine.

On the open road, my hair whips against my cheeks,

stinging my skin. The heat presses down on me, the sun glaring from a cloudless sky.

All I know from the map Chaz sent is that the bunker is deep in the desert, beyond civilization.

After riding for a while, my Lynk beeps, indicating I've hit the coordinates. I slow my bike to a stop. If they're tracking me, they'll know I'm here.

Glancing around, I scan the horizon. All I see are brown mountains, orange dirt, and sparse desert plants of cacti, Joshua trees, and the spiky mound of leaves of the banana yucca. There is no sign of a building, no sign of people, and certainly no sign of a government bunker.

As I turn to my right, something catches my eye. At first, I think I'm hallucinating, that the desert heat is producing a mirage of some sort.

A gray concrete building, not much larger than an outhouse, rises from the ground. I blink a few times, but sure enough, it's there. Once it's completed its ascent above ground, two armed men step from the doorway.

The men are young, not much older than I am. They must be hot in their dark pants and gray T-shirts. Their hands cradle large guns that they raise in warning as I hop off my bike and walk toward them. I suddenly wish I owned a gun, to make it fair.

"Stop right there," they call out.

Stopping, I lift my hands in surrender. They walk toward me, their guns trained on my chest.

"Who are you?" the one with curly dark hair demands, his face hard.

I lower my hands. "You have my mother. I want her back."

Curly scowls. "Who's your mother?"

"Vivian Preston."

He stares at me with narrowed eyes. When he doesn't say anything, I continue. "You know, bright red hair. Green eyes. She looks like me, except older."

Curly throws a glance at his buddy, the guy with a deep scar above his eyebrow. "Ever seen a woman like that?" Curly calls to him.

"Nope. Only person I've seen with that description is standing right here in front of us."

My temper flares. Before I can stop myself, I scream out, "You have her; I know you do!"

I hear the click of their guns, and I force myself to get control. It does me no good to get shot while trying to rescue my mother.

"Let me speak to your leader. Radcliffe, isn't it?"

The two men stare at me as if I've just escaped the loony bin.

"Miss, I have no idea who you're referring to." Curly laughs, shaking his head. He gives me a look of pity. "Where did you come from? Alpine House? Wayfair Springs?"

My face flushes in embarrassment. He's naming mental hospitals.

"Your leader, Radcliffe, kidnapped my mother." I lower my voice in an attempt to sound threatening. "I want her back. Now."

Curly shakes his head again and grabs his radio from his belt. He walks a few feet away, speaking low into the transmitter. The man with the scar keeps his gun trained on me but glances over his shoulder every few seconds to see when Curly will return. After a few moments, Curly replaces the radio and rejoins us.

"He's on his way," he says.

As I wait, my mind screams. *I swear, if Radcliffe has hurt one hair on my mother's head...*

The man who exits the gray building and walks across the desert sand is not the man I expect. This man is not Radcliffe. In fact, he's barely a man at all.

Not more than twenty-one, the man walking toward me is well built, with broad shoulders and a trim waist. As he nears us, smiling, I recognize the face that is too attractive to be an assassin. With deep-set eyes, a strong jaw, and a dimpled smile, Trey Winchester is not who I expect to see.

"That's not Radcliffe."

"No, it's not," Curly says. "But you asked to see our leader, and here he is."

Trey has a slight swagger to his walk, which can only be explained by an excess of confidence.

"Sienna…" He smiles. "Did you decide to join the Fringe?"

My head spins in confusion. "The Fringe? I don't understand—" I glance around. "Is this the Fringe Compound?"

"Yes. What did you expect?" Trey's eyebrows furrow, and he glances at his companions, who shrug their shoulders.

I shake my head. "The government bunker. Chaz was supposed to—" Then it hits me. "That lying little punk."

Trey laughs. "What did he do?"

"He gave me the coordinates to the Fringe Compound instead of the government bunker."

"Why?"

"I don't know, but when I find out, he'll be limping for a month," I say, seething.

Trey cocks his head to the side. "Why are you trying to locate the bunker?"

"That military colonel, Radcliffe, abducted my mother. I think they might be holding her there." Something Curly said earlier claws its way to the front of my mind. "You're the leader of the Fringe?"

Trey nods and squares his shoulders, probably an unconscious gesture. "My father was Bryant Winchester, former leader of the Fringe Organization. When he died two years ago, I took his place."

"Why didn't you tell me that when you got me out of the government facility?"

Trey glances nervously at his fellow Fringe companions, and Curly's eyebrows rise in interest. Trey grabs my elbow and steers me away from the other two boys.

"In case Radcliffe got to you again," Trey says. "I didn't want you to carry the weight of knowing the leader of the Fringe. This Radcliffe guy would have my head if he ever caught me. And he probably would do the same to you if he knew you were associated with me."

"That's why you were upset when they took your fingerprints?"

"Exactly. The Enforcers and other government officials have been trying to track our location for years. Once he realizes how close he was to the leader of the Fringe... Well, let's just say he's probably kicking himself now."

Another thought pops into my mind. "Wait. How did Chaz know the location of your Compound?"

Trey grins, showing off his chin dimple. "Because he's part of the Fringe."

My mouth falls open. "Come again?"

"You didn't know that, did you?" He laughs. "Yeah, Chaz is one of us."

Now I'm really going to kill Chaz for keeping that from me. Why didn't he tell me?

"I recruited him a couple of years ago when I found out about his mad computer skills," Trey says, his eyes glazing over in admiration. "He's phenomenal."

"So, the night of the Match 360 break-in—"

Trey nods. "Yep, I knew he was helping you. He's the one who suggested you for the job."

Now it's all starting to make sense. Wow, I never pictured Chaz as a liar, but it turns out, he's fairly convincing. In fact, he's almost as good as I am. *Almost.*

My mind shifts to my mother and the scumbag who took her. "Do you have any idea where this government bunker is located?"

He slowly shakes his head. "I don't. But if you need help—"

"Thanks," I say quickly, "but I prefer to work alone." I

also don't want to be responsible for the takedown of the leader of the Fringe.

Trey moves closer. "Well, if you change your mind, you're welcome to join us. We could always use another extractor." He smiles. "I think you'd be good at it."

Extractor?

"Unfortunately, I don't think I'm Fringe material," I say. "But thanks."

Climbing on my bike, I rev the engine. All three men stare at my Harley with lustful eyes, like they're mesmerized by a picture of a scantily clad woman. I roll my eyes, but of course, they don't notice. They are too busy eyeing her sleek, chrome frame and smooth handlebars. She is a beauty. Even I can admit that.

Once I'm a good distance from the Compound, I pull off the road where the obnoxious weeds choke the grass and any other living thing that tries to grow. I feel like those blades of grass, being choked out by circumstances beyond my control.

I have to find Mom. If she's hurt because of me, I'll never forgive myself.

I hear a noise behind me and turn in time to see a black SUV barreling in my direction. Revving the engine, I take off through the weeds and into the desert landscape. On a bike, I have the advantage. I can easily maneuver past underbrush, cactus plants, and oversized rocks, but for a car, that should prove to be more difficult.

My heart pounds in my ears as my bike speeds over the sand. I should be losing them, but when I check over my shoulder, they are only feet behind me. The windshield is too dark to see inside, but I recognize the vehicle. The one I was forced into. The one that took my mother. I'm certain if I could see inside the car, I would see the two goons in the front seat and thick-necked Radcliffe in the back.

I steer the bike around a grouping of large rocks, dirt hitting my leg as my tire catches the loose earth. I glance behind me again. Thankfully, they've pulled back a little.

Catalyst

Confidence surges, but when I turn back around, a large Joshua tree looms in front of me. I swerve too quickly, and then I'm sliding. Losing control. The bike tips sideways and the searing heat of the exhaust pipe scorches my leg through my pants. I don't even have time to scream. I'm knocked to the ground, my right leg trapped beneath the hot bike as we skid twenty feet across the sparse grass and grainy sand.

I lay there, the sun blinding my eyes, creating a giant ring of white in the sky. Pain radiates from my head to my toes, and I close my eyes until I sense the presence of someone else. He casts a shadow over me, a small respite from the sweltering heat.

Instead of the harsh voice of Radcliffe, I hear the nasally voice of one of his goons.

"Whoa, that was a purty big crash," he drawls.

"Is she conscious?" the other goon asks.

Both of them crowd out the sun. When I peer into the sky, all I see are two dark shapes hovering over me.

Pressure builds on my legs, and then sweet release follows as the bike is lifted. I fear my leg may be broken, and I don't even want to think about the searing pain radiating up my calf. It's the opposite leg from the laser-gun burn, which means I can now boast about matching scars.

Groaning in pain, I struggle to sit, but darkness crowds my vision, and everything goes black.

Chapter Fourteen

The moment my body hits the concrete floor, my eyes fling open. There's a grating sound, like something metal moving along a track, and then a door chinks closed. As my eyes adjust to the dimly lit space, I realize I'm in a small cell, and one of Radcliffe's men is leering at me from the other side of the bars.

A dank, musty odor fills my nostrils as I inhale, trying to breathe past the pain. I'm still covered in sweat, dirt, and blood, but my right leg is now bandaged beneath my pants. As I rise slowly to a sitting position, my hands scrape across something sticky. I swallow back the bile that rises in my throat.

When I look around, I see someone huddled like a scared rabbit in the corner of the cinderblock room. My eyes focus on the figure and the shock of red hair.

It's my mother.

I can't get to her fast enough. I draw her into my arms as she looks at me with wide eyes.

"Sienna? How'd you—?"

I shush her and stroke her matted hair. "It doesn't matter. I'm here now." I pull back to look at her. "Did they hurt you?"

She shakes her head. Her green eyes are tainted with tears, and a slight butterfly rash decorates the bridge of her nose and cheeks—a common symptom of a systemic lupus flare-up. My heart breaks for her. She is too delicate. Too sick. Too fragile to endure this.

I rest my forehead on my mom's shoulder and hold her as sobs rack her body. Her swollen hands clutch the bottom of my shirt like she's afraid I might disappear. Physically, she's in my arms, and yet, she's not really here. She's retreated to that place she goes when life is too unbearable.

Gradually, her crying subsides, and I can tell she's asleep. I reposition my body until I'm leaning against the hard wall, my mother's head cradled against my chest. My stomach rumbles. The darkness of the cell and lack of windows make it impossible to tell what time it is.

Closing my eyes, I rest my head on the wall as the stench of the cell fills my nostrils. A mixture of urine and body odor. I swallow hard to keep from gagging and bury my face in my mother's hair. It still smells of lavender shampoo.

A low moan reverberates down the hall, and my eyes snap open. We are not alone. Someone or something is only a few feet away. My body tenses, waiting, listening for another sound.

But there is only silence.

Metal scrapes against metal. Radcliffe stands in the doorway of the cell, freshly showered and smelling of bath soap.

"Miss Preston. How are you?" he says, directing his smirk at me. "How's the *assignment* coming along?"

I glance down at my mother, whose head is resting in my lap. Thankfully, she's still asleep. "It's not," I say. "How am I supposed to get back into Harlow's house?"

He gives me a disapproving look. "You'll have to be creative. You need to get close to Harlow. Get in on the inside, become part of the family."

"And how do you propose I do that?"

Radcliffe's mouth curves into a wicked grin. "Seduce the pants off his genetically modified son."

Seduce Zane? *Zane?* The one engaged to the perfect princess with the endless legs, tan thighs, and perfect size-two body? My lips curl in disgust. Impossible. What would he ever see in me? Pale skin, freckled nose, frizzy red hair... the list goes on.

"If that's your plan, you must be crazy," I retort.

"Don't be so hard on yourself. You have a certain... appeal to men. More than you think." His eyes rove over my body curiously, as if he has X-ray vision. Shuddering, I cross my arms over my chest.

If I thought killing Harlow was bad, seducing Zane is fifty times worse.

I can't do it. I won't do it. There has to be another way. If I can get my mother out of here, we can leave. Go someplace remote where no one can find us. Maybe somewhere up north where it's not so hot. Or someplace by the ocean—I've always wanted to learn to surf.

But then I remember the tracker inside of me. A shiver works its way up my spine. He will always have eyes on me. He will know every move I make. I can't escape because I'll never be free.

However, I can send my mother and Emily far away. To a place where they will be safe. If these men can't get my family, they can't hurt me. The greatest pain they can deliver would be to hurt my mother or Emily. My life means nothing, especially if I have to live it without them.

Mom stirs and opens her eyes. When she sees me, she smiles, but it is quickly replaced with a look of fear as she sits up and looks at the doorway.

I stand and face Radcliffe. "Can I take her home now? She's sick. And you don't need her."

He smiles, but his eyes never light up. "Ah, Sienna, surely you know me better than that by now. I've already told you, your mother serves as insurance to make sure you complete your end of the deal." He leans in close, and I almost gag on the staleness of his breath. "When Harlow Ryder is dead, your mother may return home."

My fists clench and unclench. Before I can stop myself, I lunge at him, my fingernails searching, clawing for any bit of skin they can find. They connect with his face, the skin scraping beneath my nails as I carve long marks down his cheeks.

His hand comes full force across my face, knocking me to the ground. Hot, white pain radiates across my cheek, and I gasp for air. I reach for my mother, who screams from her corner, but all I grab is concrete. My hands scrape across the ground as Radcliffe lifts my legs and drags me from the cell.

Without my blindfold, I see it all. A cell block. Filled with prisoners.

My guess is that these are all people who have gotten on Radcliffe's bad side. And I know if I'm not careful, I'll be here too. And Emily will be motherless. Sisterless. And homeless.

Chapter fifteen

The blindfold is forced back over my eyes, and the goons lead me to the SUV while Radcliffe tends to his wounds. It gives me a significant amount of satisfaction to know I caused him pain and possible scarring. I wish my aim had been a little higher. It would make my day to gouge out his eyes.

I pay careful attention to every detail I hear and everything I smell. The *plop-plop* of dripping water. From a pipe perhaps? The faint echo as my feet slide over concrete flooring, and the grainy shuffle of dirt moving with my feet. Too much dirt to be a main level floor. From the damp, musty smell, I get the impression we're underground.

The inside of the SUV reeks of hamburgers and onions. After a few seconds, my body tilts like we're driving up a steep incline or a ramp. When we reach the top, more light filters in behind the blindfold. Sunlight. I think I'm right. They must have taken me to their underground bunker. Now if I can only figure out where…

We drive for about twenty minutes, the sun warming the left side of my body through the window. Based on the position of the sun in these early morning hours, I assume we're driving south.

They drop me off somewhere in the desert. As I struggle to remove the blindfold, the car pulls away. I cry out in frustration, dirt and dust filling my mouth and nostrils. They can't leave me alone is this God-forsaken wasteland!

But as I glance around the barren landscape, I realize my bike rests beside the undergrowth. I don't know how it got there or why they left it for me, but I don't intend to question this one small token of generosity.

The burn on my leg sears beneath the bandage when I place it next to the exhaust pipe, and I squeeze my eyes shut in pain, every muscle throbbing, every bone aching. I want to go home. I need to see Emily.

When I pull up to my house, a sob chokes the back of my throat. I slide off my bike and stumble toward the front door. I'm halfway across the yard when I notice the sleek silver car parked on the dirt road in front of our trailer, as if it were accidentally driven to the wrong side of town.

Zane steps out, and I am horrified. I glance down at my dirt-stained pants, bloodstained top, burned leg, and raw hands. I want to run inside and lock the door. Instead, I straighten up, wipe a palm across my sweaty face, and wait.

He walks toward me, and my heart pounds. Why do I feel sick to my stomach every time I see him? Like I might hurl at any moment?

"Sienna." He says my name like it's the sweetest thing in the world. It rolls off his tongue like butter and honey combined.

I'm tired. I'm drained. I'm scared. But seeing Zane gives me an unexpected surge of energy, and as he walks toward me, I think, *It will all be okay.*

He has a huge grin on his face, but as he draws closer, the grin fades. His eyebrows knit together, and he stares at me. "What happened?" He's by my side before I have a chance to speak. He touches my face, my arms, and my hair. Each place he touches is like an electrical fire burning my skin. I collapse, and he catches me, drawing me to him. My head fits perfectly against his chest, and I breathe him in, an earthy, cedar mixture.

The dam bursts and the tears flow. I'm tired of being strong. I'm sick of proving myself.

Zane strokes my hair and kisses my forehead, his lips warm against my hot skin. My whole body longs for more, for his kisses to rain down on me. But instead, he lifts me gently and carries me into the trailer, placing me on the sofa. I want him next to me, but he moves to the kitchen.

Reality check, Sienna. He's engaged.

I wipe the tears from my face as he returns with a wet rag. He sits next to me, and my heart thunders. With careful, steady hands, he wipes the dirt from my arms and cleans the cuts on my hands and face. His touch is gentle. I close my eyes and allow myself to be taken care of for the first time since my dad died.

Neither of us speaks, even when he returns to the kitchen to rewet and wring out the rag. He's calm and silent, but I know he has questions. Lots of them. But he's saving them—for the right time.

His hands lightly touch my cheek where Radcliffe struck me. I'm sure it's a bruise by now. His eyes question me, but his lips don't move.

When he's cleaned off the last drop of dried blood, Zane returns the rag to the kitchen and brings back a cup of water. Wordlessly, he hands it to me, and I drink. He stares at me. Once I've set the cup on the coffee table, he leans back and crosses his arms over his chest, his eyes never leaving my face.

"What. Happened." His voice is quiet, controlled, and the words are more of a statement than a question.

I don't know what to say. I liked the silence more than his questioning eyes.

"I… had an accident. On my bike."

His eyes narrow. "The bike you rode home? It looked fine to me." He takes a deep breath and runs a hand through his hair. His gaze is unsettling. "Who hurt you?"

My voice catches in my throat. "Please. Don't ask me."

He reaches for my hand, and a volt of electricity surges

through my fingertips. *Can he feel it too?*

"Sienna, I want to help you. Please. Let me." His eyes are pained.

But why should he care? Pretty soon, he'll have the perfect genetically modified family—a model for the world. Why should he care about trailer-park trash?

As if reading my mind, he speaks again. "I care about you. More than I should. More than an engaged man has a right to. If there's anything I can do to help, please tell me."

I shake my head. That action causes a dull ache to climb from the back of my head and spread to my temples.

"Is it...?" He pauses as he struggles for the words. Swallowing hard, he continues. "Is it a boyfriend? Did he do this to you?"

The absurdity of the question produces a bubble of laughter to burst out. A boyfriend? *Ha!* I wish I were dealing with some lame boyfriend instead of the kingpin of the government hierarchy. I clamp my hand over my mouth when I see the hurt in Zane's eyes.

"I'm sorry. No, it's not a boyfriend."

A soft knock on the door saves me from his questioning gaze. I hurry to get up and go to it, knowing who it is before I even fling it open. Emily. And Mrs. Locke.

Fresh tears fill my eyes as I grab Emily and pull her into my arms. I squeeze her as if at any moment, she might disappear. I kiss her button nose, her wiry curls, and her soft cheek before setting her on the ground.

"Si-Si, who's that?" Emily asks, pointing to Zane.

"His name is Zane. Why don't you go over and say *hi* while I talk to Mrs. Locke?"

I watch her run over to Zane and place her small hands on his knees before I focus my attention on our neighbor. "Thank you for watching her, Mrs. Locke. I hope she wasn't any trouble for you." I'm glad the elderly woman has bad eyesight and doesn't notice the bruise on my face.

Mrs. Locke smiles, showing off a stained set of false teeth.

"No trouble at all. She was an angel, as always. If you need me any more while your mother is out of town, you know where to find me."

I glance over at Zane, who has Emily in his lap and is lightly tickling her. Emily giggles and swats at his hands. I smile and turn back to Mrs. Locke. "I appreciate the offer."

She leans close and lowers her voice. "What a nice young man. Is he a friend of yours?"

"Something like that."

Mrs. Locke gives me a knowing look. "Well, don't let that one get away."

Smiling, I decide it's best not to correct her. I can't let something I don't have *get away*.

Mrs. Locke turns to leave and waves to Emily. "Bye, dear."

Emily waves and resumes playing with Zane, who is now hiding a small toy in one hand and making her guess which hand it's in.

Once Mrs. Locke is gone, I shut the door and lean against it, studying Zane with Emily.

When he sees me staring at him, he flashes a sheepish grin. "I've always liked kids."

"You would be a great big brother." I sink onto the couch next to him, and he turns serious.

"I overheard you and your neighbor. Your mom is out of town?" Emily pats his face and lies back in his arms.

Pursing my lips together, I shake my head a little. "Emily, why don't you run and get Mr. Bear to show to our friend Zane? I'm sure he'd love to meet him."

Emily's face lights up, and she scrambles out of his arms. "Be right back!"

When she's out of earshot, I say, "My mother was abducted. I know who has her, but…"

"Is it the same person who did this?" His fingers touch my face again, and I flinch, not because it hurts, but because of the warmth that spreads every time he touches me.

I hesitate, my eyes shifting to the threadbare carpet. "Yes."

"But what?" His fingers slide to my chin, gently lifting it. My eyes connect with his, and I want to tell him everything. I want someone to know. Maybe if he knows, I can find a way out of this mess.

I want to tell him... but I don't.

"I have to do something to get her back."

"What?" His eyes cloud over.

Seduce you. Break up your engagement. Kill your father... *Take your pick.*

"I can't talk about it."

"Fair enough. Can I do anything?"

My mind flits to Emily. With Radcliffe out there somewhere plotting his next move, she's in danger. And truthfully, I can't protect her. What is one girl compared to an entire entourage of soldiers at Radcliffe's disposal?

"I'm worried about Emily," I say, my voice soft.

Not even two heartbeats pass before Zane pipes up, "Why don't you both come to my house? Obviously, I don't know what's going on, but at least you'll be safe there."

I shake my head. "I can't. I have to find my mother." If he had asked me yesterday, I might have jumped at the chance to get closer to Harlow Ryder, but now, there's no way I'm going through with the whole murder thing. Radcliffe will have to find himself another scapegoat. "I just need to figure out what to do with Emily."

He doesn't hesitate. "I'll take her."

"That's sweet of you to offer, but what do you know about taking care of a child?"

"I won't be alone, you know. Greta, our housekeeper, practically raised me, and I know she'd be willing to help. Then there's Arian. I'm sure she's good with kids."

Hearing Arian's name is like a knife through the stomach. Of course she's good with kids. She's beautiful and perfect and good at everything. *You lucky son-of-a-gun.*

My lips turn up into a tight-lipped smile. "It's too much to ask, and I barely know you—"

"I'll take her." He says it like there's no more room for discussion.

"What would you tell your father? Or Arian?"

He shrugs. "I'll think of something."

"I might be off the grid for a while," I warn him.

"That's okay."

"And she's not always as sweet as she appears to be." Not exactly true, but I want him to be willing to take the good, the bad, and the ugly.

Zane grins. "I'm sure we'll be fine."

When Emily runs back into the room a moment later with one hand clutching Mr. Bear, I pull her onto my lap and explain that she'll be staying with Zane and his family for a while.

"Are you coming, Si-Si?"

I hug her tight and whisper in her ear. "No, sweetie. I have to work, but we'll be together again real soon."

"But I want you to come," she whines.

"I know. But it's only for a few days. Okay?"

Her bottom lip sticks out in a pout, but she nods, her curls bouncing.

"Do you want to help me pack a bag?"

She slides off my lap and runs back to her room, and Mr. Bear is left forgotten on the couch.

Before I have a chance to stand, Zane covers my hand with his. Warmth spreads up my arm. His eyes are dark. And worried.

"Let me help you. Please. I can find your mother. I have money. And connections."

I know the connections he has. Money always equals connections. A small voice gnaws at the back of my brain, reminding me of Radcliffe's words. *Seduce the pants off his genetically modified son.*

No. I won't do it. I may now be a liar, a thief, and a cheat, but there are two things I'm not. I am not a murderer. And I am not a tramp. I cannot allow myself to get any closer to

Zane than I already am.

I force a smile. "Thank you for offering, but this is something I have to do on my own."

"I don't see why—"

I pull my hand out from under his and stand. "I just have to."

Twenty minutes later, I'm outside with Zane and Emily. I can't believe I'm about to send my sister off with a guy I hardly know, and yet, it feels right. I know he'll take good care of her.

I help Emily climb into the backseat and buckle the straps across her chest. Before I shut the door, I pull her close and breathe her in. I don't know how long it will be before I'll see her again, and my breath hitches at the thought. Heat presses against the back of my eyes, but I blink it away. I don't have time to be sad.

Zane places a warm hand on my shoulder. "I promise I'll take good care of her."

I straighten up and face him. "I know you will."

He hands me a micro-card with his info on it. "Call me. Anytime. Day or night. If you want to check on her or if you need my help."

I nod. "Thanks. For taking her. For coming by—"

"Which reminds me. The reason I came by..." He pulls a small, black device out of his pocket. The transcriber. "You left this on the veranda last night. You snuck away before we had a chance to finish our interview." His smile is sheepish. "I hope you don't mind that I activated a trace on your Lynk to find out where you lived."

Yesterday? It was only yesterday? It seems like a lifetime ago. In all the craziness, I never gave the transcriber a second thought.

"Of course not. Thanks for bringing it back." I slide the

device into my pocket. So the only reason he came by was to bring something I left? He didn't come to see me at all. Not that I should care. And I easily convince myself that I don't.

Zane stares at me until heat rises to my cheeks. I know I'm a mess. I don't need him to point it out. He looks as though he wants to say something, but then he shakes his head.

"Take care of yourself," he says before sliding into the front seat. The door automatically closes over him. I watch Emily waving at me, so small that she's practically swallowed up by the depth of the seat.

As Zane drives away, I say a silent prayer that, for her sake, I stay alive.

Once Zane's car is out of view, I pull out my Lynk and dial Victor. When I'm given the option to *view* or *listen*, I click on listen. I'd prefer *not* to see his greasy face.

"Victor…" I don't wait for him to respond. "I quit." I picture his lips puckering into a sneer.

"You don't get to quit, Sienna. You aren't finished until I say you're finished."

"That's where you're wrong. Just deposit any outstanding money into my account." That money can be saved for Mom and Emily. I certainly won't need it where I'm going.

"Sienna—" I can hear the warning in his voice.

"Goodbye, Victor." As I press *end*, I hope and pray he doesn't come looking for me. The last thing I need is another thug hunting me down.

After a hot shower, I force down a quick meal of yogurt and Meat *Gross* Delite, then lay on my bed for a few minutes. My body needs rest. I already changed the bandage on my leg, lathered on some burn cream, and popped a few expired pain pills, but my body still aches and my head pounds from lack of sleep. I can't remember the last time I had a good night's rest. Not since this whole episode with Harlow Ryder and the computer chip began. Damn that man.

But I'm too wired to sleep. Sometime between meeting the Fringe and seeing my mother in that cell, a plan has formed. I don't know if it's a good one. Not even sure if it will work. But it's the only one I can come up with. And it involves a lot of sacrifice on my part.

Today, I will give up everything I've ever known. I will become one of them.

A member of the Fringe.

Chapter Sixteen

Even though it's daylight outside, the inside of the Megasphere is pitch dark. I've asked Trey to meet me here because I need a favor. And he owes me.

I climb the stairs to the top level where the wall-to-wall windows allow the light to bathe the large room that was once a place for upscale dining. And who wouldn't want to eat here? The view must have been amazing, being able to look down the Gateway at all the lights and colorful casinos.

Several small, round tables still rest on the outskirts of the room, by the windows. A perfect place to dine at night—or remove a tracker during the day.

"Sienna?" Trey hurries into the room, carrying a small medical bag. "Is everything okay?"

"It will be, once I get this thing out." I turn my arm over, exposing my forearm.

Trey crosses the room in two strides and stares down at my arm. I can't see the device they put inside, but I can still see where the large needle was inserted into my skin.

Trey runs a finger over the site where they injected the tracker. "Is that what I think it is?" He glances up at me, his eyebrows knit together. "A tracker?"

I nod. "Can you get it out?"

He slowly exhales. "I think so." His eyes rove around the room, assessing what he has to work with. Two chairs are quickly placed at the table with the most light. He pulls out an antiseptic spray, cleans the table, and then instructs me to sit.

Taking a seat in the adjacent chair, he arranges the medical tools on the table. There are latex gloves, a knife, a syringe, and iodine, among other things. I turn my head away. It's probably best to keep him talking, so I'm distracted.

"Have you ever done this before?" I ask. I bite my lip and fold my hands to stop the shaking.

Trey raises an eyebrow as he snaps on the latex gloves. "If you're asking if I've ever removed a tracker, then the answer is *no*."

I force a laugh. "No, I mean, you seem comfortable around all these supplies."

He takes out a cotton swab and reaches for my arm. My skin heats up at his touch as he cleans the area around the tracker injection. "Lucky for you, my mother was a nurse, so I spent quite a bit of time with her in the infirmary." He shrugs. "Guess it rubbed off on me."

He lathers another cream over the site and blows on it. The cool air from his breath causes a shiver to run up my spine, but I'm not sure if it's from cold... or fear.

"Unfortunately, I can't inject this area with a heavy numbing agent or else it might mess up the tracker underneath. It's best if we leave the tracker intact." He blows on my skin again. "I used a topical numbing cream. It should take the edge off."

I nod, because my throat is too dry to speak.

He reaches for the knife and glances at me as he digs the tip into my skin right above the site.

I feel pressure, but not the pain I'm expecting.

"Okay?" he asks. The knife is now poised, ready to cut into my flesh. The first one was practice, now this one will be for real.

"Remember, the first layer of skin is numb, but after that—" He blinks rapidly, and I notice his long lashes, so uncharacteristic for a guy. "After that, there's nothing."

My breath hitches. Why is he telling me this? He must not think I can handle the pain.

"I'll be okay," I breathe. I squeeze my eyes closed and try to calm my racing heart. The pressure of the knife builds against my forearm, and I hold my breath. At first, there's only the pressure, and I make the mistake of opening my eyes.

Bright red blood oozes from the two-inch long incision. For a moment, I have an out-of-body experience, as if I'm looking at someone else's arm. Someone else who is being mutilated by a man with a knife.

The pain hits when he cuts through the next layer of skin and muscle. I cry out as heat fills the back of my eyes and tears sting my cheeks. Biting my tongue, I close my eyes again. I can't see it. I can't watch my blood spill onto the wooden table.

"I'm through. Now, I just have to find it," Trey mutters.

My eyes snap open, and I stare at him. At the concentration lining his face. I focus on the arch of his eyebrows, his thick lashes, and the dark stubble on his cheeks.

"There's too much blood."

Not what I want to hear.

Trey suctions some of the blood with a bulb syringe-type thing, and I grip the side of the chair as he sticks his fingers into the incision.

I feel dizzy, lightheaded. The pain is unbearable. It is hot, white, and it rolls through me like a thunderstorm. The thud of my heart is the thunder, and the lightning is the pain. Now all I need is the rain.

I feel warm drops run down my arm and fall onto the table beneath me, and I think the rain has come. I open my eyes, but it's not rain I see. Blood. Large, warm drops of blood. *My* blood.

I moan as darkness pricks the edge of my vision. I don't know how much more I can endure.

Before I can tell Trey to stop, the room tilts. Everything goes black. And I am gone.

Chapter Seventeen

"Sienna…" a voice calls out through the fog. I know that voice. Its melodious lilt and deep, rich tone. Zane.

I reach out for him. Surely, he's come to save me from this storm. The thunder and lightning that rages through and all around me.

"Sienna."

I can already imagine the scene. His broad chest and muscled arms enveloping me in a tight embrace. I can practically see his perfect smile, and his chocolate eyes staring into mine—

"Sienna!"

Wait. That's not Zane's tantalizing tone. Someone else is forcing me awake. I squeeze my eyes shut, intent on my vision of the genetically modified man, in all his perfectness and glory.

"It's over, Sienna. I got the tracker. C'mon, wake up." The voice sounds vaguely familiar, but it's too husky to be Zane's.

And then I remember it all. The truth flashes through my brain like a sick and twisted movie reel—my mother locked in a prison cell, Radcliffe's leering face, the tracker…

I gasp as my eyes fling open. I still feel lightheaded, probably from loss of blood, but I'm relieved to see I missed the rest of the procedure. My arm is now heavily bandaged and resting across my stomach. And I'm laid out on the ground. I try not to think about how filthy the floor is.

"Six stitches. Well done," Trey says from his perch on the chair beside me. He raises an eyebrow. "I thought I'd lost you there for a minute."

I rub my eyes with my good hand. "What happened?"

"You blacked out. It's pretty typical, though. Sometimes, our bodies want to escape the pain and don't know how else to do it."

I sit up and glance around the room. "Where's the tracker?"

"Safe—"

I move to stand, but Trey stops me. "Uh-uh, you're not going anywhere, not yet."

"But I need to get rid of the tracker—"

"Why not just leave it here? They'll storm the Megasphere, search for a few hours, and eventually, they'll figure it out, but not until they make fools of themselves." He leans closer. "Besides, you need to recover from your *surgery*."

I blink a few times as I stare at him. It's hard to believe he's the leader of the most violent group in our society. He seems so... nice. Maybe everyone has the Fringe all wrong. Maybe they aren't this vigilante group after all, but a group of misunderstood people.

His kind eyes draw me in. For a moment, I'm not sitting here with the leader of a terrorist organization, but rather with a guy not much older than I am. One whose bronze skin and dark hair accentuates his chiseled chin.

Blinking rapidly, I try to force the thoughts from my mind. I don't know what is wrong with me. I've never been the boy-crazy type, but here I am thinking about two different guys in the same sitting. Must be all the passing out I've done lately. Can't be good for the brain cells.

"Did you find your mom yet?" Trey says, bringing my focus back to the second reason I called him today.

"No. I need to find the underground bunker where they're

keeping her. And that's where our mutual friend should be able to help."

"I assume the last time you asked Chaz to help that he gave you the Compound on purpose?"

"I think so. I have a feeling he was worried about me and didn't want me to tackle the government bunker alone."

"So he sent you to me instead." Trey grins. "Smart guy."

Swallowing my pride, I rush forward with the next words. "So, will you help me? If we can locate the bunker, will you help me get my mom out?"

Trey tilts his head. "Considering I'm the one who got you in this mess, it's only natural for me to help. And a chance to stick it to the government? Of course, I'm in. I'm sure some of the other Fringe members will be eager to join us."

"Thank you, for everything." I give him a small smile. For the first time in days, I feel something I haven't felt in a while. Hope.

He ducks his head like he might be embarrassed, but I find that hard to believe considering who he is. "Don't mention it," he says before clearing his throat. He stands and crosses the room, pretending to busy himself with cleaning up, but the table looks pretty clean to me. He must have wiped all the blood up while I was passed out.

I slowly sit up. The dizziness is gone, and for the most part, I'm ready to take on the world. Trey turns in time to see me push myself off the ground.

"You sure you're ready to be up?"

"I'm fine." I finger the small, metal tube that was once in my arm and now rests on the table.

He nods to my pocket. "I think you got some messages while you were recuperating."

Zane. Emily.

I whip out my Lynk and scroll through the most recent messages. There's one from Zane. I have the option to *listen* or *view*, and I press *listen* because I want to hear his smooth, deep voice. Crushing the communicator to my ear, I lean into the wall, trying to be discreet and not blast the message for Trey to hear.

Zane's voice sounds too perfect, even through the phone. "Sienna, just wanted to check in. We went swimming, and Emily seems to be having fun. She's such a sweet girl, and no, I haven't seen that monster side yet like you warned me about." He laughs, and I can picture his perfect white teeth. He clears his throat and lowers his voice. "I hope you're staying safe, Sienna. I've been worried about you... Really worried. In fact, I can't stop thinking about you." I hear Emily's little voice in the background, slightly muffled. "Hey, I have someone who wants to say *hi*. Here she is."

"Hi, Si-Si. I love you. See you later." She's off and running before the Lynk even has a chance to settle back into Zane's hands.

"Take care of yourself, Sienna."

The message clicks when it's finished, and I press end.

Trey is pretending to study the crumbling skyline and looks at me when I finish listening to the message.

"Everything okay?"

"Yep, just needed to check in with my little sister."

Trey raises an eyebrow. "Sister?"

"Yeah, she's five."

He walks toward me. "Where is she?"

"With a friend. For now." I know he's curious, but I like that he doesn't pressure me to say any more.

Trey nods and scoops up his medical bag, while I throw the tracker in a corner of the room. When his eyes meet mine, I smile. "So, I was thinking of joining the Fringe. Do you have any objections?"

Trey grins in return. "We'll be lucky to have you."

As we exit the Megasphere, the sun is blinding, and it takes a moment for my eyes to adjust to the brightness. I hear the squeal of tires just as Trey's arm presses me behind him. A car door slams, and then another. Peeking over Trey's shoulder, I see the unmistakable image of Victor and his greasy sidekick, Carlos, making their way toward us. My heart plummets to my feet.

"I'm not here for you, Trey," Victor calls out. "I'm here for the girl."

They know each other?

"Sorry, Victor. She works for me now."

I sidestep Trey's arm because I don't need him protecting me. I can take care of Victor myself. "Victor, I told you I was done. Now go home. You aren't getting anything else from me."

Victor's lips curl back into a sneer. "Well, hello there, Sienna." He pauses, staring at me. "I told you before that you're not done until I say you're done. Remember?"

Trey's body tenses beside me. "Listen, if Sienna says she's done, then you need to leave her the hell alone."

Victor grins. "You always were a hothead, Trey. Like that time in the bar a couple of years ago—"

"Shut up, Victor," Trey warns, his voice low.

Carlos takes a few steps forward and cracks his knuckles. I'm sure these guys are packing heat. I only hope Trey is too.

Victor turns his attention back to me. "You know, Sienna, the Devil doesn't take too kindly to people breaking their promises."

Trey takes a step forward, his fists clenched. "You tell the Devil that if he has a problem, he can take it up with me."

The air is charged with tension. Every muscle in my back is stretched taut, ready to fight or run, whichever comes first. Carlos reaches in the back of his pants, but Victor's hand stays him. "That won't be necessary. Trey knows better than to pick a fight with us again."

I wonder what he's referring to, but I keep my mouth shut.

Victor stares at Trey, his eyes menacing. "I'll be sure to send *The Devil* your regards." His eyes turn on me. "As for you, this ain't over." He strides back to his pimped-out car with Carlos following on his heels.

"You know Victor?" I ask as they drive away, tires squealing and bass pumping.

"I've had a few run-ins with him here and there," Trey says, sounding vague.

"Run-ins?"

"Look, just forget about it." His eyes follow the car until it has turned the corner. "I don't trust him."

"Well, me neither, but that's nothing new—"

"No, I mean, I don't trust him not to follow us back to the Compound. I think you should head to the Compound, and I'll distract him, maybe lead him on a wild-goose chase. Will you be okay on your own?"

"Of course." And as I watch Trey stride to his black truck, I'm not worried. After all, what could possibly go wrong?

Using the same coordinates Chaz gave me before, I find the location of the hidden entrance to the Fringe Compound. I sit on my bike and stare at the desert soil, waiting patiently for the outhouse building to appear. The concrete building rises up like lava cresting the top of a volcano. Two men exit the building. The same ones as the day before.

Leaving my bike on the side of the road, I walk toward them, my backpack on my back and my hands in the air. Their guns lower as I near the concrete slab.

"Remember me?" I call out.

"How could we forget?" Curly hollers back. "You're the only chick I've ever seen ride one of those."

I stop a few feet from them and hook my fingers in my belt loops. "I'm here to join you guys," I say.

The two men look at each other and burst out laughing. "You want to be part of the Fringe?"

My temper flares. "What's so funny?" I demand.

"You. Here you are—this tiny thing with the biggest attitude I've ever seen," Curly says. "It's pretty damn funny."

I decide to ignore them and flaunt my source. "I have Trey's permission."

"Trey's not here. He's out on a supply run. Should be back in a couple of hours," Scar says.

"I know. He told me to come—"

"In the meantime," Curly adds, "Nash is in charge."

"Nash?"

"Yeah, also known as the Commander. And when you meet him, you'll see why." Curly radios to someone and requests that Nash come to the front entrance.

My heart pounds in anticipation. I don't know what to expect from this Nash guy. Trey is at least a decent person, but if Nash is anything like most members of the Fringe I've heard about, I have reason to fear.

My mouth dries out, and I have a hard time breathing when a man exits the same concrete building Trey came from yesterday. He's much larger than Trey and a little older. He looks powerful... and dangerous. Clad in gray fatigue pants and a form-fitting black shirt, he shows off each ripple of muscle. And believe me, there are many. His hair is cut in typical military fashion—short.

His eyes narrow as he approaches the two guards. They come to rest on my face, and he scowls. "What do we have here?"

"Commander, this is..." Curly trails off when he realizes he doesn't even know my name.

"Sienna. Sienna Preston." I hold my hand out, trying to be cordial, but Nash just looks at it.

He studies me with cold, gray eyes, making me wonder why he's not the leader of this group. His stare is very effective.

"Why are you here, Sienna?"

I straighten my shoulders and look him in the eyes. "I want to join your group."

He looks surprised for a moment, but then covers it with a sneer. "And why should I let you?"

"I'm fast. I'm smart. I'm brave." I pause for effect. "And

I'm a great thief."

Curly laughs, but shuts up when Nash turns and glares at him. As Nash turns, I notice a jagged white scar that begins at his ear and ends at his cheekbone.

"Well, Miss Preston, I don't know why we would need a thief—"

"I'm friends with Trey, Commander. He expects me to be here when he gets back."

He scowls. "Are you willing to complete Initiation?"

Initiation? I've never heard of it, but I wonder how bad it can be.

"I'll do whatever is required of me," I say with more confidence than I feel.

Nash smiles, and I see a row of crooked teeth. Not hideously crooked, but just enough to declare he needed to have teeth correctors as a child.

"Glad to hear you say that. Follow me."

I hang back, not sure what to do about my bike. Nash senses my hesitation. "Give the keys to one of the boys. They have experience on jet bikes. They'll park it in a safe place for you."

I'm about to argue that no one, and I mean no one, drives that bike except for me. But then I think of the words I just uttered. *I'll do whatever is required of me.* Suck.

I throw the keys to Curly, who stares at me with wide eyes before his lips split into a grin.

"If you get one scratch on her," I threaten.

"No worries," he calls back.

I follow the Commander across the sand without looking back. I can't watch someone else drive my Harley. The very thought makes my stomach clench.

We enter the gray outhouse building, which is about the size of a small elevator and large enough to house a couple of metal chairs. Like an elevator, there are a series of buttons on a control panel, which the Commander pushes. The elevator-like room descends underground. When it stops, we step out to a mini car waiting for us.

"Climb in."

Once we're folded into the tiny space—and my backpack is resting on my lap—the smart machine moves on its own, knowing when to stop and when to go. We weave through underground tunnels for several minutes, traveling a couple of miles underneath the desert soil. Just when I think we'll end up in the ocean if we keep going, the car pulls up to an elevator and stops.

"Follow me."

We take the elevator to a higher level. When the doors open, two people step aside, guns slung across their bodies. They're guarding the elevator, making sure no one comes in… or no one leaves. Not sure which yet.

The female guard, who's probably in her late teens, is tall and perfectly proportioned. With short brown hair and high cheekbones, she looks like she could be a supermodel in another life. Now she guards the elevator door wearing a gray tank top, khaki shorts, and combat boots.

The male on the other side of the door is much shorter, but well muscled. With spiky blond hair and several chains around his neck, he's like a surfer who lost his wave. Too bad he'll never find it out here in the desert.

Nash nods to the male and female guard. "Trina, Jeff, follow me, please."

Trina and Jeff file in line behind the Commander, and I bring up the rear. He leads us down a hallway of concrete flooring and beige walls. Immaculately clean and devoid of any art on the walls, this place could easily be mistaken for the inside of an old hospital.

Nash opens the door to a room on the right and ushers us inside. The room is white and empty. No furniture. No chairs. Nothing. But when I turn my head and see what rests against the far wall of the room, my heart stops. The room isn't completely empty. There are two items… and two items only.

A small table. And a pair of rusty scissors.

Chapter Eighteen

"Long hair gets in the way of what we're about here," the Commander says, holding out the rusty scissors. "Cut it."

For all the times I've cursed my hair, I've never wanted it taken from me. It may produce unwanted curls in the summer heat, but it's long and it's mine. One of the few things I own that I'm proud of.

I shake my head and wrap my arms around my body, as if I can protect myself.

Nash's eyes narrow. "Do it. Now."

The girl named Trina steps in. "Commander, is this really necessary?"

The Commander turns and glares at Trina, shutting her right up.

Choking back a sob, I grab the scissors from his outstretched hand. I refuse to cry in front of these people.

I twist my arms behind my head. Grabbing a chunk of hair, I bite my lip to keep from crying out. The scissors are dull and rip strands from my head. I blink back tears as the first hunk falls to the floor in an orange ring. By the time I'm finished, my arms ache and my eyes sting from holding in the tears. The fallen hair lies on the floor in a clump of dull red. The back of my neck feels naked. Exposed. I hand Nash the scissors.

"Better?"

He nods. "Much."

He grips my shoulder and leads me into an adjoining room. A metal operating table sits in the middle with some type of gray machine hovering over it. This machine has a long "arm" that rests at a ninety-degree angle. But that's not what strikes fear in my heart. It is the three-inch long needle sticking out of the metal arm.

"We show our allegiance by taking on the mark of the Fringe," Nash says. "Are you willing to do this?"

I nod, too scared to speak.

"Lay down," he orders.

My heart thuds loudly in my ears, but I do as he asks, placing my backpack on the floor first. The table is hard and cold beneath me, the metal cooling my skin through my thin cotton shirt.

He motions to Jeff and Trina. "Hold her down."

My eyes widen when they grab my arms and force them onto the table. A sideways version of Nash appears in my vision, and I watch as he tinkers with the large machine.

Even though I want to scream, I lay as still as I can, the world tilted on its side.

The machine starts with a whir, and Nash brings the needle within inches of my upper arm.

"This may hurt a little," he says. His eyes shift to my other bandaged arm. "But it looks like you're used to pain."

My throat closes. *What am I getting myself into?*

Trina is holding my right arm, and she gives me an encouraging smile. "It'll be okay," she says, her voice soft.

The needle punctures my skin, and the pain roars down my arm. I scream out, a mind-blowing noise that rings through my ears. Heat sears into my skin—burning, flaming, stinging. The needle moves quickly like an antique sewing machine, but it digs deep. It hits muscle, cartilage, and even bone.

My stomach heaves, and I squeeze my eyes shut as tears

sting the edges. The pain is too great. Just when I think I can't handle a minute more, there is relief. The heat is gone, and a cool compress soothes the burning site.

I keep my eyes closed until the pain settles to a dull ache. Trina pats my hand. "It's over. You did great." She helps me sit up, and I dare a glance at my upper arm. The skin is bright red and tiny drops of blood seep out of the needle holes. My stomach heaves again, and this time, I can't keep it in. I jump off the table, pain shooting down my arm, and run to the nearest trash can. The acid burns the back of my throat, and I puke until there's nothing left. I'm weak. Tired. Humiliated.

The Commander stands in the doorway, waiting for me to compose myself. His face is blank, unfeeling. Neither disgust nor an ounce of care resides between the lines of his eyes.

I wipe my mouth with the back of my hand as Trina hands me a glass of water. "Don't worry," she whispers. "It happens to the best of us."

Nash stares at us and then barks a command. "Trina, show Sienna to her room." With that, he turns and strides out the door.

Trina flashes me an apologetic look as Jeff quietly slips out of the room.

"What did he do?" I ask, wiping away the beads of blood with the towel Trina hands me.

"You now have an internal tattoo," she says. "We all have the same one embedded in our skin. The sign for the Fringe."

"What's an internal tattoo?"

"Instead of tattoos being on the surface of the skin, they penetrate deep, beyond the bottom layer. You can only see them using a black light or when it's completely dark." Trina walks over to the light switch and flips it off. The room is immediately bathed in darkness, but then I see swirls of orange radiating from Trina's arm, almost like vines snaking from her wrist and disappearing into her shirtsleeve. I glance down at my upper arm where light glows through my own skin. It's a geometric pattern consisting of overlapping circles that vaguely resembles a flower.

"What is it?" I ask.

"It's called the Flower of Life. It symbolizes our connection to life."

That's when I remember the knotted tree decorating Trey's arm the night he busted me out of the government facility.

"What's that on your arm?" I ask her.

"This is my scenery tattoo." She flips the lights back on, and it takes a moment for my eyes to adjust to the brightness. She moves to the metal table. "Usually people choose something from nature to counter-balance all that's unnatural in our world." She raises her eyebrows. "Do you want one?"

It was incredibly painful getting the small Flower of Life tattoo, and I'm not sure I'm up for something even larger. I'm about to say no, but then I think of how cool it would be to have something that defines me.

"Yeah," I say. "I think I do."

Trina pats the metal table. "Hop back up here, and I'll do it for you."

I slide back onto the metal operating table as my heart pounds. Maybe Trina will be more gentle with that thing.

"Do you know what you want?" she asks.

I think back to when I was ten and my father took me shopping to get a birthday present for Mom. For lunch, we ate at an outdoor cafe in the city. A beautiful black and purple butterfly landed on our table and I was about to touch it when my father stopped me.

"Do you know what I love about butterflies?" he'd said. Without waiting for an answer, he'd continued. "I love that they get to experience a rebirth. They start this life as an ugly old caterpillar, but when they emerge from the cocoon, they are one of the most beautiful creatures. Whenever I see a butterfly, I'm reminded of that."

At the time, my father's words held no meaning for me. But now, they do.

When a butterfly goes through its transformation and emerges from its cocoon, it is free of its old life. It is free of its life as a caterpillar and the cocoon that not only bound it, but also helped it complete its transformation. I love the idea of being free from my old life. The idea of a rebirth or a transformation. I have the opportunity to become a new Sienna, one who doesn't lie or steal to make ends meet. A new person who doesn't get her mom abducted because of her carelessness and stupidity. I can be different.

"A butterfly, please."

My "room" is more like a cell. An eight-by-eight square cement block with no windows. They might as well put bars on the fourth wall. The room is only large enough for a mattress, a blue plastic chair, and a small dresser. A crude mirror hangs over the dresser. I approach the mirror with caution, not sure what I'll think of the girl who stares back.

I don't recognize the face I see. The green eyes are mine, the full lips are mine, but that's where the similarities end. My hair is brutally short. Hacked at my ears, it sticks out in all directions. My vision blurs as I finger the blunt edges.

What would Zane think if he could see me now?

I shake my head. I don't want to think about him.

He means nothing to me.

I want to convince myself of that, and yet, he openly volunteered to take care of Emily. I will forever be in his debt.

I pull out my Lynk and speak into the receiver, recording a message for Emily. Once I press send, I wait for a response. There is only silence. *She's probably getting settled in her new place.*

Unfortunately, that thought doesn't stop the ache that

spreads in my chest. It matches the pain in my arm. I flip my light switch off and study the interconnected purple butterflies that loop and swirl up my arm. The purple glow seeps out of my skin. I now know why it burns so badly to have an internal tattoo put under your skin—because of the fluorescent liquid that's inserted through the needle tip. No wonder it hurts like hell.

Shouts and a loud noise filter through my closed door. I throw it open and watch as a dozen or so people race down the halls. Trina is one of them.

"What's going on?" I call to her.

She stops and turns. "Trey's back with another inmate. He just performed an extraction all by himself."

There's that word again. *Extraction.* What *is* that?

Curious about what's going on, I slip a hoodie on over my T-shirt—one of the few things I brought to the Compound—and pull the hood over my head, trying to hide my butchered hair. Once the door is closed behind me, I hurry down the hall to catch up to Trina. At least a dozen other teenagers jostle each other as they move down the narrow corridor. Bringing up the rear, Trina and I pass room after room until we reach an open doorway. People are spilling out into the hall, but Trina pushes her way through until she's inside. I'm grateful I'm small as I easily maneuver past the others until I'm standing next to Trina.

It's a hospital-type room with several unoccupied beds.

"Watch out," someone shouts. "Trey's coming through!"

The crowd behind us parts. Trina grabs my arm, pulling me to the side as Trey passes us, carrying a girl with a blonde ponytail in his arms. He lays the jumpsuit-clad girl gently down on one of the beds and pulls a blanket up to her chest. Her eyes are closed and she sighs, snuggling deeper into the covers. He's about to move away from her side when this girl, who can't be more than sixteen, opens her eyes and wraps her fingers around his wrist.

"Thank you," she whispers. Her hand falls back onto her

chest and she closes her eyes again, turning her head away from us.

With one finger up to his lips, Trey shoos us out of the room and into the hallway. Once the door is closed behind him, a dozen voices all start speaking at once.

"What's her name?"

"Why did you go by yourself?"

"How long was she in the lab?"

Trey holds up a hand to stop the questions, and that's when he notices me for the first time. He stares at me for a moment, a slight frown on his face, before giving a nod in my direction. He then focuses on the others scrambling for his attention.

"Her name is Kaylee. It was an emergency extraction. I received the call while I was in the city, so I didn't want to waste time coming back to the Compound for help. I know you're excited, but please, let her rest. I'm sure she'll feel up to socializing in a day or two."

With that, he dismisses everyone. Taking my elbow, he steers me down the hall away from the crowd of people. Once we're alone, he stops and stares at me with narrowed eyes. He fingers my hoodie. In one swift movement, he pulls my hood down and groans, muttering only one word.

"Nash."

I nod and self-consciously run a hand through my short hair.

Trey shakes his head in frustration. "We don't make females cut their hair, not unless they want to. I don't know what he was thinking—" He scowls and his blue eyes grow dark. "No, actually, I do. He was probably trying to get back at me for allowing you to join without discussing it with him first. I'm really sorry."

I got caught in the middle of a pissing contest? That's why I had to cut my hair? Seriously?

Trey nods at my left arm and the tattoo he can't see through my hoodie. "Does it hurt?"

I shake my head. Truthfully, it still stings like hell, but for some reason, I don't want to admit it. Like I'm tough enough to handle the pain.

He takes a deep breath and forces a smile. "Well, I'm sorry I wasn't here. Nash can be a bit… abrasive at times."

Abrasive? I was thinking more along the lines of *psycho*… but whatever.

"It's okay."

"I'll have a talk with him."

I pull the hoodie back over my head. "Can you tell me what just happened? What is an extraction? Who is that girl?"

Trey studies me. "How much do you know about Harlow Ryder's company?"

"Not much. Just what everybody else knows, I guess."

I can tell he carefully chooses his next words. "Kaylee is an inmate being held in Confinement for some stupid crime," he says. "I think she shoplifted a candy bar or something equally dumb, just like every other juvenile in there. What most people don't know is that juvenile delinquents are being transferred to Harlow's lab for experimentation."

I stare at him, shocked. "What kind of experiments?"

"Harlow believes in epigenetics, but he's taken that belief to a completely different level. Whereas epigenetics focuses on changing your environment and your reaction to your environment in order to reshape your DNA, Harlow believes he can change the actual DNA of a person by creating the right complex formula. He's trying to create GMs using already existing genes."

"Why would he want to change the DNA of a person?"

Trey's lips purse. "They're delinquents. A bane to society. If Harlow can alter a person's DNA to make them better members of society, why shouldn't he?" Sarcasm drips from his words.

"So you rescued her?"

He nods. "Listen," he says. "I know you must have a million questions, but it's almost time for dinner and I need to get Kaylee set up with an IV. But I was thinking after dinner, we should pay Chaz a visit. Figure out where this bunker is located. What do you think?"

My chest feels lighter all of a sudden. "Sounds like a great idea."

He smiles then. "It'll all be okay. I promise. We're going to find your mom."

And as he walks away, for some strange reason, I believe him.

The cafeteria is buzzing with people. Similar to a grade-school cafeteria, long rows of rectangular tables occupy the center space, and a line of people curve along the outside wall, waiting their turn to be served.

Earlier, Trina stopped by my room to bring me to the cafeteria, so once we have our trays of food, I follow her to a table where several other Fringe members are seated. Trey is already there and flashes a smile when he sees us. He motions for me to sit next to him while Trina takes the seat across from me. I recognize Jeff, who held me down during the tattoo branding, and Curly, the guard who parked my bike.

After a few bites of potatoes where I have to suppress my desire to go "Mmm" after every spoonful, I notice many curious eyes looking in my direction. As I glance around the room, I'm surprised to see a common theme among the members of the Fringe. Confused, I turn to Trey, who has a death grip on his fork and is shoveling in his food like he hasn't eaten in a year.

"Everyone looks so…"

"Young?" he says, his mouth full of food.

I nod.

He swallows and takes a sip from his water bottle. "What most people don't know is that before Harlow Ryder created his *perfect* son, he created trial batches of genetically modified until he got the formula right. Zane might be his first perfect specimen, but he's nowhere near the first genetically modified person." Trey nods to a guy with blond, shoulder-length hair who looks like he's about thirty. He's sitting at a table with a beautiful woman, and from the matching wedding rings on their left hands, I'd guess it's his wife. "He is. Paxton Reece."

My mouth drops open. "Harlow Ryder's been *lying* to everyone?" Not that it should surprise me. He did, after all, murder my father and get away with it.

"Not only that," Trey continues, "but he treated many of those in that first wave like lab rats, using them to perfect his formula, experimenting on them against their will."

"But where are their parents?"

"Many don't have any. They were test-tube babies, created in Harlow's lab and implanted in a homeless woman or some girl who desperately needed the money."

"What happened to the genetically modified babies once Harlow realized he'd failed?" I ask, already dreading the answer.

Trey pauses, his eyes shifting away from mine. "Some… were euthanized. Others were used for experiments." When I gasp, he quickly adds, "When my father learned of this, he started rescuing them. That's why he built the Compound— to create a safe haven."

I don't want to picture small, innocent babies laid out on a metal table, kicking and squealing, a scalpel raised above them. My stomach churns, and I set down my fork. I'm suddenly not hungry anymore.

Trey continues. "But there was one extraction that didn't go right. My father received intel that some of the GMs from the first wave were still alive and being experimented on at the government's AIG facility in Rubex. Somehow, the government managed to get their hands on these GMs— don't know if Harlow worked out a deal or what. Our parents knew it was a dangerous mission, not only because they were rescuing the first wave of GMs, but also because they'd have to go to the Capital." His smile is wry when he says, "It was."

My breath catches, and I whisper, "What happened?"

"During the extraction, they were ambushed by government agents. They were able to get most of the GMs to safety, but many of our parents were killed."

Stunned, I shake my head. "I can't believe this happened and no one knew it." I look around at all the young people in the room. Beautiful people. Strong people. Motherless and fatherless people. My heart goes out to them. "How many people here are genetically modified?" I ask.

"Only about twenty percent. Most of the GMs from that first wave either live here, escaped on their own, or died during experimentation. Those of us in the Compound do all we can to extract those in bad situations and provide shelter and protection for them."

"Like today. With Kaylee."

Trey's lips press together. "Exactly."

I pick up my fork again and take a small bite of chicken, my eyes scanning the room.

Trey nods toward a red-haired boy who can't be more than fifteen. "Garrett Johnson is one of those who lost his mother that day. He carries a picture of her in his back pocket to remind him of her sacrifice—that she was willing to give her life to save someone else." He glances around the room, and his face hardens. "All these people have a story. And many of them are tragic."

"But if the Fringe is all about helping people," I say, "why do you guys have such a bad rap? Why did you try to kill Zane Ryder at the Extravaganza? And why do you go around blowing things up?"

"First of all," Trey says. "We didn't try to kill Zane. That was some other crazy person not affiliated with us." He smiles. "As for blowing things up… it's a cover. If we can distract the media and Enforcers with our innocent bombings—notice that no one is ever killed—then we're able to focus on what really matters. Rescuing someone."

"Are you telling me that every time I hear on the news about another bombing by the Fringe, you're performing an extraction in some other part of the city?"

Trey grins. "Yep."

"Incredible."

I stare at the red-haired boy across the room. Garrett. *What would it be like to lose everything you love in an instant?* Pains fill my stomach when I realize how close that hits to home. Aren't I experiencing that very thing? The feeling of tremendous loss?

"Is that how your parents died?" I gently ask Trey.

He nods. "My mother and Nash's parents were killed. My father survived, but he was shot two years ago during a routine supply run." He glances at Trina. "Trina, on the other hand, has a little bit of a different story, but it's hers to tell."

My eyes shift to Trina's face, her beautiful, heart-shaped face with the long lashes and high cheekbones. I feel like a butch compared to her.

She glances down at the table as if she's embarrassed. Before I have a chance to respond, I feel a body slide onto the seat next to mine, leaning in dangerously close.

"Well, well, what do we have here?" Nash's breath brushes my ear. "Sienna." He says my name like it's dirty, like there's more meaning implied than there should be. "You seem to be adjusting to life in the Fringe."

His face is only inches from mine, clearly invading my personal space. I lean back a little and bump into Trey beside me.

Nash's gray eyes shift to the bandage on my arm. "So what happened anyway?" he asks, sounding almost too casual.

I shrug like it's no big deal. "I was in a bike accident and sliced my arm on a rock. Trey stitched me up."

Nash's mouth turns up in a crooked sneer. "You better be more careful, Preston. You wouldn't want something bad to happen to you here."

As he turns his attention to Trey, I can't help but wonder—

was that a threat?

After dinner, Trey and I leave the Compound to visit Chaz, just as he promised.

All the hallways look the same—brown, stamped concrete flooring and peeling plaster walls. There are no windows, and each hallway is lined with doors I assume lead to other cubicle bedrooms. The corridors are endless in this expansive building. How will I ever learn my way around?

"We're underground, right?" I ask Trey as I follow him through the Compound.

"Close." He glances back at me. "We're under a mountain."

As we walk through a wider corridor, Trey shows me an oversized kitchen with endless block counters and explains that we all have assignments. Some days, I will be required to help cook; on others, I will be part of the cleanup crew. For now, I should shadow Trina until I learn the ropes and receive assignments of my own.

"We want to conserve energy since we're underground," he says after showing me the laundry room where I will occasionally have laundry duty. "Showers should be short, five minutes or less, and only turn on lights when absolutely necessary. When possible, use the flashlight provided in your room. It contains a small generator, so all it needs is a good crank when the juice is low." He grins. "Think you can remember all that?"

I nod.

At the end of the hall is a metal door with a digital scanner entry. Trey lifts his shirtsleeve and flashes his internal Fringe tattoo at the scanner. The door slides open. I follow him into a stairwell where a young man is guarding the door with an AK-47 slung across his chest.

"Hey, John," Trey greets him. "How's it going?"

The boy nods. "Going good. Been pretty quiet today."

Trey clasps him on the back and smiles. "That's what I like to hear. Holler if you need anything."

We continue down the stairs, go through another door, and then we're in a large, cavernous tunnel. I squint to adjust my eyes to the thick darkness. A train track runs down the center of the wide expanse.

"Is this an abandoned train tunnel?" I ask as we walk along the tracks.

"Yep. This is the entrance we use for all vehicles and supply trucks." He nods to the line of cars, pick-up trucks, and semi-trucks parked on the side of the tunnel.

"I'm surprised no one has discovered your hideout yet."

"The cars might tip them off, but it would be hard to get inside." He glances behind him, and I follow his gaze. The door we just came out of is gone. Only the rocky side of a mountain remains.

"What the—?"

Trey grins. "Pretty cool, huh?"

"Where did it go?"

"The door has an artificial rock face, so it blends in with the tunnel's interior."

"Impressive."

"My own creation," he says lightly.

"Now I'm really impressed," I admit.

Trey winks. "Thought you would be." He walks toward a black pickup truck, the same one we hid under after he busted me out of the government facility. "We can take my truck."

"How about my motorcycle instead?" I look around the dark tunnel, but I don't see it. My throat closes as I think of Curly joy riding on *my* Harley.

"Where is it?" Trey asks, glancing around as well.

My fists clench. "I don't know. Nash told Curly to park it—"

"Who?" I see the confusion on his face. Of course, he doesn't know who *Curly* is.

"One of your guards with the dark, curly hair. He looks like he's about nineteen or twenty."

Realization dawns on Trey's face, and he smiles. "Ahh, you're talking about Jeb." He grabs his radio and speaks into it. I hear the static of Curly's voice—well, Jeb now—through the radio.

"I parked it between the two supply trucks to keep it hidden from other curious folks."

That was thoughtful. He better hope it's there.

Trey moves toward the semi-trucks, and I follow him, passing the bulky shape of two jet bikes as we go. There she sits, just as pretty as the last time I saw her. The keys are still in the ignition.

I figure Trey's awesome tracker-removal skills have earned him an opportunity to straddle my Harley and touch her throttle. When I motion for him to take the front, his eyes widen in surprise.

"You sure?"

Smiling, I pat my bandaged arm. "You earned it."

He climbs on, and I situate myself behind him. I'm not used to riding behind someone so I have no idea where to put my hands. It seems awkward to wrap them around his waist, so I settle for grabbing the bar behind me. I wince in pain as the skin pulls and stretches around the stitches.

Trey glances back and sees me struggling. "No. Like it or not, your hands go here." He reaches for my hands and pulls them around his waist.

My face flames in embarrassment, and I'm glad he can't see me. He revs the engine. Before he pulls away, I speak into his ear, my lips accidentally brushing against his skin.

"If you wreck my Harley, I'll kill you."

He laughs over his shoulder. "Trust me, if I wreck this thing, I'll kill myself."

Trey rides along the track until we exit the tunnel. The sun sits low in the sky, but it's still powerful enough to warm my face. I close my eyes and tilt my head back as Trey picks up speed. The hoodie falls, revealing my butchered hair, and I don't bother to pull it back over my head. It's the first time I've ridden my bike without long hair, and it feels wrong. The wind has nowhere to go except to my exposed face. It doesn't whip through my hair anymore, but makes it stand on end. Tears sting my eyes, and I'm not sure if it's from the wind or from emotion.

I bury my face into the back of Trey's gray T-shirt and tighten my grip around his waist. There's something comforting in knowing I'm not alone. Not right now, anyway.

When we are far enough from the Compound, Trey calls over his shoulder, "Where does Chaz live?"

"I thought you were friends," I yell back.

"Yeah, but we've only interacted in cyber space. We've never actually met," he hollers, his voice getting lost in the roar of the wind. I lean into him and give him directions.

We ride past boarded-up businesses, rat-infested homes, and condemned buildings to a cluster of apartments where Chaz now lives. After he graduated from GIGA a couple of months ago, he moved out of his parents' house to be closer to the university.

Chaz's apartment building is rundown, but nothing compared to the others around it. He answers on the third knock, just when I'm beginning to worry he's not home. His dark face breaks out into a large grin, which falls quickly when he sees my short hair. His mouth drops open in shock.

"Sienna, what happened?" His thick hands touch a lock of hair as he grimaces. "No offense, girl, but that is the worst haircut I've ever seen. I always told you white girls don't know how to cut hair."

I laugh as he encircles me in a bear hug. He then notices Trey behind me.

"Trey Winchester, good to see you, man." Chaz smiles.

"Hey, Chaz. It's great to finally meet you in person." Trey grins, clasping Chaz's hand in his own.

"Come in, come in," Chaz says, ushering us inside. Once

we're in the tiny foyer, Chaz wags his forefinger, pointing to me and then Trey. "I knew it would work."

My eyes narrow. "So, you *did* give me the wrong location of the bunker on purpose."

"Of course." Chaz grins. "I couldn't have you storming a government facility with nothing more than the clothes on your back. I knew Trey would have the weapons you need to rescue your mother."

"So, I should thank you?" I say, sarcasm dripping from my voice.

Chaz shrugs. "Sure. Although monetary donations are *always* appreciated."

I roll my eyes and glance at Trey. "You take over. I think I might strangle him."

"Chaz, do you think you can locate the government's underground bunker?" Trey asks, stepping in.

"Of course I can," Chaz says in an exasperated voice. He moves to his bedroom, muttering his indignation about us even questioning his ability to complete the task. His bedroom is where his computers and equipment are stored. I follow cautiously behind, never knowing the condition I might find his room.

Dirty socks litter the floor and empty chip bags are scattered everywhere—the nightstand, the bed, and the desk.

"Someone likes chips," Trey mutters beside me.

"And socks," I whisper back.

Trey tries to hide a smile, but I see it before he turns away.

Chaz settles his large body in front of the computer and types rapidly on the paper-thin keypad. A holographic image of the screen transfers to the spot beside him, and Trey and I are able to watch his process without leaning over his shoulder. A series of numbers and letters pops up on the holoscreen—codes of some sort. I'm boggled by it, but Chaz takes it in stride. His fingers fly over the keypad as he mumbles to himself.

"I just need to bypass the security system and I'll be in,"

he mutters. After a few more minutes of clicking away at the keys as I bite my lip and watch, Chaz exclaims, "I'm in!"

The official government logo, the triskelion symbol that represents progress and advancement, flashes onto the screen. Some say the curved symbol looks like three legs running, but all I see are three swirls or incomplete circles spreading out from one location. Underneath, the government motto flashes—Profectus est futurum. *Progress is our future.*

"If I can access the central database, I'll be golden," Chaz says, concentrating on the screen in front of him.

Trey pats Chaz on the shoulder. "So glad you're one of us, Chaz."

After a few more minutes, a new screen pops up on the holograph. This one lists the various departments of the government.

"Which one?" Chaz asks.

I search the image and see the only one that would make sense. "Try military."

Chaz clicks on it, and we enter an internal military site. After more codes and bypassing passwords, we hit the jackpot. Underground bunkers.

"See if you can pull up an aerial view," I say.

The entire desert landscape folds out before us, and we have a bird's-eye view. I close my eyes and try to remember every detail from yesterday. The sounds, the smells, and the time it took to travel in the car. My eyes flip open.

"Here's what I know. They dropped me off around here." I move to the holographic image and point to the spot I think my bike was parked. "It took roughly twenty minutes to get to this spot." I turn to Chaz. "Can you highlight the area around this point that would be twenty minutes or closer?"

"I'm on it."

An expanded circle frames my point of reference, and I begin to feel hope. There are only two underground bunkers within those parameters.

"There was a smell," I say. Trey looks at me curiously.

"In the car, there was a smell. Like onions and hamburgers. Clearly, they bought hamburgers somewhere, which would likely put them on the southern part of this circle, near Harry's Hamburger Joint."

"Yeah, but they could have gotten those hamburgers from anywhere," Trey says. "If those are government cars, they do an extensive amount of traveling. It could have been a leftover smell from days—even weeks ago."

I nod in agreement. "True. But how else can we narrow it down?"

"Can you think of any other details that might be helpful? A sound, maybe?" Trey asks.

Closing my eyes, I picture walking down the underground hallway. I'd suspected I was underground because of the grainy dirt that scraped against the concrete as I walked. It was more dirt than would be typical if it was tracked in, which led me to believe that dirt particles were falling from above.

That's it! The dirt.

I rush over to Chaz's nightstand, turn the lamp on, and sink down on his unmade bed. Carefully, I take off one of my shoes and study the bottom, holding it up to the light. I'm going off a small glimmer of hope, knowing I'm not likely to find anything. It would be a miracle.

Then I see it. Specks of deep orange embedded in the soles of my shoe. Just like the clay around the northern part of our perimeter. Clay that is more prevalent the nearer we get to the Fire Cliffs, huge rock formations made entirely of this orange, dusty dirt.

I turn to them and grin. "I got it. I know where she is." I slip my shoe back on and hurry over to the holoscreen. "Right there." I point to the bunker located in the northernmost part of our perimeter, about twenty minutes from my starting point.

"Chaz, can you get the coordinates for us? We need to know exactly where we're going," Trey says.

"Sure. I'm accessing those right now. I'll send them to

your Lynk, Sienna."

Almost simultaneously, my communicator buzzes, indicating I have a new message from Chaz. "Got it, thanks."

Chaz rests his hands in his lap and glances back and forth between Trey and me. "Anything else you want me to find while I'm on here?" he offers.

Trey shakes his head. "If I think of something, I'll be in touch."

Chaz follows us to the door, and I wrap my arms around his soft body, hugging him tight. "Thank you so much for helping me. I don't know what I'd do without you."

Chaz grins. "I'm sure you'd think of something. You always do." His face grows serious, and he pauses. "Sienna?"

"Yeah?"

"Good luck finding your mom." His eyes get all watery, and he swipes at them. "Dang, I think I have something in my eye."

I chuckle and pull him in for another quick hug. "Those are called *tears*, Chaz."

He clears his throat and steps back. "Yeah, well, I'm not used to them."

Chaz and Trey clasp hands and pat backs in typical man fashion, and then Trey and I leave.

"Now that we have the coordinates, how soon can we get a group together?" I ask once we reach the parking lot.

Trey shakes his head. "Sienna, if we're doing this, we're doing it right. We aren't going in there half-cocked. We need to come up with a plan, maybe even do a little training."

My hope plummets. "Training? Are you kidding me?"

"I don't mean intense training. Maybe a few fighting lessons, a little target shooting. What do you think?"

He has a point. These are trained military professionals guarding the facility and the people inside. But, my impatience is one of my biggest downfalls. I don't want to wait. I want to ride into the bunker with guns blazing and get my mom the hell out of there. "I think you're wasting my time," I say, my voice flat.

His face hardens. "Look, if you want my help, you'll do it my way. If not, feel free to tackle the bunker on your own." He turns away, indicating the conversation is over, and straddles the bike, leaving just enough space for me in the front.

I heave a sigh and start toward my Harley. There's no use arguing with him. He's the one with manpower, guns, and ammo, and as Chaz pointed out earlier, all I have are the clothes on my back. Trey's the leader, and that's the way it works.

That night, as I lay on my mattress, my mind wanders. Even though every muscle in my body aches, and my eyelids are heavy, my mind refuses to calm. Images of my mother in that stupid prison float into my mind, and my fists clench. Is she hurt? Scared? Sick?

Are they feeding her?

I feel useless, hopeless, and inadequate. If I could trade places with her, I would do it in an instant.

When Trey says we'll get her out, I want to believe him, but he's clearly busy with things in the Compound. I only hope that extracting my mother has become his top priority.

Chapter Nineteen

"**Y**ou need to learn a little hand-to-hand combat." Trey puts his fists up by his face. "Always protect your soft spots—your face being *numero uno*." He glances at my bandaged arm. "You right-handed?"

It's after breakfast and we're in the training facility, a large, gym-type room with thick mats, punching bags, weights, and a long wall of mirrors. The smell of sweat and stinky feet assault my nose as I stand across from him on the pile of black mats used to create a "ring". We have the gym to ourselves. Most likely because everyone else is too smart to work out right after a meal.

I nod and flex my right hand, the one that's not bandaged.

"You should be fine, then. I'll take it easy on you." He grins. "Go ahead—hit me."

I take a step back and shake my head. "I'm not gonna hit you."

He moves forward to decrease the distance between us. "I said, hit me."

I raise my arms as if I'm about to fight him, but all I can think is how much he's done to help me. How can I punch the man who saved me from the government facility, removed my tracker, and is willing to help rescue my mother?

When he realizes I won't fight, he lowers his hands. "Remember, Sienna, these men don't care that you're a girl.

They don't care how old you are. If given the opportunity, they will hurt you." His eyes harden. "Now hit me."

I punch him as hard as I can, and he's not expecting it. The force of the blow to his face knocks him backward, and my hand throbs from the impact. He looks stunned, especially when a trickle of blood makes its way out of his nose. But then he grins.

Wiping his nose on his shirt, he motions with his hands for me to come closer. "Nicely done. Now, hit me again."

Surely, he must be crazy. I'm about to walk away, but his words echo in my mind. *If given the opportunity, they will hurt you.* I can't give them that opportunity.

My arm swings out again, this time a right hook, but he's too fast. He grabs my hand and twists it at a painful angle before letting go.

"Too slow. You can't give them the chance to grab you." He nods at me. "Again."

Shaking my hand to get rid of the stinging pain, I take a stance. I try a roundhouse kick to his upper chest, but again, he's too quick. He grabs my foot, twists it, and lifts me off the ground. I land hard on my back, gasping for air. What is this? I thought he was going to take it easy on me.

"Still too slow," he says as I jump to my feet, my bandaged arm throbbing.

I shake my head and narrow my eyes. Now we're fighting, for real. I hear a door open behind me, but I don't bother to see who it is. I concentrate on the deep line in Trey's chin. That is where I'm aiming. Maybe I can cause it to split wide open...

I wait until his hands shift slightly before I make my move—a jab toward his face. I expect to feel the bone of his chin, but something stops me. His own fleshy hand blocks his face, and his other fist goes for my soft spot, my stomach. I double over in pain, and then his strong arms encircle my waist and force me to the ground. He straddles my lower body, and I'm helpless.

"If I had a knife right now, you'd be dead," he says. He shakes his head and hops up. "We have a lot of work to do."

Someone starts clapping behind me, slowly at first, and then gradually picking up speed. A deep voice booms and carries throughout the room, and my heart sinks.

"Well done, Trey. Way to beat the hell out of a girl."

I turn to see Nash striding toward us. He hops up onto the mats and takes a stance across from Trey. "Now let me show you the right way to kick some ass."

I scoot out of the way just in time to see Nash throw the first punch. Rolling my eyes, I get up and brush myself off. What is it with guys and their egos? Do I really need to watch a testosterone battle?

I lean against the wall, wishing I had a bag of popcorn. This could get interesting...

Trey ducks under Nash's arm and right hooks him in the ribs. Nash groans and throws a jab that lands on Trey's cheekbone. Trey comes right back at him swinging and lands a nice sucker punch on Nash's eye socket. I cringe because I know he will have a nice purple bruise by tomorrow.

I watch them duke it out for a few minutes and wonder when it's going to end. Trey's face is covered in sweat and blood, and I cringe every time Nash's fist makes contact. Nash is older and larger, but Trey is quick and a fighter.

Trey goes down, clutching his gut, and I let out the breath I've been holding. Finally. It's over, and Nash proved he has the bigger balls. He can walk away with that title and leave us the hell alone.

But it's not over. Nash begins kicking Trey while he's down, aiming for his ribs and the softest spot of all. Trey gasps for air and curls into a ball to protect himself.

I lunge toward the mats. "Stop, you're hurting him!" I monkey jump onto Nash's back and squeeze my arms around his neck, my stitches pulling from the strain. "*Stop*," I scream into his ear.

He shrugs me off like I weigh no more than a sack of

potatoes. And that's exactly how I fall to the ground—not very graceful at all. But it must have knocked some sense into Nash because he stops and stares down at Trey before striding off the mat and out the door. I scramble across the mat to get to Trey.

Cradling his head in my lap, I stare down at his bloodied face. My stomach turns at the sight of his eye, swollen with a cut at the corner. Dried blood is crusted under his nose. Guilt fills me when I remember I'm the one who did that.

"What the hell was that?" I breathe when Trey struggles to sit up.

He groans and clutches his side, but he manages to make it into a sitting position. "That? That was just Nash and me duking it out. You know, one of those male-domination things. Who has the loudest roar, or the sharpest claws, or..."

The biggest man parts? Yeah, I get it. No need to say it out loud.

"Sorry you had to watch that. It's kind of a family thing... We've been doing it for years."

Family thing?

At my raised eyebrows, Trey clarifies. "Nash and I are cousins. His dad and my mom were brother and sister."

My mouth forms a silent *oh*. Never in a million years would I have guessed that Nash and Trey are related. Where Trey is kind, friendly, and helpful, Nash is... not.

Trey continues. "Although, I think today he was taking out a little more aggression than usual."

"That kick to the ribs was a low blow. Literally."

Trey's mouth turns up into a smile, but then he grimaces. "Yeah, I think you're right. Definitely a low blow, even for him."

Trey moves to stand, and pain contorts his face. "Here, let me help you," I say, hurrying to my feet. I hold out my arm for him to grab.

"Thanks," he says once he's fully upright. "I'll be sore for a few days, but no big deal."

I shake my head, completely miffed. I don't understand the point of getting the crap beat out of you just for fun. "What will people think when they see you like this?"

He shrugs. "Everyone knows by now what happens when Nash and I take to the ring."

The door to the training room bursts open, and a small, dark-haired girl I don't recognize runs into the room.

"Trey," she says, gasping. "Come quick. You have to see this."

Trey takes off running after her, clutching his side while I hurry after them. I follow them down the narrow hallway to another room I haven't been in yet. It looks like a large recreation room complete with couches, a pool table, and an oversized, paper-thin comscreen mounted to the wall.

At least fifty people are crowded around the couches, staring at the screen. A young, raven-haired reporter stands in front of Confinement. The holding place for prisoners looks like a formidable fortress with its gray concrete walls and razor-sharp barbed wire. I creep closer and tune in to what she's saying.

"Officials report that yesterday afternoon, the terrorist group known as the Fringe broke in and kidnapped a juvenile inmate who was serving a five-year sentence for petty theft."

"That's a lie," Trey mutters beside me.

"This is the fourth kidnapping of inmates in recent months. You can see the imposing structure of Confinement behind me. Officials are wondering how the Fringe has been able to get in and out undetected."

"Yeah, I'm wondering the same thing," Trey says, his tone sarcastic. "It's nice to see them covering their tracks."

The camera focuses for a moment on the building before returning to the woman. "President Shard held a press conference from Rubex this morning. Here's a clip."

President Shard's face appears, his blue eyes piercing the screen. He has a head full of dark hair that's tinted with gray, and his skin is stretched too tight over his face, like if he smiles, it might rip wide open. He's had too much work done to keep him from aging, which is sad, because it's easy to see that in his younger years, he was a handsome man. Boos and hisses fill the room, and someone throws a shoe at the screen, which elicits a sharp remark from Trey.

"My dear fellow citizens of Pacifica, our society is in turmoil. We have an opposing force that refuses to see the need for change. For growth. They want us to remain *normal*. But normal is not part of our vocabulary. We are more than normal—we are extraordinary. And we owe that to Harlow Ryder, the creator of Match 360 and Chromo 120. We hope to be able to partner with him in the future to grow our society and increase our progress toward perfect individuals."

President Shard looks straight into the camera, his nose crinkling as his eyes narrow. "Fellow citizens, it has come to my attention that the Fringe is harboring fugitives. We have a disease, if you will, that is spreading out of control. The Fringe is the disease, and they must be eradicated."

Chapter Twenty

The screen clicks off. That's when I notice Trey with the controller, his hand outstretched, aiming at the screen. There is a simultaneous roar from the crowd around us. There's shouting, banging, and angry voices. I watch, eyes wide, as someone picks up a vase and smashes it, and two boys duke it out in the corner.

Trey walks over to a wooden chair, stands on it, and puts two fingers in his mouth, letting out an ear-piercing whistle. Everyone stops what they're doing, even the scuffling boys, and crowd around their leader. They wait expectantly for him to speak. I watch in admiration as Trey takes his time, demanding our attention and respect. He draws a few deep breaths, his eyes flickering to mine before he speaks.

"We have once again been falsely accused of something we did not do. Kaylee was rescued from the Chromo 120 building, not kidnapped from Confinement. I'm sick of the government making us out to be monsters."

Angry shouts radiate around the room, but Trey hushes them with his hands. "Spread the word. We will have a meeting in the cafeteria in one hour."

The cafeteria is filled with people. Angry faces mix with

raucous voices, and I search for a familiar face. A cleaned-up Trey stands on one of the cafeteria tables at the front of the room. Thankfully, his face doesn't look nearly as bad as it did. Spotting Trina near the front of the crowd, I squeeze through bodies until I'm next to her.

"Hey," I say.

She glances down at me, making me realize how tall she really is. "Hey," she replies, smiling.

"Did I miss anything?"

"Nope, I think he's getting ready to start."

As if on cue, Trey claps his hands together and then whistles with his two fingers. The room quiets down, and all eyes turn toward him. I have to admit, at first, I wondered how Trey could lead a group of people this large, but now it's clear to me. He is respected, even loved. He doesn't use force or intimidation to get others to follow, but instead, his example of compassion and kindness makes others want to be with him. To follow him.

"My fellow Fringe members, we have been accused of another heinous crime. They say we are unfeeling. They think we're monsters. But you and I both know what we are. We are *not* monsters. We are *not* unfeeling. We do care, and it is because we care that many of you are with us today. It is because we care that we cannot sit back and pretend like all is right in our world."

Someone in the crowd screams out, "Yeah!"

Someone else shouts, "Harlow Ryder is the monster!"

Trey holds up his hands to gain control. "We have the opportunity for another extraction. So, tonight, not only will we rescue someone from Harlow's clutches, but we will also send him a message. Anyone who has been approved to do an extraction, meet at the supply entrance at 23:00 hours." A few whoops and hollers follow before Trey raises his hands to catch everyone's attention. "We need to be prepared in case the government finds us. We can be sniper-skilled with our guns; we can shoot the heart out of our targets; we can have the ultimate advantage in hand-to-hand combat. If the time comes, we will protect ourselves, our home, and each other. But most importantly, we will protect all those who are with us seeking refuge."

Trey eyes the crowd. "Training will begin early tomorrow morning. If you have any questions, you can talk to me or Nash." Trey points to Nash, who is standing in the back, his arms crossed over his chest, his biceps bulging in his muscle shirt.

Yeah, I'm sure Nash is excited about the training. More blood, sweat, and tears.

Trey jumps off the table and lands lightly on his feet like a cat. I'm hoping he'll spot me and come over, but he weaves through the crowd, mingling with the others and answering questions. A particularly pretty blonde about my age hugs him and leans in to whisper in his ear, her oversized chest grazing his arm.

I roll my eyes and turn to Trina, who is also gazing after Trey. "Are you going tonight?" I ask.

"Yeah. You?"

"I don't know if I'm cleared for an extraction."

She smiles. "I think you are. But if you're not sure, just ask Trey."

"Okay, I will."

"Hey," Trina says suddenly, "do you want to get out of here? Go someplace?"

I nod, feeling a little nervous. Is this what girls do? Hang out? I'm not used to it. What will we talk about?

"Follow me. I know the perfect place where we can relax and let the sun soak up our worries."

"Sun? Are we leaving the Compound?"

Trina bites her lip and smiles, reminding me of a supermodel. "You'll see."

We make our way through the crowd of people, and I feel slightly disappointed I haven't had a chance to talk to Trey since I cradled his head in my lap.

Trina leads me down the corridor away from the cafeteria and through another door that looks like it belongs to a custodial closet. It's unlocked and Trina ushers me inside, peeking around the door to make sure no one is coming. *Is this some weird prank she's playing on me?*

She opens another door in the closet, and a steep spiral staircase extends heavenward. Her boots clunk against the metal steps as she begins climbing it.

"Wait, where are we going?" I call after her, but she ignores me. She's already halfway up. Even though my heart sputters in protest, I decide to follow her.

My hands are slick with sweat, which makes the thin handrail slip and slide under my fingertips. I climb slowly until I reach the small ledge where Trina waits. She's standing in front of a door. It isn't until I reach out and touch it that it occurs to me I'm looking at the inside of the mountain. Dirt flakes off under my fingers, and I feel the jagged edges of rocks.

"You ready?" Trina asks. She pushes the door open before she receives an answer.

The first things I think of are white and blinding. After being underground for a full twenty-four hours, it's amazing how much the sun hurts my eyes.

We are on the side of the mountain, and the desert is laid out before me. If I strain my eyes, I can see the city on the horizon. Trina begins to climb the short distance to the top, and I follow her, the tiny pebbles on the path slipping and sliding under my shoes. When we reach the top, we stand shoulder to shoulder and stare out at the vast, desert landscape.

"Only Trey, me, and a few others know about this place," Trina says. "Got it?"

"Sure." I understand the meaning implied through her words, and a warmth burns slow in my chest. I don't know what I've done to deserve her trust, but I like it.

I glance around at the blue sky, gray mountains, brownish-orange landscape, and patches of green from a stray tree or bush. "I don't understand how one minute, we were inside the bunker, and the next, we're on top of a mountain."

Trina takes a seat on a large rock and lets her legs dangle over the edge. I join her.

"Trey's father had this built for his mother, who hated the idea of being locked up under a mountain. She needed sunlight and fresh air. She would come here on occasion to escape the drudgery of being underground." Trina gives me a wry smile. "It does start to wear on you after a while."

"Were you one of the inmates who were rescued?" I ask, staring at her smooth skin and heart-shaped lips.

She purses those lips. "No. I actually escaped three years ago when I was seventeen."

"Escaped? Are you a GM?"

Trina nods and tosses a rock off the side of the cliff. When she glances up, her eyes meet mine.

"I had to get away from them. From everything they believed and everything they stood for. It wasn't right—"

"Who?"

"My parents."

"Why?"

Trina sighs and brings her knees up to her chin. "It's a long story."

"And you're going to tell me…?" I prod.

Trina laughs. "Okay, I'll give you the shortened version, but only because the sun is making me feel invincible." She closes her eyes for a moment and tilts her head back, soaking up the sun's rays. When she opens them, she stares off into the distance at something only she can see.

"I grew up in Rubex. When I was a baby, my parents had me genetically matched to a boy. All my life, I was told I would marry this boy when I turned eighteen. There was no other option. There was no discussion. That's the way it would be." Trina picks up another rock and twirls it between her fingers. "My school was gender segregated, of course, so they didn't have to worry about me meeting another student and ruining the match." When she lifts her blue eyes, there's pain inside. "But they didn't expect me to fall for my math professor."

Oh, snap.

"Nothing really *happened* between us, but it was enough to break up his marriage and for my parents to sentence me to eternal damnation."

Oh, double snap.

Trina continues, "My genetic match was still willing to marry me, but I couldn't go through with it. I'd had a taste of love, freedom, and choice, and I wanted more of it. I wanted to make my own decisions. Make my own match or, better yet, find someone who wanted to be with me not because of the DNA in my veins, but because of the love in my heart." She smiles, but there is pain in it. "So, I left. I wandered for a while. It was tough after the privileged lifestyle I'd led. I knew the Fringe existed, but they were so elusive. Plus, I thought they were some vigilante group. I didn't realize they were trying to help GMs. Then I met Trey."

"And you fell in love?" I dare to ask.

Trina throws back her head and laughs. "Hell no. Trey is like a brother to me. The best brother in the world, mind you, but still only a brother."

My heart thuds its own sense of relief, and I'm confused why I care.

"How about you? Why did you join the Fringe?" Trina asks, her eyes lighting up now that the spotlight is off her.

Hmm, where to begin. "My mom was abducted a couple of days ago by a military leader named Radcliffe. I found where he's holed up, but I need help getting her out. Trey said he'd help, but with this recent development—"

Trina holds up a hand to stop me. "Wait a minute. Did you just say that your mom was abducted?"

I nod.

"And Trey's coming up with a plan?"

"He's supposed to. He even said there might be some Fringe members willing to help. Would you—?" I break off, not sure how to finish the sentence.

"Help out?" she finishes for me. In the next breath, she declares, "Hell yeah! I even have my new combat boots with the steel toes." She models a shapely leg and winks. "Trust me, these suckers can do some damage to those sensitive man areas, if you know what I mean."

I laugh, and it feels great. It feels good to bond with another female. To share our experiences and worries. If this is what having a girl BFF is like, then I missed out all those years. Chaz just doesn't measure up.

A noise from above draws our attention to the sky. Three sleek black aerodynes fly low over the desert, heading in our direction.

"Oh, suck." Trina scrambles to her feet and practically drags me down the mountainside to the hidden door.

"What is it?"

Fear clouds her eyes. "Drones. And I don't think they're here to deliver mail."

We crouch behind a rock as the drones fly past. Even though the Compound entrance, the concrete outhouse building, is underground right now and nowhere in sight, it's clear that's where they're headed. We watch as they circle the area. They are like bloodhounds, tracking a predator with their nose. Except these drones aren't trying to sniff anyone out, all they need is their infrared element to determine the heat level. I'm sure someone is underground in that area, maybe Curly or Scar, and I'm hoping they have enough sense to take cover somewhere else.

"We're screwed," Trina moans beside me, and my heart rate picks up.

Did I do this? If Radcliffe was tracking me the day I came to the Compound looking for the underground bunker, did I inadvertently lead him here? My mouth goes dry with fear.

I half-expect the hatch at the bottom of the machine to

open and drop a bomb, but it remains closed. The drones circle the air space for several minutes, but they don't move toward the mountains. They are fixated on the hidden entrance.

"We better warn Trey," Trina says low in my ear.

We both creep to the door. Covered in fake rocks, it blends in completely with the environment. Once we've descended the metal staircase and our feet are firmly planted on the concrete flooring of the janitor's closet, we take off down the hall, looking for Trey. We practically run into the Commander as he exits the cafeteria.

"Ladies, ladies. Where's the fire?" Nash smirks.

"We spotted drones," Trina blurts out. "They're circling over the hidden entrance. There are three of them—"

Nash's eyes narrow, his smirk fading. "Have you told Trey yet?"

"We were on our way to find him."

"He should be in his room. Run and tell him." Nash speaks directly to Trina, like I'm not standing next to her. I don't mind the oversight, though. Anything to keep his eyes off me.

I start to follow Trina, but Nash grabs my upper arm. Hard.

"Let go of me," I hiss.

He drags me down the hall and around the corner as I try to dig in my heels. My heart pounds in fear, and my breathing comes out raspy. What does he want with me? Does he suspect that I led them here?

Nash backs me up against the wall and places his hands on either side of my head. He leans in close, and I try not to think about the fact that I can smell whiskey on his breath and it isn't even noon. He stares me down for a good twenty seconds. "I'm on to you," he finally says.

I glare at him and try to remain calm. "About what?"

He sneers in contempt. "Oh, I think you know. You think you have everyone fooled, but not me. Maybe Trey.

Maybe Trina. But not me. I know exactly who you are and why you're here."

I shake my head in irritation. "I don't know what you're talking about. And you probably don't either considering you've been drinking since you woke up this morning."

Nash's eyes narrow, and there's rage behind his carefully controlled face. Before I can comprehend what's happening, his hands close around my throat, and I'm lifted off the ground. He slams me against the wall, the noise echoing down the corridor. I gasp for air as black spots dot the edges of my vision and my throat burns like it was recently scrubbed with steel wool. Pain. All I can think of is the pain radiating through my head and down my throat.

I will die. Right here. Right now. My death is nothing like I imagined. It won't be at the hands of those who've threatened me. Instead, it will be at the hands of one of the men I ran to for protection, safety, and help.

A calm voice speaks from behind Nash. "Put her down. Now."

Nash turns his head, but he doesn't let go. "She sent them here. She's a spy."

Trey speaks again, this time louder and with more authority. "Put her down, Nash."

Nash snarls. "I won't allow a traitor in our midst—"

"She's not a traitor. Put her down and I'll explain everything." Trey moves forward, and I can see him out of the corner of my eye. My lungs scream for air, but I'm too weak to fight. Soon, it will be over.

Nash's hands release me, and I crumble to the ground on the cold concrete floor. The air feels too thick to breathe. I gasp and cough, each rush of air scratching against my raw throat.

Closing my eyes, I focus on breathing. *In. Out. In. Out.* It shouldn't be that hard, and yet, it is.

Heavy footsteps move down the hall, away from me. When I open my eyes, Trey is crouched in front of me, his eyebrows knit together in concern. Nash is gone.

"You okay?" Trey asks.

I nod, too afraid to try to speak. Trey slides his arm around my waist and pulls me up. Once I'm upright, he doesn't let go. He draws me closer, forcing me to lean on him as we walk down the hall. He smells like bath soap.

"Where are we going?" I manage to croak. My room is in the opposite direction.

"The infirmary. I need to change your bandage." He's quiet for a moment, and then he leans his head close to mine. "And we need to talk," he says, his voice low.

My heart pounds. What do we need to talk about? Is he going to refuse to help me rescue my mom? Maybe he thinks I should leave the Fringe Compound?

The infirmary is adjacent to the hospital room, only a see-through door separating the two. But from here, I can't see the beds, so I have no idea if Kaylee is still recovering or not.

"How's Kaylee doing?" I ask.

"Better. She's still resting."

Trey helps me up on the table, his strong arms doing most of the lifting. He stares at me until I become uncomfortable and avert my eyes to the floor. Taking my chin in his hand, he tilts my head back and studies my neck, his fingers gliding over the tender spots. His touch provokes a feeling in my belly I don't like very much. An ache, raw and deep. My cheeks flush.

Trey drops his hands, takes a step back, and clears his throat. "I'm sorry about Nash. He's ex-military, so he tends to think the worst of people. Until he gets to know you. His intentions are good—he only wants to protect everyone."

Irritation fills me. I wonder when he'll stop making excuses for his sorry-ass cousin. It seems like that's all he does—clean up the collateral damage that is Nash. Smooth things over and hope others forget his craziness. Or is Nash only like this with me and that's why it feels like Trey is constantly apologizing?

If Trey wants me to leave, I can spare him the trouble of asking.

"All I've done is cause trouble for everyone here," I say. "Those drones are probably here because of me. I should leave. And figure out how to get my mom out on my own." I move to slide off the table, but Trey's hand on my thigh stops me.

"No," he says quickly. "I don't want you to leave. Where would you go? You belong here. With us." He clears his throat again. "With me."

My pulse spikes at his last words. I don't know what they mean, and I'm not sure how I feel about them, other than the thrill of excitement that shoots through me.

"Plus," he says, "I could really use another extractor. And considering how well you did getting the computer chip, I think you'd be a valuable asset to us."

"Can I ask you something?" I say. "Why did you hire me to break in to Match 360 when clearly, you're just as skilled as I am at breaking in?"

"I don't do safes," he says simply. "Chaz swore you could handle it." Trey smiles at me. "And he was right."

"What about my mother? Are you still going to help?"

He sighs and takes a few steps back, leaning against the counter. "That's what I wanted to talk to you about. Can you give me a few days?"

"A few days?" I glare at him. "You promised you would help, and now you're reneging on that promise. I understand you have a lot going on right now, and if you can't help me, that's fine. I'll do it on my own." I slide off the table. Immediately, the blood rushes to my brain, and my knees buckle.

Trey's arms encircle my back and pull me to him. "Careful," he warns. "The last thing you want is a knot on your head."

His breath brushes my skin, and our lips are incredibly close. Heart pounding, I force my way out of his arms and steady myself against the table.

Trey heaves a sigh. "I never said I wouldn't help you." He moves to the cabinet and takes out a clean bandage and gauze. "Climb up, please," he says, nodding to the table.

I clumsily situate myself and hold out my arm. In silence, Trey removes the old bandages with the dried blood, and I glance down at the two-inch long incision. My stomach rolls at the sight of the skin separating slightly where the stitches have pulled.

"I guess hand-to-hand combat this morning wasn't a great idea," Trey says, his tone wry.

"It'll be fine. Besides, it was worth it." I touch my nose and smile.

His eyes warm as he smiles back. "Yeah, thanks for that bloody nose, by the way."

"At least I didn't kick you in your ribs."

Trey groans. "I think Nash got me good enough for both you and him."

I grow serious. "How are your ribs?" I reach out to touch his stomach, but then stop myself when I realize how intimate that gesture is.

"They're fine." He finishes wrapping my arm, and I place my hand on his arm before he can move away.

"Hey, I'm with you guys all the way. Training. Extracting. The works. Just tell me what you want me to do and I'll do it." I tilt my head and smile. "Don't forget, I'm part of the Fringe now." I lift my sleeve to remind him of my hidden tattoo.

His fingers lightly trace the scabbed-over skin, sending a tremor through me. "Let me put some salve on it. I don't want it to get infected." He removes a jar from the cabinet and spreads yellow cream over the tender areas with his fingers. The cream cools and soothes the site.

"Thanks." I pull my shirtsleeve down over the internal tattoo as he cleans up the supplies and throws away the bloodstained bandages.

"Are you coming tonight?" Trey asks, resting his hip against the counter.

"Do you want me to come?" I ask, immediately wishing I could take back the words.

"I think it will be a good experience for you," he answers, dodging the question.

"I'll be there," I say, and then pause, wanting to know something but not wanting to bug him about it. "When did you say we'd rescue my mom?"

"I didn't." Trey moves close to the metal table and rests his hands on either side of me. "Let's meet in my room after lunch tomorrow. I'll call together a few people I can trust and we'll go over a game plan. Sound good?"

My face breaks out into a huge smile. I'm so happy I could kiss him. And it takes all my willpower not to. "Yes," I say. "Thank you."

Our eyes lock, and my breath catches.

He holds my gaze for a moment, then clears his throat and pushes away from the table. I think I know his tell. His throat clearing is a sign he's uncomfortable or embarrassed. Which makes me wonder... Why do I make him uncomfortable?

Dressed in jeans and a navy-blue shirt—one of the few outfits I brought with me to the Compound—I walk toward the group of Fringe members waiting in the supply tunnel. About two dozen people showed up to take part in this *mission*. I use the term loosely, because at this point, I'm not sure what to expect.

Trina is toward the front of the group, but I stop at the back next to a red-haired boy who looks like he could be my twin. He's taller than I am, of course—I mean, who isn't?—but he's kind of gangly with super skinny arms and legs. He offers me a small smile as I sidle up next to him and wait for Trey to give us instructions.

"You're Sienna, right?"

I nod and turn to look at his freckled face.

He leans in. "I know. I've been watching you since you got here. I think Trey wants to make you one of our extractors. That must mean you're good at breaking in." He gives me a toothy grin. "Did you know I'm an extractor too? Basically, we'll be working together. I'll be the yin to your yang, the peanut butter to your jelly."

I throw my head back and laugh. "What did you say your name was?"

"It's Garrett."

I hold out my hand. "Nice to meet you, peanut-butter-yin-Garrett."

Chuckling, he takes my hand in his in a loose handshake. "You've been here your whole life?" I ask.

"Most of it. My mom was killed during an extraction." He pulls out a photo from his back pocket and shows it to me. It's a picture of a pretty blonde.

And that's when I remember the boy Trey told me about in the cafeteria. The boy whose mother died during an attempt to rescue the first wave of GMs.

"I'm sorry," I say in a soft voice.

He shrugs and pockets the photo. "Don't be. It's all part of the circle of life. We all die sometime. At least hers was a noble death."

"But doesn't it make you angry? What the government did?"

"Sure it does, but I can't change the past. I can only improve the future."

I smile at him. For a moment, I do feel as though I'm talking to a brother or someone I've known for years. "When did you become so wise?"

He shrugs, a small smile creeping to his lips. "I don't know. I think I was born this way."

I laugh again, and this is the lightest I've felt since before my mother was taken.

"So, what's your story, Sienna?" he asks. "Why did *you* decide to join the Fringe?"

Biting the inside of my lip, I'm considering how to answer his question when a loud whistle pierces the tunnel.

"Hey, everyone," Trey calls out. "Thanks for joining me. Let's go ahead and break into groups. I'll be the leader of one group, Nash the other, and Jeff the third. Make sure none of your group members are left behind. Clear?"

Trey divides the groups, calling the names of each person in the crowd and sending them to stand with their group leader. When he gets to me, I stare at him in expectation. Obviously, I'm hoping he'll put me in his group, but at the very least, I hope he has enough sense *not* to put me with Nash.

"Sienna, you'll be in my group."

Struggling to hide a smile, I move to where his group stands. Trina and Scar aka Cade, are already part of his group, along with a few others I don't know. Trina flashes me a big smile and moves to stand next to me. She introduces me to the others in our group, and I learn that the wiry, chestnut-haired boy is Samuel and the rainbow-haired girl he's clinging to is Abby.

When Garrett is called to be in Nash's group, his shoulders sag in defeat. He must dislike Nash as much as I do, but even though I feel sorry for him, I'm sure glad it's not me.

When everyone is placed, Trey calls out to Jeff and his group. "The extraction tonight shouldn't be too difficult. Only the night guards will be around. Think you can handle it?"

Jeff nods. "Sure thing, Boss."

"I'll send all the info to your Lynk. Stay safe. We'll meet you back at the Compound."

"Got it."

My group of eight moves to Trey's black truck, with Trina and Cade calling shotgun. The rest of us pile into the back. I scoot in and rest my spine against the side of the truck bed. The bumpy, uneven bed pokes into my butt, and I shift my rear as Trey pulls out of the tunnel and drives along the track with no headlights. Nash and Jeff follow us in trucks of their own. We're a caravan of Fringe stealing into the night, but to do what, I still have no idea.

"Sienna, have you met the others?" Samuel calls from his spot in the corner where he and Abby are huddled together. His arm is slung over her shoulders in a protective gesture.

"Not yet," I say as I glance at the two other people who are part of our group. The great thing about being out at night is that everyone's internal tattoos are on display.

Samuel points to the girl and boy who sit on opposite sides of the truck. "Laurel and Hank." They lift their hands in a silent greeting. Laurel is small and blonde, about my age, and I recognize her as the girl who was talking to Trey earlier after the meeting in the cafeteria. Her internal tattoo of a yellow climbing plant creeps up her arm, and the tiny flowers on the end are pretty and delicate. Hank is just the opposite. Tall, dark-skinned, and muscular, Hank looks like the type of person you don't mess with. And the orange creature spilling down his arm is proof of that.

"Hi," I say with a nod. They both nod back, and then turn their attention to the darkness that surrounds us.

Once we are on the freeway, the wind picks up and drags through my short hair. Goose bumps tickle my skin; I pull my arms in, hugging them to my body. I like the way my skin glimmers in the darkness, as if I have my own constellation on my arm. Tilting my head back, I glance up at the stars. Out here, so far from the city, thousands of constellations reveal themselves, and the sky is lit up like a gateway to the heavens.

When I was younger, I would gaze at the stars with my father and pretend that the pockets of light were small tears in the fabric of space that led to another world. Another world that looked down on us. A world that cried when we cried, laughed when we laughed, and felt our pain when we failed. But as I grew older, and life took on a more cynical spin, I realized how silly I was to ever believe such a thing. There is no one looking out for us. No one who feels our pain. There is only us, the keeper of our miserable lives.

I sigh as my thoughts turn to my mother. I don't want to think of her in that hellhole. Can't allow myself to picture her on that dirty cell floor while I'm out running around with a group of strangers. If I allow myself to go there, I will only feel frustration, helplessness, and defeat. I find comfort in knowing that, soon, we will make a plan. Tomorrow, Trey will call together a group of trusted friends and we will figure this out.

Resting my arm on the side of the truck, I stare out into the darkness. The desert shadows change as we near the city. Instead of the dark forms of Joshua trees and cacti, crumbling structures take their place. I assume we are headed to one of the government buildings in the Hollow, so I'm surprised when Trey turns down the Gateway. With his lights off, he drives past the abandoned casinos. The dark outline of the Megasphere looms in front of us, and for a brief moment, I wish I could escape there.

Our truck and Nash's truck stop in front of the Megasphere, and we all pile out. I'm tempted to run up to the top where things seem clearer. No one would probably notice I was gone.

Trey removes a large duffle bag from the back of his truck, and we all crowd around. The bag opens, revealing different kinds of explosives—dynamite and homemade bombs are the ones I recognize. Nash whistles from his spot behind Trey, and the excitement is evident in his eyes. Rubbing his hands together, he grins.

"Now this is my idea of fun," Nash says. Some of the others from his group laugh and jostle each other. My eyes connect with Garrett's. He stands only a few feet from me, and he makes a face. I can tell this isn't *his* idea of fun—he'd probably prefer to be with Jeff's group performing the extraction.

"What are we blowing up?" a blond-haired boy with

glasses asks. He's with Nash's group, I assume.

Trey looks up from his squat in front of the oversized duffle, the green tree on his arm illuminating the contents of the bag. "The biggest building on the Gateway, of course. The only one owned by Harlow Ryder."

My heart leaps in my chest and my mouth goes dry. *No. Please, no.*

The boy scans the long, deserted street, eyeing the buildings in turn. "Which one?"

I know the answer even before Trey says it.

"The Megasphere."

Chapter Twenty-one

"Nash, your group will be in charge of the explosives on the top floors—"

I hear Trey's voice giving orders, but I'm in a daze. The Megasphere. My space. The one I come to for solace. For peace, comfort, and solitude. Why the Megasphere? Do I say something to Trey? Do I beg him to choose another building? Would my pleas even matter?

Taking a deep breath, I move to Trey's side. He is busy assembling dynamite packs. "Trey," I say softly, hoping no one else will hear my plea.

"What's up?" He hardly glances my way. If I'd thought there was anything between us in the infirmary, that idea is long gone now.

"Can I speak to you for a moment?"

"Yep, I'm listening." He glances up briefly, but then resumes what he's doing. The wires of the homemade bomb are crisscrossed, and he carefully untangles each one.

I swallow hard and wipe my sweaty palms on my jeans, the material rough against my skin. "Why the Megasphere?"

He looks up at me. "Because Harlow Ryder owns it. I kind of like the irony, don't you?"

"But—but…" The right words aren't coming. "But this place has history. *Meaning.*"

With narrowed eyes, he refutes my reasoning. "To who?"

To me, I think. But that's not what I say. "To those who live in the city?"

Trey shrugs. "Looks like they'll have to find a new place of meaning." He resumes what he's doing. "Besides, this is just an old ride. It's a hazard, really."

I turn away so he can't see the tears that form in my eyes. I know it's silly. Why am I so attached to this place? Maybe because for the last year, whenever I missed my dad or felt as though life was too unbearable, this is where I escaped. And now, it will be no more.

Trey's group is responsible for setting the explosives on the lower level, but I can't help. Impulsively, I grab a flashlight from Trey's truck and sprint to the top of the Megasphere. When I reach the final floor, I burst out of the door onto the terrace. The darkness of the valley spreads out before me as I gasp for air. Trembling from exertion, my legs shake as I near the edge of the roof. I stand at the top of my building and take in the sight for the last time. The tiny pinpricks of light around the city, the radiance of the homes from Hampstead Hill. From here, I can see the glow of the internal tattoos of the Fringe members. The weaving vines in colors of red, blue, purple, orange, green, and yellow illuminate their skin in the darkness, making their moving limbs appear as if they're doing a light dance. I glance down at my own luminescence and run a hand over my shimmery skin. The trailing design of interconnected butterflies and swirls is more beautiful than I could have imagined. And purple does look good on me.

A small army of lights shimmers in the distance. I watch for a moment before realizing the lights are moving toward the Gateway. My chest constricts. Enforcers. Probably out for their nightly roundup where they gather all those who are sleeping on the streets and lock them up for disturbance of the peace or some other stupid reason they make up.

I have to warn Trey. Hurrying down the stairs, I almost run into Garrett, who is carrying an armload of explosives. The red flames on his arms match that of his hair.

"Enforcers are coming," I gasp, struggling to catch my breath.

He looks conflicted. "I'm supposed to set these at the very top. Nash is counting on me."

"Did you not hear what I said?" I cry in desperation.

"Yes," he says, sounding calm. "It will only take a minute."

"Hurry, then," I say, exasperated. I watch his retreating figure and debate if I should help him. No, I have to warn Trey.

My lungs scream for air as I bound down the stairs two at a time, the light from the flashlight bouncing along in front of me. The muscles in my legs twitch so much that I think they might give out before I make it to the bottom. But I don't stop. When I burst through the door, Trey is standing twenty feet away with a few bricks of dynamite in his hands.

"Trey," I shout. "Enforcers are coming!"

"How far?"

"I don't know. A couple of miles, maybe?"

"We need to blow this thing," he says, his face stoic. He transmits a message to Nash, who is somewhere in the upper levels of the building. "Set the explosive for five minutes, and get the hell out of there."

"What can I do?" I ask, breathless.

"Just make sure everyone is out before this thing blows," Trey says, turning away. I watch him stride out of sight, around the side of the building. Helpless, I glance around. Trina is nowhere to be seen, which makes me think she's in charge of setting the explosives on the lower level. I position myself by the exit and count the bodies as they come out. Fourteen people, not including Trey or myself. That's how many should walk out of that building.

First, the blonde, Laurel, exits and takes a stance next to Trey's truck, waiting for the fireworks show to begin. Then a few kids I don't recognize from Nash's group burst through the door, laughing and hollering. Two boys, one girl. Eleven more to go.

Trina slides through the door with a broad grin on her face. "I did it," she squeals, the orange, vine-like swirls on her arms glowing. Ten more. After what seems like an eternity, and I'm sweating bullets, five more bound out of the door—Hank, Samuel, Abby, and two girls I don't know. Four more.

Cade strides out, followed by the blond kid with glasses. Nash brings up the rear at the same time that Trey comes back to the front of the building, his hands empty.

"We all set?" Trey calls out.

I quickly count in my head. Fourteen went in, but thirteen came out. One more left. Who? Then it hits me. Garrett.

Glancing around, I double check that I didn't miss him, hoping that maybe he somehow snuck past me. No, there's no Garrett.

I rush over to Trey, my heart pounding. "How much time do we have left? Garrett is still in there."

Trey glances at the time on his Lynk. His eyes widen before he looks up at me. "Two minutes."

Fear courses through me. "We have to warn him."

"I'll go," Trey says, starting forward.

I grab his arm, pulling him back. "No, I will. I know that building like the back of my hand."

Realization dawns in Trey's eyes and his face softens, but I don't have time to contemplate his lightbulb moment. I take off for the entrance to the Megasphere, my feet pounding against the uneven pavement. As I race up the stairs, calling Garrett's name, I set a countdown on my Lynk. One minute and thirty seconds and counting.

"*Garrett*," I scream, my heart thudding loudly in my chest. "Garrett!"

I hear his footsteps before I see him. "Right here," he calls, moving swiftly down the stairs.

"We have to get out of here now! The explosives are set to blow in—" I stop and glance at my Lynk. "In less than a minute!"

"*Go!*" he yells. "I'm right behind you."

I race down the stairs, glancing behind me every few seconds to make sure Garrett is still there. When I reach the last level, I practically collide into Trey, who is on his way up. His strong arms steady me when my legs almost collapse beneath me. He takes my hand, pulling me out the door and across the pavement. The other Fringe members are nowhere in sight, and Trey's truck now sits a good hundred yards up the road. We run, side by side, and it isn't until I hear the blast and feel the whoosh of air that I turn to see if Garrett made it out. I scan the road, but it's empty.

Jerking my hand from Trey's grasp, I stop. "Did Garrett make it out?" I pant.

"He was right behind us. He should have."

Another blast roars through the building and throws me backward. I land on my rear in a daze as heat spills out of the building. Pain shoots from my butt to my legs, and I turn my head to see Trey sprawled on his side.

"You okay?" I call out.

He pushes himself to his feet and offers me his hand. Grateful, I grasp it and pull myself up. "Yeah, I'm okay," he says.

My eyes scan the area in front of the burning building. I know it's only a matter of time before another blast rips through it. "Where's Garrett?"

I shout his name and wait to hear him call back. But the only thing I hear is the roar, hiss, and pop of the fire consuming the Megasphere. Then there's another sound that makes my blood run cold. An air horn. It blows in the distance, signaling that the Enforcers are on their way. Soon, they will surround this area.

"We have to get out of here." Trey grabs for my hand.

"Not without Garrett." I rip my hand from his grasp and scan the area with my flashlight.

"He's not here, Sienna." Trey shakes his head, his eyes pained. "I don't think he made it."

"But he was *right* behind us," I protest. "What could have happened?" Then it dawns on me. "Maybe he's trapped." I sprint back toward the building before Trey can stop me.

The lower-level explosives haven't gone off yet, but I cringe as I shove open the door to the entrance, knowing they will at any moment. In the lower stairwell, I find Garrett, his leg trapped beneath a pillar.

"Sienna, you have to get out of here. The other bombs haven't blown yet."

I struggle to remove the pillar, but it's too heavy. Desperate, I shine my flashlight around, looking for something to use as a lever. Trey's large frame stands in the doorway.

"He's trapped. I can't get this thing off him," I yell to Trey. The hum of the Enforcers' vehicles draw closer and closer.

Trey moves quickly to Garrett's side. Together, we heave. A blast above us rips through the building and we're thrown backward. The stairwell fills with dust and smoke as more debris falls, leaving a wake of destruction and completely covering Garrett.

"Garrett, you okay?" I gasp, struggling to sit up. As the dust settles, I see a dazed Garrett neck deep in debris.

"You have to go. Now," Garrett says, his voice firm as steel.

"Not without you," I protest, climbing to my feet and pulling plaster and splintered boards off his legs.

Garrett reaches out a hand to stop me. "Thanks for caring, but you need to go. Remember the conversation we had in the tunnel?" He smiles. "It's okay. I'm okay with it."

I shake my head as tears form in my eyes and run down my cheeks. "No," I choke out.

"Trey, get her out of here," Garrett says, closing his eyes.

Trey looks from him to me for a moment before he scoops me up in his arms and carries me kicking and screaming from the Megasphere. "No, *don't* do this," I cry in desperation, but my sobs are drowned out by the explosive force that sends Trey to his knees and me skidding across the pavement. I lay in a crumbled heap, the world muffled around me, my body bruised and sore, and my heart aching.

Groaning, I roll over on my back and glance into the sky at the towering fireball that was once my safe haven. Salty tears fall down my cheeks as I think of the boy trapped in that burning inferno. A boy who could have passed for my twin. A boy who, in the end, saved my life.

Trey pulls me to my feet. With one arm around my waist, he helps me limp the one hundred yards to where his truck is parked. The other Fringe members pour out of the abandoned buildings surrounding the Megasphere and climb into the trucks.

The steady hum of the Enforcers' electric vehicles draws closer, and I glance over my shoulder as Trey helps me into the front seat. Five energy cars have surrounded the Megasphere, and over half a dozen Enforcers are climbing out with their laser guns drawn. Too busy eyeing the damage, they don't notice us down the dark, deserted street. But as soon as Trey starts the truck, they'll know we're here.

"Hank, Samuel, give me a push. I'll put it in neutral until we're far enough away that they won't hear me start it." The other Fringe members climb out of the vehicle, but I remain motionless on the front seat. I'm too stunned to care. Too tired to give a damn what happens now. I feel the vehicle move slowly beneath me, inching along the road. I'm sure Nash and his crew are doing the same thing.

When we are far enough away that the Enforcers won't hear the start of the truck engine over the roar of the fire, Trey climbs back in and Trina settles beside me. Orange flames light the sky behind us.

The ride back to the Compound is filled with silence. I have nothing to say. I think Trina is too afraid to say anything, and Trey is probably wallowing in guilt.

A life for a life. I only hope it was worth it.

Chapter Twenty-two

"We lost one of our own tonight," Trey says, addressing the crowd after we return to the Compound. "I want you to know I take full responsibility. I wasn't careful enough, and because of it, Garrett Johnson is no longer with us." He bows his head for a moment. When he lifts it, I see the sorrow in his eyes.

"Does anyone have anything they'd like to say on Garrett's behalf?" Trey asks. No one says a word, and I think, *Come on people, nothing? Really?*

When the silence becomes unbearable, I slowly raise my hand.

Trey nods for me to speak, and I begin, hesitantly at first, but then drawing my confidence from the type of person Garrett was.

"I didn't know Garrett that long," I start. "In fact, I only met him tonight." A chuckle breaks out from the crowd, but Trey silences the boy with a look. I feel dozens of eyes on me, and I continue. "Even in those few moments that we spoke, he made an impression on me. He told me his mom died a noble death. When I asked if it bothered him what the government did, he said, 'I can't change the past. But I can improve the future.'"

I pause for a moment, letting the words sink in. When I continue, my voice is stronger, and I only hope that what I'm saying would make Garrett proud. "Garrett understood our purpose for being here. It isn't to bomb, burn, and destroy, but to improve the future. If that means hiding GMs and rescuing inmates, then let's make it count. Garrett Johnson gave his life to save another, someone he's never even met. He'll always be a hero in my book."

Dropping my head, I turn to go inside the Compound and steal away to the quiet of my room. A voice speaks from behind me, and I stop to hear what he has to say.

"Sienna, I'm sorry."

I turn to face Trey. "It's okay," I say, my eyes never quite meeting his. "It couldn't be helped."

"No, not about Garrett. Although, I'm sorry about him too. I mean, about the Megasphere." My eyes lift to his. "If I had known how much it meant to you, I wouldn't have chosen it." His blue eyes are kind, sincere, but my heart aches so badly that I don't have room for compassion.

I shrug. "It was just an old ride. It wasn't meant to hold meaning."

Neither of us speaks for a moment, and I can tell Trey is struggling to find the right words. The ones that will relieve me of my pain—that will allow me some comfort.

"Please tell me that Jeff was able to extract that inmate," I say. *Please tell me Garrett didn't die for nothing.*

"Yeah, he did." Trey clears his throat. "Thank you for your words. About Garrett, I mean," he says.

"Somebody had to say something," I reply in a tired voice.

"Yes, but you said the *right* thing. So, thank you. Garrett would have appreciated it—" Trey breaks off, overcome with emotion. I haven't even taken into consideration how he's handling Garrett's death. Trey knew him for years, and I, only a few minutes.

I lay a hand on his arm, a gesture of empathy I somehow muster from somewhere. "I'm sorry about Garrett."

"Me too," he says, his eyes moist. He quickly rubs his eyes with his thumb and forefinger, clearing his throat again.

"Don't forget," he says finally, "we're meeting after lunch in my room to plan your mother's rescue."

"I look forward to it." I turn and trudge up the stairs to the Compound and the comfort of my eight-by-eight room. When I shut the door, I flop down on my mattress and cry until I don't have any more tears left to shed.

Chapter Twenty-three

Afer lunch, a small crowd gathers in Trey's room. When I walk through the open door, the muscles in my neck tighten. Nash is there, lounging on Trey's bed, along with Trina, who is seated at the foot of the bed. Curly has taken a stance in the corner, and two other boys I don't recognize are sprawled on the floor. Trey is leaning over his desk, a metal contraption that looks like it was ripped from the garbage. Nash's eyes rest on me as I hesitate in the doorway.

"Preston, here's a seat for you," he calls out, patting the bed beside him.

I'm about to tell him to *go to hell* when I catch Trey looking at me. He nods to the space beside him. I step over the boys sprawled out on the floor as Trey pulls out a wooden chair from under the contraption and moves it to the side of the desk. "You can sit here."

Once I'm seated, Trey crosses the room and closes the door before returning to his original spot.

"Everyone's here, so we can go ahead and get started." Trey pauses, glancing around the room. "I called you here to talk about an assignment." His eyes flicker to me for a second. "A special assignment."

At the mention of a *special assignment*, Nash sits up on the bed and leans forward, his arms resting on his knees. The two boys on the floor also perk up.

"Now, obviously, in the wake of what happened last night, I feel I should warn you about the risks involved. This will be a challenging mission, but I think we can pull it off."

"What's the assignment?" Nash calls out.

Trey continues. "A woman by the name of Vivian Preston was kidnapped by government officials a few days ago."

Nash's eyebrows rise as he turns to me. I ignore him. Let him think what he wants.

"We think she's being held in an underground bunker. We need to find a way in and extract her. Sienna has been there—"

"Hell no," Nash says, his tone flat and hard.

Trey's eyes narrow. "Excuse me?"

"I said, hell no. It's a trap. Can't you see that?" He turns to face the group. "This girl is nothing more than a spy. Why do you think the drones were circling overhead yesterday? They were looking for *her*."

"Nash," Trey threatens, his voice low. "That's enough."

"Of course, I don't expect you to see it. You've been trying to get into her pants since she got here the other day. What's that saying about *fresh meat*?"

I watch with wide eyes as Trey's jaw clenches and his hands ball into fists. *Oh no, not another brawl. Please, not another one.*

I half-expect Trey to tackle Nash, or kick him in the face, but he doesn't. I'm amazed by his restraint.

"Get out," Trey says. I've never seen him look so angry, not even when President Shard said the Fringe needed to be eradicated.

Nash rises and saunters toward the door. "You're all stupid if you're gonna go along with this. It's an ambush. Nothing more, nothing less." He stops at the door and throws a contemptuous look at Trey. "I guess I won't be too upset if you get killed." His lips curl into a wicked grin. "If you die, I'm in charge. Just remember that."

The door slams shut behind him, and I slowly let out the breath I've been holding. I'm afraid to look at Trey. Will he hate me for causing this rift between him and his cousin? I keep my head low, staring at the stamped concrete flooring and shag rug.

"Anyone else?" Trey counters. "Anyone else want to back out? Because if so, now is the time to do it."

I dare a glance at him. His blue eyes flame with rage, and his mouth is set in a hard line, making the dimple in his chin more prominent. A muscle in his jaw twitches as he clenches and unclenches his teeth.

My eyes shift until they connect with Trina's across the room. She gives me the '*Oh crap, what just happened?*' look by raising her eyebrows and baring her teeth. Not a becoming look on her.

The two boys on the floor rise to their feet and throw me an apologetic look. "Sorry," they mutter to Trey as they move to the door. It closes a little more quietly behind them.

Trey waits a few more moments, but I can't look at him. I stare at the floor, the cinderblock wall, my cuticles—anything to avoid eye contact.

I try not to think about what Nash crudely said about Trey and my pants. Why would he make that comment? It is *so* not true. And yet, just thinking of it makes me blush and that stupid ache to return to my belly.

When Trey finally speaks, he sounds like he is more under control. "I assume those of you who stayed are willing to help. Correct?"

I glance around the room at the two remaining and willing participants—Trina and Curly, aka Jeb.

"Hell yeah. I'm always up for a government beat down." Curly smiles.

"Me too," Trina says.

I flash them both a grateful smile and turn my attention back to Trey. He's also avoiding eye contact. Out of embarrassment? Anger?

He opens a desk drawer and pulls out a cylindrical box. After setting it on the desk, he presses a button, and a holographic image materializes in the air above the box. It's a picture of the inside of a bunker. The image does a 360-degree turn, and then another image takes its place. This time, it's the inside of a cell block.

"Hey, I was there," I say, excited. "That's the cell block where they're keeping my mom." My eyes meet Trey's. "How did you—?"

"You're not the only one with sources," he says.

The image spins before giving us the same room from a different angle.

"If you look closely, you can see three guards at the entrance to the cell block. They are heavily armed with AK-47s."

At each picture, Trey points out the guards and their weaponry. As I watch him, his eyes intent on the images, I realize something. He's been working on this since I first asked for his help two days ago. This isn't something he's haphazardly thrown together. This is a careful, thought-out design with a plan to go with it. I cringe when I think of his specific request to give him a few more days. Now I feel stupid for questioning him. I have a new level of respect for the guy standing in front of me. And an immense amount of gratitude.

When the last image dies down, Trey claps his hands together. "It will be difficult, but it won't be impossible." He glances around at the remaining three of us. "If you're still game, let's go over a step-by-step plan of how this will go down."

For the next two hours, we hammer out the details. We figure out who will cause a distraction, who will sneak inside, who will take out a few guards, and who will rescue my mom.

When I think my eyes might bug out of my head from staring at the sketch Trey has made on the oversized paper, and my back aches from leaning over his desk, Trey dismisses us.

"Get some rest or do some target shooting. We'll meet tonight in the tunnel at twenty-two hundred hours."

"Tonight?" Curly asks incredulously.

Trey's eyes narrow, and I'm glad I'm not on the receiving end of that look. "Is there a problem?"

"No, sir. I'm surprised, that's all. I didn't realize we were doing this so soon."

Trey shrugs. "No time like the present." He turns his back as if the conversation is over. The three of us stand and shuffle to the door, but I want to thank Trey for taking this on. He could have refused to help, but instead, he is risking his life for me.

I glance behind me at his broad shoulders and dark head stooped over the sketch. No, I don't want to bother him. He appears to be concentrating as he goes over each detail. I'm following Trina out the door when he stops me.

"Sienna? Do you have a minute?"

Trina's eyes widen, and she grins. "You go girl," she whispers before closing the door behind her.

Heat rises to my cheeks, and I try to slow my heart because it feels like it's about to thump right out of my chest. I turn to find Trey leaning against his desk, his arms folded across his chest. Avoiding looking at his biceps, I focus on his face instead.

"I wanted to make sure we're cool. I mean, I hope you don't think anything about what Nash said—"

I shake my head. "Of course not. He was just blowing off steam. I get it."

"Because I'm older than you, and it would never work out—"

"Never," I agree. My breath catches as he moves closer.

He raises an eyebrow, a smile half-curling his lips. "Why do you have to agree so readily?"

I swallow hard. "I thought that's what you wanted me to say."

He stops when his face is only inches from mine. "No, it's not."

My head spins. What is he saying? That he doesn't want me to agree with him? That it would work out?

"You're confusing me," I say, which is probably the first honest thing I've uttered in a while.

Trey laughs and takes a step back. "Sorry. I just wanted to make sure we're good."

"We are," I assure him. "Thanks for everything you're doing. I'm sorry I was such a brat before. If I had realized—I would have given you more time."

"Instead of an ultimatum?" He grins.

"Exactly." Silence follows. My eyes shift awkwardly around his room, which is significantly nicer than mine. At least his doesn't look like it belongs to someone in a straightjacket. His mattress rests on a frame with a sleek wooden headboard and several pictures hang on the wall, one of the city at the highlight of its wealth, and another of a field with a massive tree. The cinder block is painted a cool blue, very different from the stark white of my room.

"You have a nice room," I say.

He cocks his head and looks at me like I might be crazy. "Pardon?"

"Your room. It's cozy. Mine makes me feel like I'm in an insane asylum."

Trey chuckles. "How about this? We get your mom out and don't get killed in the process, and I'll help you paint your room."

My eyes narrow. "Why *are* you being so nice to me? *Do* you have an ulterior motive?"

Trey raises an eyebrow. "Like?"

"You tell me."

He winks. "I guess you'll have to wait and find out." Crossing the room, he opens the door. "See you tonight. And don't forget to wear black."

Chapter Twenty-four

Trina and I arrive together at the tunnel at twenty-two hundred hours. I'm wearing borrowed black pants and a black, sleeveless Quik-dry shirt, courtesy of Trina. Unfortunately, the one thing I didn't throw in my backpack before I left my house was my black shadow outfit. Such a shame because it would have been put to good use.

I've hiked the pants up as far as they'll go and rolled the pant legs so they don't drag on the ground. Trina promises she'll take me to the Pavilion tomorrow, the place I can stock up on clothes. A used clothing store inside the Compound, people donate old items and "trade" for newer ones. When I indicated to Trina that I didn't have anything to donate, she assured me that the first shopping trip is free.

Trey and Curly are already in the tunnel, waiting for us. Trey has a large duffle bag slung over his shoulder. He leads us to his black pickup, throws the bag in the back, and hands a set of keys to Trina.

"You two take the Silver Bullet. Sienna and I will drive the truck. Follow us closely."

I watch Trina sashay to the silver Verita, a car so sleek and close to the ground that the two passengers sit with their shoulders and head exposed. She is wearing her red "hooker" shorts—as she calls them—that barely cover her rear, and tight, black, four-inch heeled boots that extend above her knee. Her black tube top shows a tight, bronze midriff and tone shoulders. She looks good, and it's intentional. As a major component of our plan tonight, she will be required to produce a *distraction*. I suppress a smile as I think of the men who will be rendered helpless.

I notice Trey also watching Trina cross to the car, and my stomach tightens. I don't like the look on his face—appreciation and...

Desire?

"Would you put your eyeballs back in your head?" I growl as I move to the passenger side of the truck.

Trey climbs in beside me and laughs. "She did good. Real good."

Facing forward, I cross my arms over my chest. I shouldn't care what he thinks about Trina. He's known her a lot longer then he's known me. And yet, flames of jealousy lick my insides, warming me to the point of boiling.

Trey doesn't say anything until we pull off the road a quarter mile from where we think the bunker is located. When he turns the truck off, he glances back to make sure the Bullet is behind us. His eyes lock with mine. "You ready?"

A wave of nausea passes over me when it hits me what we're about to do. I lean forward, my head between my knees. If something goes wrong, if something happens...

It will be my fault.

Trey's hand rests on my back. "We can do this. If we stick to the plan, no one will get hurt."

An image of Garrett flashes in my mind—all smiles and freckles. I quickly sit up. "But what if someone does?" I inhale sharply. "I should do this alone. I can't be responsible for—"

His fingers move to my chin, forcing me to look at him. His eyes glow in the moonlight. "You won't be responsible. I will." Turning away, he hops out of the truck.

The truck bed creaks open, and I slide out of my seat. Hiking Trina's pants practically up to my armpits, I join the others at the back of the truck. Trey unzips the duffle bag and hands each of us a gun, a small, black piece that looks like a handgun, but I know instantly that it's not.

"What's this?" I ask.

"A stun gun. This is our first resort. We don't want to hurt anyone."

"And if it doesn't work?" Curly asks.

"That's why we have these as backup." Trey pulls out two Beretta pistols and hands one to Trina and the other to Curly. They begin to load them with the bullets from Trey's bag.

Trey turns to me. "You've shot a gun before, right?"

I nod, thinking of the few times my dad took me to the desert for some target shooting. He always said we were hunting snipes, but I knew the truth. Since he never had a son, he at least wanted his daughter to learn to shoot.

Trey hands it to me, his fingers lingering next to mine longer than necessary. He watches as I load the bullets into the magazine. The piece is heavy in my hands, especially compared to the stun gun. I'm hoping I won't need to use the real gun, but I will if I have to. When it's fully loaded, I tuck it into my waistband and pray I don't accidentally shoot myself.

Using my Lynk with the coordinates as guidance, Trey, Curly, and I walk the quarter mile to the area where we think the underground bunker is located. We crouch behind a strand of thin bushes. Trey dials Chaz while we wait for Trina to drive down the road.

"Okay, we're here," Trey says in a low voice. "How long will it take to deactivate their alarms and cameras?"

Chaz's voice comes through the Lynk. "A few minutes. But remember, you'll only have ten minutes before their system comes back online. In and out. Fast."

"Got it," Trey says.

At that moment, headlights appear, moving toward us. We watch as Trina drives down the road in the Silver Bullet. The car slows and gradually stops, but not before she turns the wheel so her headlights rest on the open expanse in front of us.

Cursing as she gets out of the car, she kicks the tire with one beautiful, booted foot. She sidles over to the hood, props it open, and seductively leans over. Clamping my hand over my mouth, I stifle a giggle. The car's headlights cast a glow over her legs and make them appear endless. Sticking her butt out, she lets her chest graze the engine and other innards of the car.

My eyes shift to the open expanse. *Come on, take the bait.* But there's nothing.

"What if this doesn't work?" I hiss.

"She needs to take it up a notch," Trey whispers back.

"What do you want her to do? Get naked and dance on top of the car?"

"Now, I wouldn't mind that," Curly admits. Trey remains silent.

I slug Curly. "That's from Trina." Then I pinch him hard on the arm. "And that's from me."

"Ow, that hurt," he whines.

"Children, cut it out," Trey snaps.

I turn my attention back to Trina, who must recognize that it's time to up the ante. She glances in our direction, a panicked look crossing her face.

"Come on, Trina, you can do this," Trey mutters.

Trina's forehead wrinkles in determination, and she wipes invisible beads of sweat. I look on in horror as she struggles out of her tube top, revealing a strapless bra and overflowing breasts.

"Now that's what I'm talking about," Curly murmurs. "So glad I didn't back out. *So* glad."

I turn to glare at him, and then realize he can't see me in the darkness.

"What the hell is she doing?" Trey mutters, turning his eyes away.

At least one of them has sense enough to look away.

Trina bends back over the car, using her tube top to

unscrew the cap off something hot.

"Genius," Trey says, his eyes trained on Trina again. I can't help but notice the admiration in his eyes.

"We're in," Chaz says from the Lynk in Trey's hand at the exact moment that a movement to my left catches my attention.

"Look," I hiss.

About thirty yards to the left of Trina's parked car, the ground opens up, a twenty-foot-by-twenty-foot space that slides back to reveal a black hole. Two military men creep out and sneak to the road.

"Let's move," Trey says without hesitation.

"What about Trina?" I ask, glancing back at her. She must have seen the men coming. Her tube top is now clutched in front of her chest.

"She'll be fine. As long as she sticks to the plan."

We crouch low and run toward the black hole in the ground that is quickly closing.

"Hurry," Trey says urgently, gripping my elbow.

Curly gets there first and jumps in. I hear a soft thud and a groan.

The hatch is closing too quickly. I stumble, but Trey steadies me. We're almost there when Trey hisses, "Jump!"

I propel myself forward and slide through the opening, my shirt catching on the lip of the hatch as the door closes behind us. When I jerk my shirt free, it tears slightly, exposing my stomach. I land hard on a concrete floor, my butt taking most of the impact. When I rise to my feet, pain shoots down my leg.

Overcome with the smell of damp earth and something metallic, I take a moment to get my bearings, my eyes sweeping over thick rock walls, a curved ceiling with a long strip of lights, and metal pipes running the length of one wall. A paved "road" complete with road paint runs down the center of the passage and gives purpose to the metal ramp hanging overhead. A ramp that must lower to allow military vehicles to enter and exit the bunker.

Trey stands up and brushes himself off, then moves to a control panel on the side wall. It's next to a metal ladder I assume the two men used to leave the bunker. Trey presses a few buttons and the hatch slides open overhead.

"Let's get going," he says, already moving down the corridor. His hands curl around his stun gun, and his pistol is tucked into the back of his dark jeans.

I follow his lead, keeping my arms locked, the stun gun pointed in front of me. Curly brings up the rear.

We turn a corner, pausing to make sure we're clear. Surprisingly, this part of the corridor is empty. *Where is everyone?*

An earth-shattering scream pierces the passage behind us. I freeze, my heart leaping into my throat. It's Trina.

"Help me! Somebody, please! Help me!"

I'm about to turn and run toward the sound of her voice when I remember. It's all part of the plan.

I breathe deeply, trying to ignore her sobs and screams. But it all sounds so real that I start to wonder if something bad did happen. Is she really crying out for help?

"Is she okay?" I ask.

Before Trey can answer, we hear footsteps pounding the pavement. They echo in the cavernous space, making it difficult to determine from which direction they're coming.

"Hide," Trey hisses. He pulls me behind a set of oversized oxygen tanks with the symbol of a flaming O inside a triangle stamped on the side.

We sit crouched, breathing the same air, and I wonder where Curly hid. My heart pounds louder than the feet on the pavement. For a moment, I worry that the men will track us by the beat of it alone. Trey places his hand on my head and forces it down as four men run past.

Four. That's a lot. More than we expected. My throat closes when I think of Trina dealing with them by herself.

Trey must have the same thought. He pushes himself up

once the footsteps have faded and whispers to Curly. "Go help Trina. Sienna and I will continue. Meet us by the cell block."

I take a deep breath to steady my heart. Wiping my sweaty hands on my too-big pants, I step away from the tanks.

"Let's go," Trey says.

We start to round another corner, but Trey stops me with his arm, pressing me back against the wall. He lifts a finger to his lips before peeking around the corner, his stun gun up by his chin. Pulling back, he whispers in my ear, his warm breath tickling my skin.

"There are two more guards down there. You create a distraction, and I'll stun them."

Distraction? What kind of distraction? My eyes narrow. If he thinks I'm ripping off my shirt like Trina, he better think again.

"No," he says in exasperation, as if sensing my thoughts. "Not that kind of distraction. Just think of something."

My mind is blank, like a freshly cleared desk-screen. And then it hits me. I rise and put the stun gun in the back of my pants next to the real one.

I place my hands in the air in a gesture of surrender and round the corner. "Hey boys, remember me?"

The men snap into position and raise their guns, aiming at my head.

"Well, you might not remember me, but I'm sure Radcliffe does. How's his face, by the way?"

"Don't take another step." The men keep their guns trained on me, stone-faced. These are military men, skilled and dangerous. If threatened, they will take the shot.

I venture another step closer, and Trey hisses behind me.

"I'm here to see Radcliffe. If you need to tie me up, go for it." I hold out my arms.

The two men exchange a look. I'm sure they're wondering why I would offer myself up to Radcliffe.

They move slowly toward me, their guns never wavering.

I panic. How am I supposed to do this? How do I get them to lower their guns so I can stun them?

"Arms behind your back," the one with the blond crew cut says in a crisp voice.

I move my arms behind my back, and the hard gun presses against my flesh. My heart races as they surround me, and I pray that Trey will move at the same time. My fingers close around the stun gun handle and I whip it around, pressing it into Crew Cut's chest. At the same moment, Trey charges from behind and fires at the brown-haired man with the thin lips.

Crew Cut is the first to collapse, followed by Thin Lips. Their faces are contorted in an expression of surprise, their eyes wide open.

I nudge Crew Cut with my steel-toed boot—another borrow from Trina—but he doesn't move.

"Can they hear us?" I ask as Trey bends down to grab their guns.

"Yeah, but they'll be unable to move for a while." He hands me the extra gun, an M-16 rifle, and I sling it over my shoulder. "The venom attacks the central nervous system. They can see and hear, but their muscles have shut down, similar to a stroke victim."

He pulls out his Lynk and studies the data map. "The cell block should be coming up around the next bend." His eyes flicker around the passage. "We should get moving. I'm sure Trina and Jeb will catch up soon."

Footsteps pound behind us, and Trey tenses. He pulls me against the concrete wall, in the shadows of an overhang. My body is pressed tight against his, and his hand on my back forces me to remain close. I hardly dare to breathe, partly from fear, and partly from the close proximity to him.

The footsteps draw closer, and then stop.

"Are we interrupting? 'Cause if so, we can always come back later," Curly says.

Heat rises to my cheeks, and I push away from Trey.

Catalyst

"We thought you were guards," I mumble, refusing to look at Curly.

"*Right*," he says, his voice dripping with sarcasm.

I focus on Trina, who is now wearing her tube top and a triumphant smile. "How did it go?"

"Piece of cake," she says. She strikes a pose. "I should use my assets more often."

Curly coughs and slings an arm over her shoulder. "You can practice on me. Any time. Any place."

She punches him in the shoulder and makes a face. "No, thank you."

Trey gives them an annoyed look. "You've done well so far, but it ain't over yet. We still need to get past the cell block. So, let's focus." His eyes fall on me. "Sienna, I'm gonna leave it up to you to get us through that cell block. Your distraction worked well. Maybe something similar?"

I nod.

We move down the passage, Trey and I in front, Trina and Curly bringing up the rear. We round another corner, and this hall looks just like the ones before it, except for the stainless-steel doors that line the wall every ten feet or so.

Trey's Lynk buzzes, and when he glances down at it, he curses. "Three minutes, guys. Three minutes until the cameras are back online."

Fear makes my blood run cold, but I keep moving.

We near another hallway, and Trey moves ahead, motioning for us to hang back. He peers around the corner, shakes his head, and then rejoins us. We crowd around him in a huddle as he whispers commands.

"There are three heavily armed guards at the entrance to the cell block. Sienna, you create the distraction. I'll take point. Trina and Jeb, bring up the rear. Any questions?"

My heart picks up speed as I shake my head. So far, this has been too easy, and Radcliffe would never make anything easy. I'm afraid of what might await us when we reach the cell block. I keep my thoughts to myself because I don't want to worry the others.

Taking a deep breath, I hand the M-16 to Curly, square my shoulders, and walk around the corner. With purposeful strides, I make my way to the metal bars. The three men guarding the gate don't see me at first because they don't expect me. One is drinking from a steaming mug, one has his foot resting on a metal rollaway chair, and the other is standing erect, his hand resting on his M-16. He doesn't see me because his dark brown head is turned, and he's talking to the one with the hot drink.

I purposefully shuffle my boot across the floor and watch as the three of them jump and clutch their guns. The mug crashes to the floor and makes a noise akin to a gunshot.

"What the hell? How did you get in here?" the one with a crooked nose hollers.

I hear the click of their guns as they move the bullets into place.

"I'm here for my mother," I say with more confidence than I feel.

The one who had his foot resting on the chair laughs. "Someone call the colonel. He'll want to know about this."

I can't let them call Radcliffe. He will summon the cavalry if he sees me, especially if he discovers I have the leader of the Fringe with me. I picture Trey being whisked away in handcuffs and tossed into a urine-infested cell. No way can I let that happen.

Before I realize what I'm doing, my hand reaches behind me and grips the gun. The real one. The pistol that can kill a man.

I aim at Crooked Nose's face and hold my hand steady, even though I'm terrified. I've strayed from the plan, and this could go terribly wrong. In my mind, I hear Trey cursing under his breath.

"Don't move or I'll blow his nose off," I say.

The other guard, a bald man who looks like he has a board stuck up his butt, laughs. "I'd like to see you try. We'd take you out before your finger even has a chance to pull the trigger."

"I don't think so." Trey's voice speaks up loud and clear behind me. He moves into my line of sight, and I see him clutching the M-16, the barrel pointed at the other guard.

"You're still outnumbered. Three to two," the third guard points out.

"Not exactly," Trina's voice calls out. She and Curly move into view, and I feel something akin to hope. We might be able to pull this off.

"You're the ones who are outnumbered. Drop your weapons. Now," Trey commands. He inches forward, his hands steady, his gun trained on the Bald Man.

The three guards glance at each other, but they don't move to put their guns down.

"I said, drop your weapons. I will shoot you," Trey warns.

Crooked Nose is the first to set his gun on the ground, followed by the man with dark hair. The bald man is the last to place his weapon down. They all raise their hands in the air, and we move quickly toward them.

"On your knees," Trey says.

I hurry to the metal bars, but the gate is locked. Glancing behind me, I see my three cohorts pull out their stun guns to immobilize the three guards.

"Wait!" I say.

Trey looks up. "What is it?"

I rush over to the guards. "The key. Where is it?"

"I'm not telling you," Crooked Nose spits.

Trey punches him in the face, then grabs his chin and grips it hard. Blood trickles out of the man's already crooked nose. "Oh, I think you will. Where is it?"

The man grins, but he doesn't say anything. I hear the bullet click into place as Trey thrusts the gun into the side of the man's head. "Tell us. Now!"

This is taking too long. I can see the anger surging through Trey; adrenaline mixed with fear has made him unstable. I don't want him to do something he'll regret, so I reach out with my stun gun and zap Crooked Nose in the shoulder. He falls to the side like a wet mop.

"Why'd you do that?" Trey stares at me, his eyes incredulous.

I shrug. "We weren't getting anywhere with him." My eyes shift to the other two guards, and Trey understands what I'm trying to convey. He thrusts the gun into the fleshy area under the dark-haired man's chin.

We need to find the weakest link. Then we're golden.

"I'll only ask you once. Where's the key?" Trey snarls.

The man's eyes widen, and he appears to contemplate something. He glances at the body of his military brother beside him.

"He has it." He nods to the sprawled-out man at his side. "He wears it on a chain around his neck."

Trey reaches into Crooked Nose's shirt and yanks the chain from his neck.

"This it?" he asks, holding out the skeleton key.

"Yep." He looks up at us with hopeful eyes.

Trey nods to Trina and Curly, who move forward with their guns.

Surprise flashes in the dark-haired man's eyes. "Hey, I thought—"

Trey shrugs. "Sorry."

The two remaining guards collapse in a heap of camo.

Trey hands me the key. "I'll let you do the honors."

I step over the bodies and hurry to the lock. The key fits easily and the gears click into place. I pull hard on the heavy metal bars, and the gate slides open, the screech of metal against metal assaulting my ears like fingernails on a chalkboard.

Once I'm in, I sprint down the corridor, past the cells. I hear Trey calling after me, but I've abandoned *the plan*. All I can think about is getting to my mother. Before it's too late.

I stop when I realize nothing looks familiar. Turning in

circles, I stare up and down the cell block. Gray block walls, uneven and cracked concrete floors, and crude cell chambers with metal bars are all I see. The faint smell of mildew and body odor hangs in the air.

Knowing it's stupid, but desperate with frustration, I belt out my mother's name. I expect to see a hand reach through the bars, hear a small sob—anything, really—but there is only silence. Where are all the prisoners?

My eyes rest on a cell partway open, and even though every fiber of my being screams at me, I move toward it. My breath catches as I glance inside and see my mother's silver charm bracelet—the one with the two dangling birds meant to represent my sister and me—resting on the filthy cot. Tears sting my eyes and my throat closes. Where is she?

I walk into the cell and pick up the bracelet, twirling it between my fingers. My mother never takes this bracelet off, which means that something bad must have happened.

"I see you found your gift," a voice behind me says.

I jerk up, my heart racing like a freight train. Radcliffe stands in the doorway, the claw marks on his face deep and ragged. I should be impressed with the souvenir I left him, but I'm too sick with worry to care.

"Where is she?"

"Ahh, Sienna. You didn't really think we'd let you storm our facility and just hand her over. Did you?" Radcliffe leans close. "Your little hacker may have disabled our main camera system, but we have backup cameras." He points to the ceiling in the hallway, and that's when I notice the tiny, digital cameras embedded in the ceiling. They were watching us the whole time. Waiting.

I pocket the bracelet and move to the doorway of the cell, but Radcliffe blocks me in. I keep expecting to see Trey, Trina, or Curly appear and take Radcliffe out.

Where are they? They should have caught up by now.

"I think you and I need to have a little chat." Radcliffe eyes me for a moment. "Nice haircut by the way. I hope you did it because you found out *Zane* likes short-haired redheads."

I glare at him, but I say nothing.

"How's the seduction going?"

"I've been busy," I growl.

His eyebrows rise. "I see that." He purses his lips and frowns. "Who are these people you infiltrated my building with?"

I clench my mouth shut. There's no way I'm telling him who Trey is. No way.

"You seemed quite *cozy* with the muscled, dark-haired one." He grins, and I want to punch him in his crooked smile. "I hope this doesn't put a *damper* on our agreement."

"Where's my mother?"

Radcliffe smiles and his beady eyes crinkle at the edges, reminding me he's a man well into his fifties. "I thought I made that clear. Once you've completed your assignment, she's all yours."

"I want to see her."

"She's safe and doing well. We moved her to a more… comfortable location." He wrinkles his nose. "The rats were bothering her."

I lunge at him, but he's too quick for me this time. He grabs a fistful of my hair and forces me into a chokehold. I'm helpless against his strength. He may be older, but a life served in the military has made him strong and agile.

He calls to someone in the hallway. "Bring them down."

I hear the shuffling of feet, and Radcliffe tightens his arm around my neck. Moments later, my three friends appear in the doorway, led by one guard. Their hands are tied behind their backs, and their faces are full of anger. They've been stripped of their guns, but when I see them, I remember. I still have one. And a laser stun gun.

The guard has a gun trained on my three friends, but I don't think Radcliffe is armed. Weighing the options in my mind, I make a decision. I only hope it will work.

I elbow Radcliffe hard in the ribs and slam my boot down

on his toes. He cries out and lets go of me, giving me enough time to reach behind my back and pull out both guns, one in each hand.

In my haste, I don't know which gun is which. But I hope the one in my left hand is the stun gun as I aim it at Radcliffe's chest and squeeze the trigger.

Chapter Twenty-five

Radcliffe collapses to the ground at the same moment Trey throws his head back and head butts the guard behind him. A sickening crack is followed by an inhumane howl. I glance down at Radcliffe and his blank eyes, training the other gun on the guard whose face is covered in blood. I'm fairly certain Trey broke his nose.

"Don't move," I warn him.

The guard throws his gun to the ground and clutches his nose, the blood pouring through his fingers. I move to him next, pressing the stun gun against his upper arm.

Trey nods his head in appreciation. "Nice work. I should have a knife in my pocket to cut these ropes. Can you grab it for me?"

I reach in his front pocket and pull out a blue-handled pocketknife with an engraving on the hilt.

Our choices define us.
BGW

Opening the blade, I kneel behind Trey and carefully cut off the bindings. I move to Trina and Curly's wrists and watch as the severed ropes fall on the concrete and lay like unmoving baby snakes next to the puddle of blood from the man's nose.

"We'd better hurry," Trey says when I hand the knife back to him.

Leaning down, I stare into the blank eyes of Radcliffe. I know he can see me, and it gives me great satisfaction to spit in his face.

"I will find my mother. And when I do, you'll be sorry."

The four of us take off running down the cell block, back the way we came. I'm not sure what we'll find. The guards monitoring the cameras will be after us in moments, assuming they haven't already prepared an ambush for the way out. We stop only long enough for the others to grab their guns.

When we reach the door-filled passage, I try each knob as I pass. I bang on a few and strain for any sounds.

"Sienna! Come on," Trey snaps.

"I can't leave without my mom." I try another door.

Trey runs back to me, and Trina and Curly stop and wait anxiously, their eyes darting up and down the corridor.

Trey grabs my arm, but I yank it free. "I'm not leaving without her," I say through clenched teeth.

Trey softens. "Look, you don't even know if she's here. They might have moved her somewhere else." He lays his hand on my arm, less forcefully this time. "We'll figure something out. But for now, we need to get the hell out of here."

I glance down the long corridor. If I stay to find her, I'll surely be caught by Radcliffe's men. And of course, they'll want to know who helped me break into the facility. The idea of being water tortured again sends a shiver of fear down my spine.

But if I leave, I may never have the opportunity to return. Short of seducing Zane and killing Harlow, I'll never see my mother again. Hot, angry tears sting the back of my eyes. I hate that I've been placed in this situation. I hate that someone else is controlling my life. For a brief moment, I wish the gun I'd aimed at Radcliffe's chest wasn't the laser stun.

Trey must sense my hesitation. "I promise. We'll find her." Grabbing my hand, he pulls me behind him.

As our feet slam against the concrete and echo down

the corridors, Trey whips out his Lynk and checks the data map to make sure we're heading in the right direction. All the passages look the same. With the dim overhead lights bouncing off the stone walls, shadows are thrust at us, making it more difficult to navigate going in the opposite direction. When we pass the two stunned guards and the oxygen tanks, I know we're nearing the ramp.

Near the entrance, we find the four guards, the ones Trina and Curly took care of. Thankfully, they are still stunned, but at any moment, they will gain mobility.

As Trey presses the buttons to activate the hatch, I glance around with uncertainty.

Why are they not coming after us? Where's the cavalry?

I expected gunfire to rain down on us, but it's too quiet. Eerily quiet.

Is this a setup?

Trina is the first to climb the ladder out of the hatch, and Trey nods for me to go next as he and Curly stand guard at the bottom. Fatigue and disappointment setting in, I climb as if it takes an immense amount of effort, my sweaty hands sliding off the metal rungs. When I finally reach the top, I crawl out onto the dirt and hear a scream that ricochets to my soul.

It's Trina. And this time, it's not part of the plan.

Chapter Twenty-six

Hands grab my arms and force them behind my back as pain shoots through my shoulders. My head slams into the dirt, and a filthy boot presses against my cheek, grinding my face into the grainy clay. I crouch on my knees like an animal, and I am helpless. I can't see Trina, but I can hear her struggling with her captor.

"You're a feisty one," a voice mutters.

"Yeah, I see you brought a friend to the party." Another sneers. "And I like redheads."

"You're gonna pay for what you did to us. Luring us out with your broken-down car and fine caboose." I hear a smack like he's slapping her butt.

"I didn't know chicks carried guns. Kinda hot."

Their faceless phrases mingle around me.

"What should we do with them?" one asks.

"I guess we need to call the colonel. He said to tell him if anyone was caught around the perimeter."

The other hesitates before speaking up. "Ya know, it's dark and no one's around. We could have a little fun first." The boot on my cheek shifts.

My breathing stops and I lay completely still, my heart pounding in my ears. The blood rushes to my face and causes white spots to dot my vision. There is no way I will let these men touch me. I'd rather die first.

"No, we should call the colonel."

Where the hell are Trey and Curly? If there were ever a time for a rescue, now would be it.

"C'mon, man. It's been like six months. That's like a lifetime in dog years."

The other guard snickers. "Yeah, you *would* think of it in dog terms."

I feel a hand reach into my waistband and withdraw the guns. He snaps the elastic, runs his hand down my thigh, and grips my rear. I open my mouth to scream and inhale a mouth full of dirt, coughing as the thick dust settles in my chest.

A gunshot rings out, and two things happen. The pressure on my arms releases, and the boot slides off my face.

I push myself up, staring at the figure on the ground beside me, and the dark liquid pooling around his head. My eyes sweep through the dark, and I spot Trina kneeling beside her captor. Trey is standing on the top rung of the ladder, gun in hand, while Curly is crouched a few feet away, stun gun raised.

"Thank God. Is he dead?" Trina asks, rising to her feet.

I stride over to her, kicking the guard with my foot. His eyes are open and blank, but there's not an ounce of blood in sight. "Nope, but that one is." I point to the one who tried to molest me.

Trey comes to stand beside us, and I turn to him.

"What took you so long?"

"I had to wait for a clear shot. He was hovered over you like—well, never mind. But once he started groping, I knew I had to take him out."

"You killed him," I point out. "We weren't supposed to hurt anyone."

"I was out of laser stun. What did you want me to do? Watch him rape you? I wasn't aiming for his head, but he moved."

I take a deep breath to calm my nerves. We have blood

on our hands. No one was supposed to get hurt, but now a soldier lies dead on desert soil, a bullet to the brain.

"What are we going to do? We can't just leave him here," Trina says, her voice rising.

"Yes, we can. And we will," Trey says calmly, clearly in command. "We are the Fringe, and this is what they expect us to do."

Turning his back on us and the dead soldier, Trey lifts his shoulders and strides away.

And just like that, the mission to rescue my mother is over.

Chapter Twenty-seven

The Pavilion is a large room inside the Compound with folding tables, makeshift racks, and piles of used clothing. It has an interesting smell too, kind of like a grandma's closet. Trina promised to help me shop for clothes that actually fit, and true to her word, she dragged me here after dishes duty this morning.

As soon as we enter the shop, she grabs things off tables and racks, stuffing them into my hands. A few colorful shirts peek through the pile. When she moves to snatch up a pair of red thigh-high boots, very similar in style to her own, I give a fervent shake of my head.

"No way. I'm not wearing those."

Trina sighs and places them back on the floor underneath the table. "Well, I think I found the most boring clothes possible, so you should at least like those."

A few minutes later, as we're pawing through more clothes, she nudges me with her shoulder. "You're awfully quiet."

"Just thinking."

She gives me a sympathetic smile. "About your mom? I'm really sorry we weren't able to get her last night."

"About my mom. Garrett. The soldier. Everything."

"Hey." Trina grips my clothes-laden arms and turns me until I'm facing her. "Trey only did that because he had to.

He's not a killer."

I know all this, but it's not the only thing that's bothering me. The whole ride back to the Compound, Trey was silent. And I can't help but wonder if he regrets saying he'll help me. Is he upset that he risked the lives of Fringe members for nothing? My mother wasn't there, and now I have no idea how I'll ever find her. And I'm sure he doesn't either.

Changing the subject, Trina holds up a bright pink miniskirt. "Do you have a boy you'd like to wear this for?"

My mind immediately flits to Zane, and my cheeks flush. I shouldn't be thinking of him that way when he has a fiancée. And I can't help the guilt that chews at me when I picture Trey's dimpled smile. What would he think if he knew I might have feelings for Harlow Ryder's son? Would he refuse to help me find my mother?

"You do!" Trina leans in close. "Spill. I want to know everything."

Turning away from her, I say, "There's nothing to tell." As an afterthought, I add, "He's only a friend."

"I knew it! There is someone." Weaseling her way in front of me, she blocks my path. "Tell me. Please? I told you my embarrassing love story."

I snort. "You mean your professor?"

"He was really cute," she protests.

I think for a minute, trying to figure out the best way to explain Zane. "Zane is… a friend who is taking care of my sister right now."

"Is he cute?"

I clear my throat. "Do you know Zane Ryder?"

Her eyes widen. "Zane Ryder? You're friends with him?"

When several pairs of eyes turn our way, I pull her over to the dressing room—which is really just a curtain hanging from the ceiling.

"Shh," I say. "Not so loud."

"I'm sorry. It's just that I can't believe you're friends with him. Is he as bad as his father?"

I quickly shake my head. "I don't think so."

When Trina just stares at me, I say, "Please don't tell Trey."

Trina gives me a serious look. "I won't. Trust me. He would not be happy about it."

My stomach cramps when I think of all the things I'm hiding from so many people I care about.

"But hey," she fingers a piece of my hair, "your secret is safe with me." She smiles. "And if you have a crush on him, I say more power to you."

"He's engaged," I remind her.

She shrugs. "So?"

"He's just a friend," I repeat, like the more I keep saying it, the more I'll believe it myself.

"It sounds like what you need is to see your sister." She gives me an exaggerated wink. "What do you think?"

It would be nice to see Emily… and maybe Zane too. They would both be a good distraction right now.

"I think you're right," I say, butterflies already fluttering in my stomach.

Trina grins. "But first, we must do something with that hair."

My hand flies to my hair. "Is it that bad?"

"I can make it look better." She looks down at the clothes in my hands. "You done?"

When I nod, she grabs my arm and leads me to the checkout counter where a teenage girl with purple hair is sitting, looking bored. There is no cash register, no chip scanner, nothing.

"This is her first shopping trip," Trina explains to the girl.

"Name?"

"Sienna Preston," I say.

"How many items?" she asks, her voice monotone.

Counting them quickly, I reply, "Seven. Three shorts and four tops."

The girl makes a mark on a notepad and says, "Enjoy your clothes."

Catalyst

As soon as we're in the hallway outside the Pavilion, Trina links her arm through mine and says, "Now for the fun part."

As she leads me back to her room, I wonder what I've gotten myself into.

I ride down the center of the tracks until I reach the sunlight. The sky is filled with clouds, and I love the way the light filters through and settles on the ground beneath. It feels so good to be in the sun instead of under a mountain of artificial light, so I ride my Harley faster than usual. The wind whips against my face and stings my eyes, but it feels right. It reminds me I'm alive, which causes my thoughts to drift to Garrett and the soldier, who aren't.

I can't wait to see Emily. I need to feel her small arms wrapped around me. Most importantly, I want to get the image of Garrett trapped beneath the pillar out of my mind. And for a moment, I don't want to think about the fact that my mother is still missing.

I haven't had a chance to talk to Trey yet, and even though I'm bothered by what happened with the soldier, I still want to thank him. He was only trying to protect me. If he hadn't been there… I don't want to think about what might have happened. Despite everything, I hope he's still willing to help me find my mother.

I make it to the wealthy part of the city in record time. Weaving through City Square, I'm on high alert for any government vehicles or Suits. Zane's house sits high on Hampstead Hill with other wealthy Citizens. I didn't call or message him, but hopefully, he doesn't mind if I show up unannounced.

Before I ring the doorbell, I say a silent prayer that Harlow Ryder is not around. If I saw him right now, I couldn't be responsible for anything I might do to him. Knowing what he did to the first wave of GMs, and what he's doing now to those juvenile inmates, fills me with an uncontrollable rage.

After ringing the doorbell, I smooth my hair into place. Thanks to Trina, my hair now has a style instead of a butchered look. And the blue, cap-sleeved shirt that was my bargain find at the Pavilion fits perfectly.

The Ryder's butler, an older gentleman with graying hair and a kind smile, opens the door.

"I'm here to see Zane or Emily."

"Come in, please." He holds the door open, and I enter the oversized foyer. "I think they may be in the pool. I'll let them know you're here. It's Sienna, right?"

I nod, surprised he knows who I am.

He walks down the hallway and disappears. As I wait, I gaze around the stunning home. My previous visit didn't afford me the opportunity to look around and truly appreciate it. From luxurious silks to silver candelabras, this house screams *money*. The expensive canvas artwork from artists like Baun and Gorgeman decorate the walls, and the crystal teardrop chandeliers sparkle without an ounce of dust.

I watch in awe as the morning sunlight filters through the oversized Palladian windows and hits the chandeliers, creating tiny rainbows of color around the foyer. I turn as the rainbows dance around the room. I've never seen anything more beautiful.

"It's amazing, isn't it?" a soft voice speaks from across the foyer.

My eyes light on a woman whose blonde bun is streaked with gray. She's wearing an apron dusted with flour, which leads me to believe she just came from the kitchen.

"It is," I admit. "I'm Sienna," I say, taking a step forward and holding out my hand. I wonder if this woman is Greta, the one who practically raised Zane. She seems like the motherly type.

The woman moves toward me and grasps my hand between both of hers. Her smile is warm. "It's so nice to meet you, Sienna. I'm Greta." She laughs. "We love having a child in the home again. It's been so long."

She squeezes my hand before letting go.

"How is Emily?" I smile at the sound of her name. "Has she behaved?"

Greta laughs again, a warm sunburst of a laugh. "Of course! She is such a delight. And so smart!" Greta leans in. "She's been helping me in the kitchen. I swear, if I don't watch out, she'll have my job in a few years."

My grin deepens, and I long to see my little sister. I anxiously glance around the foyer.

"They're probably drying off," Greta says. "They should be up in a minute."

A few seconds later, I hear the pitter-patter of small feet on the marble floor. I want to yell at her not to run or she'll slip and fall and crack her head open, but I bite the inside of my cheek instead.

When she sees me, Emily leaps into my arms and buries her face in my neck. I hold her so tight I'm afraid her bones might break. Her bathing suit is still wet, and it soaks through my shirt, but I don't care. She wraps her legs around me, and I cradle her like a baby monkey. Tears sting my eyes. I will do anything to keep her safe.

"Did you miss me?" I murmur into her wet hair.

She pulls back and places her hands on either side of my face. "Where did your hair go, Si-Si?"

A deep, melodious voice speaks from behind her. "Yeah, where *did* your hair go?"

My stomach tightens as my eyes rest on Zane's grin, then wander down to his bare chest and the towel slung over his shoulders. I try not to stare at his fully formed pecs, chiseled abs, and the V-line muscle that dips into his bathing suit.

A flush creeps to my face, and I bury my head into Emily's hair to hide my embarrassment. I don't mean to ogle, but it's hard not to.

"I had to cut it," I say to Emily, and then immediately regret my choice of words.

Zane moves closer, his eyes narrowed. "I'm sorry... did you say you *had* to cut it? As in, you didn't have a choice?"

I shift my weight and readjust Emily in my arms. Greta takes it as her cue to leave.

"Well, kids, I better get back to my dough. Sienna, it was a pleasure to meet you." Greta claps her hands and focuses on Emily. "Do you want to help me roll out the dough for the pie?"

I'm not ready to let go of Emily yet, but she's already squirming out of my arms, clearly excited about making a pie.

"Yes! Yes!" Emily jumps down and runs over to Greta. "Can we put sprinkles on it?"

Greta laughs and places her hand on the back of Emily's head, steering her to the kitchen. "Well, I don't think we should put sprinkles on the pie crust, but maybe we can find some ice cream for you to put sprinkles on. What do you think of that?"

Emily claps her hands. "Yes! I love ice cream. Can I have chocolate syrup too?"

"Sure..."

Their voices fade down the hall, and I turn to find Zane intently staring at me. He takes a step closer.

"What happened? Where were you?"

"Someplace safe." That's all he needs to know.

His eyes cloud over. "Why can't you let me in?"

"Why have you been lying about what's going on in your lab?" I counter.

"What are you talking about?"

"The juvenile inmates? The experiments? Ringing a bell?"

Zane slowly shakes his head. "I have no idea what you're talking about."

My eyes narrow as I cross my arms over my chest. "Are you telling me you're not experimenting on juvenile inmates, trying to change their DNA so they aren't a scourge to society?"

"What? That's the most *absurd* thing I've ever heard," he

says, his voice rising.

"Is it, Zane?" I say, sarcasm ringing through my tone. "Is it really?"

Zane stares at me. "Where did you hear this? Who told you this?"

"I think your father is hiding stuff from you," I say simply.

His eyes move to my upper arm, and I freeze. I should have picked a different shirt. The scabbed-over tattoo injection site peeks out from my cap sleeve and trails down my arm. My arms drop to my sides.

My breath catches as Zane's fingers lift my shirtsleeve, exposing the red and tender area. His fingers lightly trace the outline, sending a shiver up my spine.

"I've seen this before—" His eyes flash with anger as he takes a step back. "Wait a minute. You were with those people? The Fringe or whatever they call themselves? They're the ones feeding you these lies?" He pauses and breathes in deep. "You were with the people who tried to kill me?"

"It was a set-up," I protest. "They aren't the ones who tried to kill you at the Extravaganza—"

"They bombed the Megasphere," he says flatly. When I don't respond immediately, he continues. "And do you know what happened last night? Do you know what they did?"

My eyes widen. Is he referring to the infiltration of the bunker?

Zane crosses the foyer to a room that has a grand piano and a pair of fancy couches and picks up a handheld comscreen. "*Iris*, show me the news," he growls.

I stare at the screen in his hands, reluctantly moving toward it. I don't want to see what's on the screen. The thoughts in my mind are a torturous enough reminder of what happened last night. But Zane holds out the handheld device, and I take it.

A dark-skinned woman with her hair teased around her head in a classic fro speaks directly to the camera. She is standing in front of a desert landscape, but her exact location is undisclosed.

"Recent reports indicate that members of the Fringe broke into a secure, underground government facility and attacked several soldiers last night. At least twelve were wounded and one was killed in the attack."

Zane clicks the comscreen off. "Do you know anything about this?"

My first instinct is to lie. But when I look into his warm eyes, I stammer. I stumble. And I fumble.

I finally throw my hands up in exasperation. "Yes! Is that what you want to hear? Yes!" I take a deep breath. "I was one of those who broke into the facility."

Zane's eyebrows knit together, and disappointment fills his eyes. "Why? Why would you do that?"

"Because they have my mother."

Shaking his head, Zane moves to the couch and sinks down on it. "I don't understand," he mutters.

I wonder if anyone would care that Zane is sitting on the couch in a wet bathing suit, and then I realize that is the least of my worries.

I take a seat on the edge of the couch next to him. I can't stand the disappointed look he's giving me. Like he even has a right to be upset with me when his father is doing who knows what to unfortunate teenagers. But Zane at least needs to know the truth—or a shadow of the truth—so he can maybe understand why I've been compelled to do the things I've done.

"Look, I don't expect you to understand, but here's the truth. A couple of weeks ago, I was hired for a job. I had no idea who hired me, but I was given specific instructions on what to do."

"As a reporter?" I can tell I'm already losing him, but there are some details he just doesn't need to know. Like the fact I stole the computer chip, tried to kill his father, and should be trying to seduce him. He really would look at me as if I were nuts.

"No, a little more of a… discreet job."

Zane nods like he understands.

"I completed the assignment, but when I tried to make the exchange, I was kidnapped by a ruthless man who knew what I'd done. This man had a new assignment for me, and I felt pressured to take it because of the… delicate nature of the other job."

"He blackmailed you," Zane says, his tone flat.

"Exactly." I release a slow, controlled breath. "He kidnapped my mother as collateral to make sure I didn't back out. But I couldn't do it. It was wrong. They're still holding my mom for ransom. But they don't want money, of course. They have plenty of it. They want me to finish what I started."

"What's the assignment?"

"I can't say."

Zane runs his hands through his hair, and I admire the way his biceps flex and the muscles in his shoulder ripple. His hands fall to his lap, and he sighs.

"What happened last night?"

I tell him the most accurate account of the events I can recall. I notice how his eyes narrow when I talk about the soldier who grabbed my rear with the intention of doing more. When I tell him about Trey shooting the guard, he leans back and exhales.

"It sounds like the bastard got what he deserved," Zane mutters.

I shake my head. "No, he didn't. He didn't deserve to die. And his blood will forever be on my hands."

Zane's expression softens. "But you weren't the one who pulled the trigger."

"No, but it's because of me that Trey did."

"Sienna," he tenderly says. "You have to let that go. You didn't do anything wrong."

Oh, yeah? If you only knew…

"And then, there's Garrett." The words tumble out before I can stop them. "I couldn't save him, even though I wanted to—"

"Wait. Who's Garrett?"

I tell him all about the red-haired boy and his noble death, trapped under the pillar and begging me to leave him.

"I'm sorry, Sienna," he says, his eyes pained. He reaches for my hands. "But you have to realize, it wasn't your fault."

His soothing voice combined with the way he's looking at me, as if I'm the only person in the world, produces a vulnerability I didn't know existed. Tears well in my eyes and slide down my cheeks. I reach up to wipe them away, not wanting to cry in front of him, but Zane beats me to it. He moves closer and his fingers glide over my cheeks, his eyes never leaving my face.

I choke back a sob as his arms encircle my back, pulling me to him. Then the dam breaks loose. I sob into his bare skin, my tears mingling with the water droplets from his hair that drip and run down his body. I don't know why I'm crying. Maybe a few tears escape for my dead father, a few fall for my missing mother, and I suppose, some drop for the loss of my own innocence.

When the tears finally run dry, I wipe my face and sit up. I'm sure I look a mess. "I'm sorry," I mumble, avoiding Zane's eyes.

I feel his thumb lightly trace my cheekbone, and I close my eyes, leaning into his touch. His hands cup my chin and pull my face toward his. Heart pounding, my eyes open.

"Sienna," he says, his voice thick. I love it when he says my name, as if it's the most beautiful word in the world, one he rolls around on his tongue and wants to taste over and over again.

His lips touch mine, so lightly, so gentle that it's more of a tease than a kiss. His mouth moves into a smile when I don't push him away. When he leans in again, our lips melt together. His lips are smooth and full and he tastes like mint. I don't know what I'm doing, but it doesn't matter because our bodies seem to know exactly what to do. He moves to my jaw, my chin, and my cheek, while an ache spreads in my belly. I don't want it to end. Ever. When he pulls away, I know I have to tell him the truth. All of it.

"Zane," I whisper. "I have to tell you something."

He strokes my face with his fingers and pulls my chin closer. "Shh, it can wait. Right now, this is what matters." He kisses me again, deeper, more passionate. My hands wrap around his neck. My fingers pull through his hair and skim his neckline. His hands move to the small of my back, pressing me firmly to him. When his fingers run along the side of my waist, they cause the fire in my belly to spread deeper.

When we do pull away, my cheeks are flaming from both excitement and embarrassment. I place my hands on either side of my face to cool my steaming cheeks. Zane smiles before growing serious. He leans forward and stares at me. "Sienna, let me help you."

I start to protest, but he places his finger over my lips.

"I won't take no for an answer. Let me do this my way. No guns. No fighting. No deaths. I promise I can have your mom in your arms in less than a week."

I swallow hard. How can he make that kind of promise? He has no idea the kind of men we're dealing with. "These men are dangerous and crooked. They won't care that you have money."

"You say they work for the government?"

I nod. "Radcliffe, the man who took my mom, says he's head of the AIG."

"Then I already have him in my pocket."

My forehead wrinkles in confusion. "I don't understand."

"For years, the AIG branch of government has tried to gain access to our company. And I have some bait of my own I can use to get what I want. And what I want is your mother freed and you left alone."

It might work. It just might work.

Hope fills me like birds taking flight. I smile and wrap my arms around him, burying my face in his neck. "Thank you," I murmur.

"Am I interrupting something?" a cold voice speaks from the doorway.

I jump back, almost falling off the couch, as my guilty eyes connect with those of Steele Ryder.

"Zane?" Steele cocks his head and waits for an explanation.

Zane stands and takes a defensive stance, legs shoulder-width apart, shoulders squared. "Yeah, Steele, you are. Do you mind giving us some privacy?"

The two men stare at each other, and I sit perfectly still. Whatever is going on between them extends deeper than Zane caught with a girl other than his fiancée.

"Think about what you're doing, Zane. You're about to make the biggest mistake of your life," Steele warns before striding away.

Zane lets out a whoosh of air and sinks back onto the couch beside me. "Sorry about that."

"He's very interested in your life, isn't he?"

"Because he's twenty years older than I am, he's been more like a second father than a brother. He only wants what's best for me, but his approach is a little rough."

I think back to the words Steele said. *Biggest mistake of your life.* That's me. I'm the biggest mistake. Knowing that doesn't exactly bring warm fuzzies.

I decide to drive Steele's point home. "So, when is your wedding?" A knot forms in my stomach as I say the words. We may have kissed, but he's engaged. To someone else. A kiss doesn't change that.

Zane frowns. I can tell he doesn't like me bringing up the obvious. "In a few months?"

"You have everything picked out? Invitations, flowers, cake… *house?*" I put emphasis on the last word so he realizes this isn't a game. He's about to start a life with someone else. He'll have perfect GM babies and kiss his GM wife before he leaves for work every day.

Zane nods, his eyes dark. "I think Arian is taking care of

those things. Except the house part," he quickly adds.

I need to turn and pull the dagger from my heart, but instead, I force a smile. "Sounds lovely," I say, not even trying to hide my sarcasm. I stand quickly before I say something else I'll regret. "I should go." Avoiding his eyes, I focus on the coffee table. "Are you okay to keep Emily for a few more days?"

"Of course. And I'll work on gaining access to your mother." He pauses. "Sienna?"

I'm forced to look into his eyes, those warm, brown, genetically modified eyes. I don't stand a chance.

"Stay safe, okay?" He moves toward me and pulls me into his arms. I don't understand what he's doing. He's playing with my heart, with my emotions, and I don't like it one bit. "For me? Please stay safe."

I lean out of his embrace. "Sure I will. For Emily and my mom."

"Hey, don't be like that." His eyes search mine. "Things are complicated for me right now."

"Me too," I reply.

His arms drop, and he moves to the foyer. "You probably want to say goodbye to Emily before you leave? I imagine they're in the kitchen. It's right this way if you want to follow me." He sounds distant, not at all like the guy I was just making out with on his living room couch—half-naked, mind you.

He leads me down a hallway of pictures; pictures of Zane as a baby, a wide grin on his face; pictures of Harlow, his wife, and Steele before Zane was born; pictures of Zane and his father. But never a picture of Zane and his mother. I peer at a picture of the mother he never knew. She's beautiful, her long, dark hair framing her face and her wide blue eyes that crinkle as she smiles. She looks oddly familiar…

I gasp in recognition. The woman from the picture of my father. My father before he changed his name and identity.

My father knew Zane's mother?

"Your mother's name was Penelope?"

Zane nods. "That's why my dad created Chromo 120."

My eyebrows rise. "Why?"

"To stop the genetic spread of imperfect genes. He often says if he had only lived a lifetime ago, he could have saved my mother."

"How did she die?"

"During childbirth, but it was because of a medical condition she'd struggled with for years."

I hesitate, wondering if I should confide in Zane what I learned about my father and his mother. I'm about to, but fear that he might say something to Harlow stops me. "She was beautiful," I say instead.

"Yeah, she was," he says, his voice soft. "I wish she could be at my wedding and be there to hold my first child…" He trails off.

Even though I realize he's sharing something very personal about his mother, his words sting, and I don't know why. Maybe it's because I know those significant moments in his life will belong to Arian.

Zane leads me around a corner and through the back entrance of a brightly lit gourmet kitchen. Emily stands on a wooden stool next to Greta, carefully rolling out the crust on the large, butcher-block island that fills the center of the oversized kitchen. I run my hand over the smooth stone surface of the adjacent countertops. The last time I was in here, I was trying to poison Zane's father.

"Look, Si-Si, look what I made," Emily squeals, pointing to the crust.

"She has been such a good helper." Greta winks at me. "This is actually our second pie crust. The first is already in the oven."

"Si-Si, do you want to try my pie?"

I lift Emily off the stool and into my arms. "I need to go, Em."

"Where are you going? Why can't you stay longer? Don't

you want to try the pie I made?" She hurls questions at me like a firing squad.

Zane clears his throat. "Emily has a point. There's no need for you to rush off when there's one of Greta's pies in the oven." He winks at me. "I happen to know she makes the best pies."

Greta pats the counter and nods to one of the barstools. "Take a seat, dear. The strawberry pie will be out of the oven in five minutes and then it will just need a few minutes to cool down." She glances up at Zane. "Zane, do you think you can help whip up the meringue for the second pie?"

Zane looks down at his bathing suit-clad body. "Let me throw on a shirt first." He dashes out of the room.

"What kind of pie are you making now?" I ask.

"Key lime with a meringue topping. It's my favorite."

"It sounds delish."

"Zane has always been my helper," Greta confides, her eyes glazing over in admiration. "Ever since he was a small boy, he would come into the kitchen and watch me cook. When he was old enough, he started helping me prepare the meals." She wipes her hands on her apron and moves to the fridge, pulling out the eggs. As she sets them on the counter, her eyes meet mine. "Zane is like a son to me. His mother and I were friends back in school. When I heard about her death, I came to Harlow and offered to help. And here I am, twenty-one years later."

"Did you ever have a family of your own?"

She smiles and shakes her head. "No. Harlow has offered many times to find my genetic match, but I'm content with the life I have."

Something she said sends a trigger to my brain. She knew Penelope in school... Perhaps she knew my father as well. "Did you by chance know a man named Mitch Hoover?"

Greta's eyes widen in surprise. "Of course. Why do you ask?"

"He was an old friend of my dad's," I lie.

"I knew him very well. He and Penelope were friends for years. She's the one who helped him get a job as the geneticist in Harlow's company." She purses her lips. "Such a sad accident that man was in. Can you imagine having a seizure while you're driving?" Leaning forward, she says, "You know, this is between you and me, but I've always wondered if somehow Mitch blamed himself for Penelope's death. It just seems ironic that he would drive his car off a cliff only days after Penelope died."

My heart stops beating for a moment. "He... uh... drove his car off a cliff?"

"Yeah, saddest thing. It was said he had a seizure and lost control. But I've always wondered if it was suicide and not a seizure at all." She straightens up. "I guess we'll never know."

My father faked his own death. That must be what the Devil meant when he said he helped my father find a different venue.

My mind reels as Zane enters the room wearing a red Cybertronics T-shirt and his still-damp bathing suit.

Greta puts him to work cracking eggs and whipping egg whites, while I watch from my perch on the bar stool, trying to ingest what she shared with me. My father and Penelope were friends, and he faked his death and changed his identity only days after she died. Why?

My eyes focus on the pie making in front of me. I'm entertained by the way Greta and Zane tease and joke with one another. Even Emily is part of the teasing. And as I watch, I don't feel left out, just the opposite actually. I feel a part of something truly wonderful. A family. A functional one. It reminds me so much of how my family used to be before my father was murdered, my mother got sick, and I got caught up in all this mess. An ache spreads through my chest, but I swallow hard and force the pity from my mind.

"Greta, I think these egg whites are about as stiff as they're going to get," Zane says, eyeing the bowl. "I know you said something about soft peaks, but if I wait any longer, I'll grow my own mountain range."

I hop off the stool to take a look. Greta told Zane the meringue would be ready when soft peaks formed. I peer into the bowl. "Yep, it's done."

Zane rolls his eyes. "You say that like you're a meringue expert."

I place my hands on my hips. "Maybe I am."

Zane grins. "If you're such an expert, why don't you taste it and tell me if it's ready?" He reaches in and scoops up some with his finger. I lean back, not sure how I feel about sucking meringue off his finger. But that's not his intention.

He spreads the meringue down my nose and laughs. My eyes widen in surprise before narrowing in determination. I stick my hand in and scoop up a handful as Zane's smile fades from his face.

"You wouldn't," he says.

I smear the meringue all over his face, laughing hysterically.

Emily squeals with laughter, and Greta chastises in a gentle tone. "All right, you two, there won't be any left for the pie."

Zane reaches out to grab me, but he stops when his eyes connect with something behind the island. I turn and my heart skips a beat.

Arian.

Chapter Twenty-eight

"I'm sorry to interrupt. Henry let me in and said you were in the kitchen," Arian says, her smile hesitant.

Surprisingly, she doesn't seem upset that Zane is hanging out with another girl. She doesn't seem to care that Zane has meringue all over his face. Is this an *act* or is she really this *nice*?

When her eyes rest on me, she gives me a warm smile. "You must be Sienna."

She holds out a carefully manicured hand, and I want to sink into the floor. I lean forward and shake her delicate hand. Hands that have probably never washed a dish in her life. Zane hands me a towel to wipe my face and moves forward to kiss his fiancée on the cheek.

"Did I forget about an appointment?" he murmurs.

Arian laughs, and I get a glimpse of her blindingly white teeth. "No. Steele called to remind me about the super sale at Nelly's Catering-and-Things, and I stopped by to see if you want to go."

Steele. Of course.

Zane's eyes flit to me for a small moment, and it's clear he's uncomfortable. This is my cue to leave.

"I was just leaving, so—" I place the towel on the counter.

"But I just got here," Arian replies, pouting. "And I've been wanting to meet you."

My jaw clenches as I stare at Arian. I wonder what Zane told her about me. Why does she think Emily is staying here? I find it hard to believe she doesn't have one jealous bone in her body. Would she care to know that only moments earlier, I was kissing her soon-to-be hubby?

"And Si-Si, you haven't had any pie yet," Emily whines.

"I can remedy that," Greta croons. Like a silent cooking ninja, she's already dished the strawberry pie onto melamine plates and now hands one to each of us, saving the last piece for Emily. Zane settles onto a bar stool next to Arian and I lean against the counter, ready to make a quick escape.

"So, Sienna," Arian says, "Zane tells me you're an undercover reporter working on an assignment outside Rubex."

This is news to me. I raise my eyebrows. "He did?"

"How's it going over there? I hear there's a lot of anger from that radical group the Fringe."

Zane averts his eyes, and now I know. He's just as good at lying as I am.

I smile and try to compose myself. "It's crazy. Members of the Fringe are restless, as always." I decide to add a little pro-Fringe propaganda into this conversation. "It's interesting, though. I'm finding that the Fringe is a very misunderstood group of people."

Zane chokes on his pie, but I continue unscathed. "It's true. There have been several attacks in the past few months blamed on them, and yet, they're innocent. I've had the opportunity to get really close to their leader." I wink at Arian. "I mean, really close. And he swears they're being set up."

I feel Zane's eyes on me, but I focus on taking a big bite of my pie.

"I had no idea," Arian says, her beautiful face twisting in surprise.

"Neither did I, not until I met them and talked with their leader." I shrug. "They're actually good people who are just trying to better society."

"Well, your article will be an eye opener for all of us then," Arian says, lifting her fork to take a bite of pie.

"It's important to get the *truth* out there," I say blatantly, looking directly at Zane.

Arian doesn't notice. She's too busy stabbing a strawberry and delicately placing it into her heart-shaped mouth.

I continue eating my pie and even finish off Emily's when she hands it to me after saying she's full.

When it seems socially acceptable to make my escape, I politely excuse myself and say goodbye to Emily. Even though I don't want to leave her, based on Zane's promise, I know it will only be a few short days until we're together again.

Zane offers to walk me to the door, and even though my eyes shift uncomfortably to Arian, she seems fine with it. I say good-bye to Arian and thank Greta for the pie, before bending down to give Emily one last hug.

"I'll see you soon, okay?"

She nods.

"Now go get some clothes on. You shouldn't stay in that wet bathing suit all day."

Emily takes off running, her tiny feet pattering over the marble floors.

Zane leads me to the front door and walks me out on the stoop, closing the door behind us.

"Thanks again for watching Emily—"

Zane stops me. "Did you mean what you said in the kitchen?"

I draw a blank. "About what?"

"About getting really close to the leader of the Fringe?" His eyes narrow.

"Maybe. But why should you care?"

"I shouldn't." He shakes his head. "And yet, I do."

I cock my head to the side. "Out of curiosity, what did you tell Arian? Why is Emily staying with you?"

An embarrassed grin creeps over his face. "I told her you two are my cousins, and you needed me to watch your sister while you were on assignment."

My mouth drops open. "Your *cousin*?" Well, that explains the complete and utter ease with seeing Zane and me together in his kitchen.

"I didn't know how to explain who you are." He frowns. "What was I supposed to say? 'Hey Arian, there's this girl I can't stop thinking about and she needs a place for her sister to stay while she goes to fight the bad guys and save her mother.'" He shakes his head. "Probably wouldn't have gone over well."

"You think?" I say, rivers of sarcasm running through my voice. "And what did you tell your dad? The same thing?" I smirk.

Zane's mouth lifts a little. "Obviously not. I told him the truth—kind of. I said that Emily is the sister of a friend who had to go out of town for a few days."

A friend. Of course.

I close my eyes, suddenly exhausted. The stress and lack of sleep is wearing me down. When I open them, Zane is staring at me, his eyebrows dipping low in concern.

"You okay?" he asks.

I sigh as if the weight of the world rests on my shoulders. "I will be. All I need is a good night's sleep and my mother home again." I swallow hard. "But in the meantime, you need to find out what's going on in your dad's lab. There's some bad stuff, really bad stuff."

"Okay. I will," he says. He hesitates before glancing around and muttering, "What the hell." His arms wrap around my waist and pull me to him. I bury my face in his chest and inhale the clean, fresh scent of laundry detergent. "Five days," he murmurs. "I'll have your mother for you in five days. I promise." He kisses the top of my head and releases me.

When he shuts the door behind him, I know his promise is one I can trust.

When I get back to the Compound, I go straight to my room. The stark white walls are blinding, but I find comfort in knowing it is a place of refuge. An escape.

Lying back on my bed, I think about my visit with Zane. I don't understand why I'm drawn to him or why I feel safe when I'm in his arms. It's probably because he's a GM and everything about him screams perfection, even his stupid voice that has me practically begging to hear my name uttered again.

And there was the kiss. The one that lit my body on fire. My fingers absentmindedly trace my lips.

A sharp knock on the door startles me.

"Come in," I say, rising from the bed. I suspect it's Trina stopping by to get a full report on my visit with Emily and Zane.

However, it's Trey who enters the room and shuts the door behind him. His eyes are bloodshot, and he looks like hell.

"Hey, where were you?" he asks casually. "I came by earlier to see if you wanted to do some target shooting."

"I went to visit a friend."

He chuckles. "Does this friend have a name?"

"Yes." But I *really* don't want to tell you.

Trey shrugs and moves toward my bed. "May I?" he asks before taking a seat.

"Fine by me." I sit across from him in the plastic, sloped-back chair—the only accessory in my room.

"Sienna, about last night—"

"It's okay."

"Huh?" He stares at me, confused.

"I know you didn't mean to kill him."

Trey shakes his head. "But that's the problem, I *wanted* to kill him. When I saw what he planned to do to you—" His fists clench. "I lost it." He looks at me, his eyes full of sorrow. "I lost it. And I'm sorry." He throws his hands up. "All I do is apologize lately. First Garrett—" He chokes. "I didn't want to leave him." His eyes plead with mine. "Do you know how hard it was for me? To turn my back and watch him die?"

The guilt is eating away at him, and it breaks my heart. I move to the bed beside him, placing a hand on his shoulder. "I know it was hard. And I'm sorry we couldn't save him. But it's okay. We're going to be okay."

Trey nods and leans toward me, his eyes fixated on my mouth. His hand grazes my chin. "I know we are. I just needed to hear you say it."

He exhales, and I smell the liquor on his breath. I know I should ask him to leave, but a part of me is curious.

When his mouth covers mine, it surprises me. His kiss is so completely different from Zane's, and yet, just as thrilling. He is urgent. Excited. A little out of control. I feel his hands slide around my body, pulling me close, working their way under my shirt.

A warning flashes in my brain, but I ignore it. It feels too good. His hands caress my bare back and move to my stomach, sending a million butterflies throughout my body. When his fingers trace the underwire of my bra, I can't breathe. I know I have to stop him.

I lightly push his hands away, but he continues to kiss me, driving me backward on the bed. His hands wrap around my rear and bring me even closer to him. My mind screams at me to stop. With shaking hands, I sit up and push him off.

"That's enough," I say, my voice stern. My heart is beating fast, and the ache in my stomach has turned to a pulsating throb.

Trey sits back with a dazed look on his face. I wonder if he'll remember this episode in the morning. Will he regret it?

"I'm sorry," he mutters. "I don't know what came over me." He stands to leave. "Just forget this happened. Please." He strides out the door, slamming it shut behind him.

My fingers instinctively touch my lips, and then move to the fire in my cheeks.

I can't believe he kissed me. It was unexpected, and yet, it felt... right. Unlike Zane's kiss that can never amount to anything, this—this is real. Or it could be.

To think that before today, I'd never kissed one boy, let alone two. Two boys in one day. What are the chances?

Over the next few days, I get the feeling Trey is avoiding me. When I take a seat at the lunch table and join him, Trina, Jeff, Curly, Cade, and a few other kids that I'm slowly learning their names, he gets up and leaves the room. When I ask for help at target practice, he instructs Curly to help me. When I have dish or laundry duty and he passes by, he nods politely but keeps going.

Was it really that awful? Was kissing me such a turn off that he doesn't want to have anything to do with me anymore? I understand he's older and has more experience, but come on.

After the fourth day of avoidance, I decide to corner him. During our hour of Reflections—the time we are required to sit and reflect on how to better ourselves and the world around us—I go to his room. If he tells me I'm disgusting, or if he says he hates my guts, I'll leave him alone. But I need to hear him say it.

I knock hard, determined not to appear weak and groveling.

The door swings open, and Trey takes a step back when he sees me.

"What are you doing here?" he asks. "You're supposed to be doing Reflections."

I let myself into his room and close the door behind me. I nod to his bed. "May I?" This conversation is starting to sound eerily familiar.

He shrugs. "Be my guest." He's trying to play it cool, but there's no mistaking the second of panic that flashes through his eyes when I sit down on his bed. He takes a seat across from me in the wooden desk chair.

I stare down at my hands. I had this all planned out in my mind, but now the words fail me. I glance up at him, at his arms crossed over his chest, at his expressionless, laid-back stance. "Did I do something wrong?" I finally blurt out.

His eyes soften, but then he scowls. "No. Of course not. I did."

"Why do you say that?" I press. "I *liked* it."

His face thaws, and he chuckles. "Just because you liked it doesn't make it right."

"So now you're avoiding me because you're afraid you've given me the wrong impression?"

"Yes. I mean no—"

"Well, which is it?"

Trey sighs, all traces of hardness gone. He leans forward, his arms resting on his knees. "Listen, Sienna. When I came to your room the other night, I was drunk. I was miserable. I was feeling guilty, and I guess I was looking for comfort. I wanted to see you, but not like that." He pauses, his stare intense. "I wanted to kiss you. Hell, I *want* to kiss you. But it was wrong for me to do it when I could barely remember it the next morning."

My heart sinks. He doesn't remember it. That totally electrifying kiss that rocked my insides, and he has no recollection.

"I mean, I remember parts of it. I know it was good. But when I kiss you, I want to be fully aware, every sense heightened. I want to remember *everything*."

Before I realize what I'm doing, I stand and move toward him. Grabbing a fistful of his hair, I tilt his head back as surprise registers in his eyes.

"I remember it," I whisper. "Everything about it. And I can promise you, it was a moment I'll never forget." I bend over and kiss him lightly on the lips, which sparks a chain reaction, just as I'm hoping.

His strong arms wrap around my waist, pulling me onto his lap. He kisses my forehead, and my body tingles from the nearness of him. Tilting his head back, he stares at me with more longing than I knew a guy could possess. His mouth covers mine, and I'm lost. In his embrace. In his lips. In his hands that drag me closer until our bodies are pressed together.

Through the thin cotton of my shirt, I can feel the warmth of his hands pressed against my back. His kisses light me up, but his hands spread the fire.

When his mouth moves down my jaw, a small sigh escapes.

"Sienna," he whispers, pressing his lips to my ear.

Biting my lip to keep from kissing him again, I pull back long enough to look at him. His deep blue eyes pull me in, and I feel like I'm drowning.

"I thought it was awesome kissing you while I was drunk," he says, "but it's fifty times better when I'm sober."

"You stopped kissing me to tell me that?"

"Yeah."

"You could have told me later," I point out. Placing my hands on his cheeks, the stubble rough and scratchy against my skin, I lean in. "Shut up and kiss me."

Trey raises an eyebrow and grins. "Yes, ma'am."

Early the next morning, I've just finished dressing when there's a knock on the door. I open it to find Trey leaning against the doorframe. He's freshly showered and shaved, which makes me want to run my hands over his smooth skin.

He steps inside and pulls me to him, grinning at my surprised look. "Good morning," he murmurs against my lips.

My hands touch his face and glide over his hard jaw. He kisses my hand before finding my lips again.

"Listen," he says, pulling away. "I want you to know I haven't given up on your mom. I've been in contact with some people, but it might take some time to locate her. Okay?"

I nod. "Thank you." I think of Zane's promise—hopefully, I won't have to wait much longer. I feel somewhat bad for going behind Trey's back, but the more people looking for her, the better.

Trey clears his throat. "I was thinking of doing some target shooting this morning. Care to join me?"

"Now that you're talking to me again," I say, "I'd love to."

He winks. "I think we've been doing more than talking."

"Yeah, and now, hopefully, you feel bad for shutting me out the past few days."

His hands slide around my back, pulling me to him. "Really bad. How can I make it up to you?"

"If you kiss me again, I think I'll forgive you."

My body tingles as Trey complies, moving to my neck first and ending with my mouth. Wrapping my arms around his neck, I press my body against his. I think he's the first to pull away, but I'm not sure. I'm too lightheaded to be fully aware of anything.

Trey sighs and frowns. "I can see you're gonna be a distraction."

I step back and cross my arms over my chest, my eyes narrowing. "What does that mean?"

Trey laughs. "No, it's a good thing—well, and a bad thing."

I raise my eyebrows, not amused.

He reaches for me, but I step out of his grasp. "You have to remember," he says, "I'm the leader. I can't appear weak or no one will respect me."

"So I make you weak?" I glare at him. The more he talks, the worse this sounds.

His expression softens. "No, you make me more than..."

"More than what?"

"More than I was." He clears his throat, and I know he's

embarrassed. "We just have to be careful. No one should know."

I can't help the grin that creeps to my face. "I'm a pretty good liar."

Trey smiles and reaches for me. "So you say." His lips are warm as he kisses me on the forehead. "And now you can prove it."

Chapter Twenty-nine

Zane Ryder is a miracle worker. True to his word, in less than five days, he's able to override Radcliffe and get permission for the release of my mother.

We meet by the railroad tracks a quarter mile from the hidden entrance to the Compound. When he picks me up in his Aria, I slide into the passenger seat, my heart already pounding from nervous energy. He smiles and appears completely at ease, but I'm about to have a coronary. If this doesn't work, I don't know what I'll do.

"How's Emily?" I ask, trying to get my mind off what's ahead.

Zane smiles at me before throwing the car in gear. "She's doing well." He chuckles. "She made me have a tea party with her yesterday."

"Really? Where did you get the tea set? There aren't many little girls lurking around your house."

"Arian brought it over—" He casts a nervous glance in my direction. "Emily invited her too."

The muscles in my neck tighten. So, Arian is having a tea party with my sister while I train to fight the bad guys. Sounds fair. Not.

"I'm glad Emily is having fun," I force out.

I don't know why I should care. I've spent the past two days kissing another guy. Why shouldn't Zane have a tea party with his fiancée?

The injustice of it all stings, reminding me how different we are. I have to fight for my freedom, while he gets to lounge by the pool, drink a cold one, and have pretend tea parties. Our worlds don't even exist in the same universe.

"Hey," he says. "Wanted you to know, I looked into the whole juvenile inmate thing. Couldn't find anything—no records or such—but something weird is definitely going on. There's a locked section of the facility on the basement floor, and I don't even have access to it." He glances at me. "I haven't worked up the nerve to ask my father about it yet, though."

"Thanks for believing me. I know I probably came off a little harsh."

"Not at all. I'm glad you said something. If my dad is doing some crazy experiments on juvenile inmates, I have a right to know. Especially since I will inherit the company."

When I look out the window again several minutes later, I notice we are nearing the Satellite Government Facility—or SGF—where the exchange will happen. It's on the border of the open desert; this is the building Trey rescued me from the night Radcliffe intercepted the exchange. I never got a good look at it that night, but in the day, the large, gray structure is a formidable contrast to the desert landscape.

"I still don't know how you managed to pull this off," I mutter as he parks the car in the half-full lot.

"Well, AIG now has an *incentive* for releasing your mom."

"What's the incentive?"

"A little serum called Re0Gene."

"Well…" I wait. "What does it do?"

"It regenerates cell growth. Promotes quick healing."

"Like my miracle burn cream?"

Zane smiles, shaking his head. "This works a *little* faster than that." He reaches for a briefcase in the seat behind him. Once it rests on his lap, he types in a code and opens the clasp. A small vial of purple-colored liquid rests against a velvet backdrop. "I agreed to give them this in exchange for your mother, along with the formula to recreate it," he says, removing the vial.

My eyes widen in shock. That must be an extremely important serum for the government to want to get their hands on it. And Zane will lose the rights to the formula. All to help me?

Zane continues talking. "This serum is my baby. I started working on it when I was eighteen and sliced my head open playing rugby with some friends. I didn't want to have the scar forever, so I decided to create something that would stimulate a quick regrowth of cells. A miracle healing cream. It took me a couple of years to feel like I had a handle on the formula, and I recently perfected it. I never got a chance to bring it to market, and now, it's probably a good thing I didn't." His eyes flash with excitement. "Here, let me show you how it works. May I?" He indicates the small bandage on my arm, the one from the tracker incision.

I nod and watch as he carefully removes it. His smile fades when he sees the pulled stitches and red, fleshy wound still struggling to heal.

"What happened?"

I sigh. "Radcliffe, the man who kidnapped my mother, put a tracker inside of me. When I joined the Fringe, one of the members helped me remove it."

"Did it hurt?"

I give him an exasperated look. "What do you think?"

Concern fills his eyes along with something else. Doubt? Maybe he now realizes there is more to the story than I've told him before.

"Watch this," he says.

He unscrews the cap on the vial and dabs a small amount onto the incision. A tingling sensation moves under the puckered skin, and then snakes its way up my arm. Almost immediately, the severed skin fuses until there's no more line, pushing out the unneeded stitches until they fall onto my lap.

The redness on my arm fades away, turning my skin a pale pink, and then back to a shade of white.

I stare in amazement at the most miraculous thing I've ever seen. My fingers brush the once tender area, but all I feel is smooth skin where the incision was.

"I can't believe it," I breathe.

"Incredible, isn't it?"

I gaze at him in awe. "You're a genius. No wonder the government bloodhounds were willing to cut a deal."

Zane laughs and screws the top back on. "Not as much of a genius as my father." He flashes a broad smile. "But pretty darn close."

"Are you sure you want to do this? You'll lose all you've worked for."

Zane shrugs. "The accomplishment was the best reward. Knowing I succeeded. Besides, I can still make it for myself. I can even sell it if I want."

"But *they'll* have it."

"And hopefully, they'll put it to good use. To help others. To heal wounded soldiers. Then it would make the hours I spent in the lab worth it."

Zane takes a deep breath and puts the vial back into his briefcase. Placing his hand on the door activator, he turns to me. "You ready?"

I nod, suddenly too afraid to speak. Afraid that if I try, the tears I've been holding in will burst out like a broken dam. I'm overwhelmed by his selflessness. Here Zane sits with something amazing. Something truly wonderful. And he's willing to give it away. For me. I'm so touched that my heart hurts.

If he only knew I didn't deserve his kindness.

We walk down the curved sidewalk toward the entrance to the building, and Zane reaches for my hand. A sense of comfort washes over me. I know everything will be okay. Zane has made it okay. No more fighting. No more sleepless nights. No more threats.

Catalyst

I glance up at the flags flapping in the breeze, proudly displaying Pacifica's symbol of advancement. The thick blue vertical stripe sits beside the white stripe, which rests beside the black one. The black triskelion stands out against the large, center white strip.

Zane pulls the glass door open and follows me through. Nervously, I glance around. I don't know what to expect. All I've ever seen is the underground lair of the government, with its rock walls and cavernous feeling. Even when I was held captive in this building, I was several floors below in the dank basement. This building is different, built on the inside in a Romanesque style with rounded archways, tall, curved ceilings, and large, white columns. Our footsteps echo across the smooth, white marble floor.

All I see are Suits. Suits everywhere. They cross the foyer with stacks of papers in hand; the women Suits talk in hushed tones and raise coffee cups to lips stained the color of blood. None of them turn to us with accusing eyes as we cross the foyer to the receptionist counter that sits in the middle of the high-ceiling room. I half expect them to whip out guns and arrest me on sight. My heart hammers in fear, and I shrink back, but Zane finds my hand and pulls me along beside him. The receptionist, a blonde with an oversized chest, eyes us as we approach.

"Welcome. Zane Ryder, I presume?"

"Yes." Zane smiles. "We're here to see Mr. Chadwick."

"Of course. Follow me." The woman comes from behind the desk, moving toward the corridor on our left. I focus on the back of her white blouse as her heels click down the hall. She does this funny thing when she walks in her spiked heels, like she's smashing a bug each step she takes.

She pauses outside a room marked twelve and tries the handle. The door swings open to reveal a single glass table with four metal chairs, two on each side.

"This is it. He'll be in shortly."

When she closes the door, I have a feeling we're locked

in, and panic hits. I lunge for the door, but it turns easily in my hand.

Zane gives me a concerned look. "Everything okay?"

"Sorry," I mumble. "I thought they were locking us in."

Zane's smile is sympathetic. "Don't worry. I have everything under control." He pulls out a chair for me. "Here, take a seat. They might make us wait a while."

I sit and strum my fingers on the tabletop. After a few minutes, I scoot my chair back, making a loud scraping sound against the marble floor. I pace back and forth, biting the inside of my cheek while my heart pounds. In moments, I could see my mother. What will she think of my short hair?

The door opens behind us, and a short, stocky man with a bald head and glasses enters the room.

"Have a seat, please." He nods to my chair.

Once again, Zane pulls my chair out for me, but I hardly notice. I'm too busy craning my neck, staring at the door, wondering where my mother is.

Zane guides me onto the chair, forcing me to sit, but my eyes are still trained on the door behind us. Where *is* she?

Zane voices my thoughts. "We had an agreement. Where is Vivian Preston?"

The man smiles, his beady eyes becoming even smaller. "She will join us in a moment." He leans forward and clasps his hands together on the table. "You have something for me?"

Zane nods and pulls up his black briefcase, resting it on the table. After he types in a digital password, the lock clicks open, and there is the vial resting in the specially designed black velvet holder. Zane removes the serum and holds it up for the man to see. The bald man's eyes practically bug out of his head, and he smiles greedily. He reaches for it, but Zane jerks it back.

"No," Zane says, his voice cold. "Not until we have Vivian Preston."

The man speaks low into his watch, his eyes never leaving

the vial.

I turn my head, finding comfort in Zane's eyes and the confident smile he gives me. He reaches for my hand under the table and squeezes it, and that's when I know. Everything will be okay.

The door behind us swings open, and I whip around, almost giddy with excitement. But the person in the doorway strikes fear in my heart instead of bringing a warm smile to my face.

Radcliffe.

The blood pulses in my ears, and all I can think is that this is a setup. He's here to cart me away—put me in that underground prison where the smell of urine and the rats are my only companions.

My hands shake, and I turn to Zane with fear in my eyes. He wraps his arm protectively around my shoulders, tensing up as Radcliffe takes a seat across from us. I get a small sense of satisfaction when I see that the scratches I inflicted to Radcliffe's face have turned into deep scars.

"Colonel George Radcliffe," he says, holding out his hand. His eyes dip over me for a second, and I see the flash of hatred he covers before turning his attention to Zane.

"Zane Ryder," Zane says, his eyes narrowing. He doesn't shake Radcliffe's hand, and I assume it's because he recognizes the name. The name of the man who tortured me, threatened me, and kidnapped my mother.

Radcliffe shrugs and eyes the vial. "I see you brought us a present. May I?" he asks, his hand still outstretched. When Zane hesitates, Radcliffe clarifies, "How do I know the liquid in the vial isn't anything more than watered-down grape juice?"

Zane nods and hands it over, but he scoots to the edge of his chair as if he thinks by staying within arm's reach, he can avoid being taken advantage of.

Radcliffe opens the vial and pours a small amount on his finger, which he proceeds to spread on his scarred face. My stomach twists as I watch the skin heal. I wanted him to live with those forever, but if it means I get my mom back, then I guess it's worth it.

"Amazing," Radcliffe says, staring into the mirror he pulled from his breast pocket. As he slides the vial back to Zane, he grins. "That's quite some serum you have there." He lays a heavy hand on the table. "Unfortunately, Zane, there appears to be a misunderstanding. Vivian Preston isn't being *held* by us, she *works* for us."

I jump up, knocking my chair over, and slam my hands on the table. "*That's a lie*," I scream in his face. Spots dot my vision, and I use the table to steady myself. I knew they would twist this somehow. It all seemed too easy.

Radcliffe reaches for something inside his military uniform, a black suit with blue stripes running down the side with white embroidery. Our society's symbol, the three running legs, is embossed on each shoulder.

Radcliffe hesitates and appears to change his mind about whatever he was about to pull out. Probably a gun.

I glare at him.

"Have a seat, Preston," he says coldly.

Zane uprights my chair and eases me back onto it, but I'm so angry that I could spit fire. I feel the rage boiling inside of me, surging from the depths of my soul.

"I'll prove it to you," Radcliffe says. He speaks into his own black watch. "Abigail, can you send in Vivian Preston, please?"

Zane's hand rests on my back, probably as an assurance that I won't jump out of my seat and strangle Radcliffe. But as I turn to the door, I brace myself for how she might look. Dirty, unkempt, maybe even beaten and bruised.

I'm not prepared for what walks through that door.

Heels click, and a woman wearing a tight red suit and pearls, her red hair twisted into a classy up-do, enters the room. She carries a clipboard, and her face breaks into a smile when she sees me.

It's my mother.

Chapter Thirty

L eaping from my chair, I fling myself into her arms as her clipboard clatters to the floor. I'm so happy to see her that I don't even want to think about what gimmick they are trying to pull.

All the emotions I've been feeling for the past week surface, and hot, wet tears sting my eyes and wet my cheeks. I breathe in the smell of her, the familiar scent of baby powder and lavender. I cling to her, too afraid to loosen my grip. Afraid I might be dreaming and at any moment, I'll wake and find myself in my eight-by-eight sterile cell of a room. Alone.

My tears leave a dark spot on her red blazer, but she doesn't seem to mind. And then I remember that it isn't just the two of us. We aren't alone, but in fact, are being watched—no, scrutinized—by three other men. One good, and two bad.

I pull back, dry my eyes with my palms, and sniffle back the snot that threatens to trickle out. Her hands immediately fly to my hair—or lack of it.

"You cut your hair?" Her eyes look sad, but then she smiles. "It looks good on you."

I step back and eye her outfit. "You're wearing a *suit?*"

She hesitates, and then breaks out into another broad grin. "Yes. I wear it for work." She spins around, a little unsteady at first, but then she regains her balance. "Do you like it?"

My eyes narrow. Something's wrong. I grab her arms and force her to look me in the eyes. "Mom, don't you remember?" I turn and point at Radcliffe with an accusatory finger. "They *kidnapped* you, threw you in a cell with rats, and refused to let me take you home." I shake her. "Why are you acting like nothing happened?"

Her eyes widen and she looks stunned for a moment, but then she covers her confusion with a smile. "No, sweetheart. That was all just a bad dream. I've been here the whole time. Working."

My hands drop to my sides. I don't understand what's happening. Why is she lying for them? She *knows* what happened.

"Miss Preston..." Radcliffe's voice is cold. "It appears you are disoriented. Confused."

"I'm not confused! I know what happened," I shout. I turn to Zane in desperation. Surely, he believes me.

But Zane's face is filled with doubt.

"This isn't surprising given your condition," Radcliffe continues, completely unfazed by my anger. "You've been having these episodes lately, have you not?"

My eyes shoot fireballs of hatred. "What are you talking about? What *episodes?*"

"Have you even told your boyfriend the truth about who you are?" Radcliffe asks in a sickly sweet tone.

Oh no. I know where this is headed. My stomach tightens and my knees go weak. I place my hand on the back of my chair to keep upright.

"He's not my boyfriend," I snap. I feel Zane's eyes on me, but I avoid his gaze. I have to get Radcliffe to stop talking. This isn't how I want Zane to find out.

"Boyfriend?" Mom says, leaning back to get a better glimpse of Zane. "My, he's handsome."

"He's not," I seethe, "my boyfriend."

"Can you please stop saying that?" Zane mutters. "I get the point."

"Hey," the bald man breaks in, "is there any chance I can hold on to that serum while you all discuss this?" He flashes a hopeful smile.

I ignore him and turn my attention to Zane. He needs to hear it from me before Radcliffe twists the truth. I sink down on the chair opposite him. "Zane, I haven't been completely honest with you."

His jaw clenches, and his eyes darken.

"Preston," Radcliffe says, "why don't you tell him about sneaking into his company and stealing the computer chip." He shakes his head. "You know, it's never good to start a relationship with lies."

"Shut up!"

"Or, you could always tell him how you tried to kill his father."

My mother gasps behind me. "Sienna, is this true?"

I turn from her shocked face to Zane's hard, cold one. My head swivels back and forth between them, trying to decide who I should comfort first.

"You used me," Zane says under his breath.

"No! It's *his* fault," I say, pointing at Radcliffe. "I needed the money, so yes, I did break in and steal the chip. But he *forced* me to try to kill your father. He threatened to expose what I'd done in the Match 360 facility." I grab Zane's hands and try to get him to look at me, but he slides out of my grasp. "Zane, please, this man is evil. He's been playing me from day one."

I want him to get angry. I want him to punch something or yell at me. Call me a liar. Something. But he's quiet. Still. And that's the worst reaction of all.

Zane shakes his head and rises to his feet. "I'm sorry, Sienna," he says, "but it looks like I'm the one who's been played." He slams the briefcase shut and strides out the door.

Chapter Thirty-one

"You," I say as my eyes light on Radcliffe. Anger, like a hot fire, creeps up my spine and inches along the back of my head. I think I could kill him with my bare hands. "You did this to me."

Radcliffe smiles and clasps his hands together, resting them on the table. "No. You did this to yourself."

"Would someone mind telling me what's going on here?" Mom asks.

I glare at Radcliffe and search his face for the best place to land a punch. Where did Trey tell me to aim to render a man unconscious?

"Oh, and because of your little escapade inside my facility, I was able to pull facial recognition for all three of your *friends*." I hate the way he says *friends,* as if it's a word I should be ashamed of. "Didn't realize I had the leader of the Fringe at my fingertips."

"You leave him alone," I warn.

"Ah, seems like you have a crush on not one, but two boys." He leans forward and gives me a dirty smile. "You aren't so little anymore, are you, Sienna?"

His look makes my skin crawl.

I stand quickly and take a hold of my mother's arm. "We're leaving. Come on, Mom," I say as I drag her to the door.

She resists, and I want to smack her. "Sienna, I'm not leaving. I have work to do."

"Drop the act, *Mother*," I snap. "There's no one here to see it." I grab her arm again. "We're leaving."

Laughing, she breaks free and dances to the other side of the room. "I'm not leaving, Sienna. I don't want to."

I turn hate-filled eyes to Radcliffe. "What did you do to her?"

Radcliffe shrugs. "Nothing. Guess she likes being here more than being with you." His lips curl into a sneer. "You *are* kind of a disappointment, Sienna."

His words hit me where they're meant to. My core.

It's true. I *am* a disappointment. I've sold my soul to the real devil that drags you down to hell. I've lied, cheated, stolen, and almost killed. I'm unlovable. No wonder she doesn't want to be with me.

"She's sick. She needs rest," I say.

"She's been receiving treatments for her lupus. I'd say she looks well, wouldn't you?"

I shake my head. "But lupus is untreatable—"

"Maybe for you, but not for us." Radcliffe's grin is sly, reminding me of a fox.

I turn my attention to my mother. "Mom," I choke out, "what about Emily? Or have you forgotten all about your five-year-old daughter?"

The smile on her face freezes. "Emily?" she whispers, like she's unsure of the name.

"Yes, Emily, your daughter," I snap.

She shakes her head. "I don't have a—" She stops as recognition dawns in her eyes. "How is my little Emily?"

"Missing her mother."

Mom's eyes are pained. "I'm happy here," she says in a soft voice. "The happiest I've been in a long time." She walks over to me and pats my cheeks, so uncharacteristic of her. "I'll be home soon enough. Besides, you do a much better job of looking after her than I ever did."

"That's not true," I start to protest.

"Yes, it is, and you know it." She walks over to the door and opens it. "I think you should leave now."

I feel as though someone has taken a knife and is carving out a chunk of my heart, but all I can do is stare at her, trying to decipher her expression. If this is her choice, why do I see fear in her eyes behind that self-confident smile?

I wrap her in my arms, hoping that somewhere in there is the mother I know and love. The one who used to fix pancakes on Saturday mornings and dance around our home listening to "oldies" music while she dusted the furniture. I squeeze her tight, like I might be able to crush out the bad and replace it with the good.

When I pull away, her eyes are moist. "Good-bye, Sienna," she says before walking out the door.

I expect Radcliffe to handcuff me and take me back to his dark prison, but all he does is nod at the door.

"You may go," he says.

Waves of shock wash over me, and I stand there, my arms ready to be tied up, cuffed, or bound. I watch Radcliffe raise his arm and speak into his watch, but he doesn't come near me. Instead, he scoots back his chair and sidles out of the room, followed by a puffing Mr. Chadwick. Clearly, he's not too happy that he didn't get his serum. I sit and wait for a few minutes, staring at the blank wall. Surely, they are coming for me.

After what seems like an eternity, I realize they are indeed *not* coming for me. There is no cavalry. There is no Sienna takedown. There's no one but me.

Alone.

Chapter Thirty-two

The sunlight blinds me and sends white, glaring dots across my vision as I push open the glass door of the Satellite Government Facility. It's so bright that it hurts to open my eyes. I blink rapidly until my eyes adjust to the sun, and then I turn to scan the parking lot. I know he's long gone. I don't even pretend to believe he'll stick around.

Sure enough, the space where the Aria was parked is now empty.

A small piece of me crumbles. If I hadn't wasted the past year lying and stealing to make money, this would have never happened. If I hadn't allowed myself to *care* for him, to develop *feelings* for him, then I wouldn't be in this situation.

There's only one person now who cares enough to help me. Pulling out my Lynk, I call Trey. He's surprised I left the Compound without telling him, and I can only imagine the lecture I'll get later. Thankfully, he agrees to come get me. But not at the government facility. We decide to meet at the gas station a mile down the road.

I set to walking the narrow highway that looks like it leads to the middle of nowhere. Like a strip of gray in a sea of endless brown, the road stretches as far as I can see. It's another hot desert day, and these Pavilion-find jeans and dark purple, scoop-neck shirt absorb the heat and cause my body to burn. As the sweat rolls down my back and trickles into my eyes, I think, *Why shouldn't I be as miserable on the outside as I am on the inside?*

The road blurs a little, either from the heat rising up from the blacktop or from the tears that sting my eyes.

Then I think of Emily, still with Zane. I know he would never hurt her, but it's time for me to take her back. Maybe I can bring her to the Compound, introduce her to Trey, Curly, and Trina. Yes, first thing tomorrow morning, I'll pick her up.

I pull my Lynk from my pocket and send Zane a message, apologizing for what happened and informing him that I plan to get my sister in the morning. But of course, there's no response.

The gas station is nearly deserted, and I take a seat on the curb to wait for Trey. All of this seems too normal. I half-expect men in tinted black SUVs to pull up and nab me, or a sniper who sits a mile out to take me down. I know it sounds crazy, but I don't think I do *normal* very well. I've spent the past couple of weeks watching over my shoulder, prepared to fight, always on edge. It feels *weird* not to be that way.

I hear Trey's pickup before I see it. The only vehicle on the road, I know it has to be him. He pulls up in front of the curb, and I climb in. All I want to do is forget about the heartache I feel at my mother's rejection. Forget about how much I hurt Zane with my lies. Forget about the triumphant smile on Radcliffe's face when he realized he'd won. I played his game, and he beat me.

In order to forget, I do the only thing I can think of. I slide over to Trey and wrap my arms around his neck, burying my face in his warm skin. He must have just showered because he smells of bath soap. I pull back, and his eyes register surprise and then appreciation as my fingers brush over his strong jaw and smooth lips. My mouth finds his, and, for a moment, I *do* forget. I'm just a girl kissing a boy, and there are no GMs, no Colonel Radcliffe. No loss of innocence, no misplaced mother, and no dead father.

His fingers slide over the curve of my waist and draw me closer.

I'm breathless when we finally pull apart.

Catalyst

"I'll never get used to you doing that," he says, shaking his head with a smile.

"Good," I answer back. I know it's strange, but I do feel lighter. Like his kisses suck out all the dark, all the negative, and leave only the good parts of me.

He cocks his head to the side. "Do you want to go somewhere? Maybe get away for a few hours?"

"Can you do that?" I ask. I know he's busy training and today is Shipment Day. Even though he didn't go on the supply run, he'll need to be there to organize the goods when they get back.

He pulls my chin closer and kisses my nose. "Yes, I can. Even I need a break sometimes. Besides, Nash is there. He can take care of things until I get back."

Just hearing Nash's name makes my skin run cold, despite the heat fogging the windows. So much for escaping all the bad parts of my life. I'm about to kiss Trey again to force away the feeling of Nash's hands around my neck, but he starts the truck and pulls away from the curb.

We ride in silence, further away from the Compound. When I glance behind me, the city is but a speck in the distance. Trey clears his throat before breaking the silence.

"Do you want to tell me why you were at the SGF?" His eyes flit to mine for a moment before returning to the road.

I sigh, already knowing he won't like that I went to another guy for help.

"Sienna?"

I clear my throat. "I want to tell you everything. I do," I say. "But can you wait a little longer?"

He glances at me, but he doesn't press for more information.

It takes an hour to drive to the place Trey wants to take me. This area of the desert is more lush and green, as if long ago people cared enough to plant trees and bushes conducive to the heat.

Trey parks the truck under a low-hanging palm tree and

strides around the car to let me out. I'm already out before he reaches the passenger side. He grabs my hand, intertwining our fingers, and leads me through a canopy of trees. A shiver of delight travels up my spine as his thumb caresses the back of my hand.

We are alone out here. My heart pounds at the implication. We've stolen a few private moments in the last couple of days since our first kiss, but we've never been *completely* alone. There's always been someone knocking at his door because they need something, or someone coming down the hall. Not wanting to be discovered, we always had to pull apart. But this time, there is no one. No distractions. No interruptions. Nothing.

My stomach twists in nervousness. I don't know how I feel about being alone with him. I trust *him*, of course. But I don't know if I trust myself.

My fingers glide over the glossy, heart-shaped leaves of a hibiscus. Trey stops and snaps a yellow flower from the bush. His fingers brush against my cheek as he tucks the bloom behind my ear.

The canopy of flowers and trees open up to reveal a lagoon. With sloping dirt sides rising around it and overflowing foliage trailing all around the greenish-blue water, it looks inviting. And completely secluded.

"How did you know about this place?" I ask, bending down to test the water. It's cool enough to entice, especially on a hot day like this.

"My dad discovered it when he was scouting out a place for the Compound. We used to come here all the time when I was younger. It was my mom's favorite place. It was the one place outside the Compound that Mom and Dad could escape to."

I stand and face him. "Do you miss her?"

"Not as much as I used to. Claire was a very strong, no-nonsense kind of woman." He tilts his head and studies my face until a flush creeps to my cheeks. "You sometimes remind me of her."

I smile and wait because it looks like he wants to say more. He takes a seat at the edge of the water, patting the ground beside him. I sit and adjust my body so I face him, bringing my knees up to my chest and wrapping my arms around them.

"My mom didn't always have it easy. Being married to my father, I mean."

I stare at him, listening intently. He's never said much about his parents before.

"Their whole marriage, he was in love with another woman."

My mouth drops open. "Did he cheat on your mom?"

Trey shakes his head and glances down at the ground. "I don't know. I don't think so, but—" He pauses. "I'm not sure."

"This sounds like an interesting story," I prod.

"It's not your typical love story, I'll tell you that." He scoops up some of the sandy dirt, letting it trail through his fingers. "You remember how I had you break in to Harlow Ryder's office?"

I nod, not sure where he's headed with this story.

"Well, I wasn't completely truthful about the reasoning behind it."

Hmm… Seems like I'm not the only one keeping secrets.

"I mean, yes, I didn't want that computer chip to get into the wrong hands, but I also wanted to hit Harlow where it hurts. For more reasons than what his company is doing to juvenile delinquents."

"Why?"

Trey sighs. "Years ago, my father and Harlow were friends. Lab partners in University, actually. My father was in love with a woman—a woman by the name of Penelope Fields. He didn't have much money, so they planned to elope one weekend during their break.

"Well, Harlow set his eyes on Penelope. Somehow, he

convinced her she would be better off with him than my father. Even back then, Harlow was a wealthy, handsome man with the means to give her whatever she wanted. That isn't what drew her to him, however. Harlow also confided in Penelope that he had created a sophisticated DNA database that could track the genetic makeup of a person and determine the perfect genetic match between two individuals."

My mind reels. Penelope Fields was Zane's mother. Bryant Winchester was in love with Harlow Ryder's wife? Oh wow, the plot just got even thicker.

Trey continues. "Penelope was doubtful at first. But when Harlow offered to show her how it worked and test to see if they were a genetic match, she agreed. He took a sample of DNA from both of them, uploaded it to the database, and wouldn't you know it? They were a perfect match.

"Harlow convinced Penelope that their marriage would be more successful than their counterparts, that their children would be smarter and better looking. He convinced her that he could make her happy, not my father. Penelope believed him, and my father lost the love of his life. Harlow and Penelope were married a few months later and had a son soon after."

Trey pauses and takes a deep breath before continuing. "When she was in her forties, Harlow mastered genetic modification. Wanting to have a genetically modified child of his own, he convinced her to carry one more child, even though she had a medical condition that made it risky." His eyebrows lower and he stares at the ground. "She gave birth to Harlow's greatest creation, his son Zane, but she died right after childbirth. My father blamed Harlow because he cared more about his company than he did his own wife. My father never stopped loving Penelope, even after her death."

I remember the hall of pictures in Zane's house and the words he spoke as we looked at the pictures of his family. *My dad often says if he had only lived a lifetime ago, he could have saved my mother.*

"My mom always knew my dad loved another woman," Trey continues, "but I guess she just accepted it." He uses a stick to scratch a line in the soft earth. "My mother was a nurse when my dad met her. I think he loved her spunk. So different from Penelope. He tried to immerse himself in her love, but sometimes, it wasn't enough."

"That must have been hard for your mom. Being second best?"

"At times, I think it was. But like I said before, she was a strong woman. She didn't let things like that bother her, and if she did, she never let it show."

As I sit, reviewing what Trey told me about Harlow, Penelope, Bryant, and Claire, I realize that knowing this now makes what I need to tell Trey easier, and yet, at the same time, more difficult.

I open my mouth to speak, the truth about Zane bubbling at my lips, when Trey stands, brushes himself off, and starts to remove his shirt. My eyes widen and my mouth closes when he exposes his muscles and the two dimples in his lower back. When he turns, I get a glimpse of fully formed pecs, washboard abs, and a scar on his stomach underneath the last oblique muscle.

"I think it's time for a swim." He grins.

I've never seen him with his shirt off before. Besides his muscles and scar, I'm surprised by a real tattoo of a Phoenix on his left shoulder blade, the kind that sits on top of the skin.

Something about his tattoo catches my eye, and I stand to get a closer look. My fingers graze over the symbol tattooed on the belly of the Phoenix—interlocking triangles and spirals forming the shape of a tree. The same shape that climbs up his left arm, under the skin.

"What is it?" I ask, my fingers trailing over his back.

"A Dara Knot." He glances over his shoulder. "The Gaelic symbol is an oak tree used to represent power, wisdom, strength, and leadership."

"As if you need a symbol representing power and leadership," I tease. "It's not like you're a leader or anything."

Trey smirks. "I'm the best damn leader, and you know it."

I tilt my head and give him what I hope is a flirty smile. "Do I?"

He turns and grasps me around the waist, pulling me to him. "Do you need a reminder?"

Laughing, I move out of his reach and circle his back to get another look at his tattoo. "So, why the Phoenix?" I eye the beautiful red and orange bird with the long tail feathers that trail down his back.

He shrugs. "I like what a Phoenix represents. That no matter what we've done in our past, we have the power to change, to experience a rebirth."

That's exactly what I need. A rebirth. If I can't wipe away the past year, at least I can change. "I like that, too," I say, thinking of the butterflies under my skin.

His eyes connect with mine, and a deep flush spreads to my cheeks. "So," he says casually, "how about that swim?"

"I don't have a swimsuit," I reply, my heart picking up speed.

"Who says you need a swimsuit?" He flashes me a wicked grin.

My fingers reach out to touch the scar on his stomach, and his muscles tighten. "What happened?" I ask, my voice barely above a whisper. He closes his eyes as I run my fingers over the white mark. When he opens them, he grabs my hand and lifts my fingers to his lips, kissing each one. Slowly. Deliberately.

My knees go weak as the ache in my belly returns and lights me on fire.

Trey hooks his fingers in my belt loops and pulls me to him as my heart pounds. His lips cover mine, and I am consumed by the taste of him, the smell of him, and the feel of him. His lips move down my jaw and to my neck, and I throw my head back, clinging to his bare shoulders.

"Let's go for a swim," he says, his lips brushing my ear, his warm breath tickling my hot skin. He steps out of his jeans and dives into the lagoon wearing nothing but his boxers.

My cheeks flame and match the raging fire inside of me. I take a deep breath and slip out of my jeans. I decide to leave my T-shirt on because no matter how much I like Trey, I don't feel comfortable swimming around in a bra and panties. It's one thing to do it when I think no one is around; it's another to do it with a half-naked guy.

Trey resurfaces twenty yards out as I make my way into the water. It's a little unnerving not to see the bottom. I can only begin to wonder what kinds of creatures call this their home.

"Are there snakes in here?" I'm deathly afraid of them.

Trey swims closer and tries to splash me with a wave of water. "Probably." He grins.

I turn around and retreat. "No way. I'm not swimming in there."

Trey swims to the side and climbs out. I avert my eyes to avoid seeing the way his wet boxers cling to him. He scoops me up, my legs kicking, and jumps into the water. Squealing, I hang on to his neck as the cool water hits my skin.

He treads water for a few seconds, still holding me in his arms, before he tips me backward and dunks me. Water floods my eyes and burns my nostrils, and I come up sputtering, my arms flailing. Not very gracefully.

"You're gonna get it now," I threaten, swimming after him.

But he disappears under the water. In the murky darkness, I have no idea where he's gone.

Thirty seconds pass. Forty-five. Then a minute. I turn in the water, my shirt billowing around me, my eyes flitting over the lagoon. My heart pounds after a minute and a half. "Trey," I call out, my voice shaky with fear. "This isn't funny."

Something grazes against my leg, and I scream. I propel myself forward, but something yanks me back. All I can picture is a giant snake wrapping its body around my leg and dragging me down to the depths. When I kick as hard as I can, my foot lands against something solid. Strong hands grip my waist and drag me closer. When Trey surfaces, I punch him in the shoulder.

He laughs and runs a hand through his wet hair while I glare at him.

"That was so *not* funny," I retort.

"I think it was." His smile is playful.

"You scared me. I thought—"

"You thought I got sucked in by the Creature from the Black Lagoon?"

I want to knock the grin off his face. "You are this close," I hold together my thumb and forefinger, "to getting the teeth knocked out of your head."

His laugh echoes around the water. Encircling my back with his hands, he draws me to him. Even though I like being in his arms, it's infinitely harder to tread water when you're in someone else's space. He lifts my arms around his neck.

"Here, hold on to me, and I'll tread water for both of us." His hand slides down my arm, my smooth, scar-free arm, and he stops. "What the hell?" he says, turning it over and studying it. His eyes connect with mine, and he's suspicious. "The stitches? The tracker scar? Where is it?"

I decide now might be a good time to kiss him, so maybe he'll forget that I still haven't told him why I was at the SGF. My lips find his, and I bite down gently on his lower lip. It seems to work at first, but then he pulls away.

"That's not gonna work this time. Would you please tell me what the hell is going on?" His eyes are confused, distrusting.

I stare at him as I search for the words to say. His arms float away from my body, and he swims to the side before climbing out, pulling on his jeans, and dropping to the ground. Lying back, he rests his hands behind his head and stares at the sky.

Catalyst

I tread water for a few more minutes because I'm scared to get out and face him. What will he think when he realizes I went behind his back and asked the son of Harlow Ryder for help? Correction, I didn't ask Zane—he offered. But I didn't say no.

And why should I? This is my mother's life we're talking about. If I have to beg a dozen guys for help, it shouldn't matter, right?

I take a deep breath and swim to the side, determined to tell him everything.

Chapter Thirty-three

As I climb out, I debate whether I should struggle back into my jeans, or let myself air dry. Deciding on the second option, I take a seat next to Trey and study my hands as I search for the words I need to say.

"The truth is," I start, "I was with Zane Ryder at the government building today."

Trey sits up on one elbow and stares at me. "You know that prick?"

I nod. "But he's actually a really nice guy—" I stop myself when I see the look on Trey's face. Murderous. "And he doesn't know anything about what his father is doing to the inmates," I quickly add.

"Why were you with him?" he snaps.

"He offered to help me get my mother back." It sounds lame. This isn't coming out right. I bite the inside of my cheek.

Trey looks like he's about to say something, but he stops himself. He takes a deep breath. "That doesn't explain the scar."

"I know. But I think I have to go all the way back to the beginning in order for you to understand."

"I'm listening." His voice is so cool that it makes my stomach churn.

I exhale and prepare to take him back to the night that changed everything. The night I broke into the Match 360 facility.

But wait, it started way before that. I started selling my soul long before the break-in. So, instead, I go back to the night I found my father dead on the kitchen floor.

I tell Trey everything. How I found my father, my meeting with the Devil, my father's connection to Penelope Ryder and his identity change, and Radcliffe's revelation that Harlow murdered my father.

Trey leans back on his elbows, his shoulder muscles bulging. "Why would your father fake his death and change his name?"

"Exactly. Why would he do that? I'm almost wondering if there's more to Penelope's death than we realize."

"I wish my father were around so I could ask him. Of anyone, he would know."

Shaking my head, I offer a small smile. "That's not entirely true. There's one other person who probably knows more than anyone else."

"Harlow," Trey says. When I nod, he continues. "Maybe we need to pay him a visit tomorrow. I can think of some ways to get him to talk."

My mind flits to Zane and what he'll think if I storm his home with my Fringe companions and hold a gun to his father's head. I'll have to think about that one.

I tell Trey about Radcliffe's hit on Harlow Ryder. And how I met Zane at the celebratory ball—purposefully leaving out that I'd met him twice before.

"So, he's a friend," I explain. "Or was," I correct myself.

"But why would Radcliffe want Harlow dead if he's working *with* him on these experiments?"

I shake my head. "I don't know. I haven't been able to figure it out."

Which leads to the explanation of why I was at the SGF, my mother's strange behavior, and Zane walking out with the serum.

"So, you're telling me this Zane guy has some type of

serum that regenerates cells so quickly that you *watched* your skin heal?"

I nod. "It was the coolest thing I've ever seen."

Trey reaches for my arm and runs his fingers over the smooth skin. "Incredible," he says. "No wonder the government is dying to get their hands on it."

"But that's what doesn't make sense. Why agree to an exchange if they claim my mother has been working for them the whole time? Why the charade?"

Trey bites his lower lip while he thinks. "Maybe they just wanted to see it? To confirm?"

Anger wells inside as I think of Radcliffe using the serum on the facial scars I gave him. Is it possible he tricked us into coming just so he could get his hands on the serum? Of course. With that man, anything is possible.

I tell Trey about Radcliffe "testing" the serum on my handiwork.

"Why does it feel like that man is always one step ahead?"

"Because he is," I say. But his actions in the SGF confuse me. Why didn't he take me down when he had the chance? And what did he do to my mother?

I have a feeling Radcliffe knows more about my father's fake death than he's letting on. Because there's one thing I've realized about men like Radcliffe—the only thing that comes out of their mouths is lies.

Trey stares at me for a long moment. "I want to help you. I do. But you have to promise me something."

"What?"

"Promise me you won't go off by yourself again." His face is serious. "You do realize that every time you leave the Compound alone, you not only put yourself in danger, but you also put the rest of us in danger as well?"

I bite my lip. "I know, and I'm sorry. I just—" I take a deep breath. "I'm sorry."

His eyes soften. "I worry about you. Just promise me you won't do it again."

"I promise."

Trey pulls me to him. "We'll figure this out. We'll get your mom back. I swear."

It gives me great comfort to hear Trey say *we*. I don't have to do this alone, and he's making it clear I won't. I rest my head against his chest, my wet shirt still clinging to my damp skin. I sigh as his arms tighten around me. For the moment, I am safe. For the moment, I am not alone.

Slowing my breathing to match his, I listen to the steady beat of his heart. I don't know if it's his strong arms around me, the beat of his heart against my ear, or maybe a combination of both, but I let my guard down. I relax my body, I breathe deeply, and I find a moment of peace. I don't know what will happen tomorrow. I only know that right now, this is where I want to be. And this is who I want to be with.

Chapter Thirty-four

The Compound is bustling when we get back. It's Shipment Day, which means everyone has a job to do. I immediately feel guilty for keeping Trey from his and for shirking my responsibilities of putting food away in the kitchen.

The railroad tunnels are filled with two large semi-trucks, several pickup trucks, and at least a dozen men. After parking his truck in the underground lot, Trey kisses me quickly on the cheek and jogs away to help the others.

I make my way down the dimly lit tunnel to the hidden door in the stone wall. Climbing the stairs that lead to the Compound, I say hello to a boy no more than fifteen who's guarding the entrance with his AK-47. He doesn't know me, but he gives me a nod when I flash my internal Fringe tattoo at the digital entry scanner. The metal door slides open, allowing me access.

The hallway leading to the kitchen and cafeteria is lined with wooden crates overflowing with vegetables. Fruit in a variety of colors sit plump and ripe in wicker baskets. My stomach rumbles at the sight, and I'm tempted to swipe a banana, but it wouldn't be fair. Everything is rationed, carefully planned for. Even one banana going missing might mess up the whole system Trey has created.

Thinking his name causes a smile to creep to my face. My

fingers wander to my lips as I think about our kisses next to the lagoon and how his hands felt on my body.

"What are you smiling about?" I glance up to see Trina coming down the hall.

"Nothing," I say. I haven't told Trina about kissing Trey. Partly because that's a secret, and partly because for all her assurances that he's like a brother, I've seen the way she looks at him sometimes.

Sliding her arm through mine, she steers me to the kitchen. "You've been gone most of the day." She smiles, her eyes curious. "I find it hard to believe it's nothing." She pauses. "Did you see Zane?"

My heart drops. Of course she would think my giddiness is a result of Zane. But he probably never wants to see me again.

I shake my head. A little too quickly. She assumes the opposite of the truth.

"You did! You little sneak!" She leans in and whispers in my ear. "Did he kiss you again?"

"No. And I wasn't with Zane." She doesn't need to know all the details, but I don't want her to think for a minute that there's anything between the genetically modified boy and me. I'd hate for that to get back to Trey.

Her eyes widen, and then they narrow. "Trey has been gone all morning also." She lets the thought hang in the air like a poisonous snake ready to strike.

I shrug.

She gasps as she slips her arm out of mine. "You were with Trey?" Disappointment registers in her blue eyes, and I feel bad. How many people will I hurt today with the truth?

Tucking her short brown hair behind her ear, she forces a smile. "I didn't realize you liked him."

"No," I say, "I didn't realize *you* liked him."

Trina starts to protest, but a small smile escapes. "He's like a brother to me—"

"I know," I interrupt, "you've said that before. But is it

the truth?"

She hesitates before nodding. "Of course. And if you're happy, I'm totally cool with it."

We reach the kitchen and stand outside the door for a moment. I study her face, trying to discern if she's lying and how much I've hurt her.

"Trina." I speak in a low voice as Kaylee, the girl with the blonde ponytail that Trey extracted from Harlow's lab, exits the kitchen, carrying a basket of apples. "If I had known how much you liked him, I would have never…"

"Kissed him?" she finishes for me with a wry smile.

"Exactly," I say, and then want to bite my tongue. Now she knows I kissed him.

She grabs my hand and pats it. "I'm okay. Seriously. I'm happy for you." She leans in with a wicked grin. "So, how was it?"

"Nope." I smile. "That would be bad form to kiss and tell." We turn into the kitchen, and I glance at her. "But, if I was being truthful… it was pretty amazing."

She laughs. This time, the smile reaches her eyes. I exhale with relief.

"I never doubted that for a minute," she says, grinning.

We spend the next two hours working side by side. We slice the tomatoes and she teaches me how to can them. How to sterilize the jars, remove the tomato skins, and how to boil the jars in a water bath canner.

I'm grateful for the opportunity to keep my hands and mind busy. I don't want to think about my mother and what those military men did to brainwash her. I don't want to feel hopeless, scared, or sad.

Instead, I immerse myself in Trina's stories as she confides in me about her life as a GM and what it was like at her gender-segregated school. She talks about meeting a boy named Justin every afternoon by the fence that separated the two schools and how they would try to kiss through the metal crisscrosses.

"Weren't you scared you'd get caught on camera?" I ask, screwing the lid on the last jar of tomatoes.

A group of teenage girls at another counter giggle loudly as they slice and can strawberries. They appear to be teasing Kaylee, whose face is beet red.

"No, by then, I was beyond the point of caring. What would they have done to us anyway? Flogged us? I don't think so."

It's hot in the kitchen with the generator going and the heat rising up from the stove. For the first time since I cut my hair, I'm glad it's short.

"I used to hate girls like you," I admit.

Her eyes widen. "Why?"

"Because you're too perfect. Too pretty. Too athletic. Too smart. As a normal girl with freckles and red hair, I resented all of you who had it easier in life." My eyes lower. It's the first time I've ever admitted it out loud. I always knew those feelings were there, right below the surface, but it's one thing to think it, and something completely different to say it out loud, and to a GM no less.

"Sienna," Trina snaps.

Her tone forces me to look up.

"I don't ever want to hear you talk like that again. Look at you. You're gorgeous. You resented my kind? Well, news flash, I resented you and all the *normal* people. People who have a choice. Who are born with a lifetime of possibilities, the power to love who they want, and the ability to live their life however they choose, whether it's good or bad." She takes a deep breath. "I never had that choice. I didn't *choose* to be genetically modified. I can thank my dear old parents for that."

For the first time, my eyes are open to her life, to the life of every genetically modified child. There is no choice. It's a life they're forced into. And a marriage arranged at their birth. There is no love, no romance... no freedom.

Now I know what my mom was referring to that day in

my room when she said my dad wanted me to be free from the pressures of society. He wanted to protect me from that kind of life.

"I'm sorry," I say. "I guess I never tried to look at it from your perspective." I wink at her. "But you're still too pretty, too smart—"

She flings a wet rag she was using to wash her hands at me. I laugh, hurling it back at her as the girls at the opposite counter turn and watch with wide eyes. They are a couple of years younger, and when they see two older girls flinging wet rags at each other, they decide to join the fun. With the heat, the soaked washcloths are almost welcoming as they hit our bare skin.

I laugh and toss one at Kaylee, who hits her friend with the brown curls. The kitchen erupts in hysterical laughter, and for a brief moment, I understand what it means to be carefree. To be a teenage girl who has girlfriends who talk about boys and stealing kisses beside chain-link fences. For a few seconds, I am someone other than *me*.

"Whoa! What is going on in here?" a familiar, husky voice booms from the doorway.

All traces of laughter stop, and we all turn, wide-eyed, to see Trey standing in the doorway, a large crate on top of his broad shoulders. His eyes flit around the room until they rest on me. He smiles. "Is this your doing?"

I point a finger at Trina, who blushes. "She started it."

Trey laughs and moves through the doorway, setting the box on the far end of the counter. "Here's some green beans. Are you canning these also?"

"Probably not tonight," Trina responds. "I think Lucille is ready to get her crew in here to start making dinner." She smiles at him, and my stomach twists. "We can get to it first thing in the morning."

He returns her smile. "Thanks, Trina." Turning to me, he says, "Can I talk to you for a minute?"

I follow him out into the hallway, but not before I glance

over my shoulder to see Trina's reaction. She looks like she swallowed something sour, and guilt overtakes me. If I had known… would it have mattered?

Trey leans his side against the wall, and I take the same stance opposite him.

He speaks in a low voice. "One of our trucks didn't come back from picking up the shipment. Me and a couple other guys are going out to look for it."

My eyes widen, and my heart begins to pound like a sledgehammer in my chest. Isn't this how his father was killed? A routine supply run?

"I won't be here for dinner." He pauses and bites his lip, and my eyes are drawn to his mouth. His smooth, full lips. The ones that light me up when they touch my skin.

"Anyway, just wanted you to know so you don't wonder where I am."

"Will you be okay?"

"I'll be fine. But do me a favor? Don't tell anyone. I don't want people to worry. Yet."

My throat closes. This sounds dangerous.

"Can I come?" I say on the off chance he's feeling generous. "I think I've proven to be a fairly good shot."

"Absolutely not," he says, his mouth turning into a frown. A very kissable frown. "And hopefully, no one will be shooting anything."

His hand touches my face, and his thumb traces my cheekbone, sending a chill up my spine despite the stifling heat seeping from the kitchen. He glances up and down the hallway before he leans in, his lips teasing mine. When he pulls away, he smiles and strokes my cheek. "See you soon," he says before striding down the hall.

When I return to the kitchen, I go through the motions of cleaning up the tomato juice and washing the cutting boards. I ignore Trina's curious gaze and the whispers from the younger girls, including Kaylee, who appears the most curious of all the girls about why Trey wanted to see me in the hall.

My stomach is in knots at the thought of this rescue mission. Something doesn't *feel* right. As I wipe down the counters, I try not to think about all the things that could possibly go wrong.

Chapter Thirty-five

Bedtime tonight is pushed up by two hours due to a downed generator and the inability to light the hallways until they replace the broken one. Trina reassures me this happens occasionally. The good news is we have several back-up generators to use while the first one is rebuilt. Apparently, they use an alternating rotation so one generator is never handling the burden on its own.

I stand at the sink with a flashlight and brush my teeth while Trina showers. Trey and his crew haven't returned yet, and my heart races when I think about what could have happened. Earlier, I tried to send him a message, but so far, I've been met with silence on his end.

"Trey wasn't at dinner tonight," Trina calls casually, the water from the shower mingling with her words.

"Yeah, I think he and some of the guys had to make a run." How long do I wait before I tell the others? How long before we send out a search party?

"A run? This late? That's odd."

She's suspicious, and I don't blame her. She's been here a lot longer than I have. She knows the routine, understands the inner workings of the Compound and the people in it, including Trey.

"Yeah, that's all I know," I lie.

The water turns off and the curtain slides back, the metal

rings scraping against the metal bar. "Do you mind handing me that towel over there?" she asks, pointing to the towel hanging on the rack next to me.

I grab it and stuff it into her hands, avoiding her nakedness. I've never understood how some girls are so open with their bodies.

After Trina's dressed, we pad down the hall together, our flashlights bouncing along the concrete floor. We stop at my door and let a group of sixteen-year-old boys slide past. I recognize the boy with the chestnut hair as John, the one who was guarding the tunnel entrance the day Trey and I visited Chaz. They nod and wish us goodnight before continuing down the hall. A boy with auburn hair punches John, who puts him in a playful headlock.

Rolling my eyes, I turn to Trina. "Boys," I mutter.

She laughs. "That's right, who needs a *boy* when you have yourself a *man*?"

My eyes widen, and then a giggle escapes. I've never thought of Trey as a *man* before, but pushing twenty-two and leading a group like this definitely qualifies him as one. A man who fights his cousin for fun, and who ignored me for days when he was embarrassed for kissing me. Well, maybe he's a man with boyish tendencies.

"Goodnight, Sienna," Trina says before starting down the hall.

"Goodnight, Trina," I call after her.

I crawl under the covers on my bed because there's nothing else to do in the dark. But I can't go to sleep. My body is filled with worry, so much that I feel like my heart might explode if it pumps any faster.

How long should I wait?

I'll give it another hour. If he's not back by then, I'm telling someone. I don't know who, but someone.

Catalyst

I slide out of my room and tiptoe down the hall, my flashlight trained on the floor in front of me. Trey never came to my room, but that doesn't mean he's not back yet. I adjust my black tank top and tug at the bottom of my sleep shorts, wishing they were a little longer, but when it comes to the Pavilion, beggars can't be choosy.

Even though I try to step lightly, my sandaled feet slap against the concrete flooring. I creep down the dark corridor, my heart thumping in my chest. My flashlight creates eerie shadows on the walls, made worse by my shaking hands. The inside of the Compound has never been so quiet, but then again, I don't make it a habit to traipse these hallways during the dark of night.

I stop outside Trey's room and put my ear to the door, listening for any sound of movement inside. I hear nothing.

Knocking softly, I wait in anticipation. Nothing.

I try the door handle. To my surprise, it's unlocked. The door swings open before I realize I put pressure on it.

I shine my light into Trey's room, only to find it empty. His bed is still made, a stack of books and papers sits on his untidy desk, and a pile of folded clothes rests on the wooden desk chair.

Fear surges through me as I sink onto his bed. Do I tell someone? Do I wait a little longer?

I'll wait for ten more minutes. If he isn't back in ten minutes, I'll check the tunnel and unloading area before I wake Trina.

I nervously tap my fingers against my leg as I count in my mind. I don't know why I'm counting, maybe to help pass the time?

A noise filters down the hall—someone's coming. I hear voices, male voices, and relief washes over me. They're back.

As they draw closer, I freeze when I recognize Nash's voice. What will he think when he sees me in Trey's room in the middle of the night?

Slipping to the other side of the room, I plaster myself

against the wall. As long as Nash doesn't come in, he shouldn't see me in the dark. I don't even think for a minute how stupid I'll look to Trey when he finds me glued to his wall.

The two voices stop outside the door, and I hear Trey's husky voice mixed with Nash's nasally, cold tone.

"You don't think they followed you?" Nash asks, his voice full of skepticism.

"No. Not a chance. We lost them before we hit the open expanse."

"How's Trip?"

"He's fine. We removed the bullet, but he won't be able to walk on that leg for a while. He'll be in the infirmary for the next few days."

"That was stupid, Trey. Really stupid. You're lucky you didn't get killed."

I hear Trey laugh. "Isn't that what this life is about? Staying alive? I refuse to crawl into a hole and allow those thugs to take advantage of us. I will fight for what is ours, even if it means losing my life."

My throat closes. He was almost killed. I knew it sounded dangerous, and now my suspicions are confirmed.

"You and I are all that's left of the Hartfield clan. Just remember that," Nash says with more tenderness than I knew he could possess. I hear footsteps continue down the hall, and then Trey walks into his room. Slumping away from the wall, I fling myself into his arms. I breathe in the smell of him, an earthy one of dirt and sweat.

He throws his flashlight on the bed, the light illuminating a small corner of the room. His arms tighten around my back as I cling to him. "This is a pleasant surprise. I didn't expect to find a beautiful girl waiting in my bedroom when I got back."

I tilt my head to look at him, trying to make out his features in the shadows. "You were almost killed."

He cocks his head. "You heard that, huh?"

"I was so worried. I thought..." I can't finish the sentence.

"Hey," he says, his eyes searching mine as his fingers move to my chin, "I'm right here. Nothing happened." His lips meet mine. He kisses me hungrily, until I'm weak in the knees. When I pull back, I notice the cut above his eye.

"What happened?" My fingers graze his wound, and he winces. "You need to go to the infirmary."

"No, it's only a little cut. I'll be fine with some antiseptic and a bandage." He smiles down at me. "Besides, I'd much rather kiss you than worry about a cut."

His lips lightly touch my jaw and move toward my earlobe, sending tiny pulses of electricity shooting through me. I wish he would stop so I can concentrate. What was I going to ask him about? Oh, yes. The man who got shot...

"Someone got shot tonight?" I murmur, pulling back. My eyes plead with him to tell me the truth.

Trey sighs and drops his hands, all playfulness gone. "Yeah, a guy named Trip. Have you met him yet?"

I shake my head.

"We were ambushed." He runs his hands through his hair. "The truck sent to get the shipment from Estelle Langley, one of the farmers who raise chickens for us, was hijacked on the way back to the Compound. Three men wearing masks and carrying M-16s blocked the road. When Trip and his buddy Jason stopped the vehicle, the men boarded the truck and forced them out at gunpoint. Trip pulled a knife on one of the guys and got shot in the leg. The masked men escaped with the truck and the goods."

My eyes narrow. "What was your role in all this?"

He shrugs and moves across the room. For the first time, I see his gun slung low over his hips. He unbuckles the belt and lays it on his desk. "I did what a good leader needs to do at times."

"Did you get the truck?"

He smiles, but it doesn't quite reach his eyes. "Of course."

"Did anyone else get hurt?"

"A couple of bruises and cuts, no big deal."

I exhale slowly, grateful he's okay. Looks like I got worked up for nothing. But then, Nash's words filter into my brain, and I know there's something he's not telling me.

"Why did Nash say you almost got killed? And why did he ask if they followed you back to the Compound? Who was following you?"

Trey moves close and his fingers grip my waist, drawing me to him until our bodies are touching. "These men were professionals. They weren't thieves searching for food like the man who killed my father. These were experts who knew our schedule, knew when we'd be coming down the road. They staked us out."

I think back to Victor's threat a couple of weeks ago when he warned that it wasn't over between us. "Was it the Devil's men?"

Trey nods. "Nash was worried because I hunted them down. I went to their lair to get the truck back, which he thought was stupid. He wanted me to forget the truck."

"They followed you back?" My throat closes, and I find it hard to breathe.

"Only as far as the outskirts of the city. We lost them once we hit the open desert."

"You could have been killed," I whisper.

"But I wasn't." His lips brush against each cheek before settling on my forehead. "Do you mind if I go get cleaned up?" he asks, pulling away.

It is then that I notice the bloodstains on the front of his shirt and upper arms. "Is that yours?" I cry out as I jump back.

"No, it's Trip's, mostly." He grabs a change of clothes from the pile on his desk chair, a towel hanging on the back of his door, and the flashlight from his bed. "I'll be back in a few," he says before slipping out the door. The room is immediately bathed in darkness.

Sitting on the edge of his bed, I wait, relief filling every part of me and making me feel light, like a hot air balloon getting ready for takeoff. Now that I know he's okay, I should go back to my room. But the thought of being in his arms, his skin scented with bath soap, and my fingers curling around his damp hair, propels me to stay.

There's something he's not telling me about the rescue. He never did say what happened when he got to the Devil's lair. Did he and his men kill them? If so, how many? Was Victor one of them?

I shake my head to rid the images. There are some things I don't need to know, and with Trey as the leader of this group, there are some things he *has* to do. I try to convince myself that this knowledge is enough.

Trey's light fills the doorway before I see him. The flashlight shines on the wall behind me before he sets it on his dresser, light side up, and it casts the room in an eerie glow. Wrapped in the aroma of shampoo and soap, he wears clean clothes—a white T-shirt and a baggy pair of basketball shorts—and the blood on his arms is gone. Wiped clean like it never existed. His damp hair curls slightly at his neckline, and I have to resist the urge to run my fingers through it. When he sees me, his face breaks out into a smile. My mouth pulls up in response as my pulse quickens.

It's time for me to go.

I stand and move to the door. "Now that I know you're okay, I should get back to my room," I mumble.

Trey hangs his wet towel on the back of the door and turns to face me. "You could stay," he offers.

My eyes shift to his bed, a twin, big enough for one, or two people very close together. I should leave.

Trey pulls back the covers and climbs into his bed, scooting all the way against the wall and leaving plenty of room for me. I kick off my sandals as a chill creeps up my spine. I've never slept in the same bed with a boy before, and I'm not sure what to expect.

I slip next to him, the sheets cool and soft against my skin. His arm slides under my head and pulls me closer until my head rests on the soft spot between his chest and shoulder. My lips are only inches from his neck, and when I inhale, my nose is filled with the fresh scent of his soap. Heart pounding from the nearness of him, I try to slow my pulse by taking deep, slow breaths.

In a moment of boldness, my hands work their way under his shirt and run along the length of his scar. His stomach muscles tense in response.

"You never did tell me what happened here?"

He looks down at me and then stares up at the ceiling. "I was in a knife fight."

"A knife fight?"

He sighs. "Yeah, after my father's death, I was lost. Confused. Nash and I went to a bar in town to help us forget." He clears his throat. "I was drunk. Hit on the wrong girl—one of the Devil's girls. So his men gave me this."

The muscles in my neck tighten as I think of the scar on Nash's cheek. "Is that how Nash got his scar too?"

Trey nods.

"And that's what Victor was talking about outside the Megasphere."

He nods again. "But I'm different now. I was young. Lost. Before my father's death, I went along with the whole idea of the Fringe because he believed so strongly in it. I had to figure out what I believed."

"And now do you know? What you believe?"

"I believe these people we're rescuing deserve protection. I believe Harlow Ryder is a selfish bastard who only cares about making money, no matter who he hurts."

"I believe that too," I say.

Trey smiles, his free hand running up and down my bare arm, from shoulder to wrist, leaving a trail of goose bumps. "I like your butterflies," he says, his breath tickling me. I shiver and draw even closer to him. My lips touch his neck, then his jaw, but the stubble on his face pricks against my mouth and skin, making me wince.

Trey's hand flies to his face, and he rubs his jaw. "I'm sorry," he says. "I should've shaved."

"It's okay. I like it."

"You do?" He sounds surprised.

I kiss him. "I do," I whisper.

Trey kisses me then until I'm lightheaded and breathless. As I draw my hips closer to him, his breathing runs hard and shallow, our hearts pounding against each other. His free hand entangles itself in my hair, refusing to let me pull away. Not that I want to. Every fiber of my being is alive, every sense heightened, every inch of my skin crawling with excitement.

Trey is the first to pull away, of course, leaving me amazed by his ironclad control. I wonder if it has something to do with what happened in my room that day he was drunk. Is he afraid he'll take things too far?

I roll onto my side, away from him, and curl into a ball as fatigue sets in. Scooting closer to me, he drapes an arm across my stomach, his warm body pressed against my back.

And for once, I feel safe.

I have to pee.

Not wanting to leave Trey, I try to hold it, but the stinging sensation in my bladder only gets worse. I groan and slip from under his arm. The room is pitch black—Trey's flashlight must need a good crank. I fumble around his room until I locate my flashlight and Lynk communicator on his desk. When I click on the flashlight, a pale circle of light hits the far wall. I slip on my sandals, pocket my Lynk, and quietly let myself out.

The hallway is dark and silent. I imagine it's close to one or two in the morning. Thankfully, the bathroom is deserted. Now I don't have to crouch behind the wooden door, hoping someone doesn't see me hovering over the toilet. I've never been one for public restrooms, and here in the Compound, that's my only option.

I prop my flashlight on the ledge of the sink and let the warm tap water run over my hands. When I glance at myself in the mirror, I frown at my reflection. I never like what I see, and I'm not sure why Trey is attracted to me. Turning the water off, I stare at myself, as if seeing my face for the first time. I analyze my green eyes framed by thick lashes, my too-small nose that makes me look like a bunny when I wrinkle it, and my lips that always look like I'm pouting. My eyes travel to my hair, and my ears that stick out slightly and are more noticeable with my hair short.

The bathroom sink shakes, knocking my flashlight to the floor and shrouding me in darkness.

What the hell?

I lean over and feel along the floor for the light, hoping I can get it to work again. A low rumble fills the air. Before I can grasp what's happening, the whole bathroom shudders and pieces of the ceiling crash to the floor. My screams bounce off the tile as a large rock falls inches from my head. Fear claws at my throat as I struggle to my feet.

Using my hands to feel along the concrete walls, I stumble out of the bathroom. Screams echo down the dark corridor as another blast rips through the Compound and knocks me to the ground. My ears ring and colorful stars shoot across my vision. I crawl along the wall before pushing myself up and continuing down the corridor. Pieces of the ceiling fall all around me, and the screaming continues. But it sounds distant, like my ears are plugged with tissues. Red embers glow around me, and at first, I think how pretty they are and how nicely they light the darkened hallway. Then, I realize, the embers are starting small fires, up and down the corridor.

Another blast one hundred feet down the hall throws me backward, and I land next to one of the embers. My body throbs and my head aches, so much that I lay there for a moment staring at the fire inching its way toward me. The heat licks at my face. As if in slow motion, I groan and roll away from it. Someone runs past me shouting, but all I can think about is getting to Trey's room.

I push myself to my feet and stumble down the hall, tripping over pieces of concrete and sheetrock. There's a buzzing in my head that drowns out the yells and cries for help. The end of the hall by Trey's room is on fire.

A piece of rock or concrete falls from above and hits me in the back of the leg. Pain shoots up my leg, and I fall face-first in the hallway, crying out Trey's name. I have to get to Trey. I have to.

"Sienna, we have to get out of here!" It's Curly. His arms move under me and lift me up by the armpits.

I struggle against him. "No." My voice comes out weak, hoarse. I try again, louder this time. "No. We have to get Trey." I point to his room and the flames outside his door. I can feel the heat from here.

"I'll get him. You stay here." Curly takes off running down the hall, dodging the falling concrete and small flames.

I claw against the wall until I'm upright, and then move down the hall after him, dragging my leg behind me. I try to shield my face from the intense heat of the flames and focus on the door five feet away, instead of the pain. When I reach it, I slip inside and gasp. Trey's room is no more. The ceiling is completely caved in, the mountain blasted through. When I look up, I see the night sky and a few pinpricks of stars. His bed, dresser, nightstand, floor—everything is covered in concrete, sheetrock, and dirt. Golden embers light the room, and I know it's only a matter of minutes before this room looks like the hallway outside.

"Jeb!" I scream.

"I found him," he yells. "But he's trapped!"

I follow the sound of his voice to where the bed used to be. Curly is underneath a pile of rubble and crawls out when he sees me.

"I don't think we can get to him," he says. "And even if we

could…" His eyes glaze over.

My breathing stops, and time stands still for a moment. I know what he's saying, but I refuse to believe it.

Adrenaline, like a bolt of lightning, flows through me. I grab the first thing I see and shove it off the pile of rubble. Grunting, I hurl a large rock behind me. "Help me, please," I yell as I claw through the dirt and debris.

Curly's arms appear beside me, and he groans as he tries to remove a large slab of concrete. I grab the other end and heave, my muscles straining, the veins popping out of my neck. It moves several inches, and we do it again, and again, until we've cleared a path.

The heat is intense. The four-foot flames lick the doorframe, and the room is filling with smoke.

"We have to hurry," I say, locking eyes with Curly. Even as I say it, my voice sounds muffled, as if I'm trying to talk underwater.

Something tickles my throat, and I hunch over, my body racked with coughs. By the time I'm done gasping for air, Curly has cleared another section of debris.

That's when I see it. Trey's leg.

My heart pounds. I continue to pull rocks, scraps of metal, and parts of the ceiling off him until my arms ache. As Curly grunts and lifts the last concrete slab off Trey's chest, I shine my flashlight on Trey's face. I'm afraid of what I'll see.

His eyes are closed as if he's sleeping, but his face is covered in tiny cuts. As the flashlight travels down his body, my stomach rolls. A piece of metal rebar is sticking out of his chest right near his heart. Blood stains his shirt and his bed.

I turn away as my stomach heaves. I vomit up my dinner, the one I ate without Trey beside me. I refuse to believe what I see. The smoke rolls into the room, and I'm hit with another coughing fit. When I turn back to Trey's body, Curly is kneeling over him, his fingers pressed to his neck.

For one brief moment, my heart stops beating, and I can't breathe. *He has to be alive. He has to.*

Catalyst

But the pained look on Curly's face when his eyes meet mine causes my blood to run cold despite the heat pressing in on us. He shakes his head and stands, and I feel as though I'm having an out-of-body experience. This can't be happening. I refuse to believe for a moment that Trey—my Trey—is dead.

Curly takes my arm and tries to lead me to the door, saying something about needing to get out of there before the whole place crumbles. But I pull free and run to Trey, tripping over the piles of debris. I cradle his head in my lap like I did that day in the training facility. Stroking his scratchy face, I kiss his still-warm lips and think about lying in his arms only moments before. I tilt my head back and scream. An animalistic howl that reverberates through the night sky above us. I can't leave him. I refuse to leave him.

Curly's hands drag me to the door.

"No," I cry. "I'm not leaving without him."

Curly isn't listening. He is too strong. In a minute, I'll never see Trey again. Just like I never saw Garrett after Trey forced me to leave him. I do the only thing I can think to do. I fight.

I kick him as hard as I can in the leg. He lets go of my arm and curses.

"I'm not leaving without him," I cry. "Help me get him out of here."

Curly must think I'm crazy, and now he's risking his own life to help me, but he hesitates.

"Help me, please." Tears sting my eyes and bathe my face, their saltiness mixing with the smoke flavor of the room as they run into my mouth.

Curly turns back to Trey and climbs over the debris.

"You have to pull out the metal bar," I shout.

Curly looks at me like I'm crazy, but then he must realize I'm right. I turn away as he grips the bar between his hands. I hear him scream, and then I turn back in time to see him lift Trey over his shoulder and stumble forward. "Stay close," he says, leaping over the fire in the doorway.

I grab my flashlight and follow him. The flames singe my legs, and I look down to make sure I'm not on fire.

In the hallway leading to the exit, we stumble past bodies. This part of the Compound seems to be the hardest hit. These people were probably trying to escape when it was blasted through. I don't allow my flashlight to linger on the faces, too scared it may be someone I recognize. Most of the walls are caved in and the ceiling is missing, exposing pieces of sky, or the earthy mountain above us. Outside the entrance to the kitchen, I notice a blonde ponytail splayed out on the floor, and my breath catches. It's Kaylee. I cry out to Curly and kneel beside her, my hands closing over her delicate wrist, feeling for a pulse. It's faint, but it's there.

"She's alive," I yell. Curly waits with Trey in his arms, and I know he must be tired. I have to hurry. I slap the girl's cheeks, but she doesn't even stir. I try to lift her to a sitting position, but she slumps against the wall. I can't carry her. I'm too weak. But I try. I lift her over my back and take a few steps, but a rumble and blast in another part of the building knocks me to my knees. Kaylee rolls off my back and lies still on the concrete floor.

I join Curly. "She's still alive, but she's too heavy."

"We have two options. We can leave her here, or we can leave Trey and take her with us."

My eyes widen. "I'm not leaving Trey."

Curly starts up the hallway toward the exit. "Then your decision is made. I can't carry two people at once."

"Can we come back and get her after we get Trey out of here?"

Curly hesitates. "If we can get back in without killing ourselves, then yes."

I kneel next to Kaylee and promise to come back for her. She is still unconscious, and I doubt she even hears me. Hurrying down the hall after Curly, I almost collide into his back. "What is it?" I cry.

He turns. Beads of sweat are pouring past his creased

eyebrows and into his eyes. "The hallway is caved in ahead. We're trapped."

"There's another way out," I say, remembering the hidden staircase in the janitorial closet.

Curly looks doubtful, but he hefts Trey over his shoulder and follows me back down the hall, the way we came. Before we reach Trey's room and the fire now billowing down the hall, we turn down another corridor. In the smoky darkness, everything looks the same. Wiping the sweat off my forehead with the back of my hand, I move past doorway after doorway, struggling to remember the location of the janitorial closet. My fingers curl around the wooden doorframe that leads to the recreation room, and I know we're close.

"Sienna," a voice calls from further down the hall. A flashlight illuminates the floor in front of me, and I see Trina standing in a doorway. She has a cut on her forehead and an abrasion on the side of her face, but other than that, she looks okay.

"Trina!" I run to her, tripping over debris and falling into her arms. She's standing in the broom closet doorway.

"You remembered," she says, pulling me into the small room. Her eyes light on Curly carrying a man's body over his shoulder. "Is that Trey?"

I nod as my throat closes.

"Is he… is he okay?"

Fresh tears fill my eyes as I shake my head. Turning away from her shocked stare, I come face to face with Nash.

His face flashes through emotions faster than I can track them. Surprise turns to confusion, then just as quickly, anger blazes through his eyes, mixed with a tinge of sadness. He slams his fist into the wall, and thankfully, it collides with drywall instead of cement block.

"We have to get out of here," Curly huffs. His arms quiver from the weight of Trey.

"Here, I'll take him." Nash steps forward, takes a deep breath, and heaves Trey's body onto his own shoulder. "What happened?"

"His room collapsed. We found him trapped under all the debris," Curly says, flexing his arms.

"I'll go first," Trina says. "Follow me."

Nash goes next and Curly follows, pushing against Nash's back to give support as he ascends the curving metal staircase. From above, I hear Nash groaning and grunting with effort. My legs are like dead weights, and I drag my bad leg up the stairs behind me. It's hard to see where I'm stepping as tears blur my vision and collect on my chin. I don't let my mind wander to the reason Nash is having trouble getting up the stairs. I refuse to believe it. If I don't believe it, it can't possibly be true.

I feel the outside air before I see the night sky. The desert breeze is cool and welcoming on my face as it dries my tears. I gulp the air, trying to soothe the fire in my throat. As I stumble out of the hidden hatch on the side of the mountain, a noise thunders above. My eyes search the sky. Several red lights soar above us in the darkness, and my heart skips a beat.

Drones.

"Run," Nash yells at the exact moment the adrenaline kicks in. I stumble down the side of the mountain, tripping over rocks and roots. Nash's bulky shape is ahead of me, Trey's body slung over his shoulders.

I trip and fall, hitting my chin on the hard earth. Pain shoots through my face, and I'm certain there must be blood, but Curly is there beside me, helping me to my feet and guiding me the rest of the way down the mountain.

A large explosion causes me to turn and look, even though Curly is urging me forward. I gasp in horror as the drones drop bomb after bomb onto the mountain and our underground home.

A cry escapes my lips when I think of Kaylee and her blonde ponytail. I never had a chance to go back for her. And now, it's too late.

"Keep moving," Nash yells, already several yards ahead

of me.

 I turn my back on the home I've come to love and the people who became my family.

Chapter Thirty-six

I cling to the ground as tears run down my cheeks and fall to the earth. Voices morph around me. A girl crying, a man cursing, a boy sounding tired and confused. I don't know what they're saying, and I don't care. I want to leave this body. I want to be rid of the pain, the despair, and the heartache. For a moment, I am gone. I am in Trey's arms. He kisses my neck and whispers in my ear. *Don't give up. Don't ever give up.*

"Sienna, we have to go." Someone is shaking me. Their voice is familiar, but it isn't the one I want to hear. It isn't Trey's husky voice.

"Sienna! They're coming. We have to hide!" Curly's voice speaks low in my ear, and I turn to him, dazed.

"Who?"

"The government sonsofbitches. We have to go, now!" He helps me to my feet and pulls me along beside him. I can barely make out the shapes of Nash and Trina already running for cover amidst some Joshua trees.

"Wait! What about Trey?" I sob. "We can't just *leave* him there." That's when I see them. A caravan of government vehicles making their way toward us, their headlights bouncing as they off-road over the desert terrain.

"We have to," Curly says, gripping my arm hard, probably so I won't try to run from him. "We can't move as quickly with him. We'll collect his body after they leave."

Comforted by this thought, I run with him, tripping over low-lying cacti that infiltrate the ground. We hide behind our own strand of Joshua trees and wait as the vehicles draw closer, the gunning sound of the engine the only noise in the night sky.

The vehicles stop only a few yards from where we just stood, and my breath catches. A car door slams followed by several others, and I see Radcliffe's face as a headlight illuminates the man clearly in charge. Radcliffe moves toward the base of the mountain—or what's left of it—where Trey lies dead. He kneels by his body. Someone gives a shout, and then several other men run over. These men look like medics and carry a stretcher between them. They load Trey onto the stretcher, carrying him back to their truck.

"No," I whisper. Tears fill my eyes and sting my cheeks. I'll never see him again. I'll never kiss his lips, hold his hand, or feel his arms around my waist. The cruelty of life settles on my chest, making it difficult to breathe.

I have to resist the urge to rush forward and gouge out Radcliffe's eyes with my fingers. I would never make it within twenty feet of him before I'm gunned down.

I watch as they load Trey's body into the vehicle, and the caravan drives away. Hot tears slide down my face and run into my mouth. I allow myself to cry for a few moments, and Curly doesn't say anything, but I do see him discreetly wipe his eyes. When I'm ready, I rake my palms across my face and turn to Curly.

"What now?" My voice sounds stronger than I feel. At least it doesn't sound like my heart feels—broken, torn in two, ripped to shreds. As long as I can keep Trey out of my mind, I might be able to make it through the rest of this night.

Curly clears his throat before he speaks. "Let's go see what Nash wants to do." He pauses. "He's in charge now," he says. As if I need a reminder.

We traipse across the desert to the other strand of Joshua trees where Nash and Trina are crouched. They stand when they see us coming.

"What's the plan?" Curly calls out as we near them.

"I just got a message from other Fringe survivors," Nash says. "Apparently, there's quite a large group from the west wing who escaped before the passageway was blocked."

The news sends a tingle of relief through my body. "How many escaped?" I ask.

"A hundred, I think."

Which means a hundred didn't.

"Feeling guilty?" Nash sneers.

My eyes narrow. "Why should I?"

Nash takes a step toward me, his hands clenched in fists. "Maybe because you sent them here, you dirty spy."

"How do we know *you* didn't send them here? With Trey gone, doesn't that make *you* leader of the Fringe? How *convenient.*"

"Guys, that's enough," Trina snaps. "We have more things to worry about right now than who's a traitor, which neither of you is."

"Yeah, Commander, if you're leading us, now is the time to do it," Curly adds.

Nash grumbles under his breath before straightening to his full height. "These bastards can't get away with this. They took away our home and our leader. They killed our friends and our family. They will pay. Let's meet up with the other Fringe members and decide which government building we should bomb. In the middle of the day."

Retaliation. Of course that's Nash's plan. And you know what? Revenge has never sounded sweeter.

"It's okay. That's our man," Curly says when we spot the headlights of an approaching truck. We've been walking for a while, sticking to the abandoned tracks and keeping a look out for more drones. Per Nash's instructions, we split up. Curly and I are in charge of getting the guns and ammo from the off-site location, while Nash and Trina meet up with the other Fringe members and secure the explosives.

A white truck pulls to the side of the road, and we climb the small embankment to meet it. An older man with a ponytail hangs out of the truck, nervously glancing around.

"Just you two?" the man drawls.

Curly nods and motions for me to get in the passenger side. I scoot over until I'm only inches from the man I assume is a farmer working with the Fringe. In the glow of the overhead lights, the jeans, suspenders, and sun-aged face give it away.

"What happened?" the man asks, his voice rough.

Curly sighs. "The Compound was attacked by drones."

"How's about the shipment? All the food?"

"Gone."

The man, who looks to be in his sixties, slams his hand on the steering wheel and curses. His eyes turn to me. "Who're you?"

Before I have a chance to respond, Curly butts in. "She was a friend of Trey's."

"Was?" he asks.

"Trey's dead," Curly answers, tripping over the words.

The man lets out a cry and turns away. He bows his head for a moment, and my heart breaks. It's bad enough I have to endure my own pain, but it's even worse seeing others mourn.

Once the man composes himself, he sticks out a weathered hand. "Ray Jones. But you can call me Jones."

I place my hand in his and feel the calloused skin of a man who's spent years with his hands immersed in the soil. "Sienna," I say, my voice barely above a whisper.

Jones nods and turns his attention to the steering wheel.

On the drive to where the weapons are stored, exhaustion kicks in. I think I may be in a bit of shock. I'm surprised by my lack of emotion as my body grows heavy. I welcome sleep to take me away from this nightmare. Letting the voices of Curly and Jones wash over me, I close my eyes and tilt my head back against the vinyl bench seat.

I sleep, and I dream. Trey and I swimming in the lagoon, laughing. I reach out for him, but instead of taking my hand, he disappears under the water, as if something is dragging him down. Diving under the water, I try to look through the murky depths, but he's not there. When I surface, I yell his name, but there is only silence. I swim around, praying it's a prank, but he never surfaces. Tears streaming down my cheeks, I call his name. Scream his name. Sob his name. But there is only the sound of my breathing and the distant hum of a drone.

When I glance up, it's not a drone I see, but a beautiful, multi-colored Phoenix, its wings splayed out as it soars through the sky. The Phoenix lands on the banks of the opposite side of the lagoon and stares at me, its broad head tilted.

I wake to Curly shaking me. "We're here," he says. I sit up and glance around. The sun has risen and glows low in the sky, bathing the morning in tendrils of orange and pink. The sunrise reminds me of rebirth, which produces an ache in my chest.

Jones' farm has rows upon rows of mirrored greenhouses. They stretch for miles and mirror the pink sky, making it impossible to tell where the sky ends and earth begins. He pulls up next to a large, red barn, the kind I've only seen in old, digital images. Except this barn has a padlocked entry that Jones deftly unlocks. We follow him into the barn, which surprisingly looks more like an aerodyne hangar than a barn. An antique relic of a crop duster plane rests in the middle, its behemoth wings taking up most of the space.

"Do you ever fly this thing?" I ask, running my fingers over the dusty propeller. I'd be surprised if he did. Ever since the attack in our airspace over five decades ago, the only aerodynes allowed are the government's drones.

"Nah, 'course not. I just keep it in case the government ever comes pokin' their nose 'round here." He grins. "I just tell 'em I like my antiques."

He slides under the belly of the plane and opens a hatch in the wooden floorboards. Standing aside, he motions for us to go down. "Got ever'thing you need down there. I been storing it for Trey for years. It's all yers."

Even hearing Trey's name causes the pain to crush down on my chest. I take a few shaky breaths, watching as Curly ducks under the plane and descends the wooden stairs. I follow cautiously, the damp, moldy smell hitting me in the face as I head deeper into the underground cavern. The steep wooden stairs lead to a room about twice the size of mine in the Compound. Curly clicks on a single bulb dangling from a string in the middle, and the dirt room is bathed in yellow light. Shadows hide the corners, but even with the dark, it's easy to see the weaponry laid out on crude tables all along the room. Duffle bags overflowing with rifles lay on the dirt floor. Curly kneels by one, sifting through the contents. "Here, Sienna, help me carry some of this stuff up," he says.

I nod because I don't have the energy to say anything. It's difficult to maneuver the stairs with the bag of guns and ammo, but as soon as my head peeks out into the barn, I place the bag on the wooden floorboards and slide it to Jones. I half-drag myself out of the hatch and army crawl my way from under the plane's belly.

Curly makes a couple of trips to get the weapons and supplies we need, but he doesn't ask for my help. Maybe he realizes I'm next to useless at this point. When the truck is loaded, Jones hands Curly the keys. "Be careful out there," he says.

"You're not coming with us?" Curly asks.

"Nah, not this time. I'm getting too old for this."

I slide into the truck and wait for Curly to join me. Jones watches as we pull away, and I can't help but notice the sad look in his eyes. His body may be getting old, but his heart is still in the right place.

Leaning my head against the seat, I stare out the window and will myself not to think of Trey. I can't think about his deep voice, strong arms, or infectious grin. If I do, I may never recover.

My body feels numb. Disconnected. Sucking in air is an effort. And I think how easy it would be to just stop breathing altogether. But somewhere deep down, I know I'm stronger than that.

"Nash chose a location," Curly says suddenly. I glance over at him. One hand holds his Lynk communicator while the other rests on the steering wheel, his eyes flitting from the road to the device in his hands.

"Where?"

"The Satellite Government Facility."

No. I close my eyes and pray I didn't hear what I think I did. When I open them, Curly is staring at me.

"He can't bomb that building," I say.

"Why not?"

"Because my mother is in there."

Chapter Thirty-seven

"I'll help you," Curly says, like there's no question.

"You're willing to go against Nash?"

Curly shrugs. "I've never really liked him that much. Besides, you can't do this alone. And Trey wouldn't want you to try." He clears his throat, his eyes intently focused on the road in front of him.

Resting my head against the seat back, I try to come up with a plan. Curly and I need more manpower than just the two of us. But the only other person I can think of is Zane, and he probably never wants to hear from me again. Well, other than for me to say I'm collecting my sister. Still, it's worth a try.

Thankfully, my Lynk survived the explosions. I pull it from my pocket and send a voice-activated message. I don't know if he'll read it. Even if he does, I have no idea if he'll respond.

I'm sorry about yesterday. I know you hate me, but I need your help. My mom's in danger.

My hands shake as I wait for him to respond. When the phone buzzes, I glance down, my heart racing.

I'm listening.

I record a quick response.

Can you meet me outside the SGF in thirty minutes?

I panic when he doesn't respond immediately. But when

his message does come through, I realize he was choosing his words carefully.

Okay. But I'll be armed.

The last sentence knocks the air out of me. I've betrayed him, and now he doesn't trust me. And why should he? All I did was lie to him the last couple of weeks. He shouldn't trust me. Hell, right now, I don't even trust myself.

The parking lot of the Satellite Government Facility is already full at 08:00 hours. We do a slow drive past the building, trying to determine if Nash is there yet. It doesn't look like it, so we keep driving, parking a quarter mile down the road. I send a message to Zane with our exact location while Curly calls Jeff to find out details about Nash's plan.

"They should be at the facility in about ten minutes," Curly says once he clicks his Lynk off. "We'll only have a few minutes of a head start."

I shake my head at his use of the word *we*. "I need you to stay out here and convince Nash not to blow up the building until after I get my mother out."

"You have someone coming to help you?" Curly asks, clearly aware of the message I sent to Zane.

"Yes. A friend."

Curly studies my face for a moment, his brows furrowed. "You sure?"

I nod. "Just keep me posted."

When I look out the window, Zane's silver Aria is cruising down the road toward us. I slide out of the truck and wait in the middle of the road with my hands up. It's a gesture of innocence or surrender, I'm not sure which. I just hope he believes me.

The car slows. Zane pulls over on the side of the road, facing the truck. He steps out, his mouth set in a hard line, his eyes never leaving my face. My eyes flit to his waist and the gun tucked in his jeans. It hurts that he thought he needed it.

"What happened?" he asks, his voice slow and controlled, his eyes roving over my smoke-streaked face and singed clothes.

"The Compound was bombed. We barely made it out, and Trey—" I choke back a sob. "Our leader was killed."

His face softens. "And what about your mother?"

"She's still in there," I say, motioning to the government facility down the road. "But our second-in-command is so angry that he wants to blow the building to bits. I have to get her out before he gets here."

Zane takes a deep breath. "All those innocent people will die?"

"They aren't that innocent. They just killed at least a hundred of our people." I pause. "But if you help me get my mother out, I'll let you save as many as you want."

"What do you need me to do?"

"Help me. Maybe create a distraction so I can search the building undetected."

After what seems like an eternity, he nods. "Okay. I'll do it."

"Thank you," I breathe. I want to throw my arms around his neck, but seeing the gun in his pants reminds me of his distrust and possible hatred. But I don't care. Flinging my arms around his neck, I hug him tight. His arms hang slack at first, but then gradually tighten around my back before letting go.

"I'll be right back," I say. I hurry over to Jones' truck, my injured calf throbbing in protest. Once inside the bed, I dig through the duffle bags of guns. When I find a nine-millimeter Beretta with a silencer, I stick it in the back of my shorts before I have a chance to second-guess myself.

"Ready?" I call to Zane as I jump out.

"I'll drive?" He glances at Curly, who is still inside the truck waiting for Nash and his crew, and gives him a slight nod, like a silent greeting.

"Yeah." I stride over to his car. "But we need to hurry." Climbing inside, the soft leather of the seat rubbing against my bare legs, I realize for the first time that I'm still wearing my tank top and sleep shorts. My arms are black with smoke, dirt, and dried blood. I was hoping to walk into the government facility and pretend I worked there, but now… there's no way I can pull that off.

Zane slides in beside me and sees the expression on my face. "Here," he says, reaching behind my seat and pulling out a wad of clothes. He grabs a water bottle from the door and wets a T-shirt before handing it to me. I clean myself as best as I can. When I'm done, but still reeking of sweat and smoke, Zane hands me another shirt, this one lacy and pretty.

"What's this?" I ask, holding it between my thumb and forefinger.

"It's Arian's. She left it in here yesterday." He pauses. "I thought you might want to change your shirt," he says, looking pointedly at the blood—Trey's blood—smeared across the front.

"Thanks." I slip the clean shirt over my dirty one. It's lacy and see-through and smells of perfume, but it does help cover up some of the dirt and blood.

Zane drives the short distance to the SGF parking lot and parks his Aria in the furthest space from the building. He turns to me. "Are we just going to walk through those front doors?"

"Yep. Maybe you can go to the front desk and create a distraction, and I'll slip in after you. I'm sure they have cameras, but I'm hoping they'll be so focused on you that they won't notice me."

Zane exhales. "That's a lot of pressure," he mutters.

"You can do this. I know you can." I pause and pull out my Lynk, dialing into his. "Just keep your Lynk on so I can hear what's going on."

He takes out his Lynk, glancing at the screen before slipping out of the car and striding across the parking lot to the government facility. From my own Lynk, I hear the door open and his footsteps echo across the marble floor. The indistinct chatter of others around him filters through the earpiece, but I strain to hear his voice. When I do, it's slightly muffled, but I get the gist of what he's saying to the receptionist.

"Excuse me, ma'am."

I imagine the receptionist looking up at him. There's a soft gasp. "Zane Ryder? Are you Zane Ryder? Oh my God, I can't believe it's you!" Clearly, this is a different receptionist than the one before, which might work to our advantage.

Ignoring the pulsating pain in my calf, I get out of the car and stay low, hurrying up the path to the building—the blue, white, and black flags hanging overhead—and slip inside.

I don't even give my eyes a chance to adjust as I creep to the corridor on my left. I keep expecting a dozen pair of eyes to turn and glare accusingly, but the oversized entrance looks the same as before. No one takes notice of me. Not the woman sipping her coffee at the cafe on my right, not the man whose face is buried in documents, and not the young receptionist who's talking to Zane.

Zane's head turns and his eyes lock with mine for an instant. He gives me a small, encouraging smile before turning his attention to the dark-haired woman who's gazing up at him, all smiles and puppy-dog eyes. She's taken by him. And why shouldn't she be? He's gorgeous and practically royalty.

I rush past.

When I enter the corridor, I glance up at the motion-detection cameras. Maybe if I pretend I belong here, the guards will disregard my dirty, casual clothes and messy hair. Straightening my shoulders, I walk down the hall with false confidence. Each room is numbered, so I start with the first and peek inside, working my way down the hall. Some are similar to twelve, which is where Zane and I met with Radcliffe and Chadwick for the exchange. Others look like conference rooms with long, oval tables and cushy chairs.

High-tech equipment rests at the front of the room, and I don't even want to take the time to figure out what it is.

Frustration builds as the minutes tick by. I hold up my Lynk to see how things are going with Zane, and his voice comes through clear.

"You know," he says in his rich tone, "I'm pretty sure I can secure you an invitation to the next shindig my father hosts."

The woman lets out an excited squeal. "I'd love to meet your father! He is seriously the smartest man alive."

I move toward the stairwell at the end of the hall. Maybe the next floor will be more productive. I take the stairs two at a time but when I reach the door, it's locked, and a fingerprint keypad keeps me from gaining access.

My Lynk buzzes, and Curly's face shows up on the screen.

"Did you talk to Nash?" I ask, breathless.

Curly's eyes harden. "He says he isn't waiting."

"Why not?"

"He thinks you're about to tip off everyone inside, and people will escape before he has a chance to blow the roof off."

"Oh no." I think fast. "Let me talk to him." At Curly's hesitation, I plead. "Please."

"It probably won't do much good."

Curly hands his Lynk to Nash, and his scarred face leers at me. "What do you want?"

"Please, Nash. Give me a little more time. I have to get my mother out of here."

"Are you trying to thwart my plans, Sienna?"

I fervently shake my head. "I want the government to suffer just as much as you. But my mom is here and—"

"Ten minutes," he says.

"Ten minutes?" I repeat.

"You have ten minutes to get the hell out of there before I blow it sky high." The Lynk clicks off.

Cursing under my breath, I dial Chaz and pray he answers. When he does, I get right to business, explaining where I am and what floor I need to break into. I don't doubt for a minute that Chaz can do this; I only hope he can do it in time.

After what seems like an eternity, Chaz says in his confident voice, "Got it."

At the same time, the lock clicks.

"Thank you!" I burst through the door to find myself in a hallway that looks eerily similar to the one before. I check the first room on the floor. Instead of a conference room, this one looks like a dentist's office, complete with a chair that lays back and some kind of metal, rotating equipment. But the most disturbing part is the body in the chair. A body of a man.

I stare in horror at the pajama-clad man who lays there with his eyes wide open, staring. He's hooked to wires coming from the machine. I don't know if he's dead or alive, but I don't take the time to find out.

Each room I go to on this floor has the same dentist chair, rotating equipment, and a body. None of which are my mother. But when I reach the fifth room, I freeze. A shock of red hair is splayed out on one of those dentist chairs, accompanied by the wide-eyed, pale face, and unmoving body of my mother. Before I enter the room, I glance up at the security camera in the corner and raise my gun. The noise of the gunshot is muffled by the silencer as I shoot out the black face of the white, swiveling arm.

As I rush to my mother's side, a sob rips from the back of my throat. "Mom," I cry out. She doesn't blink or even acknowledge that I'm here. I see the rise and fall of her chest and know she's still alive, but she's hooked up to that rotating machine. Electrodes protrude from under her sweatshirt and rest on either side of her head. I grab her right hand, which has several tubes snaking out of the IV in her veins. I look her in the eyes. "Mom," I cry again, squeezing her hand. "It's me, Sienna."

She is unresponsive, unmoving. She is a shadow of the

woman I knew as my mother. The rotating machine comes into view, and I'm able to get a clear shot of it. It's a digital screen, playing images. The images are pictures of my mom dressed in business attire, smiling, happy, and working. These images fill the screen one right after the other. They don't look falsified, and yet, they can't be real. When would she have taken these pictures? Another image of my mother and a man with dark-rimmed glasses and hair tinged a distinguished gray fills the screen, followed by dozens of pictures of the two of them. Holding hands, kissing, and showing off wedding rings. Fear grips me, and I take a step back. I glance down at my mother's hand and see the diamond ring on her finger, the opposite hand of the one with the IV.

What the hell is going on? I don't have time to contemplate it. As I rip the electrodes off her, she shudders, like a shock rippling through her body. The machine beeps behind me, and the images shut down. Biting my lip, I remove the tape keeping her IV in place, and then slowly pull the tubing from her hand. Her body jerks in response.

"Mom." I peer into her eyes, searching for some form of life, but she stares at me with a blank expression. "Mom, please. We have to get out of here." I slap her cheeks as hard as I dare and shake her shoulders. "Mom, wake up, please. It's time to go home."

I stare at her face, barely breathing, hoping that somewhere in there is the mother I love, the mother who sang lullabies by my bedside and stroked my hair when I had trouble falling asleep.

"Zane," I choke out, speaking into the Lynk. "I need your help. I'm in room five on the second floor. The floor is locked, but if you can find a way in... I found her, but I need your help. We only have a few minutes."

I don't know if he'll get my message, not while he's entertaining the receptionist, so I have to try to get her out on my own.

Her body is a dead weight that I drag off the chair and

across the floor. My arms ache by the time I reach the door, and yet, I still have such a long way to go. Too much time has passed, and this place will blow any minute.

Walking backward, I drag her down the hall, my hands under her armpits. My back screams at me and my arms quiver from exertion, but I can't stop. There's no time for rest.

I'm almost to the stairwell when I hear a voice behind me that makes my blood run cold.

"Well, well, if it isn't Sienna Preston."

I lay my mother against the wall and turn to confront the beady eyes of Radcliffe. "I'm taking my mother out of here."

"And I won't stop you."

My eyes narrow in suspicion. "Why not?"

"Because now that I have the leader of the Fringe, I have no use for you or your mother."

"What are you talking about? Trey's dead, thanks to your drones."

Radcliffe's mouth turns up into a hideous smile. "He did appear to be dead, yes. But we revived him."

I gasp as his words sink in. Trey's alive? It can't be possible. Surely, Radcliffe is playing some sick game in an attempt to beat me down one more time. But what if…

"I don't believe you."

He shrugs. "You know what I like about you, Miss Preston?" He doesn't wait for a response. "You are so predictable. Like herding cattle, that's how easy it was to convince you to do what I wanted. And what did I want? I wanted Trey, the leader of the Fringe." He shakes his head with a cruel smile. "And you gave him to me. And allowed me to take out the Fringe Compound in the process. So really, Sienna, I should thank you."

"What are you talking about?"

He leans forward. "I've been using you. From the very beginning. Why else would I want a seventeen-year-old nobody to kill one of the most important men in the city?"

My throat seizes. "Using me? How?"

He grins. "The night Trey broke into the SGF, his DNA was everywhere, not to mention the fingerprints we pulled from his truck. That's when I realized your connection to Trey." He licks his lips. "I had to back you into a corner, you see. Make you feel like you had no choice but to join the Fringe."

My stomach clenches as my mind reels through the events of the past two weeks. Who did I call to help me remove the tracker? Trey. Who did I run to for help rescuing my mother? Trey. Who did I call after Zane left me at the SGF? Trey…

Like a puppet master controlling the strings, Radcliffe's been manipulating me from the very beginning. Anticipating my every move. And what did I do? I led him right to Trey and the Fringe Compound.

Radcliffe pulls out a gun from behind his back and aims it at my head. "But now, you've become a bit of a nuisance."

I stare down the barrel of the nine millimeter, my heart pounding. Pretty soon, we'll both be blown to bits.

"You know," he continues. "It's funny. You actually believed Harlow Ryder killed your father."

My eyes narrow. "He didn't?"

"Of course not. I've always been the one to clean up Harlow's messes. Twenty-one years ago. A year ago. I don't know what he'd do without me. Too bad he doesn't see it that way."

My throat closes. "You killed my father."

Radcliffe shrugs, his gun wavering with the movement. "Are you surprised?"

"Why? Why did you kill him?" My hands are shaking with anger, but I try to hide them.

"He knew too much."

The sound of the stairwell door banging open diverts Radcliffe's attention, and I lunge at him, knocking the gun out of his hands. He reaches for my neck, but I slide out of his grasp, pulling my own gun from the back of my pants. "Stop right there, Radcliffe," I say. My eyes flit for a moment to Zane, who has miraculously come through the door, and then back to Radcliffe. "I want to know what my father found out and why you killed him."

"I'm sure you would," he says, his face smug.

I aim the gun at his kneecap. Without hesitation, I squeeze the trigger. His screams reverberate through the empty hall as he collapses to the floor. "You bitch!"

"I'll ask you again," I say, leaning close. "What did my father discover? And why did you kill him?"

He stares at me, his mouth twisting into a sneer. "Go to hell."

I shift the gun to his head, my heart pounding in fury. "No, you go to hell," I say, my fingers tightening on the trigger.

Chapter Thirty-eight

"Sienna," Zane calls out.

Without taking my eyes off Radcliffe, my fingers relax. "Don't do this," Zane says. "Don't do something you'll regret. Besides, in a few minutes, it won't matter. *He* won't matter."

I take a deep breath. Radcliffe has a self-satisfied look on his face, and I can't stand it. Lowering the gun, I aim at his other kneecap. "For insurance," I say before squeezing the trigger.

Radcliffe screams in pain and lets out a string of curses, but I ignore him. I refuse to look at his blood spattered all over the floor.

"Zane, get my mom out of here. Now! I have to look for someone."

"Who?"

"I don't have time to explain, but I think Trey is still alive."

He shakes his head. "I'm not leaving you in here by yourself."

"You have to," I plead. "Please." I glance down at my mother. "Get her out of here. Emily needs her."

"Here, you might need this." Zane hands me a keycard. "I swiped it from a passing guard. Apparently, it works on the fingerprint keypad."

I take it from him and sprint to the stairwell, ignoring

the angry yells from Radcliffe. If loss of blood doesn't kill him, the blast surely will.

Once inside the stairwell, I stop for a second to decide if I should go up to the third level to look for Trey or down to the basement where I was water tortured that first night. Assuming Trey is alive, he's badly injured and would require medical attention. I don't think the basement would house the equipment needed to treat him.

Decision made, I race up the stairs until I reach the third level. Grateful for the keycard when I see the fingerprint keypad, I swipe it and thrust my way into the hallway. This floor looks like a hospital wing. Nurses in white, slim-fit uniforms roam the halls with clipboards and false smiles. Plastering my body against the wall next to a jut out, I decide my plan of attack. I don't really want to gun down a whole bunch of innocent staff, but this is clearly a secure floor and "visitors" would not be welcome.

A petite, dark-haired nurse moves down the hall toward me, and instinct kicks in as she passes. I grab her around the neck, simulating a chokehold. "You cooperate and no one will get hurt. Do you understand?" I hiss in her ear.

She nods. I lift my gun and place the barrel to her temple as I drag her down the hall. Nurses of all shapes and sizes gasp and press themselves against the wall, their clipboards clutched to their chests.

"As long as you don't try to stop me, no one will get hurt," I yell to whoever can hear me. *Well, at least until Nash blows this place to shreds.* "I'm looking for a man named Trey Winchester. He was brought here during the night."

The petite nurse in my chokehold raises her arm. I release some pressure around her neck so she can speak. "I know Trey," she croaks. "I'm his nurse."

"Where is he? Which room?"

The nurse points down the hall, and we move in synchronization. She motions to a door, and I inch closer, dragging her with me. In my excitement to peer into the room, I loosen my hold around her, and she slips from my grasp. She's like a ninja, small and quick. Her foot shoots out, sending my gun sliding across the floor. Her fist is next. It connects with my jaw. The pain radiates across my face and blurs my vision. Clearly, I've underestimated this *nurse*. And Trey would be very disappointed in me for getting my butt kicked.

I bring my fists up near my face to protect my soft spots, and I look for a hole in her movements. A quick jab to the face, which she ducks, but she comes at me with a hard hit to the stomach. My stomach muscles quiver in pain, but I stay upright and turn my fury on her face. I focus all my energy on her nose. I send a fake jab with my left, and then uppercut with my right. The crack is deafening, and I cringe as blood spurts from her nose. She screams and her hands fly to her face, her eyes glaring at me.

"Hey, I told you no one would get hurt if you just cooperated."

A low rumble shakes the building, and my heart stops. *No, not yet.*

The nurses on the floor scream, and the petite nurse stares at me with wide eyes, her hand over her nose, and the front of her white outfit stained red.

"Get everyone out of here, *now*," I scream. "This building is coming down!"

The nurse nods, grabs a towel from a rolling cabinet, and shouts for her colleagues to get their patients out. I turn to the door and fling it open. Doubt still makes me uncertain that Trey will be in that bed. But when I see him, his dark hair matted against a fluffy pillow and a white sheet pulled up to his chest, there is no mistaking that it's him. It's Trey.

I rush to his side and place my hand on his forehead, tears slipping from my eyes and falling onto his face. I'd been sure I'd never see him again, dead or alive, and now, here he is. Alive. The sheer joy I feel is immediately shattered by another blast that knocks me to my knees. If I don't hurry, this hospital room will be both of our graveyards.

There are several machines keeping him alive. One oxygen tank; an IV probably administering morphine, antibiotics, and food intravenously; a heart monitor; and something else I've never seen before in any hospital I've ever been in. As I study the machines, I pray he can survive without them.

My hands move deftly, unhooking each tube and ripping out every IV. I pause only long enough to make sure Trey is still breathing. I wait, counting the seconds, watching for his chest to rise and fall again. "Come on, Trey, you can do this," I whisper. "Stay strong for me." Then I see it. The slight curve of his chest as he begins to breathe on his own.

"Sienna," a voice shouts from the hallway.

"In here!" Grunting, I push Trey's bed away from the wall and inch it toward the door. It flings open and Zane stands in the doorway, his eyes wide. His hands latch on to the bed, pulling while I push. Once we're through the doorway, we race down the now-empty hall, the bed rolling easily on the smooth concrete flooring. I'm relieved to see everyone cleared out so quickly, which is probably how Zane was able to get on the third floor.

When we reach the stairwell, our eyes connect. He knows what I'm thinking before I even say it. He moves quickly to the bed and effortlessly lifts Trey into his arms.

"He has a wound here," I say, pointing to his chest. "So just be careful."

Zane nods and starts for the stairwell. I'm right behind him when another blast rips through, this one from underneath us. The floor crumbles beneath me, and my hands search for something, anything, to grab onto. As I'm falling, my screams ricochet down the cavernous space below. Just when I think it's too late, my hands connect with the railing on the side of the bed and close over the smooth metal. My heart pounds in fear as I dangle over the unknown below. I struggle to pull myself up, but I'm too weak. Too tired.

"Zane," I cry, my sweaty hands slipping off the railing.

Heat licks the bottom of my feet, and I close my eyes, sure at any moment I'll be consumed by the raging fire beneath.

"Sienna," I hear him shout. "Hang on, I'm coming!"

Sweat runs into my eyes, but I hold on. I can't give up now. Not after everything I've been through. And now that Trey is alive… That knowledge gives me the strength I need to hold on even though my arms scream at me to let go.

"Grab my hand," Zane says from above.

"I can't! If I let go, I'll fall."

"I'll catch you. Don't worry." I open my eyes and stare into his warm brown ones. I trust him. I do.

Letting go with one hand, I immediately feel myself start to fall. I reach out for him, sure I'm going down to a fiery grave. Just when I think I'm at the point of no return, Zane's strong arms grasp mine and lift me in one swift movement. His arms encircle me as I collapse on the ground next to him. I barely have time to catch my breath before he's lifting me to my feet.

"We have to get to a safer place," he says, pulling me through the stairwell door.

"It's no use. The entire floor below us is in flames. It's only a matter of time—"

"Don't talk like that. I think we can survive in the stairwell. Just look at all this concrete."

Trey lies on the ground in the alcove under the concrete stairs. Zane guides me onto the ground beside Trey before disappearing from sight. Fear grips me until he comes back through the door with the hospital mattress in his arms. He wedges the mattress between the two walls in the stairwell alcove and climbs under, wrapping his arms around me as another blast roars through the building. I lift Trey's upper body so that his head rests against my chest, and the three of us stay huddled in the stairwell. I hold Trey, and Zane holds me.

"You shouldn't have come back," I mutter.

"I told you I wasn't leaving you alone," Zane says.

"And now you'll die because of me," I say, tears clouding my eyes.

"Hey." He lifts my chin, forcing me to look at him. "No one is dying today. Not you, not me." He glances at Trey and scowls. "And not him."

I pull Trey closer and place my hand on his chest, anxious to feel its rise and fall. Smiling, I revel in the fact that he's alive. For now.

"You love him, don't you?" Zane says, his voice soft. When I look up at him, I see the pained expression he is trying to hide.

I hesitate, not sure how to respond. "Yeah," I say finally. "I think I do."

"You risked your life for him," he points out.

I nod.

"And I risked my life for you," he says simply, and then averts his eyes.

My breath catches in my throat. "I didn't want you to—" I start to protest.

"You don't get it, do you, Sienna?" Zane scowls. "No matter how much I don't want to like you, I do. Even when I wanted to hate you, I couldn't." He takes a deep breath. "I can't stop thinking about you. You're in every thought, every dream. When I'm supposed to be planning a life and a future with Arian, all I can think about is you beside me." He moans and runs a hand through his hair. "You've ruined me."

"I'm sorry," I say, because it's all I can think of.

"You should be," he says, his tone wry. "I'm in love with you… but you don't love me back."

Before I can wrap my mind around what he's saying, a loud noise reverberates through the air around us. A grunting, groaning noise like the building is too tired to carry its weight any more.

Zane's hands grip me harder, pulling me closer to him and deeper into the alcove as pieces of the building above us crumble. The stairwell shifts, and I'm certain the whole thing is about to tumble to the ground, crushing us beneath thousands of pounds of concrete.

Rock falls around us, but in our little alcove, we remain untouched.

With my arms still around Trey, I bury my face in Zane's neck. The ground shifts underneath us, and then we're falling as my screams rip through the stairwell. We stop abruptly, concrete slamming against concrete. We are still enclosed in our alcove, but our little fortress has moved down a floor. From here, I can feel the heat. Beads of sweat dot my skin, and my heart hammers an uncontrollable rhythm. The air feels thick and heavy, as if there isn't enough oxygen for all three of us. I breathe deeply, willing my lungs to fill with the precious air, but finding none.

I blink as fuzziness clouds my vision. And for the first time since I stepped foot in the government building, I realize with perfect clarity. There is no way out. There is no escaping the inevitable. We will die here. All three of us.

Chapter Thirty-nine

My eyelids are too heavy to keep open. I just want to sleep. Sleep sounds so good. It feels as if I haven't slept in days. And it's not fair. Trey's asleep. Zane's asleep. Why shouldn't I sleep?

Closing my eyes, I rest my head on the hot concrete wall beside me. I don't know why the wall is so hot. Maybe the sun has been beating down on it too long. Ahh, I like the sun. Especially the way it slants through the clouds and lights on my face when I ride my Harley. I miss my Harley. *Where* is my *Harley?*

I blink my eyes open and try to focus. *Where am I?*

Shouts echo through the stairwell and produce a lightning response in my brain. The events of the past twenty-four hours flood my mind.

"Rescue Services! Anyone alive in here?" someone shouts.

I open my mouth to speak, but nothing comes out. My mouth is too dry. I try to swallow, but there's no spit, just like there's no air.

"Anyone in here?" the voice hollers, drawing closer.

"Here," I whimper. "Over here."

"Hello?" a man's voice calls.

I try again. Louder. "Here. Help us, please."

"Is anyone in here?" he calls again, but this time, it sounds like he's headed in a different direction.

No, don't leave us. Please.

My fingers fumble along the concrete floor, searching for something, anything I can use to make noise. They close around a rock the size of my fist. I drag it across the ground—even this simple rock is too heavy for me to lift. Then, with power that comes from beyond me, I heave it against the wall, my fingers colliding with concrete and scraping my skin. Over and over, I bang the rock, willing the man to come back.

"Hello?" he calls. "I think I got something!" he says, and I imagine him speaking into a Lynk. I continue to bang, over and over, until warm blood runs down my arm and falls into my lap. When the man pulls the mattress off our hiding place, I collapse in exhaustion. It isn't until he pries the rock from my bloodied fingers that I realize, through my hazy world, that I'm still banging the wall.

It's too bright behind my eyelids. Too bright to be in my bedroom back home. Too bright to be anywhere in the Compound. And definitely too bright for the concrete stairwell.

My body feels light, like I'm weightless. There's no pain. No aching limbs. I'm enveloped in a softness that makes my skin want to cry for joy.

Even though my eyes feel like they're glued shut, I force them open and glance around the room. I immediately see Zane sitting in a chair. He looks perfect. Clean, fresh, and spotless. His face lights up when he sees me, and he moves his chair closer.

"Hey," he says, taking my hand in his.

"Are we—?" I croak, before swallowing and trying again. "Are we dead?"

He laughs and kisses my hand, his lips barely brushing the skin. "No, we're not dead."

My eyes scan the room. I'm enveloped in a large, cushiony

bed and surrounded by an array of pillows. The room is larger than my entire double-wide trailer and fifty times nicer. Silk curtains drape the windows, and thick, cream carpet lines the floor. It looks like we're in some luxurious suite, but then I notice the hospital equipment surrounding my bed. "Where are we?"

"My home," Zane says.

I sit upright. "My mother. Trey. Where are they?"

Zane's hands guide me back on the bed. "They're fine. They're here too."

"And Emily?"

"She's with your mother right now, actually."

"Can I see them?"

Zane nods. "In a minute."

My body relaxes, and I snuggle back against the pillows. "Why don't I feel any pain?"

Zane grins and nods to the machine pumping liquid into my veins. "Probably because of that. And because of this." He reaches over and grabs something from the nightstand. Holding it in front of me, he shows me the vial of purple-colored liquid—Re0Gene—in his hand. "It's hard to have pain when you don't have cuts and bruises."

"How long was I out? A couple of hours?"

Zane slowly shakes his head. "A couple of days."

My mouth falls open. "A couple of days? But I don't understand. The last thing I remember is a man searching the rubble for survivors. How did we end up here?"

"I came to as they were loading us into their vehicle. At my request, Rescue Services brought us here. There's been a team of nurses and doctors around the clock for the past forty-eight hours."

"And Trey's okay?"

A pained look flashes through Zane's eyes. "Yes. But there's something you should know."

My breath catches as fear claws at my throat. What now?

"The doctors did blood work on each of us, and Trey's

blood was… different."

My heart pounds. "Different how?"

"Well, I guess I shouldn't say different. It's different from yours, but not from mine."

"I don't understand."

"Trey is genetically modified." He pauses to let the idea sink in. "And not only that… he's my brother."

Chapter forty

"What?" Surely, I misunderstood Zane. There is no way, and I mean, *no way*, they can be related.

"We're brothers. We're both twenty-one. Born on the same day at almost the same time."

"You're twins?" As if this could get any weirder.

"I don't know if you can call us twins, but it definitely looks like we shared the same womb."

It must be the drugs. None of this is making any sense.

"Since I found out," Zane continues, "I've tried to talk to my father about it, but he refuses. He keeps repeating that it's a mistake. But I know he doesn't believe that. He, of all people, should know that science doesn't lie. But how could he not know about this? Did my mother hide it from him? And if so, why?"

I'm trying to focus on what Zane is telling me, but I'm still stuck on the fact that Trey is a GM. And he's Zane's twin brother. How?

I think back to what Trey told me at the lagoon about his father and Penelope. Is it possible they had an affair? But that wouldn't explain how Trey ended up sharing a womb with Zane, who is clearly Harlow's son.

A thought tugs at the edge of my brain. My father. Did he somehow play a part in this? As a geneticist, wouldn't he know how to implant two genetically modified embryos in a mother's womb? More specifically, in Penelope's womb?

"Does Trey know?" I ask. I'm not sure how he'll take this kind of news. As much as he hates the Ryders, only to find out he's related to them. Oh no, this can't be good.

Zane shakes his head. "He's been unconscious for the past couple of days. And I don't know how to tell him when he wakes up. Or if he would even believe me." He pauses. "I think it might be better coming from you."

I nod. He's right. It probably would. Trey doesn't even like Zane, so he certainly won't trust him. Besides, a shock that big needs to be delivered with something soft. Perhaps a few kisses?

I lean forward. "Can I see my mom now? And Emily?"

Zane rises from the chair. "I'll go get a nurse." He nods to the tubes snaking out of my body. "You aren't cleared to leave your room yet."

I roll my eyes in exasperation. "Can't you clear me? This is, after all, *your* house."

He laughs and leans over, placing a quick kiss on my cheek. "There's the Sienna I know." As he heads to the door, he calls over his shoulder, "I'll see what I can do."

Fingering the IV protruding from my hand, I contemplate pulling it out myself. Before I have a chance to consider it further, a nurse with short brown hair enters the room, followed by a smiling Zane. The nurse moves to my side and begins unhooking the equipment.

"I was just trying to figure out how to yank out my own IV," I say.

"I thought you might try something like that," Zane says, "which is the reason I brought Tandy to help you."

Once I'm free from the machines, I slide off the bed, suddenly aware of the loose-fitting pajamas I'm wearing. Zane is immediately by my side, his arm around my waist, pulling me to him and offering support.

"I think I'm okay," I say, slipping out of his grip. I try to ignore the hurt look that flashes across his face.

"Of course," he says, keeping his voice light.

I follow him down the carpeted hall until we reach a room adjacent to my own.

"She's still weak," Zane warns me as I place a hand on the doorknob.

"But she's okay, right?" I search his face for any indication that he's hiding something from me.

"She'll be fine. But… I just don't want you to be surprised."

"Does she know anything?"

"She knows where she is. And Greta and I have been filling in the missing pieces as much as we can."

"What about your dad? Is he upset we're here?"

Zane purses his lips together. "He doesn't get to have a say, especially since I'm the one paying for all of this."

I glance down at the ground, completely overwhelmed by his generosity. "Thank you," I say, refusing to meet his eyes.

Zane holds the door open, and I feel his hand on my back, pushing me through. As I look up, the first thing I see is a mass of blonde curls hurtling toward me. Emily throws herself into my arms, and I squeeze her so tight I fear I might break her. As I sink into an armchair by the bed, Emily snuggles deep and fits perfectly on my lap, like a little puppy. For the first time since entering the room, I turn my attention to the red-haired woman in the bed. She's pale, but her eyes are open and wide. She smiles when she sees me, my name lingering on her lips.

"Sienna. My sweet girl," she whispers. She reaches out a trembling hand, and I grasp it as tears fill my eyes.

"Mom." Holding Emily against my chest, I lean forward and run a hand over my mother's hair before kissing her cheek. "I missed you."

"Oh, Sienna," she says. "I was so worried about you."

"Me? You were worried about me?" I cry out. "Mom, I thought I'd lost you."

Tears fill her eyes. "I'm sorry." She shakes her head, her tears falling onto the soft cotton sheet pulled up around her chest. "That man—he did something." Her eyes are pained, and I wait for her to continue. "He tried to convince me I was someone else. Made me believe I was even married to someone else."

The picture of the man with the distinguished gray flashes in my mind. "I saw the images, Mom. They *looked* real."

My mother nods and turns her head away. "I know."

I have so many questions, I need so many answers, but now is not the time. So, I just ask, "Do you remember anything?"

"No." She sighs. "Just bits and pieces of being in that room with the rotating image projector."

"You don't remember that I came to the facility to get you out?"

"You came to get me?" Tears form in her eyes again.

"Several times. Different locations." I'm actually relieved she doesn't remember being abducted or that rat-infested cell. Maybe the trauma part of her brain decided to block it out. And for that, I'm grateful.

"I'm sorry," she says again.

"It's not your fault, Mom. I'm the one who should apologize for dragging you into this mess." I close my eyes, my head feeling very stuffy all of a sudden.

"You need to get more rest," she says, her voice so soft I can barely hear her.

When I open my eyes, she's staring at me through half-closed lids.

I rise reluctantly, placing Emily on her feet. "You're right, Mom." I nudge Emily with my knee. "Come on, Em. We need to let Mom sleep."

Mom tries to sit up in protest, but she falls back against the pillows. "If your father could see me now," she mutters, half to herself.

I bend down and whisper in Emily's ear. "Why don't you go find Zane and I'll catch up with you in a minute? Okay?"

She nods and runs out of the room, the door left ajar behind her.

Sitting on the edge of Mom's bed, I take her hand in mine again. "Mom, when you met Dad, did he ever mention anything about a previous job?" *Or previous life.*

Frowning, she shakes her head. "But as you can see, I'm not the best judge of character. My own husband was gambling our money away, and I never knew it."

I squeeze her hand. "Mom, I think there's a lot about Dad we don't know. But I don't think he did anything wrong."

Mom gives me a sad smile. "That's sweet of you to say, but—"

"No, Mom. I found out things about Dad that go against everything we were ever told." I give her a reassuring smile. "He was a good guy. He always was."

She blinks a few times, her eyes brimming with tears. "Thank you, Sienna," she whispers. "I needed to hear that." For a few moments, there's silence between us. This time when she turns away, her hand goes limp under my fingers, and her breathing becomes steady and even. I sit and watch her sleep, so thankful she's safe. If there's one thing I've learned in the past few weeks, it's that I don't ever want to imagine a life without my mother or Emily in it.

After placing a kiss on her cool forehead, I slip from the room. Zane is striding down the hallway toward me, his face lighting up when he sees me.

"How is she doing?" he asks, placing a hand on the wall beside me.

"Fine. She's resting now. Whatever happened in that SGF room really wore her out."

"According to the doctors, her blood work looks good, so she should make a full recovery."

I bite my lip as I stare at him. "So, no lasting effects from the brainwashing or whatever it is they did to her?"

He moves his hand off the wall and places it on my shoulder, leaning close. "She's going to be fine, Sienna. I promise."

I exhale then, all my worry, all my doubt, expelling out of me. Then I think of Trey and a new knot forms in my chest. "Can I see Trey now?"

Zane's hand slides off my shoulder as he nods. He leads me down the hall, and I can't help the grin that creeps onto my face when we stop outside the door of a room only two down from my own.

"He's still unconscious," Zane warns me. "But the doctor thinks it'll be good for us to talk to him. Might help him come out of it quicker."

"Are you coming in too?"

"No, I'll let you have some time alone. Just come find me when you're done."

I nod and take a deep breath before pushing open the door to Trey's room. His isn't quite as big as mine, but it's still rather nice with a king-sized bed and dark-stained furniture.

My smile deepens when I see Trey in the oversized bed. His face is pale, but he's been cleaned up since the last time I saw him. Instead of matted, his dark hair is now washed, curling at the base of his neck.

Despite the tubes snaking in and around his body, he looks like he's resting. As if I kissed his lips, he might wake. I decide to try.

Leaning over, I press my lips to his warm ones. It's hard to believe that at one time, I thought he was dead. Gone. Lost to me forever.

I pull back and study his features, memorizing every line of his face and yearning for the moment when he'll open his eyes and smile at me.

I'm not foolish enough to believe with Trey alive that everything will be okay. We still have displaced Fringe members, and an overabundance of hurt and anger. We've experienced tremendous losses. We need a leader. Someone who will take a worthy stand.

We need Trey.

And I know that, no matter what happens, I will be there. By his side.

The slight twitch of Trey's hand in mine causes my heart rate to accelerate. I lean closer and whisper his name, softly at first, and then louder. But he's still.

Careful to avoid the wound in his chest, I climb into bed next to him and lay my head on his shoulder. His body is familiar, the scent of his skin is familiar, and when I intertwine my fingers with his, his hands are familiar.

I don't know how long I lay there, our bodies touching, my heart aching to talk to him again, but when two nurses come in to check his vitals, I know it's time for me to leave. I whisper a soft good-bye and kiss his scratchy cheek, which reminds me of our last night together in the Compound. The same night I thought he was dead.

"I love you," I whisper.

The truth is, I do. And I can't wait to tell him.

Every day, I visit Trey and sit by his bedside, waiting for him to open his eyes, to see me. Waiting for the moment I can tell him I love him, wondering if he feels the same way. It's been three days, three long days, since I first woke to discover myself in Zane's house. My mother looks better, stronger every day, partly because of Greta's cooking and partly because the one thing Radcliffe didn't lie about was treating my mother's lupus. I don't know if she's cured forever, but she's at least better than she's been in quite some time.

Thankfully, I've yet to see Harlow, who I've come to learn spends most of his time in the west wing of the house in order to avoid all of his unwanted guests. It's fine with me. I already know that at some point, I'll demand answers from him. For now, he can play dumb, but sooner or later, he'll have to fess up what he knows about my father, his relationship with Penelope, and the genetically modified embryos. Harlow Ryder isn't the type of man who would let something like that slip past him. So what is he covering up?

It's half past noon when I enter Trey's room, anxious to see if today will be the day. I want to feel his lips on mine, his breath on my skin, and his hands at my waist. I go about my typical routine of placing a kiss on his lips and holding his hand.

"Hey, Trey, you gonna open your eyes today?" I wait a few seconds, like I always do, studying the curve of his lips, his strong jaw, and his barely visible chin dimple.

"I talked with Trina earlier, and she said about a hundred Fringe members survived. They're hiding out, just waiting for you." I lean closer, my lips brushing against his ear. "They need you, Trey. *I* need you."

His fingers twitch and his eyes move behind closed lids, as if he's struggling to find the strength to open them. My heart flutters in my chest.

"I'm right here, Trey," I whisper. "Right here."

I wait, hardly daring to breathe. After what seems like an eternity, his eyes fight their way open. Slowly. My breath catches as his deep blue eyes connect with mine. I'm taken back to that first moment I saw him, when he broke into the government facility to rescue me.

"Hey," I say, my voice soft, my lips curving into a smile. I've waited so long for this moment that my expectations are running high. I expect him to smile back. To squeeze my hand. Something. But I'm not prepared for what he does.

"Hey?" His voice sounds thick. Different. He looks at me, confusion and uncertainty in his eyes. His gaze then travels around the room. "Where am I?"

I place my hand on the side of his face. "Somewhere safe."

He studies me for a moment before he frowns. "I'm sorry," he says. "Do I know you?"

At first, I think he's joking. Or maybe he's just a little disoriented.

But I quickly realize that he's neither of those. I stare into his eyes, those deep blue ocean eyes, willing him to come back to me. When all he does is stare back with a blank expression, my hand slides from his cheek, and I lean back.

"You don't know who I am?"

He shakes his head, wincing in pain as he does. Raising his arms, he glances down at the IV. "What the hell is going on?" he mutters.

"You were... in an accident. Do you remember anything?"

When he looks at me then, I think he remembers. For one small instant, our eyes connect, and I pray it's enough. But then he shakes his head, and my hope shatters.

I try again. "What about the Compound? Or the Fringe? Or maybe Nash, your cousin? Does anything sound familiar?"

Trey closes his eyes and grips the sides of his head in frustration. "I don't understand what's going on. What are you—?" He opens his eyes and scowls. "What do you want from me? I don't know what you want me to say."

Heart aching, I rise and walk slowly to the door. It was painful enough when I thought he was dead, but this...

This is a million times worse.

"Wait! Where are you going?" he calls after me.

"To get a doctor. Someone who can help you," I say without turning around.

"But, wait—" The urgency in his tone makes me stop and turn. "Should I know you?"

My heart skips a beat. I want to shake him. I want to make him remember me—remember us—but instead, I turn away. "No. Apparently not."

I stay composed until the door closes behind me.

And then, I crumble.

Acknowledgements

There are so many people I want to thank for helping me bring this idea, this book, to fruition, and for supporting me along the way. I'm not sure where to begin, but I'll try. Great big thanks and awkward hugs go to:

All of the Clean Teen Publishing Team for believing in Sienna's story and offering me a chance to hold the book in my hands. This has seriously been a dream come true. Thank you!

Cynthia Shepp, my brilliant editor, for her keen eye and fantastic editing skills. Thank you for making me dig deeper and think harder, ultimately making the book so much better.

Whitney Royster, my publicist extraordinaire, for her determination and devotion to getting Catalyst in front of readers. Thank you for all of your help with social media!

The most wonderful critique partners in the world without whom I might never have made it this far. Leandra Wallace for your spot-on advice, ideas, words of encouragement, and general awesomeness. You are truly one of a kind—my soul sister. Thank you for not only being my close friend, but my cheerleader and my sounding board. You rock. And to Sheri Larsen, my other incredible CP who knows her way around this business better than I ever will. Thank you for all your insight and knowledge. You will always be top notch in my book!

Mark Noce for critiquing my manuscript even with a newborn baby at home and while experiencing a significant amount of sleep loss. If that's not dedication, I don't know what is! Thank you, Mark.

Jen Holl for being so excited about this story when it was only the roughest first draft imaginable. You will always be my favorite reader!

My fellow Charlotte writers, Monica Hoffman and Holly Hughes, for your endless support and encouragement in navigating these publishing waters. I love our Amelie's chats!

Charity Bradford, for being a wonderful mentor when I triumphantly finished my first novel several years ago. Little did I know then…

My dear friends, Adria Macdonald and Sandy Abbott, for rooting for me throughout this journey. Love you, girls.

My parents who helped foster my love of reading and writing at an early age. Thank you for feeding my addiction of Nancy Drew, Sweet Vally Twins, and Babysitter's Club books.

My sister, Laura Anne Moxley, who was as excited to hear about this book being published as I was. Thanks for being the best big sis.

My sons: Corbin, Hayden, Ethan, Liam, and Declan, for only mildly complaining when you had to eat another frozen pizza or bean burrito because Mom was too busy writing to cook dinner. I hope I made you proud.

My husband and best friend, Adam, for always being my very first reader and giving me your honest opinion. Thank you for letting me roll ideas off of you, especially during long road trips. And thank you for believing in me, even when I almost stopped believing in myself. I love you.

God. While I'd love to believe that this story stems from my own creativity, I have to give credit where credit is due. Thank you for always giving me the inspiration I need.

All my readers. You seriously rock. Thank you for reading my story!

Discussion Questions

1. Why do you think Sienna turns to a life of crime after the death of her father?
2. Why does Sienna agree to kill Harlow Ryder? Does she have any other options?
3. Do you think Sienna is a good person? Why or why not?
4. What do you think about Sienna's decision to join the Fringe? Was it a good one?
5. Why does Sienna decide to get an internal butterfly tattoo? What is the symbolism behind the butterfly for her?
6. What do you think of the idea of genetic matchmaking? Would you want to be matched to the "perfect" person for you?
7. Are you Team Trey or Team Zane? Why?
8. Sienna had a chance to kill Radcliffe, but she didn't do it. What do you think about her decision? What would you have done?
9. When Trey wakes up, he doesn't remember Sienna. Do you think this is short-term memory loss or something else?
10. What do you think of the idea of genetic modification? Would you have wanted your parents to choose your genetic traits, or do you think it's better to let nature decide? As a parent, would you want to handpick the characteristics of your child so you have complete control over the outcome of their genetic makeup?

11. What do you think of the idea that genetic modification can get rid of certain diseases that plague our society? Would it be worth it?
12. Sienna learns throughout the story that her father, Ben Preston, had a former name and former life. Why do you think Ben Preston faked his death and changed his name? If you were Sienna, how would it make you feel to learn that about your father?
13. What is one common theme throughout the story? What are some examples of this theme?

About the Author

Kristin Smith writes young adult contemporary and science fiction novels. When she's not writing, you can find her dreaming about the beach, beating her boys at Just Dance, or belting out karaoke (from the comfort of her own home). Kristin currently resides in the middle-of-nowhere North Carolina with her husband and five incredibly loud but extremely cute boys. To read more about her obsession with YA novels or her addiction to chocolate, you can visit her at kristinsmithbooks.com.

CPSIA information can be obtained
at www.ICGtesting.com
Printed in the USA
LVOW12s1213021116
511098LV00003B/4/P